SUP...

...JELLY

SURF WAX & VODKA JELLY

Lucy Clarke

Spring Hill

Published by Spring Hill
Spring Hill is an imprint of How To Books
Spring Hill House
Spring Hill Road
Begbroke, Oxford
OX5 1RX
Tel: (01865) 375794. Fax: (01865) 379162
email: info@howtobooks.co.uk
http://www.springhillbooks.co.uk

British Library Cataloguing in Publication Data
A catalogue record for this book is available from the British Library

ISBN 10: 1-905862-04-0
ISBN 13: 978-1-905862-04-7

Cover design by Mousemat Design Ltd
Produced by Deer Park Productions, Tavistock
Typeset by PDQ Typesetting, Newcastle-under-Lyme
Printed and bound by Bookmarque, Croydon

ABOUT THE AUTHOR

Lucy Clarke is 24 years old and lives in her hometown, Bournemouth. She studied English Literature at Cardiff University and whilst she was there, co-wrote the *Student Survival Guide* with her housemate, Jenny. Since graduating, Lucy has toured schools and colleges with her writing workshop and lectures about the university experience. She's also spent time in Hawaii and Canada, where she began writing *Surf Wax and Vodka Jelly*.

ACKNOWLEDGEMENTS

Thanks to Mum for the creative advice, Dad for the business advice, Amy Bogue for the encouragement, the Soho-Wednesday girls for the laughs and support and James for the big hugs.

ONE

Monday 16 September

2.30 pm Am in the car. Can't see out of the back window and a chair leg keeps poking me in the neck. Mum is taking me to university. She's acting very strangely, though. We've been driving for over an hour and she hasn't said a single word – not even a mention of personal safety or the danger of drugs. At first I thought she was subdued because I vetted her outfit before leaving, but now I've worked out the problem: her mothering instincts are shutting down! They peaked over the last few days with the obsessive packing and constant food shovelling, and now that I'm leaving home, Mum thinks her responsibilities have ended.

2.32 pm Oh, God. University is a conspiracy! Parents all over the country have spent the last year leaving out prospectuses, painting university as the land of young dreams and making tearful speeches about how they'll miss us. It's not because they're supportive and care about our education, but simply because they want rid of us! Am being thrust towards murky student lifestyle and expected to cook, clean and feed self – and pay for it, while Mum gives herself a congratulatory pat on the back!

2.45 pm OK, calm. Was getting carried away with self. Think I'm just a little tense about starting university. Am sure that's normal.

Wonder if it's also normal to spend three hours flinging clothes round room in search of a suitable 'fresher outfit'? Think I'm panicking because have heard that lots of students reinvent themselves at uni. I could get my hair dreaded and say my hobbies include sandboarding and base jumping – that might add an interesting angle.

No, must try and relax and be myself: I'm a single, white female who's only a couple of inches over five foot. My outfit choice is Topshop cut-offs with a Bench jumper, and my hobbies include watching *The OC* and sunbathing.

3.15 pm I'm here. At university! (Still in car, though.) OK, breathe. In. Out. Calm. I'm confident, fun-loving and approachable. My outfit choice is fine. Yes. Good.

3.45 pm Have collected my room keys from Brian, a very scary Accommodation Warden. I don't know if it was his permanent look of doom that was freaking me out, or his comb-over hair style? I was definitely unsettled when I clocked his hands: nine fingernails were cut and buffed immaculately – but the nail on his right forefinger was twice as long as the others and he kept using it to gently stroke the underside of his chin. Eek!

I stood on one side of the desk nervously chewing the corner of my accommodation letter and trying not to look at the nail. Warden-Brian stood on the other side giving me lengthy instructions about which forms I'd failed to produce. After lots of rummaging (by me) and sighing (by him), I eventually handed him the crumpled papers and, in return, Brian told me that my new address is 'South Hall, Flat 2, Room A'. It doesn't sound very homely.

He then placed a diagram of the campus on the desk between us and used his freakishly long fingernail to navigate me around the map. The campus is massive – there are four blocks of halls with 600 students in each!

Warden-Brain stabbed the A4 sheet so that his nail indent marked my new home. 'You will be living *here* for the next nine months.'

My stomach flopped uneasily – nine months suddenly seems like a very long time. Enough time, in fact, to grow a baby. (Obviously 'growing a baby' is not an official term as you don't water it and leave outside like plants but . . .)

'Twenty pounds!' Brian snapped at me.

Huh? I think I'd missed something.

'I need a twenty pound deposit for your room keys.'

I reluctantly handed over a crisp note, mentally calculating that was over three hours work at Prezzo, and then he pushed the silver keys towards me. 'Thank you,' I said politely, hoping if I was friendly enough, maybe Brian wouldn't kill me and feed me to the rest of the crazy wardens.

4.30 pm. South Hall. My new room is about three feet wider than a single bed. It smells of disinfectant with a hint of mince, and I'm a little nervous about the sludgy yellow stain by the door. The walls are painted with an anti-Blu-tack beige gloss, which complements the brown nylon carpet and sturdy grey curtains. Oh, and my view is of a Telecom pole, a railway line and one tree.

When I flung myself on to the bare mattress, wailing, 'It's worse than a prison cell!', Mum pointed out, quite rightly, that I've never been in a prison cell and then told me to 'stop being so dramatic'. (Think I need to do some hasty self-improvement before I introduce self to flatmates.)

South Hall is massive. The building is at least ten storeys high and it's split into flats of six. As you walk through the entrance to our flat, my room is on the left hand side, opposite the kitchen.

5 pm. Alone. Mum has just left. Have got those pains in my throat and temples from trying not to cry. Felt torn between wanting to bear-hug her so tightly that she couldn't leave me here, yet also subtly trying to hide her in case she did anything embarrassing in front of the other students. Actually, though, other than putting on the rubber gloves and insisting on Dettoling my entire bedroom, she was really quite well behaved.

Was definitely a bit hasty with my conspiracy theory. Mum helped me lug all my stuff up to my room and then started making my bed. 'You're going to have a wonderful time here, Josie,' she said, tucking in the corners of my bed sheet. 'You do know how proud I am of you, don't you?'

I always get a bit embarrassed when Mum says things like that, so I combined a nod and a grunt, which seemed to affirm it.

'Sorry I was quiet on the way here,' Mum told me as she stuffed a pillow into its case. 'It has finally sunk in that you are leaving home and I suppose I feel a little, well, redundant.'

Should have realised Mum was feeling sad. This morning I found her sat on the lounge floor sifting through an old photo album that showcases pictures of me when I was three and didn't mind being naked in public. Splurged around her was a heap of items and a big label that read: PACKING ESSENTIALS. Things that Mum classes as 'essential' include: a sandwich toaster, freezer bags, a colander, a travel iron, a sewing kit, vitamin C, Bach Flower Rescue Remedy, fragranced drawer liners, Toilet Duck, rubber gloves, oven cleaner, two spare light bulbs and a red screwdriver.

I hate it that Mum had to drive me up here on her own. She must have noticed the other students with both parents beside them helping them unload their stuff. Dad called from Lanzarote last night to say 'good luck' – and that has been the extent of his involvement in my university career. Really annoyed me when he tried to pass the phone over to Janine, who also wanted to wish me happiness. Felt like pointing out that neither of them were thinking of my well-being when they ran off to Lanzarote last summer. Anyway, have not got time to make mini-vodoos of Janine or Dad as must start my unpacking . . .

5.10 pm Yey! Just found Mr Tubs. *Definitely* didn't pack him. Only explanation can be that moments before I left home, Mr Tubs hurled himself in kamikaze teddy-on-a-mission style, landing snugly in my bag. It was simply good fortune that he was cushioned comfortably between a padded bra and a bag of cotton wool. Clearly, I did not pack him. I'm an independent student with no need for the reassurance of a one-eyed cuddly bear that I sometimes/often talk to.

5.30 pm Not sure what to do now. Am still here, have hung up my clothes and changed three times. (I wasn't sure about the cut-offs, so settled on jeans, Converse flip-flops and a yellow vest top from the kids' section of H&M. Am hoping the look says 'cool, yet approachable'.) I'm waiting for someone to come and find me.

5.35 pm No one has found me.

5.40 pm Stuck head out of door and flat seemed empty so I had a little look around. The corridor is a bit bleak – blue nylon carpet with overhead strip lighting. Other bad news is there are only two bathrooms and the smaller one just has a toilet and sink in. I don't think anyone else is here yet. Oh, hope new flatmates aren't at a craft fair making friendship bracelets for each other.

5.55 pm Ooo . . . can hear someone, I think! Must be brave and go and introduce self. Am friendly, outgoing and confident. Yes. Good.

Hope top looks OK.

6 pm Oops! Is a bit embarrassing, really. Found new flatmate in the room at the far end of the corridor next to the bathrooms. It was a male. Was quite shocked to be living with boys; suddenly it all felt rather exciting, except that boy was wearing a Kappa hoodie, dirty tracksuit bottoms and white trainers with a bow in them. (Still, am definitely not judging people as I'm an open-minded student and very, very friendly.)

'Hello, I'm Josie,' I said, a little too loudly, and then lunged at him for a hug.

My flatmate, who smelt of stale tobacco and dried sweat, took a step back and narrowed his eyes.

This wasn't encouraging.

'I'm Josie,' I repeated in an unusually shrill voice. 'Your new flatmate!'

Silence.

'So, you've just moved in too?' I continued. 'It's all a bit crazy, isn't it? Ha, ha! Yes, we're students! Feels strange, doesn't it? I already said that, didn't I? Ha, ha!!'

I was behaving like a drama student.

I looked at my flatmate again and then realised that he was foreign. Asian, perhaps? Maybe he didn't speak very good English. 'WHAT–IS–YOUR–NAME?' I enunciated.

Shoving both hands into his pockets, he barked, 'Aja. And I'm not moving in.' His voice was hard and there was a London twang to his faintly foreign accent. I noticed his front teeth were stained brown and his lips looked dry and chapped. He indicated through the bedroom doorway to where a slight girl was unpacking a suitcase; 'I'm just here watching Suniti move her stuff in.'

Fck, fck. This wasn't how I'd planned my first introduction. I over-compensated for my mistake by throwing my arms around Suniti too. She stood uneasily while I hugged her and then she shrunk away, nervously mumbling, 'Thank you.'

Suniti's not much taller than I am. She was wearing small tortoiseshell glasses, a long grey skirt and a black headscarf. 'It's nice to meet you,' I smiled. When she didn't reply, I asked, 'Where are you from?'

'Karachi. Pakistan.'

'Oh, how lovely.' I nodded enthusiastically, not sure I'd even heard of it. 'Good journey?' I found myself asking, surprised by my ability to make the world's most boring conversation.

Aja looked at me warily. By now my mouth was fixed in an unnatural smile and my head was moving up and down in quite a scary way. When neither of them answered, I blethered on with more questions. 'What are you studying?'

'Medicine,' Suniti replied.

'Wow, that's cool. And how do you know each other?'

'We're cousins,' Aja said firmly.

'So do you live in Pakistan, too?'

'No,' Aja replied with a stern finality that suggested our conversation might be over.

'Lovely,' I repeated. I waited there awkwardly, hoping they might ask me something too. When they didn't, I clapped my hands together like a cheesy 80s game show host. 'Well, I can see you're busy unpacking,' I said, watching Suniti pull out a yoga mat, 'so I'll catch up with you both later. Byeee!'

7 pm I almost cracked. Was sat at my desk clutching mobile, finger poised over 'Mum' in the phonebook. Kept rehearsing what I could say: 'Look, Mum, I've given it a fair try but all my flatmates hate me and I've decided I'd be better off at drama school,' or 'The uni's being evacuated because of bomb threats from, er, anti-educationalist terrorists. Could you pick me up?' Just as my index pad touched down, there was a chirpy knock on my door. I flung myself on to the bed, picked up a magazine and struck the pose of 'chilling'.

A ginger-haired boy with freckles and a sing-song Welsh accent bounced in, wearing a red zip-up top and brown cords. He gave me a friendly handshake, 'Hi, I'm Justin,' and then dashed off, whispering conspiratorially, 'Let's go and bagsie the best kitchen cupboards!'

Yes! Was so relieved that someone wanted to speak to me that I followed him into the kitchen and stood gormlessly watching him stock his cupboard (he chose the corner one as it has extra depth – very clever). Our shared kitchen-cum-dining-room is a rectangular room with lino flooring and more strip lighting. There's a large white fridge that buzzes and an empty blue noticeboard with drawing pins jabbed into the shape of a face. A table has been plonked in the middle of the room with six orange chairs sat around it. Think the design theme is 'cheap and washable'.

Justin filled me in on his life history: he's from Abergavenny (love the way he says it!); he's studying Art History, thinks Picasso is over-rated and Spider-Man is his favourite superhero. Think it's cute that Justin is a huge comic-book fan. It could be like living with my very own Seth Cohen (although Welsh rather than Californian, and ginger rather than brunette, but still, there's very good friend potential there).

When Justin went back to his room, I pressed my face against the kitchen window and peered down into the courtyard trying to spy on new arrivals. Was comforting to see other freshers looking bewildered as they heaved their belongings around while trying not to talk to their parents too much. I jumped when a voice behind me said, 'Hi!'

A very attractive girl with wavy blonde hair and a tall, voluptuous figure gave me a warm smile and introduced herself as Tamara.

Tamara is in Room B (next to mine) and seems really lovely. I've been helping her unpack and am pleased to report she has a TV (yey!) – and *The OC* box sets (double yey!). I like her taste in clothes too; she is wearing snug-fit jeans and a floaty beige top with chunky leather belt – kind of boho-chic. Am very excited as have discovered we've got lots in common: we both fancy Jared Leto, agree Warden-Brian is scary, think cowboy boots are a staple wardrobe item and believe communal bathrooms are not a good idea.

We'd just found out that we're both studying English Literature (except Tamara's doing Joint Honours with Spanish) when there was a loud beeping in the corridor. I went to investigate. 'Beep. Beep. Beep,' it continued. I

9

looked around but couldn't tell where the noise was coming from.

'Beeeeeeeeeeep!'

A red head poked out of the room opposite Tamara's: 'I think it's the intercom,' Justin suggested.

The beeps sprang into a rhythm: 'Beep-beep-beep-beep-beep. Beep! Beep!'

I pressed 'talk'. 'Hello?'

'Is that The Love Palace?' said a male voice.

'It's, er, South Hall, Flat 2.'

'Exactly!' said the voice. 'And who am I talking to?'

'Josie.'

'Well, Josie, you're about to meet your very handsome new flatmate. Let me in, will you? I've left my keys in my room.'

I pressed another button and heard the main entrance click open. Tamara and I moved into the kitchen and listened as a thundering of feet rushed up the stairway. A tall, dark-haired guy wearing too much aftershave, a tub of hair gel and a tight, black T-shirt that said 'PORN', burst in carrying a crate of Carling.

'Josie!' he said, flashing me a wide smile and shoving the beer into our empty fridge. 'I'm Matt. It's a pleasure to meet you,' he told me, while mentally assessing my vital stats.

Matt spun round, noticing Tamara by the window. 'And who might you be?' he asked her breasts.

'Tamara,' she replied coolly.

'Perfect.' Matt fetched his first beer and snapped back the ring pull. He sat himself down on a plastic chair, rested his feet on a second and took a noisy slurp. 'Ah!' he exhaled, satisfied. 'This couldn't have worked out better. I'm living with two beautiful ladies and a fridge full of beer. This is gonna be a damn good year!'

Tamara raised her left eyebrow at me: the girl-to-girl collusion of 'fuckwit'.

7.30 pm Hmmm, so, flatmates are an interesting mix. Would be nice if we could chop away at Matt's confidence and give a little to Suniti. I nipped into her room to ask if she wanted to come out tonight for our first drink at the campus bar (am excited!), but Aja was still there and insisted that she finish unpacking. Seemed bit odd really as from what I could see her one suitcase was neatly tucked under the bed. Anyway, am sure in a few days Suniti will warm up and Matt will calm down and we'll find the middle ground – the ebb and flow of the flat as it were. Yes. Is all fine. Tamara seems lovely and I've managed to curb my drama student introductions, so things are looking perkier – although we haven't met our sixth flatmate yet . . .

Midnight We've just got back from Energy, the 80s-themed student bar in the middle of campus. Was quite a fun evening meeting lots of new people. It was a relief to walk in with flatmates though, as saw several other freshers stood nervously on their own, pretending to find their drinks extremely interesting.

Has been nice getting to know flatmates better, although am not sure I like the way Matt's already taken to calling me 'Shorty'. Have told him quite firmly that I've got the same measurements as Kylie (although not quite the same following, which is disappointing). Justin and Matt are very different. Justin spotted a guy in a Spider-Man T-shirt

11

and had to tell him how 'tidy' it was, and then Matt ditched us to schmooze with a 'hot lady' by the bar.

Have read that a good way to make friends is to keep a note of facts about someone you meet, then at a later date you can casually drop them into conversation, making you appear interested and a good listener. Tried to do this with Tamara and was taking mental notes about her boyfriend, Oliver: age thirty; met him at the marketing agency she worked at during her gap year; lives in London; they've been going out for five months. Was all going swimmingly until Tamara's mobile rang and she nipped outside, hoping it would be him. . .

. . . leaving me on my own in the middle of a busy bar!

Was awful. Suddenly felt that whole bar was staring at me. I was trying to scan the room casually to find Justin or Matt, but they'd disappeared. I was a lone fresher stood in the middle of a packed room. I rummaged around in my bag pretending to look for something, then checked a non-existent text message, and finally downed my drink just so I could order a refill. Tamara still wasn't back, and after that I had nothing left to fake-do. I realised that this was it: the moment. I took a deep, shaky breath, gave myself a mental slap round the face and decided to introduce myself to someone. To anyone.

The next hour was ridiculous. I kept having the same moronic, three-questioned conversations: What's your name? Where are you from? What are you studying? There's a filter system – if you're not from a socially compatible part of the country or not doing the same course as your acquaintance, then you're filtered out. Was pleased, though, to be sieved by Sid, Middlesborough, studying Biochemistry. Got as far as a fourth question, 'hobbies', with Elizabeth,

Tunbridge Wells, Anthropology, but when she discovered I didn't have a dying passion for show jumping, she trotted off.

After shuffling from one person to the next, I found myself in the middle of a group of people who were talking about travelling. A guy with weathered skin and an X shaved into his head was relating an amazing experience he had in Bora Bora; 'I truly found my spirit among the tribal people, man.'

There was intense nodding from a girl with her lip, eyebrow, nose and cheek pierced. 'Travelling through Asia', she told us wistfully, 'has been totally mind-expanding. I find it difficult to relate to people who aren't interested in experiencing the lifestyle and values of different cultures.' Then she turned to me: 'Have you been travelling?'

Think I was mesmerised by her cheek-stud as found self nodding in agreement. 'Yes, I met some interesting locals who gave me a real insight into their culture.' Was I meaning my week-long holiday in Spain where I ended up pulling Pablo, the hotel barman?

A large girl wearing a brown flowery bandana chipped in, 'Absolutely. It's all about interacting with the locals. What was your route?'

'Erm, well,' I stalled uncomfortably. 'Europe. Yes, I wanted to experience our own continent first before exploring far-away soils. It was very enlightening,' I added. 'Ended in Spain.' This was a demi-truth: I started in England, flew to Alicante, island-hopped to Mallorca and flew back to Gatwick.

'How long did you go for?' probed Bandana Girl.

'Not long enough,' I answered quickly. 'Once you're home, you get the travel bug, don't you?'

Thankfully, I spotted Tamara who was back inside standing near the bar. I mumbled my excuses to the travellers and made my way over – and just in time. She was stuck talking to a couple of boys who were faking being freshers. Had heard myths of F-A-F (Fuck-A-Fresher), but really didn't think such desperate second and third years existed – until I was stood in front of two of them. A guy with a paunch, lank hair and a damp 'DRINK BEER' T-shirt was trying to seduce Tamara by explaining that in his freshers' week, he drank sixteen pints in one night and had to have his stomach pumped.

Tamara caught my eye and gave the 'rescue me' signal.

'Sorry to interrupt,' I smiled, 'but Matt and Justin are waiting to walk us back to the flat.'

Tamara was grateful for the escape route and, as we hurried off, we did actually spot the boys. Matt was standing at the far end of the bar downing flaming Sambucas with a group of guys in football shirts, and Justin – who doesn't have a very favourable alcohol-to-body-weight ratio – was trying to strike up conversation with a coat.

TWO

Tuesday 17 September

8 pm Have only been a student for twenty-four hours and am already exhausted. My morning began in rushed-panic after a minor over-sleeping incident involving me, my duvet and a 10 am Health and Safety talk. Even if I hadn't pressed 'snooze' nine times, am sure I'd still have been late since the campus is so huge and maze-like that it's difficult to get anywhere quickly. I live amidst three miles of Student Village: there are cafés, book shops, lecture halls, the Students' Union (SU), a pizza place, a video store, STA travel, a gym and a launderette. It's really quite amazing and best thing is that just about everyone in this village is under twenty-five!

Warden-Brian was heading the Health and Safety brief, wearing a freshly starched white shirt for the occasion. I'm sure he'd taken extra care with his hair; each of the five strands of black hair were neatly combed over the glistening bald patch. He looked pleased to be standing in front of an audience and kept using his freakishly long fingernail to drive home important points about halls behaviour.

'You must obey the following rules,' he commanded in a voice not dissimilar to Darth Vader's. 'Sellotape must not be used on the walls. Candles are banned. Absolutely no plug adapters are allowed. All doors must be kept closed as they are fire doors. And, most importantly, extinguishers must be used only when dealing with a real fire.'

Mentally pictured room with door propped open by fire extinguisher, photos Sellotaped to walls, pretty floating

15

candle display beneath smoke alarm and eight appliances attached to one plug adapter.

Brian's finale was a stark warning that there'll be a fire drill at some point in the next fortnight and we must all be outside within 120 seconds of the alarm sounding. He's so strict, it's almost as if he's wearing an earpiece coming directly from Mum.

After the talk, Tam and I went food shopping to a huge Tesco half a mile off campus. Along with hundreds of other bewildered students, we spent hours traipsing up and down long aisles filled with mystery products. Who knew super-markets were this confusing? Found self gazing about hopefully as though a surrogate parent might spring out of the dairy counter with useful culinary advice.

After momentary panics of 'I can't cook', 'I might starve', 'Where do you find the eggs?', realised that the benefit of living on my own is I can buy – and therefore eat – whatever I want. Yey! Then we both got over-excited and ended up spending £121.90 between us (mostly on sugar and alcohol: chocolate spread, yoghurts with marshmallows in, potato waffles, Ben and Jerry's, family-sized Haribo, vodka, white wine and WKDs).

Was disappointing when we realised that all our stuff had to be carried back to the flat rather than arrive magically in cupboards like at home. With so many bags and so little muscle, we decided the best plan would be to 'borrow' a trolley and wheel food to flat. Annoyingly, mulleted Trolley-Man spotted us just as we were winding our way out of the car park. It was really quite rude the way he went on about 'stealing' supermarket property and 'student vandals'. Our trolley was then confiscated and we were left with eleven carrier-bags stacked on the tarmac.

Had to struggle home, hauling the bags between us and taking rest-breaks every few steps. Managed to lighten load slightly by eating all the Haribo sweets, which also perked up energy levels. We arrived back at the flat clammy and exhausted. I wanted a sleep to recuperate but Tam said, 'We can't submit to snooze pressure as we'd be wasting important socialising time, meaning we'd miss out on meeting future friends and thereby affect our mental well-being.' She's so wise.

Instead we cooked dinner. We agreed to make a simple pasta dish, until our lack of shopping skills were exposed: we had no vegetables or pasta. We settled for spaghetti hoops on potato waffles and both felt very jealous when Justin opened his bulging cupboard and then casually threw together a gourmet meal.

(Note: Justin would be better cooking-buddy than Tam.)

8.30 pm Just called Mum. Her voice went all high-pitched when I said, 'Hi, it's me.'

'Josie! How are you? Are you happy? What are your flatmates like? Are you eating properly? You're not drinking too much, are you? Did you find the multi-vits?'

Hearing Mum's voice, I felt a wave of homesickness. Mum and everything homely feels so far away now. And I don't like to think of her padding round an empty house by herself.

'Are you OK, Mum?' I asked gently. 'I mean, being on your own?'

'Don't be silly,' she chided, 'I'm not on my own – I've got Gruff. And I don't think he'd like to hear you say that.'

Do worry when she talks about the dog like he's a person and fear it'll only get worse in my absence. She already displayed the first signs of Dr. Dolittle madness this summer: I caught her saying, 'Go on, Gruff, go and find your sister for me. Where's your sister? Where is she?' Although I wouldn't have chosen to be an only child, I'd rather not have a border terrier as a brother. Particularly as that'd make Gruff Mum's son. Oh dear.

Our conversation then deteriorated into dog-chatter as Mum told me in some detail about the dog's day. I was a little distracted by Matt, who was lingering in my doorway doing drinking-a-pint visuals and then tapping his watch.

'OK, Mum. Well, yes, I'm sure he'll enjoy that. I'd best go now as I'm nipping out for a drink with my flatmates.'

Then I heard Granny's voice in the background: 'Off, Gruff! Down!'

'Granny's here for supper,' Mum said by way of explanation, '– and she's brought Doogle.'

Mum and Granny have a long, bitter and entirely competitive feud about which of their dogs is more intelligent/attractive/well-trained etc.

'Control your dog,' I heard Granny demand. 'He's doing beastly things to Doogle!'

'Josie, just hold on a moment,' said Mum, in her I'm-going-to-sort-this-out voice.

After that, all I could hear was a lively debate about canine humping and then Granny hollering, 'How dare you! Doogle is not homosexual!'

I used the opportunity to call into the phone, 'Bye, Mum. Speak soon!'

Wednesday 18 September

10.10 am Energy was fun last night. It was just Tam, Matt, Justin and I as Suniti stayed in with Aja (who, I'm starting to feel, should also be paying rent). Our sixth flatmate still hasn't moved in so we were working on theories of why they hadn't arrived yet. Matt was keen on the idea that it's a 'she' and 'she' is late starting because of a glamour film shoot that over-ran. I'm hoping it's not a girl in case Tam loses interest in me and then I'll be forced to bumble around Energy for endless evenings talking about my imaginary travels and how I love Biochemistry.

If the room stays empty, I suggested we use it as a girls' dressing area. That didn't go down well with the boys; Justin thinks renovating it into a Chill Out Lounge with candles, beanbags and comics is a good idea, but Matt insisted he'd shot-gunned it two days ago as his Conquest Den. He described the concept: 'When I entice a lucky lady back to my room and we've interacted satisfactorily, she can then retire to the Conquest Den. This will optimise my beauty sleep in preparation for the following night's activities and in addition to this, it will diffuse those awkward morning-after moments when my beer goggles have been removed. I think you'll all agree that this is the perfect solution.'

Hmmm.

When we got back to South Hall, the whole building was shaking along to a thudding bass. Students were spilling out of the flat below ours, swarming in the corridors, blocking the stairs and surging into the courtyard outside. Our new neighbours were having a party, so we steered through the throng of people to go and meet them.

Their kitchen is a replica of ours, except the plastic chairs had been stacked up, the varnished table was pushed against the wall and there was a poster on the noticeboard of two naked girls licking cream from each other. A short guy with floppy brown hair was hunched over a set of decks, wearing a 'NO LOGO' T-shirt with scuffed-up slacks.

'Hey, there!' shouted a head of blonde dreadlocks from behind us. 'I'm Gil. Do you want some punch?' Gil pointed to the plugged kitchen sink filled with red liquid. Matt and Justin had already vanished so Tam accepted for the two of us. As Gil ladled the dodgy concoction, the sleeve of his Surfers Against Sewage hoodie dangled in the punch. He brought it to his mouth and sucked it clean.

'I think we're your neighbours,' I yelled over the music, wondering if this was a good thing. 'We live above you.'

'That's wicked,' Gil beamed. 'You're pretty.'

Oh. Felt a bit awkward as wasn't sure it would have been honest to return the compliment.

'You've gotta meet Hobbit,' Gil continued. 'He lives here too.'

Wondered if Flat 1 had bonded so quickly that they were already at the doling-out-nicknames stage? Or maybe Gil and Hobbit are actually ex-public school boys who, the week before uni, decided on a change of image, so Gil got dreadlock extensions and called himself after a fish lung and Hobbit looked in the mirror and realised, 'Good gosh, I look exactly like one of those midget people with the hairy feet.'

Turned out that Hobbit was the DJ. When he trundled over to us later it became clear that Tolkien was definitely the naming inspiration. Hobbit wasn't that big on conversation and I couldn't see any hints of a public school education, though I did learn he prefers his weed from Amsterdam: ('It's got more of a kick to it, man').

Our new neighbours gave us a tour of their rooms. Wasn't sure if it was a chat-up attempt but since their rooms were crammed with party-goers, Tam and I felt safe. Gil's bedroom, directly beneath mine, was splattered with posters of surfers and Reef models in thongs. There was a shiny red-and-chrome Chopper bike parked against the wall and a battered surfboard resting against the chair.

Next door, Hobbit's room was filled with records, speakers, DVDs and several posters of breakdancing moves. There were a couple of mediation books on his desk, and I did notice a lot equipment devoted to the art of smoking; there were bongs, pipes and, well, that's all I know the names of, but there were definitely lots of other things that Gandalf would have approved of.

After a couple more hours of drinking red stuff and chatting with other South Hall freshers, we went to find the boys. Matt was in the corridor holding a bottle of Ouzo and shouting 'Malacas!' with Yanni and Hesperos, two Greek brothers who live with Gil and Hobbit. When he saw Tam and me, he pulled us into a side room and panted: 'I've just met two girls who live in the flat above us – and they're seriously hot! One of them was wearing this pink outfit that was so tight I could see every curve of her fine body. Shame they've left, though.'

I gave Tam an 'I-wonder-why?' shrug.

'They're probably in bed right now,' leered Matt. 'Girls in pyjamas – together!' He huddled in close and lowered his voice. 'I've got something very important to ask you both. Can you introduce yourselves and then invite them over for a slumber party?'

'Good night, Matthew,' we chorused.

As Tam and I left the flat, we found Justin passed out on the stairway, hugging the fire extinguisher. As we hoisted him to his feet, Justin gurgled something about 'red liquid, veryverystrowng', so we dragged him upstairs, plonked him on his bed and put a glass of water beside him.

'Do you realise,' said Tam, as we took off Justin's Green Flash trainers and pulled the Spider-Man duvet over him, 'we're living with a comic fanatic' (Justin), 'a porn-enthusiast' (Matt), 'a shy foreign student' (Suniti), 'and our neighbours include a DJ called Hobbit, a surf-bum named Gil and two Miss World contestants that Matt wants us to have sleepovers with?'

'When you look at it like that,' I said 'I'm not holding out much hope for our sixth flatmate.'

Thursday 19 September

4 pm Ugh. Have spent five hours enrolling. First, I had to enrol to become an official student. I filled in various forms and, armed with passport and university acceptance letter, stood at back of queue that was 1,326 students long. I reached the front two hours later, only to have a university official point to the bottom of my yellow form where in tiny letters it read: 'Your application cannot be processed without a passport-sized photo.'

Grrrrr!

Was redirected into stuffy side-room filled with flustered students and one tiny photo machine. Spent a further forty minutes shuffling along and was over-heated and sweaty by time I got into booth.

I span the twizzly stool and pulled the curtains so no one could see me rearranging my hair. I dropped my coins in and smiled.

Flash!

Luckily it was an option booth as there was definitely shine on my top lip. No. 1 discarded. Next.

No. 2. Wiped away the shine. Tilted head slightly to left as is best side . . .

Flash!

Interestingly, I managed to look like a female Ricky Gervais. Hmmm.

No. 3. Final chance. Was ready this time, big smile, eyes wide open.

'Josie!' bellowed a male voice from the back of the room.

For a split second my brow furrowed questioningly and my eyes flickered from the screen . . .

Flash!

Buggery. I had a facial expression that made me look as though I'd smelt something horrible coming from the left. I didn't have any more change so had to hit the 'Accept' button and then watch the hideous photo develop four times. What made it worse was that 'Josie' turned out to be a tall girl with purple hair.

I then met up with Tam for stage two of enrolment procedure: choosing your modules. Is very exciting (in a geeky way) as there are over a hundred English Literature choices, everything from Beowulf, Chaucer and Austen, to Fiction of the Indian Sub-Continent and Gay and Lesbian Studies. Was getting confused by all the options so eventually made decisions based on length of books, start time of lecture and whether Tam's taking the module.

My timetable looks like this:

Autumn Semester
Mon 10–12 pm Shakespeare's Comedies (with Tam)
2–4 pm African American Literature
Tue 10–12 pm Twentieth Century Children's Literature
Wed No lectures

Thu 10–12 pm Crime Fiction
2–4 pm Gay and Lesbian Studies (with Tam)
Fri 12–2 pm Cultural Criticism (with Tam)

Favourite module is definitely Children's Literature as set texts for semester include *Winnie-the-Pooh*, *Matilda* and *Charlotte's Web*. While I'm very pleased with the amount of free time I've got, am wondering whether six lectures a week are really worth £3,000 a year in tuition fees? Hmmm.

Friday 20 September

2.15 pm Am rich! Student loan has arrived. Love my new free money!! Is very good timing as it's the Freshers' Ball tonight (maybe the student bar does scratchy-back favours to the LEA so the loan cheques are released on Ball night?). Now that I've left home and am a sensible grown-up, plan to budget money and not fritter away on frippery such as unnecessary accessories. Instead, will work out incomings minus outgoings and allocate self a monthly budget.

2.45 pm Hmmph! Budget is not looking perky. Once accommodation, books and food are deducted, it leaves enough money to buy one shoe. Maybe should consider taking the Ben and Jerry's back?

3.05 pm Ooo . . . Matt's told me that if you can't repay student loans within twenty-five years then the Government wipes it out. He thinks same thing happens if you leave the country for ten years. Not too convinced about this, as surely gap decades would become popular? Does sound nice though – and quite fancy an extended holiday. No! No! Must not get side-tracked by ten-year holidays as need to get ready for the Ball!

4 pm Have pulled out every item of clothing I own and paraded length of room (three and a half strides) to *Kylie's Greatest Hits*. Should just mention that I only listen to her in a self-conscious, ironic way, not because I know all the words or style myself as an olive-skinned version of her.

I discussed outfits with Tam and she thinks I should opt for my fitted red boob-tube dress that tapers nicely at the waist and ends just below the knee. She said it maximises my petiteness and red suits dark hair. She is wise. For her, I decided on a dusky pink dress with waterfall neckline that will look lovely with her curves and wavy blonde hair. I too am wise.

Is a shame that Suniti's not coming out tonight. I wondered if she doesn't drink alcohol because she's a practising Muslim, so I went to see her earlier to reassure that she could just have soft drinks at the ball. I said that Tam and I wouldn't drink either if she'd be more comfortable (hadn't actually mentioned that to Tam as think she may have cut holes in my dress). Anyway, Suniti still wasn't tempted and said she wants to get ahead with course preparation. Shame.

6.30 pm Tam and I have plucked eyebrows, waxed legs, showered, washed hair, cleansed, exfoliated, moisturised, dried hair, straightened hair, applied make-up, arranged suitable underwear, put on dresses, fastened stilettos and perfumed.

Matt and Justin have used liberal amounts of hair wax and put on their dads' tuxes.

6.45 pm Off to the Ball!

3.30 am Ijm bagck and a ittle bit dwunk. I tink i mayhave e m b a r s e d   m e s e f l   v e r y v e r y v e r y   m u c h. Ooooooooooooooopppps!

Saturday 21 September
11.25 am. In bed. Ygrrk! Head hurts. Tummy wobbling. Brain fuzzy. Sleep.

11.30 am Am still in red dress. Has twisted into compromising and blood-restricting position. Help!

11.33 am Unwelcome memories flooding back . . .

Things started well. Matt and Justin chaperoned us. (Matt actually offered to be our personal protection unit throughout the night, 'in case you get any hassle'. We politely declined as thought his type of protection might be counterproductive.) Was nice atmosphere at Ball as fake laughter and fixed smiles have calmed down and people actually seemed to be having a good time.

Gil and Hobbit were there and added their own touch of street-wear to formal dress code (tuxes with skate trainers). Gil had scraped his heavy blonde dreads into a ponytail, and immediately loped over to tell me, 'You look pretty. Do you want to dance with us?' So Tam, Justin and I threw some crazy shapes on the dance floor while they hipped and hopped. Love how Justin dances – he wiggles his whole body like a string-puppet on speed. Think I came into my own when cheesy tunes took over and, although frowned upon by rest of student body, I was pleased to have the chance to dust off my Jackson 5 routine.

Have been thinking about it and really, the name 'Freshers' Ball' is just a cover; put 4,000 eighteen- to twenty-five-year-olds in a large room, dim the lights, play music, add alcohol and you've got speed dating without the rules. The boys were over-excited by so many young, available girls in suitable education and social brackets. Must have had my bum pinched, slapped or groped over a dozen times.

Was in full flow with an athletic dance move when a pale, chubby guy sneakily manoeuvred himself behind me and lingered his fingers on my bottom. I smacked at his grubby hands and called him a 'dirty pervert', but he grinned back as though it was a compliment.

I ranted to Tam and Justin; 'The next idiot to touch my arse will get the same treatment to his balls!'

Two minutes later, I felt a strong squeeze to my left buttock. Think vodka makes me bold as I whipped round, grabbing and twisting the genitalia of the offending male. Was a bit of a surprise when I looked into the pervert's face and found he was an extremely attractive, but now wincing, blonde guy.

'Do you honestly think,' I began hoity-toitily, 'that grabbing my arse would turn me on so much that I'd melt dreamily into your arms and suggest we have sex? Your mother must be proud of raising a son who single-handedly inspired the notion of sterilisation.'

Tam clapped.

Justin looked impressed.

Chubby Guy stopped grinning.

Twisted-Balls stood shocked. Then he took a deep breath, straightened his body to full height, and then glaring at me with wild blue eyes, he bellowed; 'I am not the sort of person who grabs girls' arses. And let me tell you *honestly*, if I were about to start, it definitely wouldn't be with yours!' And he stomped off.

How rude! What's wrong with my pert derrière? He wouldn't say that to Kylie. Hmmph! I began fuming about 'the nerve of . . .' when I noticed a group of lads laughing and patting the real culprit on the back. Crap!

Tam and Justin helped me douse my embarrassment with more vodka-oranges. Think this might have contributed to the three of us ending the night on the karaoke machine performing '*Blame It on the Boogie*' as a group of drunken freshers stumbled around in front of us to the rhythm of 'sunshine, moonlight, good times, boogie'. Oh dear.

11.45 am Humiliation on so many levels. Mr Tubs says he is embarrassed to know me. Need to wake Tam and get her version of events.

11.46 am Will have to wait before conversing with witness as cannot yet co-ordinate thoughts with leg movement.

12.05 pm Desperately need to clean teeth/mouth as think Warden-Brian might class breath as fire hazard.

12.06 pm Will have to make bathroom attempt.

12.10 pm Oh! My! God! There's a naked man in our bathroom. I walked in on him showering and froze, rooted to the vinyl floor. It was Twisted-Balls.

In our shower.

Naked!

Mmmm . . . lovely pectorals, though.

'What the hell are you doing?' he demanded, water dripping all over his muscular body.

His angry voice induced flashback of dance floor attack and shook me out of gawping. 'I . . . I'm . . . I am about to clean my teeth,' I stammered indignantly. 'What are you doing in my flat?!'

'I live here!'

Brain got all fuddled and hoped I was still in half-drunk, alternate dimension. Then I remembered the Conquest Den. I looked round and, horrifyingly, door was open and belongings were inside. All came pounding into focus. The guy whom I'd twisted in a very private place, lives here, in this flat, in the Conquest Den, two doors away from mine. I was staring at a naked man who thinks I'm a sadistic lunatic and we have to live together for the next year. Buggery!

Speedily backed out of bathroom attempting apologies, but door was slammed before I finished.

12.15 pm Things have gotten worse. Caught sight of self in mirror, which cruelly reveals am still wearing red dress that has ridden up to waist exposing big Snoopy pants. Fck.

12.25 pm Climbed into bed with Tam, who must have attempted to put her pyjamas on last night but seemed to have missed her right arm, which was now pinned to the side of her body in a PJ-straitjacket sort of way. I breathlessly filled her in on identity of our new naked flatmate and she couldn't believe it either. And then promptly fell back to sleep.

Took opportunity to nosey at photos on her wall. Her boyfriend is quite good-looking, although his smile does look like a sneer and he has Spock ears.

1 pm Am back in own room. It smells like Bacardi mixed with Tangy Cheese Doritos. Need water (and to open window). Can't go into communal areas in case Twisted-Balls sees me.

2 pm Really quite dehydrated. Mr Tubs said I must pull self together as cannot hide in room for next nine months.

Small steps, one at a time. First the kitchen – will check coast is clear.

2.01 pm Can hear someone in there . . .

2.02 pm Rang Tam's mobile so she can fetch drink, but she's ignoring me. Am going myself.

2.17 pm Walked into kitchen in a 'I'm-breezy' type way. Luckily, it was only Matt eating cold pizza in a crumpled shirt and boxers. 'Hey, Shorty,' he croaked at me in a hangover voice. 'I hear you've met our new flatmate?'

'Erm, yeah.' I squirmed uncomfortably.

'Why didn't you grope me when we met?'

'I didn't grope – I twisted.'

'Feisty!'

'No . . . no! What I mean is, I thought he grabbed my arse, so I twisted his balls.'

'You saucy little minx!' he winked, sauntering out of the kitchen before I could explain.

After sipping water very gently (being considerate of thumpy head), was making my way back to bed when I saw Twisted-Balls emerge from his room and walk along the corridor towards me! The ground resisted my attempts to be swallowed by it, leaving me no choice other than to explain self.

New flatmate is called Ben. After making apologies about dance floor attack and shower exposure, he eventually stopped looking at me like I had 'mentalist' tattooed on forehead. I even managed ninety seconds of 'normal' conversation and have learnt that Ben is studying Psychology and was late starting as he's just returned from a gap year in South America. Apparently he spent six months in Costa Rica helping with turtle conservation (ah!), and then spent the last three months travelling around surfing (mmmm).

Luckily I resisted temptation to say, 'I've been travelling too.' Phew.

Don't know if it was Ben or maybe my hangover, but something made my stomach flutter. He has these really intense blue eyes and sandy blonde hair that spills messily over his face. His shoulders are broad and I could see the definition of his muscles beneath his T-shirt and he has a lovely deep tan, and there's this tiny mole below his right eyebrow that I just want to . . .

Oh, crap! I fancy my flatmate. This is terrible. Incestuous! I'm a girl raised on American sitcoms and Rule No. 1 is, 'Under no circumstances should you fall for flatmates'; it'll only lead to problems with general flat karma and end with lifelong disappointment. (Plus, I've potentially ruined Ben's chances of ever being able to have sex.) This is all wrong. Must suppress feelings. Think of Pablo. Eugh, no! Don't think of greasy Pablo. Think of other boys.

6 pm Have spent afternoon at Freshers' Fair trying to blank out alcohol headache and stirrings of dangerous new love interest. Was possibly not best hangover cure as place was packed with students, brightly coloured stands and people forcing random free stuff into my hands. I've got two carrier bags full of pointless things, including three lollipops, a deodorant for men, eighteen branded biros and a 20-page pamphlet about how joining the Territorial Army would suit me.

The Sports and Societies Fair was being held next door in the Great Hall. Third years were trying to bribe us to join their clubs with gifts of penny-sweets and promises of attractive opposite-sex club members. Tam and I decided to take a leisurely stall-stroll so we could objectively assess the different clubs and the types of people who join them.

This is what we saw: Mountaineering Society (Duke of Edinburgh die-hards), Drama Club (ADD sufferers), Medieval Society (people with plaits called Marian), Country Pursuits (William and Henry), Cheerleading Squad (Sweet Valley wannabes and Matt), Sci-fi Society (Terry Pratchett fans and engineering students), Debating Team (Arts students), Table-Tennis (Maths students), Comic Book Club (Justin), Herbalism (Hobbit) and Bell-Ringing (no one).

Hmmm. None of the above were quite right for me. Did consider Rock Climbing as like the idea of being an outdoorsy type, except fear of heights may stunt progress. Then thought about Film Society but decided films could be art-house sort and, sadly, I'm more of an Adam Sandler kinda-gal. In the end I joined the Surf Club. My reasons were:

- exciting outdoor sport
- can explore new part of British coastline
- good exercise (but not too strenuous)
- always wanted to try beach-chic
- fit boys in tight wetsuits (mmmm)
- Have persuaded Tam to join too, thus sealing friendship inside flat, on my course and in a sports club. Good

work. (Just to clarify, having 'Surf Club member' stamped on Athletics Union card has nothing to do with Ben mentioning he surfs. A decision based on two-minute conversation with object of prohibited lust would be both shallow and desperate.)

First surf is next Wednesday. Better get some waterproof mascara before then.

7 pm Got home and found Matt slumped in our kitchen, crying into a leaflet. He paid £10 for annual membership to S.H.A.G. society and has just realised it's an abbreviation for Sexual Health Awareness Group.

THREE

Monday 23 September

10.20 am. Shakespeare's Comedies. Am squashed on the end of a long row next to Tam. Not sure I like being in an echoing lecture hall surrounded by 300 English Literature students. In one sense, I do feel slightly cool – as though I've stepped on to a film set and the camera is about to pan round and see me looking studious yet suitably nonchalant. But in another more pressing sense, feel that I might be developing vertigo.

We're sat towards the back of the tiered hall and I keep peering down over sea of heads watching everyone else silently taking notes. No one's fidgeting or whispering or possibly even breathing. Just complete silence. It makes me feel anxious. Am worried that brain could suddenly malfunction and I'll throw self down lecture hall in a crowd-surfing-type manoeuvre. Would forever be known as Jumping Girl and . . . OK, take calming breaths. In. Out. Everything is fine. Breathe. Will count things to help focus mind. Row in front: One girl. Two girls. A boy wearing a trench coat. Three girls in blouses and pearls. White boy with Rasta hat and Bob Marley T-shirt. One girl wearing tiara. Two people tapping on laptops. One skater in visor and sweatbands. Good. Calm.

Don't think nerves have been helped by a panicked start to lecture. Tam and I were a little late as we weren't sure what to wear. After years of whining about sad polyester school uniforms, have now realised they are actually a brilliant idea. You don't need to spend precious morning minutes trawling though wardrobe and wondering whether denim mini skirt with Jane Norman top is too dressy for lecture. Obviously, school uniforms are designed to be hideous, but think that this is OK since hideousness is enforced on all, whereas now there is no excuse for own hideousness.

Anyway, clothing dilemmas put us behind schedule and then we got lost in labyrinth of university buildings. Did wonder if David Bowie might be waiting behind the Science Block holding a baby, ready to confuse us through song. We eventually worked out that lecture hall C/W6.1 stands for 'first floor, Humanities block' (how?). We creaked through the door trying to blend into the scenery, but, regrettably, I'd chosen inappropriate footwear which squeaked with each flip and every flop.

Rather than politely ignoring our late entrance, McGibbon – our lecturer straight from the pits of academic hell – peered at us over half-glasses and said with thespian pomposity: 'We are so glad you could join us. Do take your time and find a seat.'

Was a bit tricky as lecture hall was packed with students, all of whom were watching us creep awkwardly up the steps. We eventually spotted a couple of spare seats right at the back of the hall and caused a bit of a kafuffle by getting everyone to budge along a bit so we could squeeze on. McGibbon is now standing at the front of the hall stabbing a pointer at a list of rules he's projected on to a screen.

'One: lateness. If you cannot arrive on a Monday morning by 10 am, then please do not come at all.'

His black, weasel eyes are skittering between Tam and me.

'Two: mobiles. I do not tolerate interruptions from mobile phones or any other new-fangled electronic device.

If you insist on accompanying your phone to class, please have the courtesy to switch your phone off and yourself on.'

How witty.

'Three: midway break. At 11 am, halfway through the lecture, you will have a five-minute break where you are free to yawn, stretch, use the toilet facilities, have a fag, check your texts or leave the class and crawl back to your student digs for the latter half of the mind-numbing, mid-morning TV schedule. Outside of this five-minute allocation, I would appreciate it if you could refrain from all of the above. Any questions?'

Personally, I'd be interested to know whether the white stuff in the corners of his mouth is spittle or an accidental oversight such as miscellaneous cottage cheese or stray dollops of toothpaste.

11.25 am Someone's mobile is ringing. How embarrassing! Did they miss Rule 2? Everyone's looking round to see whose it is. McGibbon has stopped talking and is searching the room with his rodent eyes.

Bugger! It's coming from near where I'm sat. Hope no one thinks it's mine.

I've gestured to Tam with an 'I-don't-know-who's-it-is' shoulder shrug.

McGibbon's staring at me. It's not my phone!!

It's coming from right in front of me . . . It's that guy's in the Rasta hat! Why's everyone looking at me? Just turn it off, will you!?

McGibbon's giving me death stares.

IT'S NOT MINE!

Oh, God, bloody Rasta Hat Boy has now turned round to look at me – as though it's my phone! Shitting blame-shifter!

Am going bright red as if confirming guilt . . . McGibbon is pointing his pointer at me . . .

The phone has stopped. Thank God.

5.30 pm Am back in flat, wearing lip-gloss and loitering in kitchen hoping to bump into Ben. Realise this is not in the never-fancy-your-flatmate plan, but think I need the pick-me-up after today's lectures. McGibbon was bad enough and then had to suffer a second helping in African American module. Was difficult concentrating on what lecturer was saying as his voice does this weird inflection thing; he begins very softly and quietly but by the end of a sentence he ascends into over-enunciated shouting. 'Nella Larsen astutely negotiates the *question of essentialism!* This is seen through Fru Dahl's stereotyped view of blackness as something savage, primitive *and ultimately intrinsic!'*

5.35 pm Kitchen isn't comfiest loitering area since all surfaces are covered in unpleasant food remnants. Was planning to cook proper meal tonight, except Matt has dipped every kitchen utensil I own in bolognaise-type sauce and left to harden.

5.36 pm Just looked at mobile. Is on loud mode. And I have *1 missed call.* Oops!

7 pm Ben hasn't been in kitchen; instead, I was blessed with Matt's company. He burst in wearing a 'REHAB IS FOR QUITTERS' T-shirt and decided to share my pizza. I tried to make polite conversation to mask his chewing noises by asking how his first lectures went.

'Very disappointing,' he told me through a mouthful of pizza. 'You'd imagine on a Sports Science degree there'd be loads of hot, sporty chicks running round in skimpy tennis skirts. Turns out it's mainly guys. I did a count up today and there's an 80:20 male-to-female ratio. Can you believe it?'

'Shocking.'

'What's the boy/girl ratio in English?' Matt asked, stuffing a piece of salami into his mouth.

'I suppose it's mostly girls,' I mused.

'I need numbers.'

When I suggested there were about seven girls to each boy, Matt shouted 'Bollocks!' with such outrage that a piece of salami landed on the table next to my hand. 'Why isn't that in the prospectus?'

He began to toy with the idea of joining me for tomorrow's modules so I steered the conversation on to another subject. 'What do you think of Ben?' I asked, casually.

'He's sound. Very cool. Actually,' said Matt, thoughtfully picking a string of mozzarella from his teeth, 'it might be a bit of setback having Ben around when I'm trying to woo the ladies. Still, there's always Justin to make me look good.'

'Don't be horrible.'

'Maybe I should go to Psychology lectures with Ben; there's probably loads of girls there.'

Ugh. Why can't Ben be enrolled on an all-boy subject? 'Is he out with Psychology coursemates tonight?'

Matt's eyes widened with interest. 'You fancy him, don't you?'

'Shut up,' I hissed.

Matt started skipping round the kitchen, singing, 'Josie loves Ben, Josie loves Ben. Josie and Ben, sitting in a tree, K.I.S.S.I.N.G.'

It's a shame Matt's good-looking because some poor girl will meet him in a bar where the music is too loud to hear properly and then before she knows it, she'll be dating someone with the social skills of a red-arsed baboon.

9.30 pm Have been sat on Tam's bed having some 'girl time'. She was feeling a bit low as she's missing Oliver. I tried to join in by saying I miss Ben, but I got the impression that it didn't really count seeing as he's only been out of the flat for three hours. And he's not my boyfriend. Still, we had common ground when it came to Matt and Justin: Tam and I both agree that Justin is a lovely, sweet, chirpy bundle of Welsh freckles, and that Matt should be stood in a corner and pelted with Skittles for being such a chauvinist.

It's a shame that Suniti is never around for 'girl time'. I've only seen her in the kitchen twice and she just keeps herself locked away in her room. I suggested to Tam that she's probably doing yoga training, and then felt like an idiot when Tam pointed out that Suniti has a prayer mat, not a yoga mat.

I sometimes wonder if I should have taken a gap year.

Tuesday 24 September
1 pm Hmmph! Lectures are starting to compromise my enjoyment of being a student. Thought today would be easy as only had Children's Literature module. I'd been looking forward to chatting about Pooh and his buddies so was quite a surprise when lecturer spent entire two hours enlightening us about the homoerotic subtext in *Winnie-the-Pooh* and concluded that Eyeore is clinically depressed, Piglet has an inferiority complex and Tigger is gay.

Am pleased it's Sports Wednesday tomorrow as will much prefer going to Surf Club and watching all the lovely boys in wetsuits . . . mmmm! Plus, if we have freakishly good weather, it's possible that Ben may surf in boardshorts!

After thinking rationally about fancying-my-flatmate dilemma, have decided that denying feelings for Ben is unhealthy. It's clearly fate that I've been housed in the same flat as a muscular, tanned Adonis who wears DC trainers. Think the main hurdle in the way of our potentially beautiful relationship, will be that whole business of having to pretend I don't look hideous between the hours of 7 am and 10 am. Every morning I've been dashing to the bathroom to make self look respectable before breakfasting in communal zone. After such colossal efforts, is very disappointing that I hardly ever bump into Ben. We live three rooms apart. We share the same corridor. The same kitchen. The same bathroom. We are flatmates. But have I seen him naked again? Have I? No. Tsk.

Wednesday 25 September

12.15 pm. In minibus. Tam and I are on our way to the beach for our first surf. I knocked on Ben's door this morning planning to ask (very casually) if he wanted to walk with us to the surfing pick-up point – but he wasn't in. He is a surfer, so why is he not surfing? In fact, where are the triangular-backed, long-haired, sun-kissed surf boys? Gil and Hobbit are sat in front chuckling like Beavis and Butthead and other than them, minibus is mainly filled with girls! As I've said before, am purely interested in learning a new sport but did think said sport might have positive men-to-women ratio.

(Am turning into Matt?)

12.40 pm We've arrived at a very cold-looking beach and it's started to rain. Don't like this one little bit.

6 pm Have been wearing full-body rubber suit. Padded bikini was firmly zipped beneath tasteless 80s wetsuit (Day-Glo green legs and yellow flash across chest) that was still damp from the last time it was worn four months ago. The real problems started when I had to get into the bloody thing. Forgot that beaches don't have changing rooms, so Tam and I had to stoop in minibus, twisting and contorting bodies into ridiculous rubber contraptions. As soon as I'd forced both legs in and wrenched arms inside, Tam pointed out (through unhelpful laughter) that I had it on back-to-front. Then whole tedious process started again and I was sweaty and angry by the time I had it zipped up.

Wetsuits don't do much for my figure as caught sight of reflection and briefly mistook self for a nine-year-old boy. Did not feel any more at ease when Gil mentioned that peeing in wetsuits aids insulation.

The whole surfing experience didn't go quite as planned. Had imagined self doing that thing in surf movies where tanned, blonde girl jogs to beach with surfboard under arm (except I'd be nine-year-old brunette boy); but, sadly, even the surfboard bit didn't work out. Mr Tickle would have struggled to carry the beast I was allocated. Between us, Tam and I managed to lug the board to the shore where an attractive surf instructor, Robbie, was giving a lesson.

He was lying in the sand yelling, 'Paddle, paddle, paddle' and demonstrating the motion with his huge, rippling biceps. 'And stand up!' In one fluid movement he'd leapt to his feet and was poised in crouching tiger posture. Mmmm . . . so delicious with big muscles all tensed.

Then we tried it. I found it difficult just getting into the lying down position as rigid urine suit made flexing very tricky. Eventually lay on board and started doing the 'paddle, paddle, paddle' bit. Robbie bellowed, 'Stand up!' Tried to spring legs into action but wetsuit was preventing all bending movements. Unfortunately, body had already made heroic attempt to rise, only stiff legs didn't follow through so ended up in maimed tiger posture.

Even though I couldn't hang-ten on land, I quickly dunked self in sea as wanted outfit hidden underwater. Tam and her board floated alongside me. 'Are we meant to get all the way over there?' she groaned, pointing to the other surfers who were 200 feet away. Deciding that we were, we did a bit of paddle, paddle, paddling and chat, chat, chatting, when out of nowhere a huge rush of white-water rolled its way straight for us. Not sure whether we should try and surf it or jump over it, the broken wave caught us in its path, flushed us with foam and dragged us back towards the shore.

Was trying to centre self on board and also push wet hair off face when Robbie paddled over to us. 'Are you girls OK?' he asked, like David Hasselhoff but without the cheese.

'Er, yes. I think. Um,' I stuttered, confused by his attractive presence and my ice-cream headache.

Tam took control: 'We were wondering how to get past the white-water to the proper waves.'

'You need to duck-dive,' he told us and then guessed from our blank expressions that that meant nothing to us. 'When a wave breaks in front of you,' Robbie explained, 'push down on your board and it will tilt beneath the wave. Hold your breath and dive with the board under water – like a duck. Then you won't get sucked back with the wash.'

We'd obviously missed this crucial first part of his demonstration while I was mincing around putting my wetsuit on back-to-front.

'You might find it a bit tricky on those boards,' Robbie added, 'because they have a large surface area, but since the waves are tiny, I'm sure you'll manage.'

Tiny? Any lump of water that is bowling towards me in a frothing mass is not something I'd describe as tiny.

'Thanks,' smiled Tam.

'Yeah, wicked. Cool. Cheers for that,' I said, testing out my how-to-speak-to-surfers vocabulary.

As Robbie paddled away, Tam mimicked, 'Oh, Robbie, I love you. You're so big and firm, let me stroke you!' She started hugging and kissing her surfboard pretending it was him. 'I like you in that wetsuit. Rubber suits you!' We were so busy laughing that neither of us noticed another wave moving in our direction. All we heard was a loud crashing as it broke thirty feet ahead of us and the white-water came roaring our way.

'Oh, crap!' Tam stopped smooching and scrambled into duck-dive position as the water thundered towards us.

I pushed with all my might but my stupid, fat, ugly board wouldn't dive. It dipped all of two inches before the broken wave crashed on top of me. I gripped tightly as I was pounded by the water and swirled nastily.

Tried to curse, but the shock of icy-cold water immersing my head into salty oblivion caught my breath and no sound came out.

I looked for Tam and saw her splashing around with clumps of blonde hair stuck to her forehead. 'I think I've had enough exercise for today,' I shouted.

'Absolutely agree,' Tam replied, sprawling on top of her board.

'By the way, how's my mascara?'

'Fine,' she said. 'If you like it on your cheeks.'

The experience wasn't all bad. We did get invited to surfing social tonight at The Frog pub just off campus, so perhaps it's worth sticking with it for a couple more weeks?

3 am Mmmm, night out was fun. I like being in a sports club as Wednesday evenings at the pub are a very nice idea – particularly as Ben came with us, yey! He looked yummy in faded jeans that hung low over his cute bum. Have to say, although I can completely appreciate the physical aspects of Ben, this is no longer just a lust crush. We had a long and lovely conversation by the bar, which has led me to the conclusion that Ben is the nicest, coolest, most caring boy on earth. Who else asks sweet things like, 'Do you miss your family?' and then is interested in your answer?

I started opening up to him about what had happened with Mum and Dad. I don't think I've ever really talked about it with a boy before, but I felt at ease chatting with Ben. I was telling him how close Dad and I were when I was younger. On weekends he'd take me for walks to Ticky Tucky Island to try and glimpse the wizards who lived under the bridge, or if he had to work at the dental surgery, he used to let me be in charge of important tasks like filling up cups with pink water and pressing the button that made the chair tilt. When I became a teenager, things gradually changed. I felt a bit embarrassed hanging out with Dad and preferred spending more time with my friends. By then, Dad was working such long hours anyway that he didn't have time for me and we drifted apart. I sometimes wonder if we'd been closer still, maybe Dad wouldn't have decided to leave.

There's something really genuine about Ben that makes me feel like I can talk to him about anything. (Maybe being a Psychology student makes him a good listener?) Was a bit annoying though, because as Ben was starting to tell me about his family, Gil bumbled over, interrupting: 'Josie, I need to speak to you. Alone.'

Ben moved away to order another drink and Gil huddled in right next to me. All he had to say was, 'Josie, I've been thinking about it and, like, if you want any extra surfing lessons, I could always show you a few moves. You know, just the two of us.' Hmmm.

At closing, we moved on to Jive Hive at the Student's Union. I didn't get to see Ben again as the SU was packed with other sports club members. As it was the first official Sports Wednesday of the year, it meant one thing: initiation night. Had heard scary rumours about students being forced to drink the blood of small children or having snakes tattoed across chests. Luckily it was a little tamer than all that. Mostly, third-year boys were forcing their first-year team-mates to drink obscene amounts of alcohol without taking breath. Matt was there with the Football Club but didn't notice us as he'd gone temporarily blind through alcohol flooding.

Was fun being an initiation spectator. Am pleased that Surf Club isn't a song-singing, fine-giving, alcohol-poisoning kinda society because, by the time we got home, we found

45

Matt slumped outside South Hall in a shopping trolley, wearing nothing but a pink tutu and chocolate body paint.

Thursday 26 September
3.15 pm. Gay and Lesbian Studies. Our lecture is being taught by a very sassy lady in killer heels. She says that one of the ideas behind Gay and Lesbian Studies is to challenge heteronormative society. Don't exactly know what this is, but sounds like a very good idea and am sure it'll involve bringing down Matt. Talking of which, it was a shame Matt wasn't incapacitated by his initiation hangover. Just as Tam and I were leaving for our lecture, he poked Justin across the kitchen table: 'So, gay-boy, why aren't you going to study the homos, too?'

Irked by Matt's constant Gay Lord, Fairy Queen, Sheep Shagger jokes, Justin slapped down his comic and said, 'People who display homophobic behaviour often use it to mask their own sexual desires.'

'You're right,' said Matt seriously. 'I knew there was something different about me – and you've just let in the light. I'm a lesbian trapped inside a man's body! Tam, will you help me find myself?'

Tam clipped Matt round the back of the head and Justin followed it up with a slap of his comic.

'Homosexuality', the lecturer is explaining, 'is not an identity or personality label but a sexual preference. We need to employ "queer theory" to challenge texts and the naturalised assumptions within them.'

Is all very exciting. Feel more culturally aware already and am looking forward to sharing my new knowledge with Matt. And Granny.

6 pm. At desk. Have been trying to make a start with course reading, so sat down to read essay, *'Sex, Drugs and Gay Bars'*. Mr Tubs and I were quite enjoying looking academic and reading important literary essay – until I heard the three boys sprinting along the corridor and then they burst into my bedroom. (Hoped there was no incriminating evidence lying around, e.g. panty-liners, Jolen, padded bras etc.) Matt, Ben and Justin were wearing mock-army gear and war paint that looked like a combination of my eye-liner and Tam's olive green eye-shadow. Judging by the detail in their outfits, do wonder if any of them went to lectures today.

Matt was giggling like a schoolboy with Lieutenant Justin covering his right (they'd obviously made up) and Sergeant Ben (looking very dashing) to his left. Clasped in their hands were three yellow water-pistols, poised in my direction. Matt pulled a second 'gun' from his holster (pocket) and began spinning the two together in John Wayne style.

'Boys – watch and learn.' With arms outstretched and a gangster tilt of his head, he aimed the yellow plastic pistols in my direction. 'Hey, yo' mo' fo'!'

I'm a what?

'You been messin' with me bitches again?'

Am I missing something?

'Shizzle ma nizzle yo' punk!'

You'd like me to what?

'Yo' gotta be taught a lesson! Bassht bassht!' Matt made a machine-gun noise as a weak squirt of tap water reached my shoulder.

'You're a knob.'

'Don't blame the playa, blame the game.'

Justin and Ben stood to his side with guns in *Starsky and Hutch* poses and Matt said, 'Cool, eh, Josie? We look like something out of—.'

'*The Beano*?' I suggested.

'There's nothing wrong with *The Beano*,' interjected Justin.

'We were thinking more like *Bad Boys*,' smiled Ben.

'Exactly,' huffed Matt. 'I see you don't appreciate our efforts to initiate you into the dark, underground world of violence, where yo' gotta have someone watchin' yo' back.'

'Don't worry, Matt. If I need protection, I've got a five-year-old cousin who's a mean shot with a super-soaker.'

The water-pistol crew have retreated and taken their mission elsewhere.

Mmmm . . . Ben even looks cute in face paint.

Friday 27 September
6.10 pm. In room. Have been ambushed three times on way back from lectures. Discovered that SU shop has been selling water-pistols for £1 and the male student population has found something other than carbonated alcoholic drinks to invest their loans in. Am now back in room, wet and exhausted, and if any of my flatmates dare to come near me with a water-based weapon, I will fight.

So pleased that first week of lectures is over, it's been an exhausting ride of the mind. Climaxed today with Cultural Criticism, which was basically a two-hour debate on 'Defining postmodernism in the twenty-first century'. If I'd brought my dictionary, I could've put an end to it and been home in time for *Neighbours*. Was particularly annoyed as was sat next to spikey-haired girl wearing a 'BAN CON-FORMITY!' T-shirt; each time lecturer paused for breath, she'd raise an additional issue, using vocabulary such as 'sublime' and 'transcendent' to make a random point about something no one other than the lecturer understood.

Two hours and a numb brain later, conclusion of debate was precisely that postmodernism is indefinable. A little ironic twist for us under-graduatelings.

7 pm Hmmph. None of flatmates are home. Really wanted to go for drink to celebrate the end of our first week of lectures. Know Tam has gone to visit Oliver for the w/e (Boo! Hiss!), but the boys never mentioned any plans. Maybe they've discovered Toys Я Us has got a half-price sale on super-soakers?

Ooo . . . maybe Suniti is in?

7.08 pm Can confirm that she is, although had to wait in the corridor for two lonely minutes while she unlocked the door. Got the impression Suniti didn't want to chat, but decided to be confident and friendly so made self comfy on her bed anyway.

Conversation was a bit one-sided really. Suniti stood awkwardly by the window adjusting her hijab, while I quickly exhausted my questions:

'Do you like your course?' (she finds Medicine very interesting).

'How many brothers and sisters do you have?' (three younger sisters).

'Are you homesick?' (she isn't).

'Have you been to the UK before?' (she hasn't).

'Do you watch *The OC*?' (she doesn't).

'Would you like to share a frozen lasagne?' (she didn't).

I paused, hoping Suniti may ask me something back, but when she didn't, I bumbled on with more questions:

'Don't you like frozen lasagne, or are you vegetarian?' (no and no. She only eats Halal meat).

'What that?' (meat that's been ritually slaughtered).

'Do you get much of it at the campus shop?' (no).

My questions weren't really going anywhere, so I tried volunteering some useful background information about self, but I only got to age six before she asked me to leave.

Am now sitting in my room with Mr Tubs, experiencing a strong surge of homesickness. Whole buzz of freshers has been dampened by reality of lectures and my lovely student loan has pretty much vanished already. Am also finding it quite tricky living with someone I fancy. Every time I come back to the flat, my stomach is dancing with expectation: Will Ben be home? Will he be in the kitchen? Will he be wearing the white Volcom T-shirt I can see his muscles through? Then, when he's not in, I have sad, bitter, lonely thoughts and flop on to bed imagining that he's cheating on me. (Not sure cheating is the technical term, since not really going out.)

On top of all this misery, the unglamorous realities of student life are coming to surface: I only have economy beans left in the cupboard and no clean plates to eat them from; the quilted toilet roll supplies from home have already run out and now we're down to the thin stuff; and this morning there was a hair on my face flannel that I know did not grow on a face. And one more thing: why is there always a piece of onion on our kitchen floor?

FOUR

Monday 30 September

11 am. In bed. Ugh. Body falling apart. Have been like this for three days now. Whole flat has caught Freshers' Flu. We're blaming Matt who, as Mum would put it, had 'relations' with a germ-bearer from North Hall (we don't like anyone from North Hall as they have en-suites and call South Hall 'the ghetto'! Hmmph). Flu is spreading madly and symptoms include: exhaustion, liver damage, dependency on Aspirin, delirium about Vitamin C intake, delusions of grandeur that your mum is on her way to look after you, and an unwavering belief that you're actually dying of meningitis.

Ah, if I was at home now, Mum would have me wrapped in a snug dressing-gown and be feeding me chicken soup by drip. In hideous student reality, am lying in foetal-position in my 1960s cell, intermittently shivering and sweating into my coat and hoping it is meningitis so I can get a bed on a ward.

Tuesday 1 October

11.30 am. Still in bed. Head hurts, body aches and bladder is full. Cannot go to toilet as am too tired, weak, achey etc. Is interesting, I keep ringing Mum to update her on my illness but during my last call she sounded as though she had better things to do. Feel let down, abandoned, orphaned.

4 pm Have been to doctor's. The moment I threw away form 23.A: 'Registering with a Doctor', I had a vague premonition that I'd be ill. All new students are meant to register with a GP so if they do get ill (ahem) they aren't dragging their sick bodies round in alarmist mode, thinking they're going to die without a doctor present. Me, along with everyone else that didn't get round to finding a GP, turned up at the campus clinic begging and pleading for a free appointment.

After an hour and a half of collecting more germs, the doctor finally saw me. He prodded me a couple of times which seemed to confirm I had Freshers' Flu. The only thing he could suggest was fluids: 'You need to drink a lot.' Then he added, 'You realise I mean water, don't you?'

Why does general population assume all students are alcoholics? Is completely unfounded; I mean, look at our flat: Suniti is teetotal; Justin and I and can manage a shandy between us; I haven't seen Ben drunk yet; Tam can occasionally show control and Matt – well, yes, he's probably an alcoholic. Actually, this afternoon he rounded us up (excluding Suniti who's chosen to have minimal involvement in flat life) and we sat in the kitchen, huddled in duvets listening to his lengthy instructions about our Saturday night plans. (Did he miss the fact it's only Tuesday and we're all ill?)

'Prestige, popularity and a lot of pints await,' he said, pausing for a minute to hack up some phlegm. Even when poorly, Matt still has the energy to coat his entire body in Lynx, put on a 'SLEEP IS FOR LOSERS' T-shirt and harangue the rest of us. 'This Saturday is the annual Beer Race. What's that, I hear you cry?' Matt held a hand to his ear, pretending that we were actually excited by this, 'Yes, you're right! We shall be fully recovered by then; we will be the winning team and yes, Josie and Justin – you two shall still be standing.'

Hmmm.

'Please familiarise yourselves with the rules, which I have posted on the noticeboard.'

Hate it when Matt gets like this. He puts on his 'proper spoken English voice' to sound important and then witters on about lukewarm beer like it's his lifeblood.

The rules, as ripped out of our student newspaper, read:

1. Every team must have a fancy-dress theme.

2. Each team member must drink a minimum of one alcoholic drink in each of the ten pubs on the Beer Race route.

3. 'Beer Race Winning Team' title will be awarded to the first complete team to finish their drinks in destination number ten, with fancy dress intact.

Am really not sure I want to race around streets dressed as something ridiculous while trying to pickle my liver. Oh, God, actually – am worried about how well I'll be able to hold ten beverages. Have tried to avoid drinking too much around Ben because when I have more than five drinks, I tend to get a little over-friendly. By drink six I could be telling Ben he has lovely pecs, by number seven it'll be 'I love you' and beyond that, well, it's just plain dangerous.

5 pm Oh, God! Matt has decided that our fancy-dress theme is 'Slags and Drags' . . .

Wednesday 2 October
11.40 am Still ill. Body aches so much that even showering is like Chinese torture chamber with little water droplets pelting fragile body. Is very boring being ill. Mr Tubs and I have officially run out of things to say. I went through the pros and cons of Beer Race with him and discussed whether a 'slag' outfit could work in my favour, but he thinks class is the way to go for a boy like Ben. Damn.

Would be nice to chat with Tam, except she's become addicted to morning TV and I'm not allowed to interrupt her before 12.30 pm. Keep hearing snippets from her bedroom like Trisha saying diplomatically, 'No one's judging you,' to a woman who thinks having sex with her daughter's husband is perfectly acceptable.

12.30 pm. Justin's room. Am hanging out with Justin, who's using his ill-time to read old comics. I tried to get involved, only I kept reading the speech bubbles in the wrong order and got all confused. Decided it would be more medicinal to talk about Ben. Was trying to explain to Justin what it is I like about Ben ('it's the way his smile tilts slightly to the left; how when you talk to him he really listens; that he has a deep, warm laugh that makes you feel special'), but then realised Justin wasn't concentrating and was trying to lift a box of Kleenex off the desk with his toes. Was actually quite challenging and between us it took seven attempts before we could get the tissues all the way to the bed without dropping them.

1.15 pm I've just been to make Lemsips for Justin and me, and found Ben sat in the kitchen chatting on the phone to his dad. He looked really sweet as his skin was all peaky and he had bed hair tufting everywhere; even the tiny sleep indents on his cheeks looked cute. I could eat him.

I accidentally (on purpose) listened in to his conversation and then felt guilty when I realised they were talking about Ben's sister who'd been in an accident at school. All I could gather was that she'd fainted and as she fell, she cracked her head on a desk. The flow of the conversation suggested she'd been taken to hospital but that it wasn't too serious. Ben was quite adamant that he wanted to go home and check on her, but I could hear his dad eventually manage to dissuade him. It was weird as, seeing Ben look so strained with worry, my stomach knotted and I had the overwhelming urge to hug him.

I guessed Ben might find it a bit strange if I suddenly lunged at him whilst he was on the phone, so I tripped back to Justin's room with our Lemsips.

Every tiny insight about Ben just makes me like him more. I tried explaining this to Justin, but by then he was trying to see whether he could drink Lemsip whilst lying down.

Thursday 3 October
2 pm I've turned a corner. Body no longer aches all over, only in key places: namely head, temples and throat. Actually got dressed for first time in six days and managed to make it all way to the shop for medical provisions.

Friday 4 October
11 am Feeling better still. Knew Galaxy had healing propensities. Even contemplated going to first lecture of week, but Matt banned me as apparently I must reserve my energy for the Beer Race tomorrow night. Hmmm.

3.30 pm Went to see if Suniti wanted to be involved in the Beer Race (I guessed what the answer would be, but I thought it'd be nice to ask). I can't seem to work her out; she's not rude or unkind, but there's just this evasiveness about her, like she wants to keep her distance from us all. Her door is always shut – not propped open like the rest of ours – and her room is bare, except for an alarm clock, her prayer mat (ahem) and a shelf full of medical books. It worries me that I haven't seen her mixing with anyone other than Aja. I know her English is brilliant, but I worry that she's struggling to adjust here with all the cultural differences. At the Freshers' Fair there was an Islamic Society stand, which I mentioned to Suniti – but she wasn't interested in joining. I hope she'd feel she could talk to me if she was having problems.

Saturday 5 October
11 am Am properly healthy again! Tam and I are going shopping for whores' clothes!

12.30 pm Er, now we're going shopping. Forgot about Tam's morning TV schedule.

4 pm Think Oxfam's been accepting donations from local brothel. Managed to pick up fantastically sluttish skin-tight leopard-print dress and Tam got a leather mini, a 'HELLO BOYS' top and red stilettos. Am not too keen on musky charity shop odour but since I don't have time to wash outfit will spray perfume and hope for the best.

Matt and Ben have been scouring our wardrobes for 'drag' outfits. Lust for Ben dipped slightly when saw him wearing one of Tam's halter-neck dresses. He then wanted to borrow a bra so he could fill it with socks and had momentary panic at thought of him trying one of mine, only to discover they come already filled: padding, gel, chicken fillets etc.

7.30 pm We're ready! Have been comparing outfits with our drag queens, who are looking very fetching. Matt has bought huge blow-up boobs that are shoved beneath a Lycra yellow top and finished with a navy netball skirt. He's done his make-up in pantomime dame style to make sure everyone knows, 'This is just pretend – we're not gay or anything.'

Justin looks amazing in a fuchsia pink A-line dress with matching pointy-toed shoes. As he stood in dress and elegant heels, did wonder, looking at self in own leopard-print atrocity, if Justin looked prettier than me.

Matt's bravado began immediately, 'Nice dress, Geri. Pink suits you.'

There was some back and forth between them and then conversation took the natural course and deteriorated into 'your mother' jokes.

Things looked like they could get rowdy when Matt mentioned 'incestuous Welsh sumo bitch', so Ben had to step in: 'Girls, girls, put your handbags away. Isn't it time we took our slags to the prom?'

Love Ben. Diffused situation perfectly. Wouldn't mind being his slag . . .

3 am Slutish boys adn bitchy bwunny reabitts! Am fwurios!!!!!!!!!!!!!!

Sunday 6 October
7 am Am unhealthy again. Yggrk.

7.02 am Why would body wake self at this unnatural hour?

7.03 am Am still wearing leopard print dress, which indicates I wasn't in a very sober state when I got home. I'm not sure all details of night will be accurate, but here goes . . .

Pub 1, The Frog: 'Our furnishings are from a pawn shop'

Felt very self-conscious walking into pub 1, stone-cold sober and dressed as a slag. Wanted to apologise to the non-Beer Race partakers and reassure them that I'm actually a nice girl from a good family.

Was very impressed by other fancy-dress efforts; there were doctors, nurses, cowboys, Indians, schoolgirls, schoolboys, Charlie's Angels, musketeers, pirates and even the Ghostbusters. One team had called itself: 'Freshers with Fetishes'. A tall boy with a quiff had tailored his own suit from porn magazines and the other (eugh!) had attached a gold shower to his head with thin sprigs of yellow tinsel hanging over his face, and a sign on his chest read, 'Golden shower, anyone?'

Matt was kicking himself.

Pub 2, The King's Arms: 'Old Man Ray's hangout'

Bumped into the boys from downstairs who were dressed as the A Team. Hobbit was in his element as a short B. A. Baracus, blacking out his face (not sure how PC this is?) and styling his hair into a mohican. He was telling anyone who'd listen, 'I pity the fool!' Gil tried to look smooth as Face, although his dreadlocks didn't quite go with the image, and Hesperos and Yanni were Murdoch and Hannibal. The whole team used vodka-filled water-pistols as imitation weapons and were running around air-slapping hands after every successful shot. (I haven't seen the A Team do this.)

Gil was very friendly and seemed excessively interested in my slag outfit. Every five minutes or so he'd bound over, put a big hand on my shoulder and say: 'If you have a problem, if no one else can help, and if you can find them, maybe you can hire the A Team.'

Pub 3, Stylers: 'Cool is such an elusive concept'

Matt learnt a hard lesson in Stylers. Wearing his drag outfit he managed to sneak into the ladies' toilets but was disappointed to find that we don't walk around naked, patting each other on the bottom.

Pub 4, Remix: 'We still do the time warp, yeah!'

After drink 4, my face started to feel a little numb and kept finding myself smiling very wildly at Ben and laughing a little too enthusiastically at everything he said. Justin was feeling the effects too; I saw him dancing the Macarena to Snoop Dog.

Matt was behaving lecherously towards anyone who happened to show an interest in his outfit. We caught him sidling up behind a Charlie's Angel and placing her hands on his blow-up breasts, giving his best, 'aren't you naughty' smirk. He kept glancing at Tam and me and then shimmied over to 'Sex Machine', turned his back, stuck out his bum and hitched up his netball skirt to reveal a black lace thong of Tam's.

'You pervert! You've been sneaking around my room!' she fumed.

'I wouldn't call it sneaking, Tamara. I was just working on my research of the female form and their habitat.'

'Wanker!'

'Yes, that is a pleasure I enjoy pursuing. Particularly in these sexy panties.'

'Aaagh!' She pushed past him and out the door.

Pub 5, Brian's Bar: 'Your alcohol in a plastic beaker, sir?'

We entered Brian's establishment as a fragmented slag/drag team. We slurped our drinks from plastic glasses and teetered straight on . . .

Pub 6, Yates: 'Who let the townies out?'

. . . to Yates, where we drank bottles of something sickly, which made my legs go a bit silly.

Pub 7, Incognito: 'We put lime in your drink and charge an extra £2 for it'

By pub 7, Tam and Matt seemed to have made up or just forgotten what they were arguing about. After a round of Shooters, I was feeling wibbly and wasn't sure I'd make it any further.

'Where's your fighting spirit?' Matt reprimanded me as I lurched on to the pavement outside. Hoiking me on to his back, he carried me past the kebab shops with the other slags and drags following behind. 'Remember, Shorty, a chain is only as strong as its weakest link. Our ginger queen is still standing so I expect a little more co-operation from you.' Am sure his hand was moving gradually up leopard-print thigh, when he stopped dead in his tracks and said firmly: 'Get down!'

'What?'

'Gerroffme!' he growled.

Matt shrugged me off and I stumbled in my heels and fell inelegantly against Justin's legs, which were surprisingly smooth.

'Ding. Dong. Would you look at that?' Matt woofed.

I glanced up to see two girls in immaculate pink bunny-girl uniforms, tripping their way prettily towards us.

'Hubba, hubba,' Matt was repeating to himself.

Was watching Ben closely for any sign of letchiness and, although my eyes were finding it difficult to focus, am fairly confident that he didn't show excessive interest.

Unlike Matt, who, stepping forward, said: 'Helloooo, ladies! May I say, you are looking extremely beautiful tonight.'

This was received with demure giggles.

'Everybody,' he addressed us. 'I'd like you to meet Jasmine and Chloe, our neighbours from upstairs.'

Misery!! I'm trying to strike up a relationship with possibly the loveliest boy on earth, and he happens to be living below two mannequin-styled goddesses who Matt wants us to have slumber parties with.

Jasmine is about six foot with flowing blonde hair, huge pert boobs, cartoonishly long legs and a sunbed tan. Chloe is a virtual clone, except she has cat-like green eyes and short platinum hair spiked out with ubër-cool brown undertones. Is so distressing; all previous notions of attractiveness have been shattered. Have been kidding self that you can't be skinny *and* have big boobs. I got skinny, Tam got the boobs, and then the bunnies mince along and completely destroy that reassuring illusion.

'I believe you have already met Ben and Justin?' Matt smarmed.

'Yes, we have,' they tweeted. 'It was a pleasure.' (When have they met before? Why was it a pleasure??)

'And these two,' Matt shrugged, 'are my other flatmates, Tamara and Josie.'

'Hi,' we said, and they smiled at us tightly.

'Ladies,' he addressed the bunny duo. 'It would be an honour if we could chaperone you to the next bar.'

Pub 8, Betty's: 'You wouldn't go there sober'

Staggered into pub 8 to see Matt generously buying a round of Campari for bunny-girls. (Funny that, seeing as he can't even afford to buy loo-roll for the flat.) Tam and I dived straight into toilets, locked ourselves in a cubicle where I pontificated, 'Grrrrughmmph!'

Then the main door opened and we heard the twittering voices of the bunny-girls.

In my slightly woozy state, I decided it would be a good idea to spy on them, so Tam gave me a leg-up on to the toilet seat and then I pulled her up too. We clung together drunkenly and peeked over the top of the cubicle.

Jasmine and Chloe were stood in front of the large mirror re-smoothing their eyebrows and pouting at their perfect reflections. Jasmine tweaked her bunny-tail and said coquettishly, 'Our outfits have so impressed everyone!'

'Totally,' agreed Chloe, spiking out her salon-chic hair. 'Matt was virtually salivating when he saw us!'

'Did you see what their flatmates were wearing? I, like, realise it's fancy dress, but would you seriously make yourself look that bad?'

'And, hellooo!' sung Chloe to the mirror. 'What about those red stilettos? How 80s!'

Tam's face expressed outrage: her eyebrows clamped down, her mouth gulped shut and she breathed out dramatically through her flared nostrils.

'Totally,' agreed Jasmine, swinging her golden locks over her shoulder. 'You know, I was thinking that Ben is pretty hot.'

'Matt told me that his flatmate, Josie – the thin one in the hideous leopard-print thing – fancies him!' Then they both laughed sharply.

'I think it's my duty to prevent a messy flat relationship,' snaked Jasmine. 'Don't you?'

My face expressed irate-woman-about-to-spew-fire: teeth bared, eyes narrowed and nails out, but then legs wobbled slightly causing a tumbling-off-toilet-seat effect.

The next thing I heard was one of the bunnies trilling, 'I think it's time we were bought another drink. Lip-gloss check.'

'Mwah! Perfect. Let's go.'

Tam helped scoop me up off toilet floor, but body was now numb and found it difficult to remember where legs were. 'It's my duty to prevent it?' I ranted.

'The thin one!' raged Tam.

'And "that hideous leopard-print number!" It's bloody-well fancy-dress, you bloody, prissy Sloanes! I was going for the 1980s slag look. And your red shoes are bloody cool. In fact, I'd like to borrow them. Can I borrow them? I've got lovely feet. Size four, actually.' Full-blown drunkenness was swooping in (alongside stray thoughts of prising little bunny-ears off and ramming them down poisonous Chanel throats).

We skulked back to the bar and slumped in a corner with Justin. We filled him in on bunny-girl horrors while he clumsily dabbed at his pink dress, which seemed to be wearing his last pint. 'Well, I feels shorry for anyone—' he pointed a finger nowhere in particular, '—who can't sees through their transparent act.' Was quite difficult to understand Justin, as apart from him slurring and me being drunk, his Welsh accent gets broader with alcohol. 'Bloody steaming fakes!' he suddenly yelled. 'They're nhos proper beauties like mygirls. Heresh to mygirls, Tamara and Josie!' Justin toasted us with his empty pint glass.

'Yes!' I agreed readily.

Tam fetched us both glasses of water and watched us drink them before leaving the pub. OK, we didn't make it past pub 8, but to be honest, I think pubs 9 and 10 would be thankful for that.

The three of us waited, shivering, for the night bus, looking like a bunch of washed-up prostitutes. I passed the time gibbering about my disillusion with 'bweer races', 'bwoys' and 'bwunny girls'.

'I don't know why I keep getting my mords wuddled up,' I said, clearly rather annoyed about it.

'It's because you're drunk,' Tam explained gently.

'Ha-ha-ha-ha,' sniggered Justin. 'I'm as jober as a sudge.'

'I'm just going to say one thing.' I swayed unsteadily, 'I got to seven drinks and did not throw myself at Ben. Yes! Oops.' I toppled forwards into them both. Tam caught me under the arms, and Justin leant his head on my shoulder. 'And one more thing,' I hiccupped. 'I loves you both.'

BRRRRRRRRRRRRR. BRRRRRRRRRRR.
BRRRRRRRRRRRRRRRR.

BRRRRRRRRRRRRRR. BRRRRRRRRRRR.
BRRRRRRRRRRRRRRRR.

What the bloody hell is that?

BRRRRRRRRRRRRRR. BRRRRRRRRRRR.
BRRRRRRRRRRRRRRRR.

Oh, shitting bollocks! It's the fire alarm!

8.30 am Have been stood outside South Hall for thirty minutes wearing leopard-print dress, laddered fishnets and furry slippers. Has sort of ruined the morning-fresh look I've been working on. Did chuckle, though, when Tam appeared with ponytail flopping to left side of head, looking like an extra from *Drunk and Dangerous*.

Only good thing was that everyone looked rough: the Ghostbusters were pale, the Musketeers were drawn and the nurses felt ill. Matt must have fallen asleep in his outfit as he stumbled from flat with one deflated boob and his netball skirt crumpled into its own pattern of pleats. Ben staggered out moments later with Justin in a fireman's lift.

Ah, our boys.

Amid hangover debris, out bounced the bunny-girls in little pink slips and full make-up. I felt a wave of nausea. Their teeny-weeny nighties fluttered in the October winds and a flash of sun-bedded skin caught Matt's attention. 'Morning ladies,' he leered, rearranging his boobs and straightening out his skirt.

'Morning,' they cooed.

'I had this incredible dream last night that I met two stunning bunny-girls. I hardly wanted to wake up.'

'Oh, behave!' Chloe gave him a playful punch on his arm and giggled too much.

Jasmine sidled over to Ben. 'Did you have fun last night?'

I got the intonation. What does she mean by fun?

Luckily, Ben missed the point entirely. 'Yes, it was a good laugh. Thanks.'

Approve use of 'laugh'. Oh God, though, hope nothing happened between them. Think I'd rather not know as whole purpose in life would be pulled from under me and would no longer have reason to put on padded bra in mornings.

After twenty minutes of shading daylight from our eyes, Warden-Brian announced fire alarm was a practice run and we could all go back inside. The sneaky bugger! Would like to shove that fingernail where the sun doesn't shine. (Ugh, horrid, scarring image in head! Unvisualise. Unvisualise!)

As we trudged back into halls, I overheard Jasmine whisper to Chloe, 'I'm, like, so pleased we were tipped off about the practice. I'd have been mortified to be seen in public looking like that.' Her symmetrical face tilted in my direction.

The cheek! Was still toying with idea of ramming bunny-girl accessories in certain places, until Tam said in a loud, confident voice; 'Come on, Jos, we'd better hurry. It's the boys' turn to make us breakfast in bed.'

Good work. As if. But good work.

FIVE

Sunday 13 October

4 pm Hmmph! Since Beer Race, life has turned into a horrible cycle of bunny-girl monotony. Matt has spent most of this weekend prancing upstairs to their flat pretending to need a spare tea bag or such like, then running (giggling) back to Ben, relaying detailed bunny-girl info: what they were wearing, how they smelt, where they were sitting etc. Am not happy about any of this. Do not like the idea of Ben being corrupted by sex-obsessed idiot flatmate who wears 'I LOVE LESBIANS' T-shirts.

Wish Tam was around so we could have a whinging session and then do room-dancing to cheer selves up. Instead, she's been away since Friday doing coupley things with Oliver. Is rubbish that she has boyfriend/old-man-friend, as every weekend I'm left to entertain myself.

To pass the time, I've mostly been behaving sluttishly around room, striking random poses in mirror and flinging self on and off bed for no other purpose than entertainment via self-exhibitionism. Things got so bad earlier I ended up watching breakdancing videos with Gil and Hobbit. Have now seen the same fat man spinning on his head twenty-seven times. Why would you want to watch that? And then watch it again? Why?

All things considered, w/e confirms that am neither a sex-goddess-style-bunny-girl nor one half of a contented couple. Hmmph.

6 pm Self-pity has been interrupted by major flatmate crisis. Tam's back from Oliver's; she opened my door, kicked off her shoes and fell on to my bed in a puffy, red-eyed heap. Oliver has told her they need to take a 'time out' as he feels their relationship is holding Tam back at uni. All seemed very noble of him until it later surfaced that he'd been sleeping with his admin assistant, Tina May.

Tam is devastated; she thinks it was a mistake to come to uni as she's been neglecting him. Neglecting him? Have told her firmly: 'Oliver is delusional. He's been seduced by the notoriety of fresh flesh, which blurred all rational judgement, leading to his monumentally bad decision. You are beautiful, intelligent and funny. He is a big knob that looks like Mr Spock.'

Enough is enough! Am not having Tam weeping all night because of two-timing idiot. Have formulated an emergency break-up plan: am going to buy triple-chocolate-chip ice cream, a bottle of wine and *OK!* Magazine, and then we're watching *Dirty Dancing*. Yes. Brilliant!

8 pm Break-up management is going well. Already completed Stage 1: passing tissues and eating ice cream.

8.30 pm Stage 2: trashing people in *OK!* to increase own shaken confidence – finished in record speed!
Page 1: 80's haircut, saggy arms
Page 2: too much make-up, boob job
Page 3: big eyebrows, slutty dress
Page 4: hideous shoes, long ear lobes
Page 5: frizzy hair, chipped nail varnish
Page 6: terrible roots, wrinkly armpits etc, etc.

9 pm After confidence building, Tam was ready to progress to Stage 3. The list: pros and cons of splitting up with Oliver.

So far, we've come up with these . . .

Cons
1. Goodbye regular sex.
2. Hello Valentine's Day misery.
3. No raunchy Sunday mornings in bed.
4. No one to take you out for dinner.
5. No boyfriend to call last thing at night.

Pros
1. No boyfriend to call last thing at night.
2. More time with the girls (yey!).
3. Big knickers can replace scratchy thongs.
4. Discard all painful hair removal products (tweezers, epilator, wax kit) and revert to natural womanly state (hairy).
5. Save money on phone credit, rail tickets, Valentine's trash etc.
6. Never again have to feign interest in football, Quentin Tarrantino or Led Zeppelin.
7. Can concentrate more on studies and become world leader.
8. Roam free among plentiful male students filling campus and achieve temporary ho-status under guise of 'rebound'.
   List went well. More reasons to be happy than sad!

Midnight Stage 4: escapism. We put on PJs, moved Tam's TV into the kitchen, opened white wine, dimmed lights and watched *Dirty Dancing*. Pure pleasure. Think wine may have gone to heads as by the 'Hey Mickey' scene, Tam and I were crawling around on all fours, singing:
   'Sylvia?'
   'Yes, Mickey.'
   'How d'you call your lover-boy?'

'Come here, lover-boy.'

'And if he doesn't answer?'

'Oh, lover-boy.'

'And if he *still* doesn't answer?'

'I simply say, baby, oh baby, my sweet . . .'

Beautifully tuneful duet was interrupted by sniggering. Matt was stood in kitchen doorway surrounded by six football lads. 'I'm proud to introduce my flatmates, Josie and Tamara. These are the two I was telling you about who've just been let out of the *hospital*.'

Would usually be embarrassed by slightly compromising first impression but what with wine, Patrick Swayze miming to us and a large dose of confidence-building, we just carried on dancing. Turns out football-team-boys enjoy the company of PJ-clad girls – especially when crawling on all fours . . .

Monday 14 October

9.30 am Tam is doing well this morning, although freakishly swollen eyelids do hint at a little unhappiness. For this reason, she's decided to stay home from lectures, and like a true friend, I am joining her. (Also, have slightly fragile stomach after wine and do not think it'd be wise to be in close proximity to McGibbon's spittling mouth.)

6 pm Is a terrible thing to admit, but I've found a tiny part of me that is pleased about Tam's break-up. Is obviously horrible seeing her unhappy as really, her eyelids are very scary, yet at same time is rather nice not feeling urgent need to throw self into steady relationship just so I have someone to spend weekends with. We've had a very pleasant day being single, talking hypotheticals and devising our Top 3s. Mine is looking like this:

> 1. Ben (wanted to position him as my no.2 and 3, except Tam wouldn't allow it as rules of Top 3 indicate that all positions must be filled by different people).
> 2. Bar Boy (fit barman at Energy).
> 3. Pablo (out of pure desperation as can't think of anyone else).

Tam said it was too soon for her to have a Top 3 as she didn't think about other boys while being with Oliver. I insisted. In four seconds she rolled off these:

> 1. Robbie (instructor from surf club. Ooo . . . good choice!).
> 2. Pete (captain of football team).
> 3. Spanish lecturer (how come she gets a fit lecturer and I get spittler?).

9 pm Tam and I have been gorging on spaghetti bolognaise à la Justin. Is interesting how when I make spag bowl, I fry mince and add Dolmio, whereas Justin's tastes like he's actually an Italian chef simply masquerading as a Welsh comic-book geek. It has been a nice evening hanging out just the three of us. Ben's been out with some coursemates (hope there were no girls present) and Suniti has been at the late night library. Was not quite so nice when Matt strode in from football training and gave Tam and me muddy bear-hugs. He then started irking Justin by commenting on the Fairy Queen's aromatic spices cupboard. There was a short repertoire of mutual abuse, which ended with Matt claiming to be a dazzling chef and Justin challenging him to cook for us all tomorrow night.

'Tomorrow night?' mused Matt. 'Now, let me check my diary.' He performed a detailed mime of opening up a diary and reading the entries. His fingers paused mid-air and he sighed heavily. 'Oh, shucks, it seems I'm washing my hair. Oh, now, hang on a minute!' Matt glanced back at the invisible diary. 'That's your diary, Justin! Mine says, "Have rampant sex with mysterious beauty." Tam, Jos – either of you free?'

We gave him looks to suggest we'd sooner hitch up our skirts for John Prescott.

'Well, then,' he continued, 'it looks like I will be free to feed you lot. We should all take it in turns to cook for the whole flat once a month, like a flat-bonding night. What do you reckon?'

Am quite excited by Matt's suggestion; monthly flat meal is lovely idea and am always keen for extra flat (Ben) bonding.

Tuesday 15 October

2 pm Poor Tam. We'd arranged to have lunch together to help keep her mind off Oliver. We met in the Humanities Café and were immediately put off our baguettes by the presence of McGibbon who was drooling in the flapjack section. After he slithered away, enjoyment of baguettes was totally ruined as Tam got a text from Spock.

'Hi, my little sex kitten. I really enjoyed last night!! Meet me by the photocopier at 3.30 pm. Oli x'

Was meant for office hussy! I suggested it could be a Freudian message-slip – though think is more likely that Tina is next to Tam in his phonebook. Tam was really miserable and said they used to meet by the photocopier.

Wednesday 16 October

10.45 am All boys are rubbish! We had our first flat meal last night, except it wasn't quite the cooking/bonding experience we were promised: Matt bought Chinese and invited the bunnies. Am pleased Suniti worked late in the library again, as don't think she'd have enjoyed the evening. The bunnies had barely parked their pert behinds before the jibes began. Chloe, wearing a minuscule black dress that looked like it'd been sprayed on, patted Tam briskly on the arm. 'Sweetie, how are you?' she asked with fake concern. 'Matt told me your boyfriend dumped you. You poor thing!'

'At least you've got your little friend to look after you,' added Jasmine.

Did not appreciate her using the word 'little', or the way she accompanied it with an exaggerated stretch of her telegraph-pole legs. Hmmph!

I spent most of the meal trying to ignore Jasmine drawing attention to her body. 'Oh, I just spilt soy sauce on my top,' (her top was actually a wisp of material, barely containing her boobs), 'I'd better wipe it off slowly and seductively. Oops! A little bit was on my breast!' (OK, is possible she didn't actually say that last bit, but I definitely saw her fluttering her eyelash extensions at Ben, which was bad enough.)

The night took a turn for the worse when Matt fetched his drinks tray. The sound of bottles chinking must have carried downstairs, as within sixty seconds Gil and Hobbit had bundled into our flat, settling their orange chairs around the table. Matt, wearing a bright orange 'I LIKE TO GET DRUNK AND HUMP THINGS' T-shirt, stood at the head of the table and roared: 'Let the drinking games commence!'

And so it began.

Tam and I were saying yesterday it's strange that Matt and Ben get on so well. We spent twenty minutes trying to think of things they had in common, but all we came up with was willies. Tam says it's like yin and yang: Matt is the knife to Ben's fork; Ben is the salt to Matt's pepper, etc. Then I started to wonder whether I could be the conditioner to Ben's shampoo, but Tam said a lot of boys don't use conditioner and then I felt sad.

By midnight, we were all very merry. In an airy voice, Jasmine giggled, 'Let's play truth or dare!'

Before anyone had chance to object, Chloe clapped her hands together in excitement and fired the first question. 'Truth or dare?' she asked Matt, pouting through baby pink lip-gloss.

'Truth,' he leered.

Chloe twisted a portion of her hair into a tight spike: 'What is your favourite sexual position?'

I noticed that Ben rolled his eyes! Does this mean he also thinks the bunny-girls are simply mannequins of beauty with no depth? Or was he wondering about the burgundy stain on our kitchen ceiling?

'That's a tough one,' said Matt, making a big show of mentally flicking through his shag reference library. 'Mm, that position was good . . . now she loved that . . . but I think that might have been illegal . . .'

Tam yawned.

'No need for jealousy, Tamara. You can be added to my memory bank, if you want? Right, I'll narrow it down.' He looked directly into Chloe's sharp green eyes. 'I'll go for girl on top.'

Chloe looked satisfied with his answer and the game continued.

Whole notion of truth or dare is hideous throwback to being eleven years old and having to confess in front of half the class that I hadn't snogged anyone yet.

University version wasn't much of an improvement. The game spiralled into a confession session and have now learnt that Matt's had sex with a minor ('Cool, man,' from Gil), Hobbit's been involved in a spit roast ('A what roast?' from Justin), Jasmine and Chloe have snogged each other ('Praise the Lord,' from Matt) and all the girls own a vibrator – except me (is like being eleven again).

I was already feeling uncool before Chloe asked, 'Josie, when's the last time you were with somebody?'

Hmmph! Was not about to be made to look inexperienced by the bunnies (who, personally, I think are rather slutty). 'Well,' I said, with the air of a high-class madam, 'one of the last people was actually somebody I met abroad.'

Hah, that pricked the bunnies' ears!

'Yes, I met Pablo in Spain. He's very special.' I wondered where I could go next with the story. I didn't want to look like I was too keen on Pablo in case it put Ben off, but a little adoration from a Spanish suitor might give his affections a nudge. 'It wasn't anything too serious – although he'd have liked it to be.' That wasn't strictly true, either. Pablo had asked for my address but only so he could improve his English – and I never heard from him anyway. It was one of those convenient holiday flings: he gave me free cocktails and an excuse to escape Mum, and I gave him a couple of snogs and a bit of help with his verbs.

'So what does Pablo do?' Jasmine smiled slyly, hoping to catch me out.

I thought of the cocktail bar and Pablo mixing Screaming Orgasms for chortling forty-year-olds. That didn't sound quite right. 'He owns a small chain of exclusive hotels,' I said lightly.

Gosh, I really was getting a lot of mileage out of my package holiday to Spain. The bunnies seemed satisfied and then Justin caught my arm. 'Josie,' he slurred, 'can I have your go? I want to ask the next question.'

Am very pleased I said 'yes,' and I shall love Justin eternally for this: 'I dare you,' he addressed Jasmine, hiccupping into a pint of beer, 'to act like a chimpanzee for one minute.'

Was brilliant! A huff of contempt escaped Jasmine's painted lips. Eventually, she stood up, positioning herself in the centre of the kitchen and lifted her hands under her armpits. She managed a couple of half-hearted 'oh oh, ah ahs', a twirl on the spot and finished with a sulky mime of a chimp eating a banana. I was embarrassed for her, yet obviously very pleased also!

Jasmine settled herself down and, crossing her long legs slowly, addressed Ben. 'Truth or dare?'

'Truth,' he answered.

Jasmine held a manicured finger to her lips, striking a contemplative pose. 'If you could kiss one person in this room, who would it be?'

What an obvious agenda! Seeing Ben sat between two immaculate bunny-girls, I couldn't bear to hear his answer. I needed to get out.

Scrambling to my feet, I murmured, 'bathroom', and lurched out of the kitchen.

The cool air in the corridor hit me and I clung to the wall to steady myself. Feeling dizzy and woozy from too much alcohol it took me a moment to regain my balance. Just as I was moving off, I heard Ben's voice; it was thick and heavy – and quite definite. 'It would be *you*, Jasmine.'

Misery!

11.15 am Tam has crawled into my bed with the alcohol blues. Feel bad as have been jabbering on for last half-hour about own trauma re: Ben picking Jasmine, and didn't even ask how she was feeling re: Oliver/Tina fling.

It wasn't good news.

After I went to bed, Tam left him a drunken phone message. She said it went something like this: 'You're probably shagging Tina May right now, and if you are – congratulations! I've also been having a wonderful time getting extremely drunk with my exquisite flatmates who are into liberal shagging and plenty of vibrator usage. You were holding me back at uni after all! One more thing, I thought you might like to know that Josie and I call you Mr Spock. Hah!'

Oops.

Feel terrible for deserting Tam in her hour of phone protection need but am quite pleased I left when I did as 'truth or dare' ended with Gil doing a naked lap of the courtyard. Tam said that by the time he came back, panting, the bunny-girls had left in disgust and Matt had passed out under the kitchen table.

11.20 am Tam is asleep on my left arm.

11.30 am Justin has also snuck into my bed and is lying in his pyjamas with his head on my legs. He's depressed, too, as he got so drunk he threw up on his Volume 1 Spider-Man collection. Room has turned into gloom corner. Legs and left arm are now numb. Meant to be going to Surf Club in half an hour but think will give up. Am too miserable for frolicking around in sea to impress a certain boy who prefers a certain bunny.

12.05 pm Eugh! Justin dribbles.

Tuesday 22 October

3 am Last six days have flown by in haze of misery: Tam is still upset about Oliver, Justin's been bleating on about his comics and I've exhausted all hypothetical analysis of how life could've turned out if Jasmine didn't exist. However, fifteen minutes ago, own misery was interrupted by petrifying middle-of-the-night experience.

I needed a wee, so felt way along corridor to bathroom. Was sat on toilet in semi-darkness, when noticed something hanging from ceiling above the bath. I blinked twice to try and wake eyes and then the shape started to take focus. It was a body!

Oh, God! Tam? I thought. She could have been sent over the edge by Oliver's desertion! Why didn't I see the signs?

Or Justin, even? The ginger jokes and comic disaster were too much!

I sprang from the toilet screaming wildly, but tripped over my PJs, which were round my ankles, and landed with a thud on the floor. I was flailing around in the corridor, sobbing and crying out for help.

Woken by the commotion, Ben burst from his room and found me in a heap at his feet. Grabbing me by the shoulders, he asked urgently: 'What's happened? Are you OK?'

'A, a b-b-body,' I squealed, motioning towards the bathroom.

Ben rushed in and flicked the light switch. I covered my eyes, preparing self for horrendous image of dead flatmate swinging flaccidly from ceiling.

'Oh, God!' Ben cried.

My stomach tightened. I knew from that moment, life as a student had changed forever. There would be inquests, police interviews, the funeral, questions from mourning parents: 'Could we have done more? Why didn't we see it coming?'

'It's my wetsuit!' Ben laughed. 'Shit, Jos – I thought you were being attacked!'

I opened my eyes, and there, hanging above our bath was a black, lifeless wetsuit, draining from a coat hanger.

I had four feelings in this order:

1. Relief that Tam and Justin were still alive.
2. Embarrassment that I'd had histrionics over a wetsuit.
3. Love for my hero who leapt to my rescue.
4. Horror that bathroom light had spilled into corridor, revealing PJs still round my ankles and big, Snoopy pants sagging over bum! (It's the second time I've been exposed in greying cartoon pants, which is ironic really as would quite like Ben to see me in underwear, though preferably when it's intentional and a black-and-white beagle isn't snoozing on my arse.)

Did have a fifth feeling:

5. Lust. Bathroom light also illuminated Ben in delicious Calvin Kleins and bared, bronzed chest. Was worth 1 to 4 just to see that. Mmmm . . .

Swiftly pulled up PJs to try and regain some decency and Ben reached out his hand to help me up. 'Are you OK, Jos?' he asked with concern.

'I'm fine,' I replied sheepishly, folding my arms over my chest as I wasn't wearing a padded bra. 'Sorry for waking you,' I added, in a whisper, conscious that I'd been shouting in the corridor.

'It's my fault. I shouldn't have left my wetsuit to drain there. Really, are you OK? I can make you a hot drink, if you'd like?'

I didn't accept. *Whywhywhy?* I just politely shook my head and said, 'No thanks, I'm fine, really.' Have gone insane, surely! Ben was offering me a drink in the middle of the night – and I said, 'No'. This is why opportunity-seizers like Jasmine will end up with delicious boyfriends, whereas I'm destined to spend my life with Mr Tubs. Agh!!

Wednesday 23 October

10.30 am Am trying to put aside frustration of not accepting drink and instead am focusing on yummy image of Ben coming to my aid wearing only boxers! Have decided to reinstate Surf Club membership immediately!

10.35 am It took some gentle persuasion, but Tam has agreed to come surfing too. Think it will be good for her to concentrate on sport not Spock. Plus, need Tam there to assess any signs of chemistry between Ben and me. Gave her the breakdown of Ben/wetsuit/dead body drama and she thinks his reaction is a definite sign of interest. Yey!

5 pm I stood up on a surfboard! Love surfing. Am becoming a mermaid! Today it may have been some shaky standing up in white-water, but in near/distant future I'll be gliding through barrels giving the high-five sign to fans on beach. Hah! Was also a lovely day as Ben was at beach too and looked especially good in snug-fitting wetsuit. Am very impressed with the way he carved through waves doing swirls and twists.

On top of all this joy, Tam and I have been invited on the uni surf trip this weekend!! And there's a Hawaiian party in the evening! Very excited. I am perky. Tam is perky. We're going on a surf trip with surfer boys – and Ben. Mmmm . . .

SIX

Friday 25 October

6 pm I've spent my day shopping for the seducing Ben trip. Did I write that? I meant surfing trip. Silly me! Bought aquamarine flip-flops, two toe-rings, an anklet and seashell-coloured toenail varnish. Feet will look beautiful.

7 pm. Packing. Just had a fraught discussion with Mr Tubs about his inclusion in my weekend bag. He says he should come because he's been a pillar of support in previous Ben moments and it would be disloyal to leave him behind now due to image concerns. Is a fair point. But then he overdid it by adding that I 'need him' and couldn't cope spending a night on my own. Hmmph! Since he's come to uni, he's been so cocky. Have decided a night apart will do us both good – and tonight he's sleeping on the windowsill as a draft excluder. Hah!

Saturday 26 October

8 am. On coach. Dreadfulness has occurred en-route to surf trip. Jasmine is on coach! Heard pitter-patter of kitten-heels and in minced princess Jasmine wearing tight white jeans and a low-cut pink jumper. 'Hi, boys,' she trilled, strutting up the coach aisle and ignoring the other seventeen girls. Then she spotted Ben three rows behind ours and sat herself next to him. Was wondering when, how and why Jasmine joined Surf Club, and then she leant across the aisle and twittered to Robbie, 'Thanks for inviting me, sweetie. You're a fantastic cousin. Mwah!'

So Robbie has got Sloane blood! Hmmm, well, I'm not quite so impressed by those biceps any more; although, his thighs are also very muscular and . . . anyway, think Tam saw my horror as she immediately grabbed my hands to stop me doing throttling actions. She has since declared this a boy-free weekend; I'm not allowed to witter on about Ben/triangular-back/toned body fantasies and Tam will not cry over Oliver/on-the-photocopier/in-the-lift/with Tina night-mares.

8.45 am. Still on coach. Time is dragging, especially because behind me I can hear the tinkling of Jasmine's laughter as she enjoys Ben's witty and charming company, and in front I've got Gil and Hobbit who keep turning round to ask questions like: 'What's the difference between a thong and a g-string?'

11 am. Rickety caravan. Forgot we are not in foreign country and while there is pretty sand and blue sea, am still in England. In autumn. In flip-flops. My seashell toes are freezing – will have to change into trainers. Oh, though, Ben won't be able to admire toe-rings and anklet! Tsk, such waste!

Sleeping arrangements are not good either. Am sharing a cramped caravan with twenty other students and Ben has chosen to sleep in the opposite caravan to me. The same one as Jasmine. (Am just writing this as fact. Information does not concern me on an emotional level. Honestly.)

5 pm Brrrr . . . am back from surfing. Robbie gave us a refresher course and I managed to take more of it in this time as am no longer distracted by his muscular arms.

Jasmine did not surf. (Weakling!) She wandered around the beach (heels sinking in the sand), twittering, 'Oh, it's so cold,' and then saying, 'I couldn't possibly,' when all the boys offered their jackets.

Decided to get as far away from bunny queen as possible, so me and my board swam determinedly out to sea. Was happily singing *'Everybody's Going Surfing'* and enjoying thoughts of Ben and me surfing in California. When final verse ran out, I glanced back to shore and was surprised to see that the people now looked more ant-sized.

Actually, looking around, I realised there weren't any other surfers nearby. A trickle of fear ran through me: do they know something I don't? The water did look very dark and scary . . .

. . . and fishy!

The Beach Boys segued into the *Jaws* theme tune and a ripple in the water ahead made me cling to the board. I remembered reading that you can get sharks in the UK. I began to panic. I was all alone. In middle of big, cold, shark-infested sea.

Can sharks smell fear? What about urine-tinged wet-suits? Quickly pulled arms out of water, removing all body parts from shark exposure. Sat up on board and held knees to chest hoping board and I might float back to shore.

After a few minutes of drifting in the wrong direction, the sea started getting rougher. This wasn't a good sign. The rocking grew stronger as a wave began forming in the distance. Oh, crap! The wave was definitely getting larger and gaining momentum. I needed to take action. Against my better shark-judgement, I plunged my arms back into the sea, then turned my board round and paddled manically towards the wave. It wasn't so much a brave attempt to surf a gigantic wave, as a glimmer of hope that if I paddled fast enough, I could glide over it before it broke on top of me.

Heart was beating rapidly. Paddle, paddle, paddle. The wave was thundering towards me now! Paddle, paddle, paddle. A huge, powerful lip was forming . . . Paddle, crapping paddle . . . The face was too steep to float over; *Oh, God,* I thought, *I've got to duck-dive!* I pushed heavily on my forearms, trying to force the board beneath the surface. The wave was looming over me . . . The board wouldn't dive . . . The wave was breaking . . .

FWOOOSSH!

It crashed on top of me, sucking me from the board and rolling me madly underwater. Hadn't prepared self by taking a breath and wave was turning and spinning me roughly, exhausting the air from my lungs. Wondered if I was going to die as body was being rolled quite nastily. After a further pummelling, I was finally tossed back to the surface, gasping for breath.

Aaagh! All body parts open to attack in deep water!! Frantically splashed about looking for my surfboard so I could get back to safety. Then a bolt of fear stabbed me: I saw something else moving in the water. Shitting hell! A shark fin! It was protruding from the water only ten feet in front of me. I screamed – but only a fearful gurgle came out.

I tried desperately to swim away, but my arms were stiff in the wetsuit and splashed at the sea heavily. I wasn't moving fast enough. Suddenly, a tight pain shot round my ankle. It had hold of me and was dragging me under the dark sea. My free leg and arms were flailing furiously, lunging for the surface. I burst up choking with lungs full of saltwater. But it still had hold of me.

This is it, I thought. I'm going to die. Was surprised that life wasn't exactly flashing before eyes as I'd imagined. Brain was still humming Jaws soundtrack and was firing images of open shark mouths, spiky teeth and bloodied human limbs. It flicked over to newspaper headlines: 'Freak Shark Attack' and 'Surfer Girl's Body Mutilated by Great White', and then focused on my funeral and lots of weeping friends and what Ben would say about me.

Was snapped out of death contemplation by sight of a surfer paddling towards me. I might be saved! I shouted at the figure to hurry.

It was Robbie.

'What is it?' he called out.

'Shark!' I screamed desperately.

Shark? Had rare burst of clarity. If my foot was in a shark's mouth, surely I'd be in excruciating pain? Adrenalin might blank some of it out and I was wearing a wetsuit, but wouldn't I feel something? I peered over shoulder to see if I was about to be eaten – and the fin was still there bobbing around. Then I noticed there were three fins. Very close together. And one had a white pattern on.

'What is it?' Robbie called out again.

I strained to look at the fins. The pattern seemed to be a sticker. It read: 'Quiksilver.' It was my surfboard – upturned and attached to my ankle by the leash! Thank the sweet . . .

'Did you say shark?' Robbie was by my side.

'Erm, no. Um . . . I said, sharp pain in my leg. Cramp, I think.'

'That sounds like some pretty painful cramp. Are you OK?' he said, his wet skin glistening.

'Yes, yes, it seems to be easing a little now, thanks.'

'Even so, let me help you back to the beach.' And with that, Robbie helped me on to his board and paddled me and my sharky surfboard back to shore with those big, musclely arms. Mmmm.

7.30 pm Tam enjoyed my surfing escapades and seemed to have fared much better by bailing out of surfing and spending afternoon in the pub. Hmmm. We're getting ready for tonight's Hawaiian party but I'm not feeling very tropical: I've got sore nipples from wetsuit chafing and a dollop of water lodged in my ear from shark attack. Am a casualty of my imagination. Have hula-ed on regardless and am now wearing a yellow sarong, turquoise top, lei of flowers, flip-flops, toe-rings, anklets etc. Tam is in pink beach shorts, a pair of coconuts and a lei of flowers too. We're freezing.

2 am Is just, well, unbelievable. Evening was like eating a delicious éclair and getting halfway through before realising someone has spat in it.

Organisers of the Hawaiian party used the term loosely. It was a room in a pub with a dustbin full of 'tropical' punch and a horizontal pole replicating limbo. I was making a point of ignoring Jasmine looking all Hawaii Five-0 in grass skirt and teeny bikini. Did not see her sashay up to Ben or feel pangs of jealousy when she cavorted under limbo pole, arching svelte body.

Have decided that limbo is ridiculous game invented by bendy girls to flaunt their flexibility. Didn't do much for my sexability since Round 1 started at 5 feet 3 inches and I didn't need to bend to get under. (Was fine, though, as was taking deep breaths and thinking of Kylie.) Several more rounds of exhibitionism flew by and I was still in the competition by

Round 4. This time, though, full body suppleness was required and I tried to force spine to bend unnaturally and toppled over on to my arse in a comic, yet painful, way.

After the pub shut, we moved out to the beach and sat round a fire Gil and Hobbit had proudly made. Was nicely warming up my toes (frrrreezing in ridiculous flip-flops), when I realised I hadn't seen Tam for past half-hour. Best friends have duty to watch out for each other. I wandered the beach straining eyes in the dark to look for a pair of large coconuts. I rounded a corner, and there, in hand-over-mouth surprise, was Tam in a cosy embrace with Robbie!!

The minx! Actions were in clear breach of 'no boys' rule, but then this was Robbie and ooo . . . she was squeezing his biceps. Rather than waiting for them to see me gawping like some Peeping-sarong-wearing-Tom, I headed back to the fire.

There was a small group of people spread out around the heat of the beach fire. I noticed Ben leant against a large rock, slightly away from the others. He smiled when he saw me and moved along, indicating for me to sit next to him.

Yes!

It felt so comfortable, just chatting and spending time together on our own. Ben was telling me about his year abroad, which sounded amazing: white sand, warm sunshine and perfect surf. Love it when he gets enthusiastic, as he does this big, open smile that tilts slightly to the left. I was vaguely aware of the low hum of chatter of the people surrounding the fire, but I felt as though we were in our own bubble, just Ben and I.

We talked about everything: our courses, flatmates, friends, futures. I think I mentioned something about family holidays, because Ben's warm smile seemed to fade away. He began tracing a finger in the cool sand as he quietly explained, 'It's just my dad, sister and me. My Mum died four years ago.' His face looked strained from the memory.

I was shocked that Ben didn't have a mum. He hadn't mentioned it before – and no one in the flat seems to know.

'Do you mind me asking what happened?'

Ben looked up at me. 'Course not. I guess I don't tend to talk about it because it can make people feel awkward. You know, people aren't sure what to say.' Ben continued gliding his fingertips across the small section of sand that separated our bodies. 'My mum had breast cancer. They found out very late – and the cancer had already spread.'

I don't know why, but I instinctively put my hand on top of his and squeezed it. 'I'm so sorry, Ben.'

Our hands rested together in the damp sand.

'How did you cope?' I asked gently.

'It was pretty difficult at the time. People tend to think that cancer is a long drawn out illness, which it can be, but that wasn't the case with mum. She died within eight weeks of being diagnosed and for most of that time she wasn't herself because of the medication. Dad was amazing with her,' he said thoughtfully. 'He was so positive and loving – but I don't think he ever really believed he was going to lose her.'

Ben's eyes looked tired, sad. I wanted to take his face in my hands and kiss his cheek, his forehead, his lips, to make that pain go away.

'Afterwards, Dad just, well, he basically fell apart. He couldn't go back to work for months, and eventually he lost his job. Mum and Dad both grew up in Cornwall – they actually met at the beach that our house now overlooks. Dad spent a lot of time just sitting out there – remembering.'

'They must have had a special relationship.'

'Yeah, they did. Dad misses her like crazy. It took him a long time to pick himself back up. He's got a new job now and is managing a lot better. In a weird way, we're all a lot closer because of it.' Ben paused and looked at me once again. 'Thanks, Jos, for asking me about it. I don't talk about Mum much. I think sometimes it's good too.'

I smiled at Ben.

'A lot of my friends from home never bring it up. I guess they think you want to forget – but that's the thing that scares me. Forgetting.'

I'd been so absorbed by what Ben had been telling me, that I didn't realise I was shivering. 'You're freezing.'

Ben leant forward and pulled a chunky jumper over his head, leaving him in a T-shirt and boardshorts. 'Here, wear this.' The jumper was warm and smelt delicious – fresh soap and a hint of mint. 'Jos,' Ben smiled warmly, 'it's been really nice hanging out with you.'

'Yeah, with you too.'

'By the way, those toe-rings are cool.'

He noticed!

The mood seemed to change between us. It became light and fuelled with an exciting tension.

'Here,' Ben said as he put his arm out and pulled me into his chest. The left side of my body was pressing against the right side of his. My thigh against his thigh; Ben's arm around me; his hand resting on my waist; my face leant into his chest.

I could feel flutters of longing dancing through my body and my pulse was racing madly. In the stillness I became aware of Ben's heart thudding against his chest. Then I felt his hand tighten around my waist and his bicep tensed as he slowly pulled my body closer to his.

Everything felt like it was happening in slow motion. I could feel Ben's eyes on me as his face moved closer to mine. His free hand reached forwards and rested on my cheek. My breath shortened as he tilted my face towards his. I looked up into his eyes and was unable to blink and was aware only of being drawn into him.

'You are beautiful,' he whispered into my lips.

I closed my eyes and my lips parted as Ben's mouth slowly pressed itself against mine.

The kiss was soft and light at first and then he coaxed my mouth between his, exploring it with his tongue. It was . . . sensual . . . delicious. My body was melting into his. His fingers traced my cheek and slid down to the nape of my neck, spreading into my hair and lulling my face closer still.

After a long and hungry kiss, Ben moved his head back to look at me. I couldn't help giving him a huge, happy grin. It felt perfect.

Out of nowhere, Gil's cold hands were pulling us to our feet – bursting our bubble. Hobbit was noisily rounding up everyone else by the fire. Inspired by a hallucinogenic thought, Hobbit announced: 'Let's all take a skinny-dip. Last one in has to wash the wetsuits!'

Skinny-dipping in October was not his best idea but there was a fusion of movement as people leapt to their feet, sand flying everywhere in the darkness.

Think excess dopamine from kissing-high swamped brain, as all I could do was panic. If I skinny-dipped, everyone would see me naked (padded-braless and exposed)! If I didn't go through with it, I'd look like I had something to hide and would have to spend my Sunday wringing urine out of wetsuits. There was only one thing I could do: I'd have to be the first in the sea and hide in its darkness.

I ran and ran and tripped and carried on running, yanking off clothes as I went. I heard the others catching me up. My sarong flew off; Ben's jumper was left on the beach, my turquoise top strewn in the sand.

I ran straight towards the water and leapt in. God! It was freezing. It took a moment to catch my breath. There was loud splashing all around as everyone else followed behind, yelping with the cold.

My nakedness was out of sight. Phew! I trod water for a moment and then brain went – Clunk! How was I going to get out of the sea without being seen?

'You're brave,' said Tam, swimming up beside me in shorts with her coconut shells floating.

'Hey – you're cheating!' I said through chattering teeth. I glanced around and everyone had cheated. They were all wearing clothes or underwear at least. And I was swimming naked!

'You go, girl!' said Tam in the spirit of camaraderie.

'I'm just doing what we agreed: going for a skinny-dip.'

'Honey,' Tam soothed, 'Hobbit said, "Let's take a late-night dip." Are your ears still blocked?'

Aaagh! I'd left a fireside kiss to catch naked pneumonia. In some perverse attempt to make me feel better, Gil swam alongside me, pulled off his shorts and threw them in the air, shouting, 'I'm skinny-dipping too, Josie!' He dived under, scooped my body out of the water and then dunked me again with his wet dreadlocks smacking against my back. And now everyone's seen me naked. Crap!

With my nakedness issues pissed in the sand, I swam to shore, staggered out of the sea and hurried up the beach trying to cover all private areas with one hand while slinging on clothes with the other. It wasn't my most elegant moment and certainly wasn't helped by Hobbit, who commentated on my naked run for the benefit of the other forty surfers.

The sandy clothes were sticking to my salty, wet body and I ended up putting my top on back-to-front and Ben's jumper inside-out. At least I was semi-dry and no longer naked. I took some deep breaths. Calm. You're OK.

Bloody hell, though, that wasn't how I'd envisaged the moment-after-kiss to go. In fact, where was Ben? I hadn't seen him in the sea and he wasn't by the fire any longer. I was very keen on continuing with our kiss, so I rushed towards the caravans hoping to find him there.

Yes! I caught sight of him on the path ahead and jogged to catch him. I was waving and hollering – but he didn't seem to hear me. As I got closer, I could make out two shapes in the darkness. He was walking back to the caravan with someone else. It almost looked as though he had his arm round her. It was a few more steps before I could make out the silhouette – the tall, slender frame and long legs.

Jasmine.

Ben's arm was holding her tightly to him, her body leaning into his. My brain was fuzzing out of control – surely I'd got this wrong? I stood watching them walk away from me. They moved towards the caravan, arms entwined. My heart was hammering at my chest. They stopped outside the door and I watched in the darkness as Jasmine turned to look at Ben. Her face moved towards his – as mine had done – and he put his hands up to meet it. And right there in front of me, they kissed.

Felt like I'd been punched in the stomach! My body hunched inwards and I leant over and heaved into the cold sand. My heart had clawed its way into my throat and I could barely breathe.

Ugh! No – this wasn't real.

Wiping at my mouth, I looked up again and caught a final glimpse of Ben as he pulled the caravan door shut behind them.

Misery . . .

2.30 am Is all so awful! Can't believe Ben is with her. I feel like I'm going mad. How could he have been so tender with me – sharing his feelings about his mum – and then minutes later, be kissing Jasmine? Am sat on caravan floor wearing his jumper. The smell is making my chest ache. Have been trying not to cry but stupid tears are bubbling down cheeks and nose keeps on snivelling. He's with Jasmine!

2.31 am Wish Mr Tubs was here . . .

Sunday 27 October
9 am Woke to blissful seven seconds of ignorance, then stomach lurched cruelly remembering Ben/Jasmine silhouette. Head feels heavy and tense from over-crying and eyes sting when I blink. I know we only had one kiss – and I can't even explain – it just felt completely right. It was perfect.

9.02 am Bet they're lying cosily in bed right now giving each other little Eskimo kisses, saying, 'You're beautiful', 'No, you're more beautiful', while I'm lying – not so cosily – on a caravan floor with six, seven, eight . . . nine other bodies. Gil has rolled over and is snoring into my sleeping bag and

Hobbit has tucked himself on my other side and is making mutting noises. They might look all dozy and innocent but I've not forgotten Beavis and Butthead's role in bursting my Ben bubble.

9.03 am Tam is fast asleep on sofa wrapped in Robbie's arms. Even though I'm consumed by own misery, am big enough person that I can look at Tam and find happiness for her deep, deep down inside me. Although, might be nice if she wakes up soon.

9.04 am No. Be strong. Let her slumber in happiness. You can do this on your own. Breathe.

9.05 am Whatshallido? Whatshallido? Should I confront Ben and demand explanation for heart-shattering two-timing? But perhaps I'm blowing this out of proportion? This is university – we're meant to be out there pulling lots of people and having fun, which is exactly what Ben did. What I don't understand is why he was so intimate with me before? After talking by the fire – I, I thought he cared about me. Maybe he felt comfortable talking about his mum with me – and then the kiss just followed on. Nothing more than an embarrassing mistake for him.

9.06 am Yikes . . . caravan door is opening. Is Ben!

9.30 am Was terrible. He came to tell everyone there's breakfast laid on at the pub. He saw that I was awake and darted his eyes away, pretending not to notice. Was not having that! Brushed Gil's snoring face and Hobbit's furry arm off sleeping bag, stood up and said, 'Ben.' Hadn't really thought of what to say next, so used upward inflection to turn it into a question, 'Ben?'

'All right?' he said quietly, barely moving his lips.

'Yes.'

We stood in silence for a moment looking at each other. 'Sleep well?' he asked finally.

'Fine, thanks. You?' (Subtext: Did you have a good sleep with the bitch-ho?)

'Yeah, fine,' he replied, shifting uncomfortably from foot to foot. He shoved his hands into his pockets and there was another long silence as he studied the ground.

I wanted to confront him about Jasmine, to ask him how he could kiss me so lovingly and then be with her, but I knew that would make flat life awkward. Ben has gone through a lot in the last few years – and just because he'd opened up to me, it doesn't mean we have a connection other than on a friends level. As much as this hurt right now, I needed to salvage our friendship, so I gave him a get-out clause. 'I guess we were pretty drunk last night,' I said, laughing weakly and attempting a smile.

Ben jumped on it. 'Definitely,' he agreed firmly. 'Must have been the punch.'

Managed heroically to swallow crying lump that was threatening to choke speech. 'Yes, that must be it,' I replied. 'Let's just forget about it.' (Subtext: I'll obsess about this for eternity.) 'Oh, and here's your jumper.' I handed it to him hoping my nose had dripped on it. But then, as Ben reached to take it, his hand rested on mine making my stomach do flippy electric things that I'm going to have to put a ban on in future.

'Thank you,' he replied tying the jumper round his waist. Then he smiled sadly at me and left.

And that's it. One magical, momentous, mind-altering kiss and then – nothing.

2 pm. On coach. Jasmine is sat next to Ben, swinging her long hair smugly. She keeps playfully touching him as if marking her territory. I've always prided self on being kind and caring but something must have snapped because current thoughts are about a giant mannequin with peroxide hair and FF-cup boobs falling from sky and flattening Jasmine.

Can't even share the misery of evening with Tam as she is sat shrouded in Robbie's big arms. Only Gil and his smokey dreadlocks are keeping me company and after telling me about his abstract dream involving me, a limbo pole and coconuts, he's fallen asleep on my shoulder.

5.30 pm. Bedroom. We're back in the flat now. Still haven't had chance to speak to Tam. She got a call from Oliver as we were getting off the coach and has been locked in room ever since.

5.33 pm Am miserable, undesirable and forty surfers have seen me naked.

5.34 pm If Tam marries Robbie, she'll be related to Jasmine. Eugh!

5.45 pm Tam is still on the phone. How much is there to say? She's lovely and he's been a complete knob-head.

5.46 pm Ah, will go and see Justin!

6 pm Hmmm. Boys are useless. Is like Justin lives on his own little comic planet. He kept on making obscure references: 'It's like Spider-Man. Jasmine is the Black Cat and you are Mary Jane.'

'Why does Black Cat sound so much cooler? I want to be the cat.'

'You've just got to think of *Amazing Spider-Man, No.42*,' he said vacantly, picking at a TippEx stain on his cords. 'Be confident with Ben and tell him straight, "Face it, Tiger . . . You just hit the jackpot."'

I mean, really, what the fuck is he talking about?

6.10 pm Eyes have actually run out of tears but body is doing phantom crying and performing hiccupy-breathing flutters at random. Mr Tubs has been quite supportive and a great listener but I can sense a degree of smugness.

6.11 pm Phone is hermetically sealed to Tam's ear.

6.14 pm Will ring Mum.

6.40 pm Mum was brilliant. She listened quietly as I sobbed my way through the details of the weekend and then she said firmly: 'Josie, you are a beautiful and charming girl. You're witty and intelligent and very special. If Ben cannot see that, then, frankly, you are better off without him.' Hah!

7 pm Tam is finally off phone. Oliver called to apologise for his 'irrational decision' (as I said) and to beg Tam to go out with him again. She said, 'yes'! After the heartache! After the Spock message! After beautiful Robbie!

'But those biceps . . .' was all I managed to splutter.

'Hm?'

'You – Robbie – his arms. What are you thinking?'

'I know, I know,' said Tam twiddling a blonde curl in her fingers. 'Robbie is lovely – gorgeous, but, well, Oliver – I don't know, there's something . . .'

'Evil about him?' I offered.

'Something addictive. I know he's been an arse, but he really regrets it. He thinks what we've been through could make us stronger. He's even taking a couple of days off work next week to visit me – so we can make it up in person.'

Hmmm. Am unconvinced about the regretfulness of Spock, but guess I have to support Tam's decision. But what wastage with Robbie!!

Then focus of conversation shifted to my news re: Ben situation, or lack thereof. I couldn't tell Tam about Ben's mum, but I filled her in on all the other details. Tam was shocked by his awful behaviour and agreed he's acted completely out of character. She said, 'Males are the weaker sex and cannot control their lust.' Was nodding firmly in agreement but then she started going on about forgiveness and male infidelity being expected. 'Oliver was telling me that there are studies that prove males are naturally unfaithful.'

I bet he has! His theory is probably based on the findings of a polygamous male scientist who watched a group of boy rabbits springing around shagging all the other pretty bunnies. The boy rabbits eventually bounce back to their original partner and scientist then makes sweeping generalisations about man imitating nature and neatly concludes it's perfectly normal for men to be complete bastards.

Tam has been brainwashed! Must help her. Although she does look worryingly happy again. Is tricky as am not entirely sure if I want her to be single for slightly selfish reasons e.g. someone to do Top 3s with while drinking vodka. Should try not to influence her decision as she'll see in own time that Oliver is bad and I am good. Yes.

Will also move forwards with own problem. Kiss with Ben was (very, very) pleasurable but was (unfortunately) a one-off and completely meaningless (for him). Did expect more from Ben but is clear that for one night he was a rabbit that saw some bunny action and took it. However, I am a strong enough person to look beyond his wrongdoing and not dwell on issue as will only ruin general flat karma. It would not do if I were stomping round halls, slamming doors and swearing, when can save that for privacy of own room.

In conclusion, Ben has got to get snog-around phase out of system before he is ready to settle down (with me – if in time I decide to forgive him). Therefore, I shall act like beach-kiss never happened and be breezy, popular flatmate. Yes!

7.06 pm Will start tomorrow. Tonight I'm hiding in room. Puffy eyes and hiccupy breathing could shatter breezy illusion.

SEVEN

Monday 28 October

8.55 am Good. It's a new day. Am popular, fun-loving and very, very breezy. Am feeling calm. Breathing is good. Have showered, changed, breakfasted and packed books. I'm off to lectures to learn and be fulfilled through education. Yes! Tam, on the other hand, is ditching Shakespeare for a bikini wax because Spock (Boo! Hiss!) is arriving tomorrow. This is what happens when boys enter life – all rational, independent thought vanishes and you end up paying people to rip hot wax from body.

8.55 am. Empty lecture theatre. It's still 8.55 am. Buggering clocks went back yesterday! Is typical, the one day I'm five minutes early rather than rushing around hysterically as though McGibbon will behead me for being 0.1 of a nanosecond late, I'm actually a whole hour and five minutes early. Is particularly annoying as after hellish weekend, do not feel safe spending excess time alone with self as will no doubt lead to miserable over-thinking about Ben/Jasmine duo of doom.

9.45 am Couldn't stop it. Tried annotating *Twelfth Night* to prepare for lecture, except annotations turned to doodles and before I knew it, was writing 'I heart Ben' and designing instruments of torture for Jasmine. Tsk.

I'm supposed to be in prime of dating life but have spent first month as a student obsessing over flatmate. Is ridiculous. Well, that's it! Have scribbled out Ben doodles and am literally drawing a line under crush. Am going to move on, branch out and think of new boy options. Hah!

Although, the thing I find a bit tricky in dating world is trying to curb pickiness. For instance, will be chatting along nicely with someone who'll laugh at a witty joke I make and, as they throw their head back in 'ha-ha-ha' type of way, I clock a freaky wolf tooth poking out from corner of their mouth. Then cannot stop thinking of, or trying to look at, freaky wolf tooth and spend rest of evening peering over top of menu or imagining our children as werewolves.

Pickiness is shallow and wrong. Must broaden horizons: will not be put off by pointy teeth, white trainers or Ben Sherman shirts. Nor will I mock boys who tie shoelaces in a bow, smell of Old Spice and wear sovereign rings. I will become less fussy, more available and possibly end up dating someone who wears a Burberry cap. Good God!

10.15 am Lecture has begun and am now sat in front row after arriving late . . . I know! My mistake was doing a quick bladder squeeze as lecture hall was filling up. Suddenly panicked that I might not be able to hold it for entire hour so nipped to the loos at double-fast speed. By the time I returned, the lecture had begun so tried to sneak quietly to an empty seat, except tiptoes tripped over bag, which went hurtling down steps, spilling contents (books, tampons, magazines etc.) over lecture theatre. McGibbon silently contemplated my death as I hastily scrambled and gathered belongings – was very nerve-racking having 300 pairs of eyes watching me stoop for my Tampax. With reddish tint to cheeks, tried to slink off to the back of the hall, but McGibbon took pleasure in redirecting me to a front-row seat.

Am now sat at close range from his mouth, which is generating a worrying amount of foaming white spittle. Is also difficult to check for potential dates in front row position. From here, I can only see Rasta Hat Boy, Trench Coat Guy and one other male who's wearing glittery eyeshadow.

10.58 am Eugh. Spittle is out of control. Wonder if McGibbon has some type of medical condition? Am in permanent state of unease in case spittle comes loose and launches in my direction. How am I expected to learn in the face of such distractions?

11 am Thank goodness. We're on our five-minute break now and McGibbon's taken a couple of steps backwards. I can relax for a moment. Actually, he's rummaging around in his satchel. Please be a tissue. Please be a tissue . . . No, it's not that, but he is carefully unwrapping something . . . It's a square of flapjack! He's looking at it lovingly. Now what? . . . Something else is coming out of the satchel . . . My God! It's a handkerchief! . . . Is he actually going to . . . I think he might . . . yes . . . he's doing it . . . He's wiped away the spittle! He de-spittles for flapjack but not for students? Wow, that's an insight.

Tuesday 29 October
8.30 am. In bed. Alarm is telling me to get up and go to Children's Literature, but the extended hypertension from yesterday has put me off lectures for life. Think I need a little more sleep. Yes. Is good to soothe mind ready for a productive day of intellectual . . . mmmm, sleeeeep.

9.30 am. Still in bed. Beep! Beep! Beep! Nasty intercom is being noisy. Am asleep. Please answer it somebody else . . .

9.31 am Grrrrr! Somebody else isn't listening. Going sleepily myself.

10 am Shock! Horror! Intercom was Pablo. Pablo was at door. Person at door was Pablo. Four-day-fling-in-Spain-Pablo, who was definitely never meant to visit, has flown over to visit ME. He is currently having a shower and then is going to unpack his stuff into MY room.

Regret past association with Pablo and his free cocktail bar.

10.02 am Just cannot believe he is here! Pablo said he's been thinking of me constantly (his exact words were 'I think many many of you'). He'd lost my address but remembered me mentioning where I was going to university. He booked a flight to England, got a coach to the university and then asked around campus for me. And now he's in my bathroom! (Is quite nice that I'm well-known on campus though! Maybe I'm an iconic figure on Top 3 lists everywhere?)

Remember him as Spanish Adonis with long dark hair, a tanned and muscular body and wearing a cute barman outfit. Seems he may have been liberal with the alcohol-to-mixer ratio as in cold light of (sober) day, he has since lost his tan, shaved his head and grown a goatee. Know I've been wittering on about being less picky, and Pablo's arrival is possibly a sign from the gods, but now have that sick, desperate 'Get-me-out-of-here!' feeling in pit of stomach, not yummy butterflies-maypole-dancing flutters like when kissing Ben. Just cannot do it. Am going to have to leave university.

10.45 am. Tam's room. Pablo came back from the bathroom with only a towel around his waist, exposing a disturbingly hairy chest. 'Pretty Hosie,' he told me with a big smile. 'I come to England to surprise you!'

It's all very well having a couple of cheeky snogs with a twenty-five-year-old barman, but when he's standing in your student room without the sunshine or the Spanish backdrop – and without the cocktails pumping through your system – it's really not the type of surprise a girl wants.

Thought I was going to throw up, so dashed next door for a crisis meeting with Tam.

She was in the middle of plucking her eyebrows as Oliver's taking her to a fancy Italian restaurant tonight. 'It's good,' she said, squinting in the mirror at her brow, 'because, ow! Bastard!' She plucked at a tough one. 'Oliver is really trying to make it up to me. It's so sweet of him to take me out to dinner.'

What is the girl thinking? As if a plateful of linguini is going to make up for him dropping his pants on the photocopier. Even as she stood there in her saggy tracksuit bums and white vest top, she still manages to look lovely. She's far too good for Spock.

Tam stopped pruning and sat herself on the bed next to me. 'What is it, honey?' she asked, probably noticing that my mouth had started to foam. 'Is it Ben? Have you seen him with the bunny?'

'Pablo is here,' I whispered anxiously and pointed towards the wall. 'In. My. Bedroom.'

Tam raised her nicely shaped eyebrows at me, as if to say, 'Who?'

'You know: Pablo. Spanish guy from my summer holiday.'

'Oh, the hotel-chain owner.'

Buggery. I'd forgotten about that.

I explained about my slight exaggeration and then focused on the more pressing problem of what I should say to someone who's flown hundreds of miles to see me, but who makes me feel sick.

'Ooo! I'm going to check him out!' Tam said, rather unhelpfully and then nipped into my room under the pretext of 'borrowing a hairdryer'.

I heard Pablo prattling; 'I am very sorry but I know not what this is.'

'Never mind! Thanks!' said Tam, who quickly returned and whispered, 'Josie, seriously, what were you thinking?'

'I know.'

'Tell me you didn't do the beast with two backs together?'

'Eek! Of course not!' I cringed at the thought. 'Look, it was a holiday fling. I was partially insane from sunstroke and partially pissed from the free cocktails and we ended up having a couple of snogs. That's it.'

'Phew.'

'So what am I going to do?' I begged.

'It's a bit awkward, isn't it?' Tam grossly understated.

Was hoping for a little more than that. Maybe an invisibility cloak, a loaded gun or even a solution would do it. Eventually she got the idea I needed help. 'Right, just be firm and tell him he can't stay. You don't have room, you didn't know he was coming and you have important work to do.'

OK. Good. That's what I'm going to do. Deep breath. Go.

Midday Um . . . this is how it went.

'Pablo?'

'Yes, pretty Hosie?'

'It's lovely that you've flown over to visit me – and it definitely is a surprise. The thing is, I'm incredibly busy with my studies right now and on top of that there is nowhere for you to stay here.'

'I stay here?'

'Erm, no, Pablo. There is not enough room,' I said, gesticulating wildly as though this might penetrate the language barrier.

'In your room? Hosie, you have the very pretty eyes.'

I faltered, smiling for a moment and then managed to gather myself. 'Non,' I said, hoping that was Spanish. 'Pablo, we had fun on holiday but now I am at university and very B-U-S-Y. I do not want you to be my boyfriend.'

'Me your boyfriend? Pretty Hosie is girlfriend and I stay in her room.'

So that went well.

6 pm Pablo is staying. Seeing as we don't have anything in common other than he makes cocktails and I like to drink them, I decided to take him to a cocktail bar in town. We took it in turns to smile uneasily at each other and then carry on slurping Sex On The Beach, which somehow felt a bit shady at three o' clock on a weekday in October. At least it gave Pablo a chance to use his English vocabulary; he'd occasionally pick something up and say, 'This is the lime' or 'This is the straw'. After the fourteenth time of nodding encouragingly, I felt self getting very irate and wanting to shout mean things at him. (Realise this was horrid of me and although Pablo wears his trousers above his belly button, am sure he's a very nice person.)

I was sipping on a Slippery Nipple when Mum called: 'Josie, are you in a bar?'

How does she do it? Swear she has supersonic hearing – or maybe telepathic powers?

'You do know it's the middle of the afternoon? I've just read a report about girls your age binge-drinking. It's very unladylike.'

I decided to go along with her drinking theory rather than explaining about Pablo. If I mentioned, 'By the way, that barman from Hotel Fiesta turned up this morning,' think Mum might have a brain power-down by all the potential threats this causes: 'He could be a rapist, carry scabies, try to involve you in a cult, pressurise you into drug-taking . . .'

After Mum had quoted some statistics from the *Daily Mail* (29 per cent of teenage girls are binge-drinking), she then told me: 'I'm going away for a couple of days on a life drawing course.'

Oh dear. Sounds like this is Mum's autumn fad. Since Dad left, she's taken up a new interest with each season. In Spring it was Pilates and summer was the Alexander Technique, and now we've got life drawing. Great.

'I was just calling to check you were OK about the 'Ben' situation.' She whispered his name like it was a dirty word. 'Remember: keep focusing on the positives.'

Right, I sat across the table from Pablo and started taking calming breaths and trying to think positively about current situation. Actually, cocktails really promote clear thinking as all of a sudden I realised Pablo's visit could be a good thing. Having a foreign lover will suggest to Ben that I am popular and also enjoy snogging around. He'll assume I have other suitors, become outrageously jealous, realise he's had enough of being free and single; he'll declare his undying love for me and then we can get married, have children and live in a house on the beach with a shower radio. (Although, of course, having firmly drawn that closure line, am simply hypothesising about alternative lifestyle with a random partner.)

Told Pablo he could stay on my floor for three nights; it's enough time to make me look popular in front of Ben, but not so long that I'm tempted to throw myself into the path of haulage lorry. Immediately regretted it, though, when Pablo did not so much as offer to split the cocktail bill with me. Am not sure that this is what lovers who have flown from foreign countries do? Especially not rich hotel owners. Hmmm.

11 pm Was a little nervous about introducing Pablo to flatmates after my truth and dare embellishments. Did try and encourage him to buy some new clothes that were perhaps more hotelier-like, but he seemed keen on his snugly fitting black trousers. ('Snug' is being polite – they are so ludicrously tight that he has a VPL.)

We were eating an omelette in the kitchen when Matt and Ben arrived back from their food shop. It was the first time I've seen Ben since the surf trip and, annoyingly, my body turned against me and began quivering. As he unpacked tins of beans, even the sinews on his thick wrists made me want to tip Pablo out the window and run into the hills screaming, 'Take me now, Ben!'

At first, the introductions seemed to go well and Ben looked suitably interested that my Spanish lover had come to visit. Things got trickier when Matt started asking questions like, 'How's the hotel business?'

Thankfully, Pablo didn't understand fully as Matt was talking through a mouthful of Monster Munch.

'Yes, Hotel Fiesta,' he smiled eagerly.

Matt shoved another handful of crisps into his mouth and, seizing my opportunity, I told Pablo he could ring home from the phone on the stairs and then shooed him into the corridor.

To keep the boys distracted, I asked, 'Have either of you met Tam's Oliver yet?'

'Absolute wanker,' Matt said, screwing up the finished Monster Munch packet. 'Old. Pretentious. Flabby. Boring. Butt-ugly. Dresses like a ponce.'

Hmmm. Am sure Matt's judgement is a little harsh. 'What do you think?' I asked Ben, who was unpacking a sack of value pasta shells.

'I don't know,' he said, reaching to his cupboard. 'It's not up to me who my flatmates dick around with.'

Huh! Was furious about loaded connotations of 'dick around' which suggest I'm being sluttish with Pablo. Well, if that's what he thinks, I'm surprised he's not throwing himself at me as from where I was stood on Saturday night, it seemed like he enjoyed the company of sluts!

'Talking of "dicks",' I spat back, 'have you seen Jasmine recently?'

Ben slammed his cupboard too and spun round to face me. I stood my ground. Ben glared at me. I glared back.

Then Justin burst through the kitchen door. 'Who's the dude in the tight trousers?'

Wednesday 30 October

1.30 pm The dude in the tight trousers is driving me insane. He snores. He doesn't get up till midday. He takes three-quarters of an hour in the shower. He wears Y-fronts. He plucks his eyebrows and has put on a fresh pair of even tighter black trousers. Plus, am not sure he's having the desired effect on Ben. Was hoping more for a little stab of jealousy leading to Ben being extra sweet and trying to woo me, rather than him fuming at me and insinuating that I have loose morals.

Have whole day looming ahead with Pablo. Haven't got any lectures to escape to and can't go to Surf Club since I've given up. (Tam and I discussed it on Monday and we made a mutual decision to ditch the wetsuits and waves: she can't go back because of the Robbie situation and I don't like sitting in a minibus full of people who've seen me naked.)

5.30 pm Ugh. Have been roped into cooking roast chicken for seven people. Justin said it's my turn to do the flat meal so have been traipsing round Tesco looking for roasting-type ingredients. Must note, am appalled at price of free-range chickens. Always nag Mum to buy them after reading scary battery report, but today I shamefully sacrificed principles as free-range were twice as expensive.

What with the murder of a caged and force-fed bird, and the two impostors (Spock and Pablo), am really not looking forward to tonight. It isn't even a proper flat meal as Suniti's not coming. I tried to gently encourage her – and even bought a nut roast (I thought it might be easier than ritually slaughtering a chicken) – but she said she's going away for a few days. She wouldn't tell me where, which seemed a bit odd. I do worry about her; I never see her with any friends

111

and she spends all her time in the library or locked in her room. Really hope she isn't lonely.

Oh, maybe I could lend her Pablo?

6 pm. Kitchen. Have sent Pablo off to explore campus so I can get on with cooking. Is strange, really, as he doesn't seem desperately in love with me. He hasn't tried to kiss me (thankfully) and just seems very interested in the housing and job climate. Hmmm? Anyway, must focus on meal. Have recipe in front of me and big, battery chicken on oven-tray. 'Baste chicken in olive oil.' Don't have olive oil but am sure I Can't Believe It's Not Butter will do same job.

6.30 pm Nasty smoke pouring out of oven. Put grill on by mistake! How are you supposed to know the difference? Chicken's buttered-back is singed. And still raw inside. Must be salvageable? Best ring the Roast Queen.

6.40 pm Granny was cooking fillet of beef for Doogle and seemed distracted. She instructed me to cut out remaining good chicken and stir-fry with marinade and vegetables. A small change of plan, then. No problem.

6.45 pm Not much good remaining chicken and no marinade to be found. Have improvised by sprinkling lots of salt and pepper – very rustic and this season. Am bit low on oriental-type vegetables, only have sprouts and cauliflower to go with roast. If I cut them up small enough am sure it'll taste fine.

7.15 pm Put chicken, vegetables and more margarine in the pan. Looks a little dry and cauliflower still hard. Will add wine.

7.45 pm Lovely! Have placed rice in a circle and positioned chicken in middle hoping neat presentation may distract from taste. Is ready!

10.30 pm. In bedroom. Am searching for Rennie tablets. Meal was hideous. Think combination of dry food and stress of being cook and hostess brought on a very painful bout of trapped wind. Is awful affliction because you can never openly say, 'I'm in agony as I've got a nasty fart lodged in my gut between a roast potato and mouthful of chicken leg.' Have locked self in room as think it is the sort of thing best dealt with in private.

Doubt I'll be asked to do flat meal again. Tried to mask taste of disastrous cooking by pouring numerous glasses of wine for us all. Everyone was polite (perhaps not drunk enough?) and Justin did say that roast chicken in red wine sauce with stir-fried cauliflower and sprouts was 'an original and very inventive dish'. But then he ruined it by laughing.

Wish I'd never bothered with the meal, as clearly no one appreciates my efforts. Don't think Ben's said a word all evening. I'm annoyed with myself because I started to feel bad for having Pablo here – when I'm not the one who's got something to feel guilty about. I've got mixed feelings about Ben at the moment. On the beach kiss evening, I felt we made a connection, sharing things that you'd only speak of with someone you could trust. Then within the same hour he'd dropped me and was being intimate with Jasmine. But even though I've been hurt, I still want to be there for him. Ugh, why are boys so confusing?

Talking of which, I finally met Spock – and, oh my God, he's practically an OAP! I know Pablo was a mistake but at least I can blame that on alcohol, but Tam's got no excuse. Spock is thirty and has got one of those trendy London haircuts and a slightly squidgy office figure to match. And those ears – pointy doesn't even cover it! Think he's a bit of a fashion try-hard as he wore a beige suit with an open-necked yellow shirt and brown heeled shoes. I hardly recognised Tam either; she'd swapped her jeans and flats for a chic dress and heels, and her tousled blonde hair was straightened and sleeked to match.

Really don't like it that Spock's been smoking throughout meal. Is horrible breathing in second-hand Marlboro fumes that have been banging around his decaying lungs. Secretly wonder if Matt's assessment of him was correct. Spock was definitely being pretentious and kept yakking on in business-speak about 'key players' and 'brand positioning' and describing everywhere as being either 'South or North of the river'.

Did make an effort to remain enthusiastic and friendly as we are all at different stages of life and it's important to be understanding, but that was before he slated English Literature degrees.

'I mean, babe,' he said to Tamara, blowing a lungful of smoke across the table. 'English Literature? You can't tell me that's going to help you get a job. In three years you'll be 15K in debt and what will you have to show for it?'

Don't like the way Oliver asks lots of questions but never lets you answer.

'Absolutely fuck-all else,' he continued, 'than a shelf full of Charlotte Austen.'

'Erm, it's Jane Austen,' I ventured, 'and Charlotte Brontë.'

'My point entirely – who even knows about this shit?'

Also do not like his excessive swearing. Although am not exactly headed for a career in academia, did feel a bit defensive of our great literary canon being described as 'shit'.

Phrrrummp!

Oops . . . think my trapped wind has passed. Glad only Mr Tubs witnessed that; what with binge drinking, farting and my regular reliance on Jolen, seems entirely possible that I'm turning into a man.

Suppose I should go back to the kitchen and check if anyone else needs a Rennie.

11.45 pm I'd only been gone for fifteen minutes but that was long enough for a full-scale ruckus to break out. I walked through the door to see Justin, red-faced and full of rage, sprint across the kitchen and launch himself at Matt.

I quickly side-stepped out of the attack zone and backed over to the table.

Justin made a heroic attempt to rugby tackle Matt to the ground; he was latched on to his waist, snarling like a rabid animal with the effort of trying to floor him.

'What's going on?' I whispered to Tam, who was perched nervously on the edge of her seat.

'Your flatmate,' Spock butted in, 'wrote a supposedly hilarious "Shout Out" about the ginger one—'

'Justin,' I corrected him.

'And now "Justin" is a little pissed off.'

115

Tam slid an open copy of the student paper along the table. As she did, I noticed with a sinking heart that Ben had already left. I tried to push aside the thought that he'd gone to visit Jasmine.

The 'Shout Out' section is a page where students can post their thoughts or messages each week, such as: 'Hi to the girl in the SU on Monday wearing the blue top. P.S. Nice tits!' [Ric Bream, third year Engineering student].

Pablo pointed to Matt's entry: *'I'd like to take this opportunity to apologise for my very small penis.'* [Justin Grange, first year Art History student].

Matt is unbelievable – as if anyone would see the funny side of that. Suddenly I was rooting for Justin.

'Grrrrr! Aaarrrgghhh! Grrrrr!' he growled, hanging on to Matt's legs and trying to force them to bend.

'God, it's pathetic,' Oliver sniped at Tam, as if the dispute was her fault.

'Yeah, you're pathetic, Geri,' Matt taunted in a mock Welsh accent. 'I think you wanna take those girlie mitts off me.'

Justin's cheeks were blood red and he panted with exertion. He looked about ten years old in his Tiger Balm T-shirt and little brown cords.

'That's a "No", is it? OK, babycakes. You're not going to like this.' In one swift manoeuvre, Matt unclamped Justin's arms, flipped him on to the kitchen floor and sat heavily on his chest.

I know that Matt and Justin have a love/hate relationship and playfights are all part of it, but I had a strong feeling that Justin was taking it seriously.

'Matthew Rowsell has Justine in a powerful body lock,' Matt commentated into an imaginary microphone. 'We've got one,' he said, slapping the ground in WWF style.

Justin's legs were kicking ferociously in a bid to free himself.

Tam was looking anxiously towards Oliver who kept doing loud executive scoffs at the spectacle. Pablo, who was smiling enthusiastically at the fighters, suddenly didn't seem so bad in comparison.

'We've got two . . .' Matt hit the ground a second time. 'The crowd's never seen anything like it. Justine is doing her best to fight back, but is there time?'

'Get your arse off my chest!' bellowed Justin, flinging his head from side to side as though fitting.

'And three!' Matt slapped the kitchen floor. 'Rowsell is crowned King of the Kitchen and Justine has been beaten once again!' Matt farted on Justin's head and then bowed to the audience with a self-satisfied smile.

'We're going to bed,' Oliver instructed Tam, standing up from the table. 'I'll leave you kids to it.'

As if proving a point, Matt yelled, 'Wedgie!!' and ran at Justin.

Justin was back on his feet now, his face fixed in a black grimace.

Matt came lunging towards him laughing.

'Noooooo!' Justin bellowed.

Matt had a hand on Justin's underwear and began yanking at them. It must have been the alcohol, but I could have sworn his pants were red satin.

The next few seconds seemed to happen in slow motion. Oliver had turned to watch Matt with a disgusted expression; Tam was cringing silently; Pablo's eyes were out on stalks. I held a hand to my mouth, knowing Justin had been pushed too far.

Justin's face was contorted. With an almighty effort he managed to break free of Matt's grasp. His fist followed through and swung at Matt's face.

I held my breath.

To everyone's surprise, his fist made contact.

Thwack!

The punch landed in the middle of Matt's forehead. He staggered backwards into the kitchen table, knocking a full glass of wine into the air. It seemed to hover for a moment and then came plummeting down and sloshed across Oliver's groin.

'Fuck!' said Spock. 'I've got fucking wine on my suit. You fucking sons of bitches!'

Everyone ignored Spock, except for Tam who leapt to her feet and grabbed a cloth from the sink.

Matt breathed out shakily and felt for his head. 'You punched me,' he said, disbelievingly.

The colour drained from Justin's cheeks. 'I'm . . . I'm really sorry.' Justin rubbed his damp brow anxiously. 'You shouldn't have wedgied . . .' he tailed off.

'Get that off me!' Oliver snapped viciously at Tam who was trying to dab at his suit with our kitchen cloth. 'You're fucking useless.'

Matt's eyes narrowed. 'Who the hell do you think you are?'

Justin stepped back: 'I know, I got out of hand – I really am sorry.'

'Not you,' Matt hissed from the corner of his mouth. 'You!' he said, taking a step towards Oliver.

'What was that?' Oliver said, jutting his chin in the air.

Tam watched anxiously as Oliver moved towards Matt.

'I said,' he repeated slowly, 'who the hell do you think you are? Nobody speaks to my flatmates like that!'

Pablo and I remained motionless at the table, eyes flicking between Matt and Oliver.

Oliver squared up to him. They were the same height – Matt more of an athletic build but Oliver had the extra weight.

Matt leant in closer.

Justin took two steps back.

Tam's soft eyes were wide with anxiety and she held both hands to her chest. 'Please, Oli. Don't,' she begged.

Oliver ignored her and pushed his face towards Matt's. 'Come on then!' he roared.

'Matthew, please . . .' said Tam, her voice quiet and full of desperation.

Matt kept his position, his whole body taut with fury.

'Please,' she begged again, shaking her head sadly.

Matt sucked in the air and then there was silence. His eyes flickered sideways to Tam.

He breathed out slowly. 'Another time,' he warned.

Oliver laughed arrogantly and then shoved past him and out into the corridor.

EIGHT

Thursday 31 October

10.30 am. Crime Fiction. I stepped on Pablo's fat head three times this morning. Is very difficult trying to navigate around already tiny bedroom when a hairy body is taking up all the floor space. Is actually very nice to be sat calmly in Crime Fiction lecture – away from Spanish impostor and mad punching flatmates.

Actually, was quite funny this morning; while general flat relations are miserable (Tam hates Matt, I hate Pablo, Ben hates me, Matt hates Oliver, Oliver hates us all and no one knows when Suniti is), Justin is walking around like he's Jackie Chan. Suppose throwing your first punch is like a rite of passage into full-blown manhood. (Am not going to mention that aiming for a nose, cheek or even chin is generally preferable to a thud on the forehead, but it was a start.)

Saw Matt in the kitchen and he seems fine about the whole thing. 'I'm pleased that Geri's got some balls. I was starting to wonder about him what with all his comic book shit and there's just something so girlie about a Welsh accent, don't you think?'

Hate it when Matt tries to collude with me on racist/sexist/fascist/gingerist subjects.

3 pm. Gay and Lesbian Studies. Tam hasn't been to lectures today as she's seeing Oliver off at the station. We haven't spoken properly since last night and I'm not quite sure how to broach the subject of, 'By the way, Tam, your boyfriend is a complete knob-head. We were all wondering, what do you see in him?'

I'm mean, really, though, what *does* she see in him? Yes, he wears suits and flashes the cash, but he's so patronising. Can only think the attraction comes from that whole position of power thing. Unless he has an exceptionally big . . .

Oh, bugger!

Just remembered it's Halloween! (Er, it's purely coincidental that thoughts of Spock triggered the Halloween link.) For last hour have been sat next to a boy wearing fangs and a cloak, but just presumed he was another arts student trying to be alternative. We're all meant to be going to the Halloween party at SU tonight, but I haven't even planned a costume. Wonder if I can be creative with existing wardrobe; is there any way a hula outfit could look slightly spooky?

6.30 pm The very presence of he-whom-I-shall-only-refer-to-as 'The Spaniard' is driving me insane! He is worsening already shaky flat relations. Came back from lectures to find Ben stood in middle of corridor holding a can of shaving foam. He looked angry. 'Can you tell your boyfriend to buy his own shaving foam? He's used mine and put the empty can back.'

Have never seen Ben like that before. I admit, at first I almost liked it; he looked so wild and manly. Maybe it was the stubble? Tried to clear head of images of Ben ripping open his shirt to expose bulging muscles in manner of Incredible Hulk (although obviously not green, or a monster) and suggested reasonably, 'Perhaps it wasn't Pablo? It could have been Matt or Justin.'

'I've already asked Matt, and Justin hasn't hit puberty yet.'

'Fine.' Was clear that Ben was not going to rip shirt from body, so got rather annoyed myself. 'As it's obviously a problem, you can use my shaving foam in the meantime.' I opened the door to my room, grabbed the foam from my wash-bag and let the door swing to as The Spaniard was halfway through saying, 'Hola, pretty lady.'

Ben snatched the foam, gave a curt 'Thanks' and went into the bathroom slamming the door behind him.

Am back in my room stewing. Ben is being intolerable and The Spaniard, worse. Room is lined with empty mugs, cereal bowls and crisp packets. My tweezers, cotton buds and moisturiser are spread across desk and Pablo is happily lying on bed flicking through my *Cosmopolitan* collection.

'Pablo!' I exclaimed hysterically, spinning round and absorbing the chaos. 'You, you . . .' I was going to shout 'you lazy fuck-head' but managed to hold my tongue. Instead, I banged around my room stroppily clearing up his mess.

Am sure Pablo thinks he's the star of *A Spanish Lover* and he's here to liberate me from our repressive English ways. He sat himself up on my bed and said, 'Hosie, in Spain we are very, er, very free. Open. You must speak how you feel.'

Fine,' I said defiantly. 'You make me feel sick. I don't like the way your hair is the same length all over. You wear your trousers too high. You use tweezers. You don't own a hotel. You haven't even bought me a present and I'm going to cartwheel round the kitchen the very second you leave!'

Not sure how much Pablo understood, but he looked hurt. I was actually being very horrible. Pablo is on holiday and trying to have a good time and I'm hysterical about a couple of dirty mugs. Am ashamed. It's like the kids in *Lord of the Flies* who turn wild and savage without adult supervision. Is happening to me. Am cruel and . . . mean and . . . Be calm. Breathe.

6.45 pm Is all OK. Was just momentary lapse into meanness due to pressure of flat guest. Is fine now. Have apologised to Pablo and am going to be very nice to him for rest of his visit (though, luckily, he's leaving tomorrow)!

7 pm. Tam's room. We're getting ready together for Halloween party. Tam and I are doing a very good job of pretending the flat meal never happened and not talking about Oliver. I've been really quite legendary as, on way back to lectures, managed to pick up brilliant Halloween outfits. I got two cute black dresses from Primark and we are wearing witches' cloaks, pointy hats and fake noses – with dreadlock wigs, fake nose rings, sweatbands and leg warmers. We're wicked witches! Justin doesn't get the concept and I've tried to explain we're wicked-cool rather than wicked-evil, but it's lost on him.

7.20 pm All is not OK. Tam is locked in bathroom crying. She broke the silence and asked me what I thought of Spock. Was awful as couldn't lie to best friend, though also did not want to offend her with the truth. Tried to bluff my way through by calling him 'independent' and 'strong-minded'. Then she asked specifically: 'What did you think of him last night?'

'Erm, I thought he was kind of, well, you know, a bit rude to you,' I said tentatively.

'I know, I know,' Tam mumbled, fiddling with her new dreadlocks. 'He did apologise and make it up to me. I think he just feels insecure because he never went to university.'

'Right,' I said, understanding a bit more. 'The other thing is – and I really don't want to upset you by saying this – but I thought that you were different around him. Normally you're more outgoing and relaxed, but you seemed quite tense while Oliver was here.'

'Oh, it's probably just the Tina May stuff,' Tam smoothed over. 'I know you didn't see him in the best light, but he is really sweet when it's just the two of us.'

Without knocking, Matt strolled straight into Tam's room, hijacked her supply of loo roll and then looked around and said, 'Has your fuckwit of a boyfriend left yet?'

Hence the crying and the bathroom barricade.

7.40 pm Tam has finally come out of toilet with black witchy make-up smudged down cheeks. Had to put cucumber on the puffy eyes and then set to work doing a repair job with my concealer.

Matt eventually apologised. Think he was a bit embarrassed that he'd upset her so much. 'Listen Tam, I'm really sorry to have made you cry. I didn't mean to be an idiot. I guess me and Oliver got off on the wrong foot. I'm probably jealous of him because you look so be-*witchingly* beautiful!' Then he gave her a big hug and I think they're friends again.

So now we're all ready; the three boys have dressed as Egyptian mummies (several loo rolls wrapped round body); Tam and I are looking wickedly witchy, and Pablo hasn't dressed up but manages to look like the devil incarnate.

(I retract that last comment. The 'I'll try and be nice' thing slipped my mind.)

Midnight Ugh! Am back already. I'm very unimpressed with SU's efforts to transform bar into Halloweeny venue. We paid £2 extra for paper spiders stuck on the walls, less lighting than normal and the DJ mixing the odd *'Thriller'*-type song into his standard, Abba, Prince, Gun's 'n' Roses medley.

Knew night would turn out horribly as within 60 seconds of walking into SU, I clocked both bunnies contorting on dance floor in skimpy devil outfits (appropriate, I thought). I haven't seen Jasmine since surf weekend and my stomach was churning madly. Have to say, though, the girl might have a good figure, but she can't dance. She was trying to be very sexy in designer red dress with flashing 'I'm-horny' horns, but she was a steady half-beat behind every song! Hah! My dancing-smugness only lasted a moment, as suddenly she was skipping prettily to the other end of the room where she saw Ben. Hmmph.

Tam and I kept the barman in wages for most of the night. We solemnly slurped our drinks while watching Matt and Justin throw beer at each other to see whose outfit would disintegrate first. Was quite cruel knowing Ben was also wrapped in thin sheets of toilet roll as mind couldn't help considering it'd just need one snip and the whole thing would unravel.

'Would you rather,' Tam asked, launching into round seventeen of our evening's hypotheticals, 'live with Pablo next year, or Jasmine?'

Hmmm. Was a tricky one. Had just seen Pablo doing cheesy snake-hip dancing which further turned me against him, but then Jasmine has the depth of a plate. Then, speak of the devil, Jasmine teetered over in red mini-dress and swishing devil tail.

'Hey, girls,' she smiled narrowly.

Hey, cowbag, I thought meanly.

'Is everything OK?' she asked me, swinging her blonde hair like the star of a Pantene ad. 'You know, like, isn't that your boyfriend over there with someone else?'

Oh no, oh no! My eyes darted round the room. Where's Ben? Who is he with? Is she prettier than me?

'There,' Jasmine pointed. I followed the direction of her talons towards a booth by the dance floor.

She meant The Spaniard.

Oh. Of course. Ben isn't my boyfriend.

Pablo was squashed into the booth snogging the face off a skeleton. I couldn't tell who it was – they were wearing a full black body sock with UV white bones painted on – and I didn't even care. The sight only confirmed my suspicion that Pablo is here for a free holiday and that Jasmine is an evil mannequin posing as a university student with a lifelong campaign of punishment planned for me.

'I can't stop and chat,' she smirked. 'I must get back to Ben. God, he's such a sweetie!' Jasmine giggled pointedly and then she and her cattle prod minced off to cause devastation elsewhere.

'Shall I kill her for you?' asked Tam, putting a comforting arm around me.

'Yes, please.'

'We can wipe our dresses on her: she'll probably melt if anything from Primark touches her.'

I tried to laugh, but all I could feel was little bubbles of anger starting to rise inside me. It was everything: Oliver treating Tam like shit, Ben ditching me for Jasmine, and now Pablo snogging Funny Bones. I'd had enough! I stormed across the dance floor with my witch's cloak flapping furiously. I reached The Spaniard and rapped him on the shoulder.

'Oh, Hosie,' he said guiltily, removing himself from the skeleton, who immediately crept off.

'*Chico Diablo!*' I yelled. (Tam had been prepping me on Spanish swear words. I was hoping to learn 'wanker' or 'bastard', but the meanest thing she could think of was 'Devil boy'. I think it still made a point.)

'I very sorry for the kiss of R . . .'

'Don't be,' I interrupted. 'You are welcome to each other! I shall leave your stuff outside my room. Ciao, Pablo.'

Bugger. I think 'ciao' is 'goodbye' in Italian.

Friday 1 November

10 am Have calmed down this morning. Pablo arrived fifteen minutes ago looking very sheepish. He apologised repeatedly for the kissing incident and I actually ended up feeling a bit sorry for him. Suppose he was just after a bit of fun and I hadn't exactly been the friendliest of holiday hosts. I made him some sandwiches and tucked a map of the city into his bag, so now I think we're even on the free cocktails.

'*Adios,* Pablo.' (Yes, better.)

So I'm now sat in my room with Mr Tubs who looks pleased to be living in a Spaniard-free zone. I really could do with hoovering my floor as keep getting Pablo's chest hair stuck to my feet. Eugh. Don't think I've got the energy to do it right now. Just feel so exhausted and miserable after the craziness of the last couple of weeks. Jasmine hasn't helped feelings of doom by hinting that she and Ben are an item. Is all so miserable and . . . ooo, phone.

10.10 am Yey, it was Mum! It's like she has an unhappiness radar tuned in to me. Tried to sound perky but was obviously a waste of time as she's been trained in the art of deception and immediately knew I was faking. She's prescribed a weekend of TLC at home. I made a weak protest out of self-respect rather than any real desire to stay in halls. Luckily, Mum insisted, so I will soon be whisked away to a happier, cleaner place.

Before putting down the phone, Mum whispered, 'Josie, did you realise that life drawing means sketching nude people?'

Sunday 3 November

8 pm. On train back to uni. Ah! Was so lovely being home. The house was immaculate. The fridge was bursting with food. There were fresh flowers. The lights didn't flicker or buzz. I could walk barefoot and there were eighteen toilet rolls to choose from. Heavenly!

Was also lovely to be spoilt by Mum. Have realised that since going away, my whole role as daughter has changed. Now my only duty is to eat. For breakfast, I was given two slices of toast, three rashers of bacon, two eggs, numerous mushrooms, a grilled tomato and a side of beans – washed down by a glass of protein juice.

Did all the things I wouldn't do at uni. Had a long soak in bath and enjoyed the absence of stray dirt and body-hair floating alongside me. Then Granny came over and talked me through her Church cell-group meeting and think I managed to sound alert and interested. Have much higher tolerance threshold when seeing relatives in small doses. I even found it comforting to go up to my room and find the customary *Daily Mail* article left on my bed. This time, it was a piece entitled: 'A New Generation of Sex-Crazed Students: The Risks.' Think it will go nicely in my collection alongside 'Smoking: The Facts' and, my personal favourite, 'Dabbling in Drugs: Dabbling with Danger'. May need to take a blood test before can prove am not a drug addict, a chain smoker or pregnant.

Was really a lovely refreshing weekend, right up until the hour where I did something awful. I'd go as far as to say I committed the student cardinal sin. Mum and I were having a coffee when it happened. Without thinking, I said (cringe), 'I need to finish packing my things ready to go home.'

Mum's eyes widened in horror.

'I didn't mean *home*! Er, I meant to say, "I should start packing for university".' But it was too late; Mum had already started crying large, round tears into her mug.

'I'm sorry, Mum, are you OK? Do you want to talk about it?'

'No, no,' she insisted. 'It's just, I've recently had a lot of time to look at my life and I've been asking myself, what have I really done with it? There's something missing, Josie. There's a gap in my life.'

'Well, I'll be back in the holidays,' I reassured her.

It turned out – rather disappointingly – that I wasn't the gap. Apparently, Mum's been feeling like this for a while. 'Since your father left,' she told me sadly, 'I feel adrift. I'm not sure I know who I am anymore.' Hearing Mum, I felt livid with Dad for what he's done. She's lost more than just him; when Dad left it's like he took her confidence and self-esteem with him.

'With you being away at university,' Mum continued, 'it's forced me to take a look at myself and to question who I really am. I've seen myself as a wife and a mother for so long, that I've lost sight of who I am. I think I need to spend a bit of time finding *me*.'

Was thrown off-balance by emotional outpouring from parental figure. I tried to quash my panic and in a mature and kindly way patted Mum on the back of her hand, hoping to stop the tears. When it didn't work, I tried patting the top of her head. Her crying ceased for a moment while she looked at me, but then the tears came again, heavier this time. I was aware that I needed to catch my train, so, in a moment of desperation, I asked, 'Why don't you visit me for a weekend and we can talk about it properly?'

Mum agreed a little too hastily and is coming to stay in three weeks' time. Feel mixture of pleasure and horror at this prospect. Pleasure that I am brimming with daughter-helping-mother goodness. And the horror is obvious. What am I going to do with a parent at university? I couldn't even cope with a Pablo.

NINE

Friday 22 November

5 pm Eugh! Have just finished cleaning our flat bathrooms. They were getting to the stage where we could have been cultivating biological weapons without realising it. Hasn't been a very relaxing end to week as I've been whooshing and flying around, disinfecting toilet seats, hoovering up dustmites and removing icky stains from kitchen floor. Mum arrives in less than twenty-four hours. It's taking a huge amount of frantic cleaning to elevate flat from slum-style living to clean and hygienic place for parent to stay.

Matt is not helping. There are two weeks' worth of his filthy, meaty pans and baking trays lining our kitchen surface. Told him earlier in an 'I'm-serious-about-this' way, that his washing-up must be done by tonight.

9 pm All pans have been removed from side and are now heaped in sink.

Barged into Matt's room, mop in hand, and found him lounging on his bed reading *Boys Toys* magazine.

'You do realise,' I huffed, 'that moving the pans from one place to another doesn't count as washing-up?'

'Chill out, Shorty. The pans are just soaking, you know, so the little bubbles can eat all the grease.'

I looked at him suspiciously.

'Josie, you seem very edgy today. Why don't you sit down? I'll give you a massage and we can talk about it.'

Is very difficult trying to think of clever and forceful retorts when plastered across Matt's wall is a poster of a woman bending over in a furry pink thong.

'Just do the washing-up,' I huffed crossly, avoiding eye contact with the walls.

'The problem I have, Jos, is that washing-up is historically women's work. Who am I to flaunt hundreds of years of great British tradition simply to soothe a female flatmate who appears to have PMT? I think we both know it would be wrong. I'd end up hating myself.'

'Aaarrgghh!' I fumed. 'You are an arrogant, self-obsessed chauvinist beyond all comprehension!'

'And I've got a great body. But enough of the small talk.'

'Do your washing-up, else I'll ram this mop up your arse,' I said, shaking it threateningly like some mad 1940s housewife in a hairnet and a pinny. 'And when you've finished, could you please fill the fridge with something other than alcohol? What will my mum think!'

'Is she fit?'

Matt always manages to confuse me by changing the subject mid-rant. 'What? No! Er . . . well, yes. She's attractive.'

I left his room hoping I'd made myself clear.

11 pm Am in shock – Matt's dishes have gone. He actually listened to me. Am experiencing a wonderful sense of calm; the bathrooms are clean, the kitchen tidy, my room immaculate and Matt – for the first time in the history of us living together – has actually done what I asked.

Saturday 23 November

12.15 pm Mum's here. She stepped out of the car in a cloud of Izzy Miyake perfume, wearing stylish olive green trousers and a matching fitted shirt. Her hair was pulled off her face in a wooden clip, exposing her elegant neck, and it was clear no outfit-vetting was needed today. She looked lovely.

Because you never see anyone over twenty-five on campus, people kept staring at us both. Think Mum quite enjoyed the attention as she kept checking, 'Have any of the other parents stayed in digs before?'

'Mum, it's "halls",' I reminded her gently. 'And no, you're the only one.'

She then looked rather pleased with herself and began dropping words like 'cool' and 'wicked' into her sentences.

As we walked into the flat, I spotted Matt strolling down the corridor in a 'M.I.L.F HUNTER' T-shirt. I swiftly steered Mum into the kitchen and left her with a cup of tea while I went to coerce Matt into changing (via nipple-twisting). I did a final scan over my bedroom to check there was no incriminating evidence to suggest I've been enjoying myself (empty wine bottles, leopard-print dress, etc.) and then went back to find Mum.

'Darling,' she smiled, putting down the navy mug, which I just realised had 'SPANK ME' written on the near side, 'I've had a lovely chat with your flatmates.'

Who? Who? I panicked, thinking she might have seen Ben and made him stand in the naughty corner on one leg.

'Suniti, the lovely foreign girl.'

'She's from Pakistan, Mum.'

'Yes, that's right. Quite shy, but then I expect you're all still finding your feet. And very intelligent. Did you know she has thirty hours of medical exams at the end of the year? Imagine that. And Justin is brilliant, too! What a wonderful sense of humour. He really had me in stitches with his Spider-Man joke.'

'He wasn't joking, Mum. Justin loves Spider-Man.'

Mum wasn't prepared to concede this so she focused on our noticeboard, which displays Matt's tally sheet of who's missed the most lectures this semester. Luckily, Mum misread it. 'So this shows your attendance rate and then the winner gets a prize? That's fantastic! Oh, gosh, Suniti might want to put in a little more effort next term for her exams. There are a lot of ticks by your name, Josie. Well done!'

Um, yes . . .

'Oh, and I met Ben, too. Lovely boy.'

What? When? How does she know everyone already? I only left her alone for ten minutes.

'I can see exactly why you like him. What beautiful eyes. You shouldn't give up on him, Josie. I don't think it's anything serious with this other girl.'

I hate it when Mum does this. In a time of desperation (i.e. after the surf trip) I give her the tiniest, briefest of insights into my world and then she feels like she can bring up the topic whenever she pleases as if she's my new confidante. Mum is not even up-to-date. It's a month since then and I'm doing very well without Ben. (And, actually, he seems to be doing very well without Jasmine. I haven't seen them together and Tam said she overheard a conversation on the stairs about Jasmine sleeping with her Business Studies lecturer. Yes! Yes!) The tension over Pablo has died down too and I think – touch wood – Ben and I are friends again. The last thing I need is for Mum to stick her oar in and ruin things.

'You didn't say anything to him, did you?' I hissed at her.

Mum looked as though nothing could have been further from her mind. 'Of course I didn't,' she snapped. 'I simply mentioned what a lovely girl you are.'

Oh, no.

3 pm Mum and I have been for lunch at a nice restaurant in town that I always walk past but can never afford (note: one advantage of occasional parental visits). We were happily chatting away when Mum casually mentioned, 'Your dad called last week.'

This was a surprise. Dad hasn't called Mum in months. When he first left for Lanzarote, he used to ring her every week. I would sometimes watch Mum on the phone to him; her face seemed to glaze over with a detached expression – distancing herself from the memories. She'd remain polite and pleasant, but refuse to give anything of herself. Dad would sometimes try and bait her into fighting with him; I think he felt so guilty that he almost needed Mum to punish him for it. Eventually, Dad stopped calling. It was obvious that he regretted leaving and I guess he found it too hard speaking to Mum.

'What did Dad want?' I asked.

'To know if I'd give him a second chance.'

I dropped my fork into the Caesar salad and stared at her incredulously.

It'd taken me a year to get used to the idea that Dad doesn't live with us, and now he wants to come back? 'What did you tell him?'

Mum placed a black olive in her mouth and chewed it slowly.

Did Mum want him back? I know she must be lonely by herself at home, but could she forgive him? I thought back to last summer when he broke the news of his affair; Mum sat calmly on the sofa, hands folded in her lap. She listened silently as he explained about his affair, and then she said: 'I'm very sorry to hear you're leaving us. As you've made your decision I'd appreciate it if you'd pack your things and go immediately.'

Mum – who will weep during Animal Hospital – never once cried publicly about the affair, but I haven't forgotten the weeks afterwards when I'd wake up in the middle of the night to hear gentle sobs muffled in her room.

Mum carefully removed an olive stone from her mouth. 'I said "No",' she told me eventually.

For some reason, I felt a stab of disappointment. I wasn't expecting that. Maybe there's also a part of me that's always hoped for a fairytale ending. I'm not quite sure how it would resolve. Dad would have to say something along the lines of, 'I tripped and ended up in Janine's bed and then I was so concussed for the next year I didn't realise she'd kidnapped me and forced me to live in Lanzarote.'

Mum put her hand over mine. 'Josie, I still care about your father, but I think I'm finally happier now on my own.'

'But what about the gap?' I asked quietly.

'Your dad didn't leave the gap; I think it's always been there. With Dad leaving – and you being away too, I've just had more time to notice it. Like I said, I need to spend some time on "me" – and that's what I told your dad.'

8 pm Oh, God! Parent/child roles are getting very blurred. Am in bedroom getting ready for a night at the SU with Mum!! Hellish thoughts of Mum shaking her booty on dance floor are flooding brain.

Will kill Matt.

He instigated the night out through his highly inappropriate flirting with my mum.

'Josie,' he smiled, sauntering into the kitchen, interrupting our Chinese takeaway. 'You told me your mum was visiting, not your sister.'

Mum started crowing with delight. 'Oh, stop it!' she cried, touching the back of her hair to check it was in place.

'Cathy, it is my pleasure to make your acquaintance,' he said, reaching out his hand. 'I am Matthew Roswell.' Am really not sure where Matt's formal voice springs from, though is quite a welcome change from him running down the corridor shouting, 'Who's the Daddy?'

'So, Matthew, why are you dressed from head to toe in green?' Mum asked.

He explained about the traffic light party at the Students' Union. 'The idea is that you wear red, amber or green to mark the colours of traffic lights. Red means "stop" – not interested; amber stands for "get ready" – possible interest; and green is "go" – on the pull. Of course,' said Matt, 'I would have worn red, except all my clothes are in the wash and this was the only thing left.'

'I see,' nodded Mum. 'And how do you explain the green face paint?'

'Paint? Oh no, I'm just feeling a little off-colour. Too much studying, I think.'

Matt's attention shifted to Tam who walked into the kitchen wearing a deep red dress that fell just below the knee. She gave Mum a big hug, and Matt watched eagerly as the dress tightened round her bum as she leant forward. 'Tamara, seeing you in that dress makes me wish you were wearing green,' he cooed suggestively with his eyes sliding down her body.

'And, Matthew, seeing you in that outfit makes me wish you were wearing red,' Tam retorted neatly.

Did feel a little envious when Ben and Justin also came in dressed for the party (am hoping Ben's T-shirt will look on the blue side of green in the SU lighting).

'Why don't you go out too, Josie? I'll be fine by myself,' Mum purred sadly, working my flatmates from the sympathy angle.

Of course, they fell for it and immediately began cajoling Mum into coming too.

She took fourteen seconds to convince.

It feels very wrong for a parent to stay at university, and even more wrong for Mum to go to traffic light party wearing olive green two-piece!

2 am I take it all back – has been brilliant night and Mum was fantastic! She drank shots, danced to the Beastie Boys and resisted filing a sexual harassment complaint when she had her bum pinched. Flatmates were lovely with Mum, particularly Ben (why does he tick all the boxes, except for the 'I want a relationship with Josie' one). He looked after her when Glitter Boy from my Shakespeare module dragged me on to the dance floor to get funky to '*Superstition*'.

We got back from the SU about 20 minutes ago, and now Mum is downstairs having a nightcap with Gil and Hobbit! Tam and I were with them, too, but there's just been an Oliver crisis. A few minutes ago Tam's phone beeped and, as she read the message, her face drained of colour. She stood up sharply and had to hang on to the kitchen sink to steady herself. Then she stumbled up to her room.

I followed her upstairs and she handed me her phone.

'*Babe, I can't do this anymore. Think it's better 4both of us if we end r/ship. I know it's right decision + u'll get over me in time, I promise. Oliver.*'

'Fuck you, you fucking fuck!' Tam shouted at the phone. Yikes!

'Isn't he?' she bellowed, this time at me.

'Yes, he's a fucking fuck,' I repeated quietly in case we woke Suniti or the boys.

Tam, not on quite the same wavelength, grabbed the phone and threw it wildly at her wall, yelling 'Bastard!!' It was a good effort, actually, as the phone hit a photo of Spock where he looks exceptionally knobbish (sat outside a bar in sunglasses and work suit, doing an 'I'm-an-important-businessman' pose).

I went to say something soothing but Tam got there first. 'Fucking Spock doesn't even have the guts to tell me face to face. He has to do by text. That's got to take some beating.' Then Tam wobbled towards me smiling. 'I'll give him a beating, Jos.' She hunched her back comically pretending to be Mr Burns and said, 'Yeah, Spock, I'm gonna give you the beating of your life! Thwack! Thwack!'

'That's a good idea,' I said, trying to placate her. 'For now, though, why don't you hop into bed and get some sleep.' I directed her towards her bed, edging her onto the mattress. 'In the morning, you and I will have a good chat and sort things out.'

'Nooooo,' drawled Tam. 'I'm forgetting Oliver. No more wasting tears. I'm moving on and forgetting him,' she repeated as she slipped under her duvet and reached for a piece of hair to twiddle.

I was about to turn off Tam's lamp when she sat bolt upright in bed and yelled, 'Beam him up, Scotty!'

Better go back downstairs now and find Mum. If she spends too long in Beavis and Butthead's company she might realise that uni is making me regress educationally!

3.30 am Oh! My! God! Mum is stoned!!

I walked into downstairs' flat and the whole kitchen was filled with the heady smell of marijuana smoke. At first, I was horrified that Hobbit and Gil had the nerve to smoke in front of Mum and I imagined her stood staunchly in centre of kitchen, quoting statistics from 'Dabbling with Drugs: Dabbling with Danger'.

Instead – and to my absolute jaw-dropping horror – Mum was slumped in a plastic orange chair in the middle of their kitchen with a large joint between her pursed lips. She smiled at me peacefully and said, 'Josie, darling, Hobbit's showing me what it's like to have a mind-expanding experience. Wonderful, isn't it?'

What happened to: 'Just say no'?

I looked to Hobbit – to Gil – and back to Hobbit again. They were both smiling sweetly at me, as if they'd just baked Mum some delicious brownies rather than encouraged her to smoke a fat reefer at three in the morning. I rubbed my eyes vigorously, but, no, Mum was still sat there, hair falling over her face and both shoes kicked off.

'Gosh, you look shattered, darling,' Mum smiled, seeing me rooted in the doorway looking bemused. 'I think it's time I got you to bed.' It was disconcerting to hear Mum using her 'I'm-your-mother-and-I-know-what's-best' voice, and then watch as she took a final drag on her joint, stretch over to Hobbit and says, 'Here you go dear, you best take care of this.'

I moved out of the kitchen in a daze.

'Oh, Hobbit,' Mum sang as she followed behind me, 'I'll text you with those numbers.'

What numbers? She doesn't even have a mobile!

3.45 am Mum has raided our kitchen. She went through my cupboard, giggling as if tins of sweetcorn are hilarious. 'Ha-ha-ha! The Green Giant! Look at his face! Ha-ha-ha-ha! He's so big. I wonder how much sweetcorn he ate?' She is currently leaning against kitchen-sink in crumpled two-piece, no shoes and dishevelled hair, eating my alphabetti spaghetti straight from the can with added sweetcorn.

Maybe this is all a big joke – possibly was a fake joint and a hilarious TV presenter will burst out of fridge at any moment, beaming, 'You've been had! Ha ha!'

3.46 am Have checked fridge and there's no one in it. Oh.

4.20 am Mum has fallen asleep on my bed. Am living in nightmarish parallel existence where mother figures have reversed roles and are hanging out in bars, getting drunk and smoking weed, while student daughter must tend to parental munchies.

Sunday 24 November
11.45 am When I woke up, I kept my eyes squeezed tightly shut, hoping beyond hope that Mum wasn't lying on my bed, fully-dressed and with a spaghetti hoop stain on her trousers. I opened my eyes slowly, and, yes, she was on my bed and there was also a piece of sweetcorn stuck in her hair.

I skulked into the kitchen and padded around mis-erably, considering whether or not to phone Child Line. After eating a bowl of soft Sugar Puffs, I took a carton of long-life orange juice from the cupboard and sat at the table sucking on it hopelessly.

'Josie,' trilled Mum, 'where are your manners? Get a glass!'

I almost choked. Mum, now fully made-up, hair combed and sweetcorn removed, was banging around our kitchen, opening and closing cupboards and tutting that I didn't have any filter coffee.

I sat there, waiting for her to apologise for traumatising me and then give me a lecture about saying 'No!' to drugs. Instead, she carried on rummaging and finally found two Tesco value eggs. Even though I insisted quite clearly that I'd already eaten, she scrambled the eggs with some milk and butter and then plonked the result in front of me, chirping, 'Eat up!'

Can't believe Mum wasn't even remotely embarrassed about last night. In fact, she looked positively radiant. Just as I started to confront her, she scooped up her handbag, gave me a big kiss on the cheek and said, 'I've had an extraordinary weekend and I'm pleased to see that you've made such wonderful friends here. Righty-ho, I better dash as I said to Granny I'd pick Gruff up before three.'

1.30 pm It's all so wrong. My mum, stoned? What will Ben think about my upbringing.

I went downstairs to talk to Gil and Hobbit about their terrible behaviour, but they were singing Mum's praises so much I couldn't get a word in.

'Your mum is a legend, man!' raved Gil, while scratching his armpit. 'She said we could come and visit. That'd be awesome – your place sounds totally lush.'

'Yeah fully,' agreed Hobbit. 'She's a serious playa. Your mum's got the G-dog in her!'

Don't know what the G-dog is and I really hope Mum doesn't have it in her!

3.30 pm Aaagh! On top of all this trauma, have just been in kitchen to get a nice ice-cold glass of water to help soothe mind, but when I opened the cupboard below the sink, it was filled with Matt's pots and pans festering there – unwashed!

4.04 pm Stormed into his room but he was in middle of telling Tam, 'He's an idiot if he doesn't want to be tied down with you.' Had to do a double-take – Matt being sensitive?

Feel bad as, with all the Mum problems, hadn't checked to see how Tam is post-Oliver. I took her into my room for a relationship post-mortem. She seems to be doing quite well except for hangover head and broken phone. We were discussing tactics now that Tam's joined the single club, when Justin bounced in: 'Jos, I heard your mum got stoned last night. I didn't know you were into that?'

'I'm not! I didn't know my mum was either.'

I filled them both in on what had happened. They were very calming and Tam said I needn't worry. She thinks that Mum was just letting her hair down and that by the time she gets home, she'll have sprung back to her normal self.

Tam is so wise.

Monday 25 November
1 pm Have just come out of McGibbon's lecture and checked mobile. I've got a blank text message. Strange.

1.10 pm And another. How odd. I don't recognise the number.

1.20 pm Is Mum. I got three more messages of random punctuation marks and then a final one that included her initials. I called to explain texting basics (e.g. don't send it before you've written the message), then had an odd conversation in which Mum told me she'd rather work it out for herself as the journey is as exciting as the destination.

She chattered on about what a wonderful time she had at the weekend and how it's really opened her mind to new possibilities. Am starting to suspect that Mum may not have sprung 'back to normal' quite as hoped. She ended the call very suddenly, saying she was going to be late to meet someone. When I asked who, she behaved very suspiciously, using roundabout phrases and then eventually said, 'I best be off then. Bye for now!'

Please don't let it be a rendezvous with drug dealer.

Wednesday 27 November

9 pm All my fears have been realised. Granny called this evening and I knew immediately that something was wrong. Granny is from the generation who distrusts mobiles. 'How can something the size of a Jacob's Cracker let you speak to a person a hundred miles away?' After repeating my name five times, Granny was finally convinced that, yes, the phone did work and, yes, it was actually me she was speaking to.

'Josie,' she said stroppily. 'Do you know why your mother is behaving so strangely?'

I suddenly had a very bad feeling about things.

'Since she visited, your mother has been uncontactable in the evenings. She won't tell me what she's up to, but yesterday I bumped into her walking Gruff with two very unsavoury types. I hardly feel safe leaving Doogle with her.

'Would you mind telling me exactly what happened during her visit? All I got out of her was something about meeting Hovel. Whatever it was that he "introduced" her to,

144

it seems to have triggered an epiphany. She keeps saying he's helped "uncover the gap" and she's been describing her state of mind as . . .' Granny paused thoughtfully. 'Now, what did she say again? Ah, yes: chilled out.'

Thursday 28 November
5 pm Cannot get hold of Mum. Have called on the hour, every hour all day and there's no answer.

Oh, God! Maybe she's having an affair with Hobbit and they've disappeared? Although suppose it's unlikely as Hobbit is 5 feet 4 inches and hairy. Is possible they'd want a platonic relationship. They could have run off together to a doss-house in East London and be making a life together smoking roll-ups and discussing Tolkien's state of mind when . . . Stop! Am being ridiculous. Brain is out of control. Need to calm down. Will check on Hobbit just to be sure . . .

5.15 pm Hobbit is not in! By now they could be on their way to Morocco looking for the hippie trail!

Friday 29 November
1.30 pm. Cultural Criticism. Lecturer is talking about hermaphrodites, which for some reason reminded me of my dream last night about Frodo and Pippin dancing around Morocco together.

I finally managed to get hold of Mum this morning. 'I'm worried about you,' I chided. 'Granny's been telling me you've been out every night this week.'

'You know how she likes to exaggerate. She's just annoyed because Gruff outran Doogle on Monday.'

Would that really bother anyone?

'Look, Mum, I need to ask you something. It's been preying on my mind ever since you stayed here. You know what you did with Hobbit?' (I couldn't quite bring myself to say the words: Mum, you know when you smoked dope with my friends?) 'You haven't done it again, have you?'

'Of course I have! Josie, you don't need to be so cagey about the whole thing. It's a wonderful experience – mind-blowing! I'm surprised you're not into it – Gilbert and Hobbit both are.'

Oh, God! Mum is trying to encourage me to take drugs. Is terrible. She'll move on to harder stuff and before I know it, be dropping an 'e' at my graduation.

'Mum, are you smoking large quantities?'

'Smoking?'

'Please tell me you're not using a bong?'

'A bong? Goodness, no! I don't think you necessarily have to take drugs to reach a higher state of consciousness. If you are disciplined, meditation is a very rewarding experience on it's own.'

'Meditation?'

'Yes, darling. Hobbit helped me realise what the gap in my life is: spirituality! And meditation is part of my path into spiritual fulfilment.'

Hobbit? Spiritual fulfilment? 'But what about smoking that joint? So you're not turning into a dope-head?' I asked, entirely unconvinced about this spiritual journey.

'Don't be a wally! I know I had a quick puff on the old wacky backy, but that's nothing to worry about. It was just a bit of fun to remind me of my college days.'

'You smoked drugs at college?' I asked, appalled.

'Who didn't? I think it's the only thing I can remember about being a student!'

Oh, God! My Mum used to be a wild, drug-crazed youth and I'm a non-drug-taking student, who pays her accommodation fees on time and doesn't even own a vibrator!

TEN

Sunday 1 December

1 pm Mmmm . . . it's Christmas month! Yey! Mince pies, mulled wine, log fires and reindeer. Lovely, lovely. What is not quite so lovely is the thought of spending the Christmas hols with an insane spiritualist. Still, I've got a couple more weeks left at uni to build up my strength ready for that merry onslaught.

To get in the festive mood, I bought my flatmates advent calendars. (I included Suniti, as although she doesn't celebrate Christmas, I figured that a Dairy Milk calendar isn't exactly an obvious celebration of Christianity.) Think calendars are a lovely gesture as it's like giving people a tiny present every day of the month. Was nice as felt a bit like Santa handing out gifts and enjoying the 'thank you' hugs I got – particularly from Ben.

Recently, things have been a bit better between us. I'm no longer in a constant 'Why-did-Ben-kiss-me-and-then-pull-Jasmine?' state of misery, as I've been trying to concentrate on getting along as friends. Was tricky though when Ben hugged me to say thanks for the calendar. He'd just come back from a bike ride with Gil and his T-shirt, damp from the exertion, clung to his delicious body. Admit that I was very much enjoying being pressed against it, and memories of our beach kiss made my body do giddy internal cartwheels. Hmmm. Must try not to regress into Ben fantasies and stay focused on being friends. Plus, I've agreed with Tam that now she's single, we'll pool our resources to concentrate on new boys.

Am so pleased that Spock is no longer infringing on our fun as it's much nicer going on manhunts together. Did worry that pairing up might lessen our chances, but we discussed it and don't think it should cause too many setbacks since we have very different looks and boys who like blonde curvy girls don't usually go for dark petite girls etc. (Except for Matt who said he'd be happy with us both, but I think he meant at the same time.)

4 pm Ooo . . . Ben has offered to cook a big Christmas dinner as his flat meal contribution. We're going to have it on the last night before the hols and make it a proper festive evening with roast turkey, tinsel and Christmas songs! We're also doing Secret Santa present-giving (suppose it isn't entirely 'secret' as we all know who we're buying for). We picked names out of a mug and I got Justin, so need to rack my brain on comic-book accessories. Possibly Spider-Man outfit?

I'm really pleased Suniti is taking part too. I think this is the first flat thing she has done, so it'll be cool to hang out all together. Matt said he's worked out why Suniti's so shy. I was actually listening to him, mistakenly thinking he was going to say something sensible. 'She fancies me. It's so obvious. My huge, rippling muscles make her feel nervous.' Hmmm, anyway, am also very excited because Ben picked my name in Secret Santa! Wonder what he'll buy me? Would almost like it to be something handmade and thoughtful, or, better still, one of those chequebooks of sexual favours, e.g. 'This cheque entitles Josie Williams to a year's supply of massages.'

Oh, damn, damn! Am meant to be concentrating on manhunt for other boys. Is very difficult trying to be less picky and source distinctly average boys, when I already live with complete sex god!

Monday 2 December

8 pm. Bedroom. In bloated state. Ugh! Time of the month has struck! At least this explains emotional instability of yesterday's hug from Ben. How am I expected to be breezy, strong and confident when confined by the shackles of unpredictable hormones?

PMT has not been helped by receiving random texts from Mum every half hour. She manages to completely defy texting convention and create her own language: 'J, Mum hr txg u! Hv bn t Reiki 2dy +nw exprt!! Wll rng whn nx3. Lv Mx'

Tuesday 3 December

11 am. In bed. Not at Children's Literature lecture. Loss of iron in body is causing high-level demand for chocolate. Need to call out for delivery since unable to leave flat as too ugly/upset/tired/emotional to be seen in public. Even simple questions like, 'Would you like anything else with your Minstrels?' may seem leading and provoke unwanted replies of, 'Yes, I'd really love a boyfriend who enjoys holding hands in public and thinks butterfly kissing is a rewarding experience.'

11.02 am Discovered a silver lining: haven't opened my advent calendar today!

11.05 am Mmmm . . . so delicious, yet so small and moreish. Think perhaps will have tomorrow's as well, since by then cravings will have lessened and chocolate replenishment not so critical.

12.15 pm Overpowering feelings of guilt (and slight twinge of nausea). Have eaten whole of December, including a double-sized chocolate for the day of Christ's birth. To be honest, I didn't even enjoy it after the 15th but fell into the mindset, 'Well, I've started so I'll finish'. I even closed all the little calendar doors again to try and pretend this sorry business never happened. Am shocked by my own gluttony and in a double bind where I feel the need to tell someone what I've done to relieve burden of guilt, yet am too ashamed to do so.

3 pm To quash guilt-pangs have thrown self headlong into reading Kant's ideas on 'sublime' for Cultural Criticism lecture on Friday. Was hoping it would be intellectual equivalent to eating an apple after grotesque over-gorging, as if apple/Kant can cleanse sin in a replacement therapy-type way. However, have discovered that Kant and I are on very different wavelengths and am struggling to understand what he's harping on about.

Wednesday 4 December
10 am. Hiding in room. Big spot has arisen overnight on chin! Possible correlation between this and chocolate break-in? Worse still, no chocolate in advent calendar to take away misery. Getting out of bed with a chocolate incentive is so much easier. Why don't they make calendars for every month of the year? That is a brilliant business plan! I could make samples and sell idea to important investor and become millionaire student! Oh – but then if had a year's supply of chocolate in room and suddenly got cravings, is possible that I'd eat my way through at least a couple of seasons in one sitting.

11.45 am Hobbit keeps popping up to room to ask me to decode various messages from Mum. Is very annoying, particularly at the moment as I have to do an awkward hand-over-chin gesture to hide ugly spot. Latest text after translation read, 'Hobbit – have had Chakras rebalanced. Feel fantastic. Thanks for tip. Next time you meditate, think of the white ball – will blow your mind. Peace.'

Hmmm . . .

Thursday 5 December
9 am Just felt for chin and spot is still at large. Can't look in mirror as am afraid of image that will be reflected.

9.09 am Looked in mirror and spot is so big it obscures face. This isn't a job for cream; it isn't even a task for cover-up. The only option is surgery.

9.15 am Ow, ow, ow. Oh no, oh no. Bleeding spot. Very red chin with white fingernail marks. Feel even more guilty as know it'll grow to twice the size. Thought spots were for fourteen-year-olds with braces? Maybe I'm a late developer and have only just hit puberty? Ooo . . . that would explain a lot.

Friday 6 December
9.30 am. In room with mountain as chin. Spot is out of control! Can only leave flat with big plaster on chin in manner of Whackaday contestant. Cannot even go into kitchen for fear of bumping into Ben who would probably vomit on the spot (ha-ha) if he saw my chin. Is typical as I've got my Cultural Criticism lecture later and is first time I've actually prepared work in advance.

9.35 am Maybe I'm being paranoid and spot is probably not that visible. With a splash of cover-up, I'll be fine.

11.30 am Have devoted best part of morning to not noticing spot. Came out of room and Matt was walking past on his way to lectures, 'Hey, Josie, nice blimp!'

Saturday 7 December
9.20 am Spot is finally clearing. Thank goodness. Think I'll brave the outside world again and go Christmas shopping. Only one week till Secret Santa!

9.32 am Have checked bank balance to assess Christmas present fund and it's not looking good. Wonder if I could reintroduce the idea of making gifts this year? Used to be so good at pasta-art that it seems shame to lay talent to rest. Is a double shame really as all the things I excelled at during school – playdough figurines, hopscotch, join the dots – don't have much use in day-to-day life.

9.40 am Rang Mum to suggest pasta-art idea. She said: 'Josie, it is the thought that counts,' which was very noble, until she added, 'But I have seen a beautiful set of essential oils in John Lewis.' Hmmm.

5 pm Have bought Secret Santa pressie! Am very pleased with self. Managed to find a comic-book shop tucked away in underground venue at the back of town. Imagined I'd be served by geeky teenage boy in black-framed glasses, but was actually a woman behind counter. She was engrossed in a conversation about telekinetic superpowers, which sounded quite cool and then I found self staring at an

Incredible Hulk comic to see if I could make it fly (I didn't, but if you look at the Hulk for too long, he looks very similar to Antonio Banderas). Anyway, the shop lady eventually came over, so I explained about Justin's Spider-Man obsession. She suggested buying a 5-foot poster of Spider-Man jumping down from the New York skyline. Justin's going to love it!

Did get a bit carried away with shopping high and bought a couple of tiny Christmas presents for self, too. Loan has since vanished, savings non-existent and overdraft is overdrawn. Even my credit card is in debt. Only foreseeable solution is to open another bank account, get £50 student incentive and use that overdraft to pay off credit card. Good thing is that, in the face of adversity, my genius always shines through.

Friday 13 December
5.30 pm. In room. I found out during today's lectures that for each module we've been assigned a 2,000 word essay for each of our English modules and they have to be handed in on 23rd January. Have always been told that uni is much easier than 'A' levels, but somehow am not convinced that knocking together a total of 12,000 words in five weeks will be easy. Am annoyed about the workload as everybody knows that the holidays are designed for workers and students to relax, get merry and pretend they don't have jobs/studies to go back to in the New Year. Is serious infringement on Christmas celebratory rights!

Will stop the moaning now as at least we've finished all our lectures, which means it's Secret Santa tomorrow. Wahoo!!

Saturday 14 December

2 pm I've been in the kitchen with Ben as he's preparing our Christmas dinner. Asked if I could be of any help, but he said, 'After your sprout stir fry, I think it's best if I fly solo on this one.' Hmmm, did not exactly wow him with culinary capabilities, then. Ben assigned me to decorations, so I've spent the last half hour draping tinsel all over the kitchen. Have to admit, hormones are leaping like lords as kept finding everything Ben did intensely sexy.

I was balancing on a chair, trying to tie some silver tinsel onto the window handle when Ben asked, 'Will you see your Dad over Christmas?'

It was a surprise to hear him bring up the topic as we haven't had any close chats since the beach kiss. Being alone together in the kitchen stirred up memories from that night and my mind was blurred with that beautiful kiss. I still can't make sense of what happened between us; how Ben – seemingly perfect in every way – behaved like that. My eyes started stinging, so I quickly looked up focusing on the tinsel again to stop them from welling.

'Dad's going to be in England for a few days,' I managed eventually. 'I think I'm meeting up with him the day before Christmas Eve.'

'How do you feel about it?' Ben asked warmly.

It was a good question. I don't really know how I feel about my dad. I love him, I know that, but most of the time I'm not sure that I like him. As I finished hanging the tinsel, I found myself telling Ben stuff that I don't usually share with anyone; how I'm disappointed and angry with Dad; how I want him to be happy but that I'm not sure I want him back in my life; how I worry about Mum growing older without somebody.

Ben was really sweet and just listened as I talked. When I'd finished he told my gently, 'It's really natural to have a mix of feelings. I think you're handling things brilliantly.'

'Thanks,' I smiled. 'I imagine it'll be hard for your family too over Christmas – without your Mum,' I ventured carefully, not sure if Ben would talk about her.

'It gets a bit easier every year,' he said openly. 'Mum died on 18th December, so the first couple of Christmases were pretty difficult. We're getting ourselves together more now – although Christmas lunch definitely isn't as good without Mum there,' Ben joked.

My chest started to ache. I just wanted to hold Ben – and be held by him. He's the person I feel most comfortable talking to, yet I can't tell him the one thing that's really on my mind: how I feel about him.

Matt bounded into the kitchen. 'Josie, why does our flat look like Santa's Grotto?'

3 pm I can't stop thinking about Ben. I can't even pack ready for the hols as my mind keeps strolling off into Ben-thoughts. Have filled Tam in with developments. She listened patiently as I performed the usual verbal Ben-dance: I start with how amazing he is and how much I want to be with him. Then I remember why I'm not allowed to be with him, so I go through the process of reliving the beach kiss betrayal, right up to the point where I felt crushed when I saw him kiss Jasmine. Usually Tam just listens and then at the end confirms that, 'Yes, Ben is no good for you.'

But tonight she interrupted.

'Well, I'm not sure you could call it a betrayal, Jos,' she said as diplomatically as possible. 'Because in fairness to Ben, it wasn't like you were an item.'

That's true. 'We weren't together – but he had still hurt me.' I stared round Tam's room, noticing empty spaces where the photos of Oliver used to be. 'Do you think I'd be able to trust him?'

'I've got to be honest', Tam said, 'there aren't many good ones out there – but I think Ben is one of them.'

And bang! There I was – right back where I started: single and falling head over heels for Ben.

'So what,' I said, confused. 'Do you think I should try again with Ben?' This conversation was unsettling me. Tam is the person who's meant to steer me clear of Ben.

'I think maybe you should.'

'Seriously? Oh God, though, what do I do then?'

'We need a plan.'

'I know. And quick. We're going home for the holidays tomorrow and . . . oh no . . . he'll probably meet up with his home friends and then fall in love with some laidback surfer girl who doesn't have to sew pads into her bikinis and—'

'Sssh! I'm working on my plan.'

'What is it?' I asked hopefully.

'I'm not there yet.'

'How about something festive?'

'Oh, yes! Something needs to happen tonight at Secret Santa.'

'Mmmm . . . that would be nice.'

'Ooooh!! Got it,' squealed Tam. 'Spin the mulled-wine bottle!'

'Nah. I'd probably end up kissing Matt and Justin, which would cancel out the pleasure of kissing Ben.'

'True.'

Then brilliant inspiration came to us in the form of Cliff Richard's 1988 classic hit, 'Mistletoe and Wine'. We worked

157

out that a combination of both mistletoe and wine could create perfect Ben-me-kiss situation! The idea does involve a small amount of manipulation, which really is fine since all good relationships are based on game-playing, apparently. It does not mean I'm desperate and willing to go to any lengths to ensnare a boy who prefers kissing bunnies. Nope, that is not what it means at all.

I'm going to hang a bunch of mistletoe above the fridge. As the evening progresses and everyone's relaxed after meal and present-giving, I'll casually ask Ben to fetch me something from the fridge – except that the item I've requested is not actually there. Hah! Very sneaky! Ben will probably say something like, 'I can't find it,' which is my cue to walk over in a sexy, enticing way and help him search.

Seeing Ben and me positioned beneath the mistletoe, Tam will say – in a very natural and non-practised voice – 'Oh, you guys are under the mistletoe. Pucker up!'

And there it is! Ben and I kiss and he'll be reminded of what a wonderful kisser/person/ lover I am. Is perfect.

Right, must go and buy mistletoe!

6 pm Think everything is set. Luckily campus shop still had some mistletoe left (plastic, obviously), which is now stuck to our kitchen ceiling (I got Tam to do it as she's three foot taller than me, plus if Ben caught me sticking up mistletoe, plan would be exposed as a plan).

Am very excited, only an hour to meal and presents and Ben. Mmmm . . .

Sunday 15 December
10.30 am I got a kiss . . .

The evening started in a very civilised way with friendly banter and chilled white wine. Ben cooked a delicious roast and a veggie version for Suniti, which has only heightened my love and respect for him. Justin was put out that he's not the only master-chef, but then I told him about my shepherd's pie attempt last week (burning the mince, making the potato too soggy, etc.) and he perked up again.

Matt ensured the evening was lively by attaching mistletoe to his head in a hat-cum-pucker-up contraption. Was quite scary to be swaying along gently to 'Winter Wonderland' and then find Matt lurking behind shoulder, saying: 'Oh, look! We're under the mistletoe. What are the chances of that?' Hmmm. (Am bit annoyed I didn't think of idea. If only Cliff had called his song 'Mistletoe and Hats', I'd have been in with a better chance.)

It was nice hanging out together. Although Suniti didn't say much, I think she enjoyed being part of things. It's a shame she doesn't like to get involved normally, as it was fun all being together. Do think it must be hard for her fitting in over here, particularly when numpties like Justin ask, 'So what are you getting for Christmas, Suniti?'

'Justin, you knob-jockey,' said Matt, 'Christmas is a Christian celebration – so I doubt Suniti's written a long list for Santa Clause.'

Suniti looked embarrassed. 'We do not celebrate it,' she said, fiddling with her headscarf. 'Although the presents would be nice.'

I think that's the first time I'd heard Suniti attempt a joke. It felt nice. Not wanting to lose the momentum of Suniti being involved in conversation, I said, 'I bet you're looking forward to seeing your family.'

Suniti smiled – a proper big smile that I've never seen before. 'Yes, I am very much looking forward to seeing everyone.'

'Is Aja going back with you?'

But just as quickly as it arrived, the smile seemed to vanish again. 'No,' Suniti said, 'he does not come back to Karachi very often.'

'How come he moved to the UK?' Matt asked, not noticing her change in tone. 'Did he study here?'

'No.' Suniti picked up her plate and hurried over to the sink. 'I'm finished. Thank you for the meal, but I think I better pack for my flight tomorrow.'

She made her way towards the door; 'But we haven't done presents yet,' I pleaded. 'Shall we just do those quickly before you go?'

Reluctantly, Suniti sat back down. She looked uncomfortable with us again and quickly unwrapped the gift she was passed. It was a pair of woollen gloves which we knew were from Matt as he'd wrapped them in kitchen roll, secured by rubber bands. Suniti said, 'Thank you' and then quietly passed Ben his Secret Santa present. I'd tipped her off about a Jack Johnson album, and when Ben unwrapped it, he beamed and leant down and kissed Suniti on the cheek.

'That's wicked – exactly what I wanted! Thanks, Suniti.'

Was half tempted to shoot my hand into the air and yell, 'It was me! Mememememe!' but thought I might be accused of glory-hunting and, anyway, was happy for Suniti as she smiled again.

'If you do not mind,' Suniti said, standing up once more, 'I must continue with my packing. Thank you very much for supper.'

After Suniti left, I was the next person to be given their present. I tried not to explode with excitement when Ben handed me two parcels. He got 6/10 for presentation as he'd managed to use wrapping paper, but I'd seen it in discount store when buying calendars. Even so, I neatly picked at the Sellotape, wanting to save the wrapping for my 'memory box' (geek). The first present was the *Lonely Planet Guide to South America*. Was very sweet and thoughtful since I might have given the impression that I'm strongly considering planning a trip there myself.

Then Ben handed me the second present. Everyone was watching as I unwrapped a mysterious ball of sweet-smelling waxy stuff.

My heart hopped a beat: across the surface it read: 'Sex Wax'.

Ben had bought me a sex product! Wow! I wasn't exactly sure what sex wax was, so I gave Tam a look that said, 'Should I be excited by this?'

She raised her eyebrows to say, 'Oh my God, he's bought you something from a sex shop. Hot!'

My heart was beating rapidly. It wasn't Ben's style to be so upfront about things, but if he was going to be, then I would be too! Sod the mistletoe plan. I looked at him seductively through narrowed eyes.

Ben stared back at me. 'Don't you know how to use it, Jos?'

Erm, well actually, I didn't. I'd never even heard of it before. I didn't want to look sexually incompetent so I scanned the label hastily to see if there were any instructions. 'Mr. Zog's original. The best for your stick.' So it's something for his pleasure then? Oo er!

'I haven't used this particular brand,' I said cleverly, coupled with a sexy pout.

'I can show you some time, if you like?'

Gulp. How forward! 'Well, maybe we can use it together,' I winked suggestively, shocked that we were having this outrageously flirtatious conversation in front of our flatmates.

'It's really cool stuff,' Ben said enthusiastically. 'It helps you get a firm grip and it builds friction for a longer ride.'

I was almost fainting with excitement. Did he really just say that to me? I glanced at my bottle of wine to check I hadn't finished it without realising. It was half full and I was awake, sober and talking about using Sex Wax on Ben! Yes! Yes! Yes!

'When you go for your next surf,' Ben continued, 'give me a shout and I'll wax up your board for you.'

Er . . . next surf? . . . What's that got to do with . . . wax up your board? . . . Oh, crap! He's given me sodding surf wax!

Face immediately flushed deep red with the embarrassment of what slurry pit mind had been thinking. Tam started sniggering and had to fetch a drink to stop her snorts.

Luckily, Matt provided a distraction when he opened his present from Tam: a year's subscription to *Playboy*. He performed a sort of whooping dance around the kitchen and grabbed Tam's face in both hands and planted a big kiss on her forehead. Am not sure if subscription will be a healthy platform to release his lust or whether it may encourage his deviancies further?

Justin screamed so girlishly when he unwrapped my Spider-Man poster, that Matt held him in a headlock for thirty seconds. Then he bounced around ecstatically, but no one could understand what he was saying as he slipped into supersonic Welsh mode.

Justin gave the final Secret Santa present to Tam. He'd bought her a beautiful set of chiffon and lace underwear – in her exact size. We were all staggered by his retail capabilities and I'm sure Matt would have put him in a headlock again if he hadn't been so busy running round with Tam's new knickers on his head.

Just before midnight, Ben got up to put a glass in the sink. Although I was still stinging from the Sex Wax humiliation, I realised that if I wanted the plan to work, this might be my only chance. I took a deep breath and said: 'Ben, while you're over there, could you grab my wine from the fridge?'

'Sure,' Ben replied. He rummaged through the shelves for a moment and then called out, 'I can't see it.'

'Here, I'll have a look.' I gave Tam a gentle kick in the shins as a reminder and then walked over gracefully and leant into the fridge all sexily and pert.

Tam cleared her throat: 'Hey, look, you two are stood right under—'

'Hey, Jos babe, can you whack these bad boys in there?' Gil burst through our kitchen door with Hobbit in tow. Ben was forced to take a step backwards to let them through and, as he did so, Gil placed a heavy crate of Bud in my arms.

'—neath the mistletoe,' finished Tam.

'So we are,' beamed Gil, who bent down and kissed me full on the mouth – with tongue!! Aaagh! I couldn't even push him off as had an armful of beer. 'Merry Christmas, you sexy lady.' He grinned at me.

'Get me some of dat!' Hobbit clapped.

Couldn't believe it! My plan was foiled and sweet lover replaced by a dreadlocked goof with beer breath. Twice he has thwarted my chances of a happy and fulfilling life with Ben.

Tried to gauge Ben's reaction (hoping possibly for a flicker of jealousy), but he'd sat down at the table with his back to me. Ugh, disappointing. Was so close to kissing Ben that stomach had actually started to flutter. Then when Gil's chapped lips pushed against mine, stomach flutters were all confused and started grinding at stomach lining. Is horrible and a misuse of mistletoe.

If I try to focus on the positives, all I can think is that Gil looked very happy about it.

What with it being Christmas and the season of goodwill, I almost felt a twinge of forgiveness when Hobbit handed me a large present.

'No! No,' he interrupted as I began tearing at the paper. 'It's for your mum.'

Hmmph! Can't believe Mum gets Christmas presents from my neighbours when I don't.

Actually, best remember to check in case it's a bong.

ELEVEN

Friday 20 December

7 pm. At home. I've been here for five days and I'm already pining to be back with flatmates. While it's very nice to be in a clean and comfortable house again, living with a mildly insane mother slightly overshadows the brief joy a power-shower can bring.

Since Mum's 'mid-life discovery' (her term, I use 'crisis'), things at home have become very strange. The festive preparations aren't like last year's: carols by The Choir of Children with High Voices have been exchanged for whale song and our Christmas tree is now a bonsai version because Mum thinks 'the mindless growing of fir trees for decorative purposes is damaging to the planet'. She plans to nurture the bonsai as 'a symbol of life and tenacity'.

At least it's nice to see Gruff again. Poor dog is really bearing the brunt of Mum's pathway into spiritualism. Apparently he's been looking a bit miserable for the last fortnight, and Mum – rather than attributing it to the forest fire of lavender incense sticks she's been burning – took him to a psychic healer. Apparently, Gruff used to be a horse in his former life and is missing the wilds of the forest, hmmm. Since the diagnosis, Mum's been getting up at six every morning to drive him out to the forest where she lets him run around with the ponies. Am just relieved he's too small for Mum to get a saddle on him.

Saturday 21 December

4 pm Have had some very bad news. Feel like whole world has shifted and no longer know my place in it.

I'm not getting a stocking this year.

Just cannot believe it. Stockings are a part of the Christmas heritage of our family. Over the years, satsuma's have been replaced with CDs, silly putty with hair products and sugared mice with jewellery. Dad was always the stocking filler, but last year Mum took over the role to compensate for the empty seat at Christmas lunch.

Think the whole, 'we'll-try-and-make-this-as-easy-on-Josie-as-possible' thing has worn off. This morning Mum barged into my room looking harassed and started telling me off. 'Josie, I'm not doing you a stocking this year. I don't have the time. If you really want one, then speak to your father.' And then she stomped downstairs to meditate.

Just because I'm eighteen, I've moved out of home and am officially an adult, does not mean that my red reindeer stocking shouldn't be filled with small but expensive presents. For goodness sake, where do you think Mr Tubs came from? We're both devastated.

I had a cry and eventually managed to control emotions by thinking of the less fortunate people who won't be receiving any presents. Like Mum if my overdraft doesn't clear.

Actually, think I best write my Christmas list now in case she tries to spring any more present surprises on me.

Dear Santa,
There are three things I'd really like this Christmas. Please could you,
1) Pay off my student loan
2) Pay off my overdraft
3) Pay off my credit card.

Thank you very much. Love,
Josie Williams

Think that list is good as am not getting bogged down by material goods; am simply hoping Santa might help me start the New Year in a debt-free way.

Sunday 22 December

5 pm Dad's back in the country for a few days so we arranged to meet for lunch to catch up. He chose the Fox and Hounds, which is a dingy pub that seemed to suit his mood. It's been almost six months since we've seen each other and Dad was very pensive and kept asking me lots of questions; 'So, you like the social side of uni? What else do you enjoy? Would you say you're an outgoing person?' I felt really awkward. It was as if Dad didn't know me and was desperately trying to fill in all the blanks.

Once he'd run out of questions about my hobbies, diet and social habits, he asked, 'How is your mother?'

I decided not to mention the spirituality quest or the drug episode as always like to make out that Mum is doing fine without him and very much in control of her life. 'She's great, thanks. She visited me at uni a few weeks ago, which was fun. My flatmates loved her. She's really happy at the moment.'

I immediately felt mean, as I knew Dad was hoping to hear that she missed him. I'm always torn between wanting to punish him for his ridiculous decision to leave us for dental-assistant-hussy, or being extra kind to compensate for that vague and distant look in his eyes.

Next time round, I decided on kind. 'How's Janine?'

'She's OK,' Dad told me, toying with his beer mat. 'Well, to be honest, things aren't great between us. I've messed up, Jos.' Dad seemed nervous and was fiddling frantically with the beer mat as he tried to find the words. 'I should never have left you and your mother,' he suddenly blurted. The beer mat slipped out of his fingers and fell to the floor. There was an uncomfortable moment when Dad leant down to get it, and in his fluster, banged his head on the table on his way up.

'Ow.'

'Are you alright, Dad?'

'Yes, yes. Just a little knock,' he said, pressing the top of his head. 'Anyway Josie, what I wanted to tell you is that, well, I love you. I know I've made some bad decisions in the last year or so, but you need to know that I love you more than anything in this world.'

Feel really confused. Have spent so long trying to hate Dad, that it's quite hard to hear him say things like that. He gave me a hug when he left and said he's flying back out to Lanzarote on Boxing Day. 'I probably won't be back in England now until summer, but if you ever need me – I'm only a phone call away. Take care of yourself.'

Was left with a real lump in my throat. I've got so many feelings knotted up inside me, I don't know what to think. As I sat in the pub on my own, the one thing I knew was that I wished Ben was there to talk to.

Tuesday 24 December, Christmas Eve

4 pm Is Christmas Eve. Mum is running round cleaning the house, leaving out glasses of sherry for Santa and carrots for the reindeer, and shredding M&S packaging so that she can pretend in front of Granny that she made the Christmas pudding. In between the standard Christmas hysteria, there's whale song blaring out of our kitchen and every now and then, Mum drops the Hoover and dashes off to chant in lotus position on the lounge floor. (Seeing her in any type of bendy position is not pleasant and think that kind of thing can do long-term damage to a sensitive child.)

6 pm Am going out with all my home-friends tonight for Christmas Eve drinks. I'm really looking forward to catching up, although, feels a bit weird getting ready without Tam bursting in with a clothing dilemma, or Matt running down the corridor singing 'Ride the punnai!' Miss flat life. Particularly miss seeing Ben emerge from his room in a delicious T-shirt and messy hair that he's attempted to wax. Actually, have been reading that South America book this afternoon (like to imagine we are planning trip together – very sad) and noticed inside the cover he'd written: 'To Josie, Happy Christmas, Love Ben.'

'Love Ben'. Am sure that is very friendly and, er, loving. Yes! You see, maybe there is a chance that he's still interested? Shame that Sex Wax thing didn't work out . . .

2 am Oos, milittle bitsy phisssed! Wher's stocking???????

Wednesday 25 December, Christmas Day
7.30 am Think I'm dying. Sleeeeeep.

11.30 am Bugger! Have over-slept quite drastically.

11.31 am Oh, no. It's Christmas and almost midday – and I'm still in bed. What's happened to my room? My drawers have been pulled on to the floor and there are socks and tights everywhere.

11.32 am And why is Mr Tubs squashed into a pink sock?

11.33 am Oh, that was it. In some drunken delusion, thought Mum might have secretly done a stocking and hidden it in room. Guess when I found out she hadn't, I tried to make my own. Hmmm.

11.34 am Anyway, last night was fun. It was great to catch up with home-friends. Have to say, to begin with, conversation was a little stilted as we haven't got much shared news: 'It was hilarious on Thursday, we went to this club – you haven't been there, with a couple of friends – you don't know them, and I was wearing those crazy new boots – you haven't seen them.' A couple of drinks helped us find our swing again and our friendships soon slotted back into place.

Everyone's changed loads during the past few months, particularly Sarah-Jane who has swapped her sixth-form council image for cat-eye contact lenses and green hair and was wearing a petticoat with wellies. Even Mum, who lived the student lifestyle for one night, has had radical university-enhanced transformation. Only noticeable change within self is I now appreciate the difference between two-ply loo roll and double quilted.

1.30 pm Mum is annoyed with me. On top of getting up late, when I came in last night I apparently drank Santa's glass of sherry and ate half the reindeer's carrot – and then put the leftover in the Christmas pudding. She's managing to put on a brave face and smile at me because it's Christmas day and everyone must have the best day of their lives, or else!

6 pm Granny, wearing a burgundy pleated skirt and a matching silk blouse, arrived with Doogle who was wearing a Christmas bow. The timing was perfect: Mum was right in the middle of her 'no-one-appreciates-me' ritual. She was refusing to have a rest as there was 'too much to be done', yet wouldn't allow me to help, preferring instead to drag herself around the house to make me feel bad. (Possible sign of return to former self?)

Lunch went quite smoothly considering Granny – otherwise known as the Bearer of Doom – was actually rather chirpy. Of course, she pointed out that meditation and Reiki were for Pagans, but Mum, with carving knife in hand, gave a firm speech about 'spirituality is all-encompassing, be that God or other forms.' Was very impressed and realise now where my tendency to rant comes from. (Do think holding the knife gave Mum the edge.)

Granny was keen to hear all about university. I shared the abridged version that left out Spanish visitors, slags and drags, skinny-dipping, and Matt. Thought it would be wise to keep focus firmly on lectures, so tried to educate her on why homosexuality should not be seen as a personality label, rather a sexual choice. Think my efforts were misconstrued as Granny said, 'If you think you prefer girls, Josie, you don't. It's just a phase. We've all experienced sexual feelings for our own kind, but it's about controlling them and not giving into your sexual urges.'

Am horrified that Granny, even in twenty-first century, does not believe in existence of homosexuality and am almost as horrified to hear her say the word 'sexual' twice in one sentence. Is it also possible that she is a closeted lesbian? Is too shocking for Christmas Day.

Conversation then flitted from homosexuality to Charles and Camilla, which was an interesting new direction, but just as Granny launched into a spiel about 'Cruella', I pointed out that one of the dogs had weed on the carpet. Mum denied it would be Gruff and then Granny insisted that Doogle is potty-trained. They both kept smiling tightly and using each other's name rather forcefully.

'Mother, Gruff would not wee in his own house!'

'Ordinarily, he may not, Cathy. However, with the excitement of Doogle visiting I think he may have forgotten himself.'

I wondered briefly if maybe Gruff *was* responsible and this was the wild horse coming out in him?

Granny got down on her hands and knees to sniff out the culprit (I kid you not) and Mum stood behind her huffing, with hands on hips. I decided this would be a good time to disappear, so I grabbed my bag of Christmas presents and slipped off upstairs to open them.

6.30 pm Hmmm. Mum got me a meditation tape and some healing crystals, which would have been very thoughtful if I was interested in either meditation or healing. Granny gave me a red cushion which bears the gold-embroided message: 'You have to kiss a lot of frogs before you meet your prince.' (Where's a cushion that says, 'I kissed my prince and then he turned round and snogged a bunny'?) There was a card and cheque from Dad, too. His message made me feel really sad; 'Josie, I'm sorry that I'm giving you money rather than a gift but I know I'd only choose the wrong thing. Please spend it on something special. All my love, Dad.'

I texted Dad to say 'thank you', and for the first time in 18 months, I added, 'I love you.'

Saturday 28 December

11.30 am Drone. The excess of Christmas is over and we've now hit the bleak 28th of December – the most boring day in festive period. It's no longer Christmas and it's still not New Year. All friends are locked away in tight-knit family sufferance circles, while own family activities have ceased. Have been aimlessly traipsing round house, dragging feet on carpet and watching Christmas TV (reruns of *Back to the Future*).

Mr Tubs has suggested that I take advantage of current free time and get a head start with essays. But then he is a teddy bear and they're obviously not aware of the unwritten rule that says you are not allowed to do any work between 24 December to 2 January inclusive. It's a blackout zone.

Sunday 29 December

6 pm Good thing is, Tam is equally bored with her home-festivities. We've spent most of the day on Messenger imagining we were back at uni.

TAM: Hahaha, what's your display pic of?

ME: Hideous, isn't it? That's my Gran doing a charade of *Free Willy* on Christmas Day.

TAM: Sick!! I can't wait to get back to uni. Is it normal for parents to go to bed at 9.30?

ME: Sounds about as normal as seeing my mum chanting in the lotus position.

TAM: Yeah, you win. Pulled quite a fitty last night . . .

ME: DETAILS???

TAM: Tall, nicely built, cute dark eyes (little close together), training as fireman :›)

ME: Oo er!! Hold on – is this a one-off or are you now waiting for the phone to ring?

TAM: One-off, definitely.

ME: Good! Am quite enjoying having someone to share the single life with. How come though?

TAM: He had small hands.

ME: Eugh, turn off at the next left . . .

TAM: Exactly. And they were limp!

ME: :‹(

TAM: Shit – look who's just signed on . . .

ME: Ben – oh God! Oh God! Do I look OK? Should I change???

TAM: Ha ha!

ME: Mmmm . . . have you seen his display picture? Must be from when he was travelling. Oh, bugger – I've got that photo of my Gran on still!!!

TAM: Hahahaha!!

ME: Shall I change it or will it look sad and obvious?

TAM: Sad and obvious.

ME: OK, just reassure me here, there's no way that Ben can read our messengering?

TAM: Course not. PARANOID.

ME: I know, I know. Tam – shall I messenger him???????

TAM: Yeah, do it.

ME: What shall I say? Oh, God, mind's gone blank.

TAM: 'Happy Christmas' should do it.

ME: Good thinking. Right. OK. I'm going to . . . Or should I wait for him to messenger me?

TAM: Do it! Do it! Do it!

ME: Yep, I can do this. Will report back . . .

* * *

ME: Hi Ben, Happy Christmas!!

[Ridiculously long pause before I saw 'writing message' flash up]

BEN: Thanks! You too. Have you had a good one?

ME: Well, my display pic shows my Gran doing a charade of *Free Willy*. I think that neatly captures the standard of entertainment this year.

BEN: Ha ha! You're funny!

[Yes!]

ME: So what have you been up to?

BEN: Not much – hanging out with the family, catching up with mates back here, etc. I went for a surf this morning.

ME: Cool, were the waves clean?

[Why, why did I say that? Is clear I am not a surf chick, so why do I keep pretending otherwise?]

BEN: Yeah, the surf was good thanks. What are you up to for New Year?

[Crap, I don't know – I haven't got anything good to say. Think of something exciting and cool . . .]

ME: A friend of mine's having a big house party – it's a parent-free zone so should be a lot of fun.

[Parent-free zone? I sound fourteen!]

BEN: Sounds good. I've gotta sign off now, my sister needs the net . . .

ME: OK, bye.

[Bye. I love you.]

I messengered Tam back and filled her in on my parent-free clanger. Still, I'm focusing on the positives: he did say I was funny.

Oh, though, wonder if that was 'funny ha-ha' or 'funny weird'?

Tuesday 31 December, New Year's Eve

4.40 pm Still don't have any plans for New Year's Eve (other than imaginary party in a 'parent-free zone'). As usual I've been waiting around, not committing to invites in case I hear of that magical party which all my friends are going to, where Kylie will be making a guest appearance and there is free entry, a free bar and all the boys wear boardshorts. Then at last moment, only hours before Big Ben starts chiming, I realise magical party is elusive dream that is never going to happen, so desperately ring back friends to accept original invites – which, of course, are now booked up. Seems there is no room anywhere in the UK for me to celebrate New Year.

Except, that is, the village hall where Mum and Granny are going. Have resignedly accepted their invitation to spend the night with a pitiful bunch of over fifties, dancing to Dennis's Discotheque, drinking warm shandy and eating pickled herrings entrees.

Wednesday 1 January, New Year's Day

10 am Am going to make one very important New Year's Resolution, which is critical to my future well-being, my happiness as a student and my ability to form functional relationships with members of the opposite sex:

DO NOT USE MOBILE WHEN DRUNK

10.05 am Last night I sent this message: 'Happy New Year, Ben! I've been wanting to tell you this for a while, so here goes: I think I'm in love with you. Jos xxx'

Dreadful, dreadful, dreadful!

Worse still, he hasn't replied.

After three long months of faking breeziness, I manage to ruin it by one stupid, drunken, foolhardy text message. I blame the tedium of New Year's Eve party.

Village hall was overflowing with old people that I didn't recognise but who kept insisting I looked like Mum (it was as if they wanted to destroy me from the start). With the exception of a fifteen-year-old waiter, I was the youngest person by a quarter of a century. Was almost like being a fresher again as kept having the same repetitive conversations:

'I can't believe you're a student! It only feels like yesterday that you were this high.'

Yes, that is the downside of senility.

'You're studying English, eh? Well, have you read . . .'

Let me stop you right there. I've read nothing by James Clavell or Alice Sebold. Except for books I'm forced to read due to a set syllabus, my 'reading for pleasure' list includes: *Fantastic Mr Fox*, *The Twits*, three Point Horrors and most proudly, a yearly subscription to *Cosmopolitan*.

Managed to keep thoughts inside, as realise this is not the friendliest way to see in the New Year and am also worried that my dark side is getting too much exposure.

It's bad enough spending New Year with your parents, but is much worse being a single girl, spending it with her single mum and her single granny. Am sure people were looking at us pityingly: 'Three generations – and none of them can find a man.'

Granny was doing her bloody best too, though. Wearing an ankle-length paisley blue dress, she was cavorting on the dance floor with our local newsagent who is twenty years her junior. And gay (Granny didn't twig). Surely old people should be asexual?

Only small joy of whole evening was the free bar. Kept imagining Matt's face hovering over me, instructing me to consume as much alcohol as physically possible. Is hardly surprising, then, that I grossly abused the generosity of the village people and got incredibly drunk at their expense. I saw in the New Year doing 'Auld Lang Syne' with the old folk holding me up. Worse still, got text messages from Tam, Justin, Matt and Gil, along the lines of: 'Happy New Year, Josie. I am having the best time of my life doing young, crazy, fun things that I'll remember forever. Hope you are too?!'

Felt sad, lonely and slightly unwell from wine with pickled herrings combo. I was sat at table dejectedly making origami from paper tablecloth, when the young waiter came over and politely asked me to stop. 'Do you fancy me?' I slurred at him.

The poor boy went bright red, hurriedly cleared away some empty glasses and mumbled he had a girlfriend. Had honestly not sunk so low I was coming-on to a schoolboy; was just hoping for a little confidence boost from someone who might find the age gap attractive. Except he didn't.

With a ban on origami and a rejection from the waiter, I had no way to vent my drunken boredom, so rooted around in handbag and found mobile phone. This discovery ended with a succession of very loving texts to everyone between A and F in my phone book, including my very unbreezy message to Ben. Oh dear.

12.30 pm Must messenger Tam. She's wise and sensible.

ME: You won't believe what I did last night . . .

TAM: Pulled a 76-year-old?

ME: Worse: I texted Ben at two in the morning to tell him 'I think I'm in love with you'.

[Giant pause from Tam]

ME: Are you there?

TAM: Yes, I was trying to think of something positive to write.

ME: It's bad, isn't it?

TAM: I can't lie to you. It doesn't look good.

ME: Is there a damage limitation angle on this?

Tam and I then spent an hour and a half bashing out ideas to make this better. We've narrowed it down to three choices:

1. Pretend phone was stolen by silly, drunken friend who sent similar message to half of phone book.

2. Ring Ben and tell him I do in fact like him and hope he feels the same.

3. Send apology text, e.g. 'Think I may have sent a few random messages last night. Hope you weren't one of them!'

Thursday 2 January

11.15 am After sleeping on it, have decided that no.1 sounds like obvious and childish lie; no.2 is possibly most mature, honest and sensible, so I'm going for no.3 – the recovery text.

11.30 am Have sent text to Ben and received nothing in reply.

1.50 pm Nothing. Nada. Zilch. Zerooooooooooooooooooo.

4.00 pm Perhaps he didn't get text?

4.20 pm Have sunk very, very low. I re-sent the message. And, selected 'request upon receipt'.

4.35 pm Message has been received by Ben. No return message to Josie.

Friday 3 January
10 am Still nothing from Ben, but I'm fine with it. Really. Have already wasted first two days of fresh year and will not waste any more of life.

Am not completely surprised that the new year has started badly as everything following Christmas is a disappointment: the nice food has been eaten and it's back to the healthy stuff; the festive parties have ceased; the Christmas films finished and even *Eastenders* – peaking on Christmas Day with high tension glory – has since become a misery show as people cry over dead husbands, injured siblings and torched businesses, etc.

Will use this lull in activity as an opportunity to get on with important business of English essays. Yes. Right, then.

Erm, where did I put my essay questions?

Friday 10 January
6.20 pm Working at home is not easy. Have spent past week trying to stitch together various loose arguments for each of my essays. Is all a bit tricky when haven't quite got round to reading set texts. Plus, am sure my academic brilliance is being thwarted by distractions in working environment. Is very difficult trying to stay focused when Mum keeps floating round the house, wafting incense sticks. (Hobbit's

Christmas present for Mum was patchouli incense sticks with a wooden holder. Hmmm.)

Rather than getting very angry with Mum, decided to include her in uni world by reading the beginning of fantastic African American essay. She feigned mild interest but when it came to my surprise Q&A at the end, it was clear she hadn't been listening. Tsk.

Monday 13 January

2.30 pm 'Hakarit, Hakarit, Hakarit, Hakarit.'

Grrrr! Mum is chanting mantras in lounge. Noise is reverberating through walls and seeping into room to destroy my soul. Her interest in spirituality is growing to obsessive proportions. She's going on a three-day retreat on Wednesday and am worried she might come back levitating.

3.30 pm 'Mum,' I said stroppily after a further hour of mantras. 'I have about a zillion more words to write and if you'd like to see me holding one of those pretty degree certificates with the red ribbon on, then, please, no more chanting?'

'Darling,' she replied, placing her hands on my shoulders in a I'm-going-to-transport-peace-into-you way, 'you do seem tightly wound. I think I know what the problem is. All this work is making you tense. Why don't you sit here with me and we can practise some mantras together?'

'Nooooo!!! I just want you to stop chanting. I don't want to join you. I have work to do!'

'Come on now, Josie, this is silly. I think you need to take a chill pill.'

A chill pill? Who has she been mixing with?

3.32 pm Oh, yes. Hobbit.

Tuesday 14 January
11 am As another day passes with me trying to do work while Mum wanders the house chanting, am trying to remember that I had a very good and happy childhood. I must hang on to those precious memories as, clearly, the best is behind me.

Good news is, her retreat starts tomorrow. While am nervous about what new ideas may be sowed into her mind, am very grateful for three whole days of bliss.

Wednesday 15 January
3 pm Mmmm . . .

Thursday 16 January
5 pm . . . the silence . . .

Friday 17 January
7 pm . . . was short-lived. Mum is back. She came through the front door wearing hemp slacks and sandals. I felt that familiar trickle of fear; I scanned her for henna tattoos, piercings or the beginnings of dreadlocks.

'How was it?' I asked nervously.

'A disaster,' she replied, theatrically slumping on to the sofa.

'Why?'

'Well,' she sighed heavily and pressed at her brow. 'For a start, they wouldn't let me wear my Carvella shoes because they're leather! I was outraged, as you can imagine. While there were some very lovely and spiritual people, they really haven't a clue how to dress. We were all made to wear these old trousers so we'd look the same!

'I could just about live in the slacks and sandals, but when it came to meal times, I realised it wasn't for me. There was no menu; we were all given the same food (some lentil-based business with no marinade or accompaniment), which we were expected to eat for three meals a day! It was appalling. As I sat down this lunchtime for yet more refried beans, I thought to myself, is this really me?

'Now don't you start grinning,' she scolded. 'I am not giving up on spirituality. I am simply taking a step back. It's wonderful to have a quiet meditate now and again, and to pop along to the shiatsu masseuse, but I think, for now, that will be enough. Anyway, I'm not going to have time to fit it all in. I've decided to join the Samaritans!'

TWELVE

Sunday 19 January

11.30 am. Train. Am on my way back to uni. Have got over initial shock of Mum becoming a Samaritan and am almost coming round to the idea. In a strange sort of way, I think Mum will be really good at this; she's a great listener and very empathetic – and she loves to be on the phone. I haven't made much progress with my essays as spent the weekend helping her research the volunteer programme. Was not entirely selfless as was thinking of the bigger picture: Mum will be doing an eight-week training course and then busy with Samaritans shifts, leaving very little time for further spiritual quests or trips to uni to see Hobbit. Yey!

Actually, think the old Mum might be slowly returning as she was lecturing me all the way to the station about eating properly and have just found triangular-cut sand-wiches and a box of homemade flapjack tucked inside bag. Mmmm. Now feel a bit bad about my ruthless bout of cupboard looting. Home shopping is addictive; it's so much easier than plodding round supermarket and the bonus is, it's free. Mum pulled a face as I started filling my rucksack, but when I reminded her that I could still be living at home – permanently – she piped down. So am now stocked-up on all things edible. Admittedly, the fruit and veg section (pantry) was a little low, but the chemist (bathroom) was well supplied and it was good to have a rummage through the off-licence (drinks cabinet). Now Mum can rest easy in the knowledge that I'll be clean, fed and drunk for another semester!

Am looking forward to seeing flatmates again, though don't know what to do about Ben situation. Maybe it's best to pretend text message thing never happened and if he does bring it up, I'll just feign complete ignorance.

Oh, what about my recovery text? Things could get complicated if I go down the route of a phone poltergeist.

10 pm. Flat. Yey! Is so nice to see flatmates again! Do have that slightly disappointed feeling as Ben is the only one not back yet. Got into a spiral of panic like: Where is he? Why is he not here? Has my text made him move to North Hall? Was tempted to pump Matt for Ben-whereabouts-intel but Tam reassured me that Ben's probably working from home and will be back later in the week. OK, good.

Has been nice catching up with everyone else. We've all been sat in Matt's room eating Domino's pizza. Matt left a chicken in the fridge over Christmas and now our whole kitchen stinks. He paid for Justin's jalapeno pepper pizza as a bribe to get him to decontaminate the fridge but I think it's going to take a few days for the smell to pass. Justin seems quite pleased with the deal as he's been all smiles and giggles since getting some special edition Spider-Man comic for Christmas. We tried to look interested whilst he briefed us excitedly on being one of only twelve collectors to have a copy.

'Shit – that's not the comic on your desk, is it?' asked Matt, his eyes glimmering with mischief. 'Only, I think I've left my mug on it. What? I didn't want to get ring marks on your desk.'

Matt's been wearing his latest T-shirt as bought by his little brother. It reads: 'WARNING! CHOKING HAZARD' and a large arrow points towards his trousers. Another tasteful Christmas presents is stuck to his ceiling. It's a life-sized poster of a blonde girl cupping her very generous breasts towards the camera. Worryingly, we all agreed it looks a bit like Tam. 'That's why I chose it!' Matt smirked, and then Tam clipped him round the back of the head and took his last bit of pepperoni.

Has been lovely seeing Tam, particularly as she confirmed that she hasn't finished her English essays either (deadline Thursday), so at least we'll be retaking the semester together.

We were all discussing whether Justin's new blonde highlights worked when Suniti arrived back, followed by her cousin, Aja. I was expecting her to look healthy and glowing after a relaxing few weeks in Pakistan, but her skin seemed tired and her eyelids were red and swollen.

'Hi,' Tam beamed and went to give her a hug.

Suniti looked horrified and took a step back, virtually pressing herself against the corridor wall to escape contact.

'Did you have a nice time catching up with your family?' asked Justin.

Suniti looked at Aja, as though searching out what to do. 'Yes, thank you,' she said eventually and, grabbing her small suitcase, scuttled off to her room.

Aja followed behind, leaving a stench of stale smoke. When he got to Suniti's door, he looked back at us and then slammed the door too, locking it from the inside.

He's so weird. Suniti seems uncomfortable talking to us in front of him (more jokes from Matt, 'It's not that; it's cos I'm wearing this new T-shirt, she couldn't control herself'). She keeps running back and forth to the bathroom, so maybe she's just unwell? Or she could be homesick or stressed out with essay deadlines coming up. I would go and have a chat with her, but Aja is still lingering around and he gives me the creeps.

Monday 20 January

9 pm. In bedroom. Ben is still not back. I was unscrewing the cap from a bottle of cheap red wine when Matt skidded across the kitchen floor in his football socks. 'You've done well, Shorty.'

'Hm?' I muttered.

'I'm impressed. You haven't asked me where Ben is yet. But being the nice guy that I am, I'll put you out of your misery.'

I poured a large glass of wine and pretended not to be interested.

'He's away snowboarding and isn't due back till Friday.'

Ugh. That's four more days. While am desperately pining to see those lovely pectorals, am also very nervous about his reaction to the text. It's like a seesaw of emotions living with a sex god but being a crush twit.

'I know it's hard keeping your teenage lust under control, but please don't forget where my room is in times of need.'

'Shut up,' I huffed and then glugged my wine.

'That's the hurt talking, baby,' Matt said in an American accent. 'On the subject of hot girls in tight Lycra – oh, we weren't, were we? Have you seen the beautiful laydeez from upstairs yet?'

Hmmph! The bunnies. Had forgotten about them. Then was suddenly gripped by irrational panic that Ben was actually on holiday with bunny-duo. Grabbed my bottle of wine and retreated to room.

9.30 pm Mmmm . . . wine is really helping stir creative essay juices. Tam and I have been working and drinking together as it helps stimulate literary thoughts. Think in the past we've been too strict with selves, which is probably why essays have not been blossoming with original thought. An evening with Tam, wine and my Children's Literature essay will be very good and fruitful. Yes.

10.15 pm Tam's gone to fetch another bottle as we're planning on having a long and productive night of work.

10.45 pm Writing is flowing freely and quite brilliantly. Is fantastic. Tam and I are really very clever. Am churning out *Winnie-the-Pooh* essay at high-speed and Tam is doing very well on her Shakespeare one. It's like we're true academics except we look much cooler.

11.15 pm I need a wee but Suniti is in main bathroom and Aja is in other toilet (erm, why is he still here?). Tam says I'm pissed and that it's not polite to ask people if I can join them while on loo. Only wanted to have a girlie chat with Suniti and find out how her trip home was over Christmas. Don't think she was very keen to swap stories with a pissed essay writer who was carrying Mr Tubs.

Oh, think I might also have tried to strike up conversation with Aja by asking him why he does evil stares at me . . . eek!

Midnight Pooh Bear – I loves you. Shorry, Mr Tubss!

Tuesday 21 January
8.45 am Ygrrk! Head poorly. Tiny bit more sleep . . .

Midday . . . Oh crap!

12.02 pm Have overslept rather a lot and important essays still need to be written. Probably will not help that brain is thudding against skull and eyes keep making objects swirl in a dizzying way.

12.05 pm Oops . . . Can see two empty bottles of wine next to crumpled copy of *Winnie-the-Pooh*. Am slightly nervous that Children's Literature essay is not as good as perhaps thought when writing it.

12.15 pm Um . . . yes . . . it does need a little tweaking.

Have noticed some pages of essay are decorated with doodles of Tam and me in bikinis. Oh, and others seem to be scattered with hearts and the word 'Ben'. Ahem. Think intelligent notes I wrote must have been the ones that are now obscured by red wine stains. Yes. Definitely.

12.20 pm Deciphered a few scribbles but am not sure essay has quite the right tone. Seem to be a lot of comparisons between Pooh and Mr Tubs, which is not strictly keeping on track with literary criticism.

Realise that last night wasn't very beneficial to essay progress. Now have a hideous, acidic hangover and only two days till deadline. Is not looking good. But must stay positive. Right then. Will have a cold shower to wash away hangover debris and get going. Yes!

1 pm Tam was staggering out of bathroom as I walked in. She looked at me and shook her head ashamedly. 'Jos, last night – did we actually write any of our essays?'

'Tam, I don't think we did.'

'Oh.'

'Yes,' I agreed, then wobbled into the bathroom and plonked self on side of bath, contemplating how I was going to get through the day.

'You look like shit,' Matt said, waltzing in, undoing his flies and taking a piss right in front of me.

I concentrated on not retching and by the time I'd vocalised, 'Use the other toilet . . .' he'd finished, flushed the loo and walked off without washing his hands.

Wednesday 22 January

6 pm Am in state of utter panic. Essays must be handed in by midday tomorrow and have only finished two of them. Yesterday was a write-off (ha-ha), as hangover blurred all perspective on life and the only thing of any urgency seemed to be sleep. On top of lack of work, think alcohol has been killing brain cells and I need those little fellas at the moment.

Do admit that have brought this on myself. Have always been a firm believer in the last-minute essay-writing philosophy, because when brain is under immense deadline pressure, adrenalin kicks in and brain spectacularly rises to the occasion. Only trouble is, today brain seems to have malfunctioned and while body is reading all the signs of essay panic – increased heart rate, shortness of breath, sweaty palms, flinging books around room etc. – brain refuses to kick into genius mode and instead is frantically fretting about obscene amounts of work still to do.

Oh, God! What if I fail essays and have to redo them in summer while other students are at beach getting tans? I'll be pale and anaemic-looking from too much time indoors and will get depressed and become a recluse. Mum will follow me up to uni and try and counsel me in Samaritans' way; she'll meet up with Hobbit again, get lured back into spirituality, have a platonic relationship with the halfling and then skip off to Morocco in search of marijuana fields – all due to my poor organisational skills!

OK, calm. Have been here before. Clearly, imagination is running away with self. Must breathe. Good. And will take one day at a time and not look ridiculously ahead into future.

In one day's time all essays must be finished . . . Aaagh!

7 pm Right. Am going to be calm and do a status report on essays to help clarify position, then can focus on what needs to be done.

Crime Fiction: Finished. Very good.

Gay and Lesbian Studies: Finished and bang-on word count. Brilliant.

Cultural Criticism: Finished. 300 words below word count. It'll do.

Children's Literature: Needs tweaking. A lot.

African American Literature: Just need to add conclusion, and possibly also a middle.

Shakespeare's Plays: Haven't started. Bugger.

11.55 pm Is nearly midnight and have lots more work to do. Have managed to finish Children's Literature, which now leaves African American improvements and Shakespeare essay. Think everything is going to be OK as can just do a late-night essay stint and am sure in a few hours' time, essays will look lovely and I can have a little sleep before handing them in. Yes. Will get coffee and carry on.

Thursday 23 January

12.04 am Saw Tam in kitchen also making coffee. Was some comfort that she hasn't started her Shakespeare essay or Spanish comprehension! Yey! (Not that I'm revelling in other people's stress. That would be mean.) Will do hourly updates to check on own essay progress.

1 am OK, African American is looking good. Have finished writing about primitive racism examples and must just quickly knock out conclusion.

2 am Hmmm. Was tricky trying to think of punchy conclusion under deadline pressure so have simply summarised what have previously said in essay. Think that this will be OK and also means I can move on to Shakespeare. Then am finished!

3 am Bloody hell! Has taken me an hour to pick question as was struggling to understand any of them. Have chosen: 'Gender differences in the Renaissance are polarised and hierarchical. Discuss in relation to two Shakespeare plays.' Although have not quite pinned down meaning of 'polarised', think I've got the general idea. Best just get on with it since it's three in morning. Yes. Rather than panicking, which I'd be very much entitled to do, I'm staying positive and hoping that miraculous last-minute panic adrenalin is going to kick in soon and make me genius essayist who can also touch-type.

4 am Sometimes wonder if my life may have been easier if Shakespeare had decided to be say, a pig farmer rather than a playwright?

5 am Mr Tubs is looking very cosy tucked up in bed. Would like to sneak in and have a snooze too. But mustn't! Will soldier on. Aided by lots more coffee. Yes. And Red Bull. Good . . .

6 am Suniti was also in kitchen with red, caffeineated eyes. At least we're all doing the late night stint together – yes, comrades etc. Now have funny feeling in heart like it's beating five times faster/harder/stronger than usual. Maybe that's the genius in me about to take over?

7 am Is like I cannot squeeze another paragraph out of my head for love nor money, nor fear. It's a shame, then, that I'm 1,000 words short of deadline.

8 am Is OK, came up with solution. Have gone for triple-spacing and 14pt font. No one will ever know. Thank goodness then – am finished. Will check on Tam, then go to computer room and print essays ready to hand in with hours to spare. Brilliant!

8.10 am Knocked on Tam's door to gloat about finishedness but she looked grey with stress and there was coffee dripping over desk. Gradually backed away as she yelled, 'Fucking footnotes and buggering bibliographies!' Was clever how she used alliteration in speech, but there was no time to appreciate language complexities as have done neither my fucking footnotes nor my bollocking buggering bastard bibliography.

9 am Oh, for the love of God, who said, 'I think, therefore I am'?? Freud? Descartes? Lacan?

9.02 am Phoned Tam on mobile (was too scared to go next door). It was Descartes.

10 am Think essays really are finished this time. They all have bibliographies (some books may have been slightly made up but am sure lecturers can't have read them all).

10.05 am Must get to computer room and print! Will fetch Tam . . .

1.45 pm Has all been very, very stressful. Edging its way out of computer room was a curling queue of at least fifty haggard students. No one ever uses the uni computers as they are so lumbering and out of date, but it was clear on deadline day that not many of us own printers.

Was a terrible sight; people were sweating and fainting under the weight of their rucksacks. Some students were trying to bribe people at the front of the queue and others were quietly swearing to themselves. Felt very uncomfortable being in public wearing yesterday's clothes, with terrible coffee breath and shaking from caffeine overdose. Think I looked like a drug addict. And Tam looked worse with coffee spillage all down her jumper.

It was 11.45 am before I was finally sat in front of a computer screen and hit the print button. By 12.03 pm we were bounding down the Humanities corridor at full pelt. With only paces to go before reaching the essay box, a grey office door swung open and out stepped McGibbon. It was like a horror movie. His gnarled face and gangly figure seemed to cast out the strip-lighting.

McGibbon stooped to the ground and gathered up the essay box. He hugged it greedily to his chest just as we skidded to a halt at his feet.

'Going anywhere important?' he asked, with a ball of spittle in each corner of his mouth.

'Handing essays in!' panted Tam.

'It's 12.04 pm,' McGibbon informed us with a wicked flicker of his left eye. 'I'm afraid you've missed your deadline. Wa-ha-ha,' he cackled like an evil professor. (Or maybe he didn't do the laugh.)

'We're only four minutes late!' I protested desperately, with red cheeks and perspiration lining my top lip.

'Four minutes, four hours or four days – it makes no difference. You have missed the deadline.'

If McGibbon hadn't been a lecturer, he's the sort of man who'd clamp cars for a living and then say things like, 'There's nothing I can do about it – my hands are tied.' Would liked to have used my freshly printed essays to papercut him into submission, but decided the technique might not be effective enough.

We begged and pleaded, explaining about the printing queue, but we could sense McGibbon was enjoying our torment. Then I remembered something about evil people – it's a power game.

And I had an idea.

From out of my bag, bathed in glorious golden light and surrounded by cherubs singing hymns, I pulled out Mum's homemade flapjacks presented in a lovely Tupperware box. McGibbon's eyes fixed on the sweet oats.

'You can have this, if you read these,' I gestured from flapjack box to essays.

His eyes narrowed at me and then fastened on the flapjacks.

I opened the lid slightly and hoped they were still fresh enough to let out that sweet honeyed fragrance.

McGibbon drummed his fingertips together in contemplation. Then he nodded and motioned towards the heavenly Tupperware, and, with it, we handed in our essays.

God bless Mum.

3 pm Oh, no! Ben is back from snowboarding trip and saw me in hideous two-day-old essay clothes. I was sat in kitchen holding my eyelids open while trying to eat a miserable cheese sandwich (very tricky actually and only managed to hold one eye when taking a bite). Ben came in carrying his rucksack and snowboard and looking gorgeous. His face was sun-kissed, with faint goggle marks, and his thighs looked very muscular after a couple of weeks on the slopes. Mmmm. He immediately came over and gave me a peck on the cheek. 'Hey, Jos, you all right?'

I was horrified. Was so tired and hideous after essay all-nighter that I wondered if this was just a mirage. The first thing that came into my head was: Did he get my text?

Not only did it come into my head, it also spilled out of my mouth. Oh, fuck, fuck. Can't believe I blurted that out!

Ben was looking at me strangely, which wasn't a good sign. Figured that he either got the text and thought I was a knob for sending it, or my coffee breath was killing him.

Pulled self together and realised I needed to do some major back-pedalling.

'Yeah, that silly message on New Year? I sent loads of them out: "I love you, Justin", "You're amazing, Suniti", "I want your babies, Tam!" Hahaha-hah!' Was actually laughing quite loudly in a forced way and kept mentioning, 'I was sooooo drunk!'

'Jos, I don't know what you're talking about,' said Ben looking confused.

'You don't?'

'I lost my phone over Christmas.'

'Oh.' Realise that if I were a rational person rather than an insane hyper-analyst, I might have thought of this possibility. I tried to regain control on situation via an avoidance tactic. 'So, Ben, how was your New Year?' I asked in a glossy Stepford-wife type way.

'It was fine,' he replied. 'I just went to a mate's house as she was having a fancy-dress party.'

'Cool,' I said, casually. OK, I was back to being breezy once again. I did not ask any questions about level of attractiveness of party-giver or number of females present. But then bloody Ben came back to the text message thing.

'You sent a text, did you?' he smiled at me, looking lovely.

'No! No. Well, er maybe, yes, I can't remember. I sent a few drunken New Year's messages to my flatmates saying "Hi!"'

'And "I want your babies"?'

'Um, yes. Er. Oh, is that my phone ringing? I best get it!' I said, in a strangled, high-pitched way. And I left – just like that – to the sound of no phone ringing.

THIRTEEN

Monday 27 January

9 am After mad panic over Autumn Semester essays, the English Department gave us about forty seconds to recover and then sent us home with a list of new modules for the Spring Semester. This time round I am wise to their sneaky ways and know that behind the interesting-sounding titles lurk months of torment and brain strain. I've decided to pick modules that are assessed by exam as not sure nerves can stand any more essay all-nighters. New timetable is below:

Spring Semester
Mon 10–12 pm Feminism and Literature (with Tam)
Tue 9–11 pm Shakespeare's Tragedies
1–3 pm Sex and Sensibility in *Clarissa* (with Tam)
Wed No lectures
Thu 11–1 pm Charlotte Brontë: Fictions of Empire
Fri 10–12 pm Nineteenth Century Children's Literature
2–4 pm The Mid-Victorian Novel (with Tam)

University is different to school as we only have two semesters. I've got twelve weeks of the above modules (with Easter in between) and then some exams – and that's it. My first year will be over.

Am looking forward to Feminism lecture today. Tam's chose the module too as we agreed it'll improve flat relations; instead of listening to Matt's sexist blethering and thinking of a comeback five minutes after he's left the room, we'll reclaim the power by responding with something intellectual and witty. Failing that, Tam and I can hit him over the head with *The Madwoman in the Attic* set text.

Really, though, have had enough of slipping into role of vulnerable, weak girl: glaring at mobile waiting for texts, being forced to live in unhygienic kitchen because of boys, or getting kissed against one's will by dreadlocked goofs. Tam needs help too, because going out with Spock for six months indicates signs of brain damage. We are throwing selves headlong into feminism and the boys will quake with terror in our wake.

Wonder, though, how feminists view padded bras?

11.15 am. Feminism and Literature. Lecture isn't quite how I'd pictured it: there are boys present; there's been no advice on female world domination, and lecturer hasn't once triumphantly announced, 'Men are bastards!' (possibly because he is male?). Instead, terms like 'subordination', 'subversion' and 'subjugation' have been pinging around lecture hall and are making me salivate for a Subway lunch (terrible proof of consumer brainwashing, but mmmm . . . that ranch dressing!). And what has the 'reification of gender relations' got to do with kicking boys' asses?

Lecturer is quite fit, though. Think he must be in his late twenties as he's just finished a PhD here. He's wearing Diesel jeans with a battered blazer thrown on for a trendy yet intellectual look. He's so cool that he hasn't even bothered telling us his surname, 'Just call me Dylan.' Was very embarrassing for girl in front wearing yellow pashmina. She forgot she was at uni and called him 'Sir'. Cringe! Nobody wants to remind yummy, cool, feminist lecturer that we are only just out of school; it's on a par with calling your primary school teacher 'Mum'.

11.55 pm Lecturer-Dylan is not so cool. He's just split us into groups and given us a fortnight to prepare a presentation on 'the role of feminism in modern literature'. I've been assigned with Tam, who's spent most of the lecture drawing cartoons of my Saturday night dance moves, and the girl on my left, who has blue and pink hair and is wearing a badge that says, 'I hate myself and want to die'.

7.30 pm Kitchen. I'm eating lasagne (ready-made, obviously) and watching Matt eat spaghetti hoops on toast with his mouth open. 'Josie, I've got a question for you.'

'What is it?' I said, trying not to look at Matt's spaghetti churner.

'How many feminists does it take to change a light bulb?'

'I don't want to hear it. I am a feminist and I'm likely to find your humour offensive.'

Matt ignored me. 'Five. One to change it and four to form a support group and blame the whole thing on men in the first place!'

'Feminism is not a support group, you complete knob!' (My witty and academic retorts have not been honed yet.)

Ben walked in as I huffily banged my empty plate on the side.

'I've got those snowboarding photos to show you, mate,' he told Matt, placing the pack on the kitchen table while he poured a glass of water.

Think lasagne must have had too many preservatives as started to drift off into fantasy starring Ben. Was imagining him in one of those bottled water ads where he's just run to the top of hot, barren mountain and then strips off his top to reveal a hard six-pack of taut stomach muscles and smooth, tanned skin. Then he opens the chilled bottle of water and pours it into his mouth, enjoying the sensation as it spills down his hot body . . .

'Cool, let's take them to the pub.'

After Matt shovelled three more forkfuls of spaghetti into his mouth without chewing, the boys walked off – forgetting to take the pictures with them.

Now an entire pack of Ben-photos are sitting on the kitchen table, staring at me.

7.40 pm I know it's terrible and wrong and a breach of trust etc., but I'm not sure I can stop self. Ooo . . . pictures of Ben!

7.45 pm Mmmm, photos are lovely . . . Ben carrying snowboard . . . Ben and other boy in chair lift . . . Beautiful snowy mountains . . . Ben in lovely ski pants . . . Sunset over chalet . . . Ben doing big snowboarding jump . . . Ben drinking in mountain-top café . . . Aagh! – Ben drinking in mountain-top café with very pretty girl . . . Very pretty girl dancing . . . Ben and very pretty girl dancing, fck, fck . . .

Oh, God, not sure I can look any more. Is like the pillow-in-front-of-face syndrome. Am too scared to look any further, yet curiosity is getting better of me . . . I'm going to look . . . I'm looking . . .

Very pretty girl blowing a kiss at camera . . . Ben cuddling very pretty girl!

Misery.

8 pm Fetched Tam immediately. She thinks it looks bad too. The sheer quantity of pictures of them together confirm I have something to worry about.

I don't like the fact that Very Pretty Girl is, well, very pretty. She's tall (I hate her already) and dusky blonde (more so) and she looks really athletic with glowing tanned skin (grrr). The worst part is that she's not even wearing make-up in the photo; she's just got that natural, ethereal beauty – the type of beauty where you can imagine butterflies wanting to land on her. And she's pressed up cosily next to Ben!

We have studied her intensively to try and find flaws. Rather soul-destroyingly, all we came up with is her lips looked slightly chapped.

Thank God I've got feminism now.

Tuesday 28 January

2.15 pm. Sex and Sensibility in *Clarissa*. Tam told me to pick this stupid module as there is only one set text. We did not bloody realise that *Clarissa* is 1,536 pages long. Do not need this kind of trauma on top of Ben potentially dating a supermodel.

2.30 pm Unless I'm having a momentary lapse into insanity, am sure that the guy at the front of lecture hall in a red 'P to the ERV' T-shirt is Matt.

2.31 pm Have pointed him out to Tam and she is gawping and then keeps swinging round to stare at me, saying, 'Why? Why?'

2.33 pm Oh, I've got it. He found our module list and didn't read the 'sensibility' bit.

3.05 pm 'Matthew,' Tam called as we filed out of the lecture hall. 'What are you doing here?'

'What a pleasant surprise, girls,' he said sweetly.

'Well?' I tutted.

'I had a little tip off about a hot chick who'd signed up for this class. I confess that I'm bored with picking up girls in bars. It's too easy. If I can get a neurotic English student to do the dirty with me, then I've achieved something.'

'Neurotic?'

'Yes, Josie. That is what N.O.R.M.A.L. people like me call C.R.A.Z.Y. people like you.' Matt patted my head in a very patronising way. 'Boring, though, isn't it? English Literature. The lecturer didn't even mention sex. Oh, here comes Lu-Lu. My new hottie.'

He pointed to a girl with a bob of jet-black hair whose boobs were bouncing out of a tight white top. I'd seen her in the Humanities café before. She's always wearing baby-pink mules with matching handbag, so I'd just assumed she was a Business Studies student who'd strayed into the arts quarters.

'All right?' she said loudly, slapping Matt's arse. 'Is it just me or did you think there'd be a lot more sex in this book?'

As Matt led her away, he turned back to us and mouthed, 'I love this girl!'

Wednesday 29 January

9.05 am. In bed. Was dreaming about Ben and Very Pretty Girl walking hand-in-hand along beach, and me running behind them trying to find nice shells to give to Ben. Woke up to find Tam, wearing a long Rainbow Bright T-shirt and nothing else, standing over my bed shouting: 'Shagging!'

'Did you hear it?' she yelled at me. 'Did you?'

Wasn't sure what she was talking about and hoped if I shut my eyes gently, she might disappear.

'They were shagging all night and did she try and keep the noise down? Did she fuck!'

Was a little scared by Tam's swearing so I tried to retreat further under the covers.

'I walked into the kitchen just now,' Tam told me loudly, 'and I found her sat on the table in one of Matt's T-shirts and a pair of French knickers. It's disgraceful!'

I was going to point out that this is actually more than Tam's wearing, but when she started to bare her teeth, I decided against it.

'She didn't even care,' Tam continued, now on a roll. 'She just sat there, eating toast with my sodding Marmite on! You know how funny I am about people using my Marmite!'

I didn't, but I'll be careful in the future.

'All she said to me was, "Do you do that Victorian novel module? Could you be a sweetie and pick me up some lecture notes?" Then she wiggled back to Matt's room. The cheek of it! What kind of name is Lu-Lu?'

'Erm, a sluttish one?' I ventured.

'Exactly!' and with that, Tam stomped off.

9.15 am Matt, barely containing a smug grin, has just walked into my room, also oblivious to the fact that I am still in bed. 'Did you have rampant sex all night?' he asked, standing at the end of my bed with hands on his hips.

I looked at him and wondered whether his mother had taken a lot of drugs while pregnant.

'Oh, no,' Matt said, slapping his forehead. 'I'm getting you confused with me. Yes, Josie, that's right. I was ragging all night – and, FYI, I'm a demon in bed!'

Then he sauntered out singing, 'Ride the punnani!'

Thursday 30 January

4 pm Every time I see Ben, I have to refrain from blurting, 'I looked at your photos . . . I've seen Very Pretty Girl . . . Is she your girlfriend? Is she?' Really don't trust self after text message thing. Am avoiding a combination of Red Bull, coffee and sleep deprivation – just in case.

The thought of Ben going out with Very Pretty Girl really bothers me. With Jasmine I could at least make self feel better by knowing she is a manicured beauty: dyed, buffed, tanned, polished and plonked in kitten heels. But Very Pretty Girl actually looks Very Lovely too. The idea that her and Ben were having cosy little chats together (and more), makes my chest ache.

Must not waste energy on negativity. Need to focus mind on feminism. Our presentation is in ten days' time and we've got our first meeting tonight. Should really try and find out what feminists do.

9 pm Sheree, the tall girl with the 'I hate myself' badge, came round to the flat wearing blue DMs with black tights, a red woolly jumper (covered in more badges) and a thick gold tie. I was a bit worried that she might be as intellectually incapable as Tam and me, so it was a relief when she emptied her 'Barbie is a bitch' backpack on to the table and out spilled a dozen books on feminism. Not sure our kitchen is best working environment as Matt's posters of 'Ten reasons why a pint is better than a woman' could be seen as slightly degrading.

Sheree seems very nice. She is clever in that sort of scary way that makes you just nod a lot. She started talking about the heterosexual matrix that underpins society and Tam and I were doing a very good job of 'uh huh'-ing in the right places.

Matt ruined our intellectual façade when he burst through the kitchen door wearing an 'I DO ALL MY OWN STUNTS' T-shirt, then ran at the wall and flipped mock-Keanu style. 'What's this about sex in the *Matrix*?' he panted eagerly.

The presence of our sub-normal housemate in front of our very intelligent feminist presentation partner was a little uncomfortable – particularly when he introduced himself by saying: 'Hi, I'm Matt. I have a twelve-inch tongue and can breathe through my nose. Who are you?'

Although chat-up lines like that seemed to have worked very successfully with Lu-Lu, we are intellectual feminists and do not find it amusing.

'Matthew,' Tam growled under her breath. 'Go away. We're busy doing important work.'

'Baby-doll, if you insist on being in the communal areas, you must accept a little interaction from your flatmates.'

Sheree was glaring dangerously at Matt so I tried to give the impression of doing important work by clearing my throat and saying: 'Yeah, no, yes. So, let's take a look at that feminine idea, er feminist idea about women. Yes, no.'

'We need to ascertain our stance,' Sheree said, talking above my prattlings. 'Are we arguing from the viewpoint of postmodern feminism, radical feminism, pro-sex . . .'

'Pro-sex! Pro-sex!' said Matt, shooting his hand up and down.

Ignoring him and taking out a pink furry notebook, Sheree asked Tam, 'do you have a preference on which position —?'

'Tam likes it doggy-style, don't you sweetlips?' Matt interrupted. Then he woofed around the kitchen, until I stood by the door and eventually managed to herd him out.

Hmmm.

Friday 31 January

12.15 pm Sheree rang fifteen minutes ago. I panicked that she was going to ask to change presentation groups, but luckily she was letting us know that essay results are out. Tam and I rushed over to the Humanities block and are now anxiously scanning a huge noticeboard to see whether writing essays while drunk is a good idea.

12.17 pm Found mine. I got a third. Not even sure what that means but Tam got the same, so I'm guessing it's not that good.

12.20 pm I asked a boy in a Metallica jumper and apparently it's very poor and is between 40 and 50 per cent. He said it counts as a pass, though. Hmmm.

12.22 pm Sheree got a 1:1 (boy in Metallica jumper says it's the top grade and she must have an inhuman super-brain). Did I mention how pleased I am that she's in our presentation group?

Monday 3 February

10.20 am. Feminism in Literature. Mmmm . . . Dylan is wearing crumpled cream shirt with thick brown tie and jeans. Again, very stylish in his sexy scholar way.

Today he's teaching us about gender-bending. I really wanted it to be fun, but the academic reality is it's a complicated theory about the performativity of gender. Really need to concentrate as presentation is this time next week. Yikes! Thing is, I'm so tired because Matt and Lu-Lu's nocturnal activities have been keeping me awake. Things got so bad last night that Tam actually top-and-tailed with me.

When we confronted Matt about the noise levels he almost exploded with joy that he'd instigated our girl-on-girl experience. Hmmph!

Is this weird: while the sex noises were filtering through my room, I was imagining Ben imagining them having sex. And then I was getting annoyed imagining Ben imagining them – in case he was imagining Very Pretty Girl. And then I just felt sad. And slightly confused.

Tuesday 4 February
1.10 pm. Sex and Sensibility in *Clarissa*. Just to note, Lu-Lu is not in lecture. (Nor is Matt obviously.) And Tam and I are not picking up lecture notes for either of them. Hah!

Wednesday 5 February
7 pm We've had three feminist meetings so far and this afternoon's was the penultimate one (I learnt that from Sheree – it means one from the end, and it makes me sound clever). We've been sat in Tam's room for three hours, running through ideas with Sheree. Three hours! Brain briefly expanded and then collapsed from unaccustomed exertion.

Presentation is based around discussing gender portrayals in my *Cosmopolitan* collection. Was embarrassed at first when I had to admit that the most recent thing I've read was a magazine, but felt better when Sheree said that would be a perfect case study for discussing feminism and gender.

As we were pouring over *Cosmopolitan*, Justin let himself into Tam's room and flopped on the bed too. 'It's miserable being a redhead!' he wailed in his Welsh accent. 'Superheroes are always dark and suave and muscular and—'

208

Justin suddenly caught sight of Sheree and blushed bright pink. 'Sorry, I didn't realise you had company.'

'This is Sheree,' I offered.

Sheree awarded him a rare smile. 'I think red hair is beautiful. I'm actually a red-head underneath all this,' she said, running her fingers through her mop of blue and pink hair.

Oh my. Ginger alarm bells ringing!

A moment later, the hair colour conference was interrupted by Matt who, seeing Tam's door open strutted in: 'Ah, isn't this cosy, all girls together,' he said, looking at Justin.

'Matthew,' snapped Tam, 'we are about to run through our feminist presentation so would you mind fucking off?'

Do like it when Tam says 'Matthew' and then swears. She's been doing it a fair bit recently; think it's all part of reclaiming the power.

'Benny-boy – in here, mate!' Matt shouted ignoring the request.

Ben wandered in wearing a faded T-shirt that had tucked under itself in one corner and was exposing the tiniest glimpse of firm stomach. 'What's going on?'

Mmmm . . . lovely Ben.

Sheree continued talking about images of women in suits with cropped hair and quiffs. 'These portrayals are positive for feminism as they suggest the fluidity of gender. Gender becomes nothing more than a performance.'

Matt burst out laughing. 'Hold on; you lot are arguing that gender doesn't exist because of a crossdressing photo shoot in *Cosmo Girl*?'

'It's *Cosmopolitan*,' I corrected him. I didn't want Ben to think I was still reading magazines about hitting puberty.

Sheree looked fiery. 'That argument would obviously be one-dimensional. We will be discussing how crossdressing can be used to expose gender as a series of actions that are learnt and performed.'

'Absolutely,' agreed Justin, crossing his arms triumphantly over his Spider-Man T-shirt.

'If gender is a performance, then, Geri, you're a fucking terrible actor!'

Justin scowled at Matt.

There were six of us crammed into Tam's room and it was starting to get very hot.

'Well, how do you explain hermaphrodites?' barked Sheree. 'They are ascribed a gender at birth and are able to learn it.'

'What's a hermaphrodite?' said Matt. 'Anyway, how do you explain this: girls cannot lift, run, throw, park or punch. They know nothing about cars except for their colour and they can't get told off without crying.'

I noticed Ben was wearing a half smile throughout Matt's little lament, so I asked, 'What do you think, Ben?'

'Er. Well, I'm not sure,' he replied uneasily, fiddling with the neck of his T-shirt.

'Come on, we'd all be interested to know,' I said, putting his sexist smirk on the spot (and wanting to punish him for Very Pretty Girl).

'Well, I suppose some gender traits are learnt, like, you know, boys are given cars and stuff to play with and girls are given dolls – so you pretty much learn some of it from being a baby. But, then, I don't reckon it's all learnt, as girls just seem a bit more thoughtful than guys, and a bit more gentle, you know?'

There was something very sexy in the way Ben said it all, looking a bit unconfident like he wasn't sure if he was about to be lynched. Then he quickly said, 'anyway, I best be off. See you all later.'

And he was gone.

Leaving Matt and Sheree to finish the debate with endearing terms such as 'anally retentive feminist' and 'patriarchal cultural philistine'.

Friday 7 February

1.15 pm I haven't seen Ben since Wednesday night. His room is locked and he hasn't eaten breakfast for the last two mornings – not that I know exactly what times he gets up and what he eats (8.15 am and three slices of peanut butter on thick-cut wholemeal).

The other weird thing is, Gil came up to our flat this morning to see if Ben wanted to go for a surf. Ben never misses good surf. I've spoken to Tam, Justin and Suniti – and none of them know where he's gone. I could ask Matt, but then I'll have to suffer days' worth of 'Josie-loves-Ben' abuse. Though maybe it's worth the sacrifice since brain is toying with crazy conspiracy theories like he's visiting his lovely girlfriend whom he's about to have copious amounts of sex with . . .

1.30 pm Matt really isn't himself. I nipped into his room to ask about Ben and found Matt sat quietly on the bed, staring into space. Think his activities with Lu-Lu are leaving him drained; the two of them have been locked in his room since yesterday lunchtime and she's only just left now. 'She must be a nymphomaniac,' Matt said, almost to himself.

When I asked where Ben was, there was no gloating, torture or smugness. He just told me weakly, 'Dunno exactly. He mentioned something about going to see someone in London.'

Saturday 8 February
10.30 am This is the third morning Ben's been without toast. Please come back.

2 pm Intercom buzzed and I rushed to answer it, hoping Ben had lost his keys and had been waiting patiently for me to give him a loving hug as he walked through the door. In one heroic movement, Matt leapt across the corridor and rugby-tackled me to the floor before I could press 'Talk'.

'Noooooooo!' he bellowed. 'Don't answer. It'll be Lu-Lu . . . I can't take any more, Jos. Please, don't let her in . . . she'll maul me.'

'You've only been going out with the girl for a week . . .'

'I'm not "going out" with her,' he corrected me sharply. 'It's a sex thing!'

'Well, it can't be very good if you're cowering behind the intercom.'

'It's just . . . I think I've got groin strain,' Matt said hastily. 'I need a night to recover.'

'No problem,' I smiled in a very understanding way as I wriggled out of Matt's clasp. 'Oh, by the way, did you clear that washing-up from yesterday?'

'I've told you, Jos, it's women's work.'

'Oops!' I said as my hand slipped on to the intercom: 'Hi, Lu-Lu. Yes, do come in. Matt's been so looking forward to seeing you.'

Hah!

Sunday 9 February

2.45 pm Ben is back. He walked in twenty minutes ago and didn't even mention where he'd spent the past four days. Doesn't he realise I have my feminist presentation tomorrow? I don't have time for obsessing over his whereabouts.

He seems different too – a bit vacant and withdrawn. I got Tam to find out where he'd been but all he told her was, 'I just went to see someone.'

'Someone special, was it?' Tam replied, angling for further details (as prepped by me).

'Yeah, it was actually,' he said quietly, and then left.

Oh no . . .

10 pm Oh, God! Oh, God! It's the presentation in twelve hours' time. We've had a final run through but I couldn't concentrate because of Ben trauma. If I fail my feminist module and become a sexist instead, it'll be Ben's fault and I'll have no choice but to hunt down Very Pretty Girl and shave off her eyebrows.

Monday 10 February

8.30 am Couldn't sleep properly as was dreaming about Ben kissing Very Pretty Girl, which morphed into them watching me do my feminist presentation, naked. For some reason Rasta Hat Boy was there too and was laughing a lot. Spoke to Tam this morning and she had a similar 'naked presentation dream', except the audience supported her decision to go nude and she ended up having sex with Dylan. She's so much cooler than I am.

Justin popped into my room to wish me luck for the presentation. Thought it was sweet and caring until he added, 'Can you pass it on to Sheree? Make sure you tell her I said, "good luck".'

10.20 pm We're bloody geniuses!! (OK, Sheree is, and Tam and I are just riding on the back of her glory.) Presentation went like a dream! I did a brief intro, placing *Cosmopolitan* in its cultural context (e.g. it's a girlie mag), then Sheree presented the middle (all the big-worded, theoretical ideas), and Tam read the conclusion (summarised what Sheree said, then waited for people to clap).

Dylan was very impressed and said our presentation 'expressed complex ideas through a modern medium'.

Hah! I really am a feminist!

FOURTEEN

Tuesday 11 February

11 pm Tam and I have spent the evening in the student bar celebrating presentation success and talking tactics for the next important event.

Valentine's Day.

And Tam had some bad news to break. 'Jos, I've got something to tell you which isn't exactly great. Do you want to hear it or not?'

'Not.'

'OK,' said Tam, sipping her vodka orange. Then she got out her Juicy Tube and started to reapply.

'Of course I want to hear it!' I shrieked.

'OK, OK,' said Tam, waving his Juicy Tube placatingly. Well the thing is, this morning Ben asked me if I knew where you could order flowers from.'

'Right,' I said calmly. I could cope with this news as I'm very rational and it's quite possible the flowers are for (a) his little sister, (b) a female relative, or (c) a female friend.

'And then I heard him order,' Tam continued, 'and it was for a dozen red roses to an address in London on Valentine's Day.'

Yes, we were in agreement that this didn't look so good.

I'm feeling really down about Ben at the moment. Before Christmas we were just starting to grow close again, but since he's come back from snowboarding with Very Pretty Girl he seems different. Maybe he did get my text and is embarrassed now that he has a girlfriend? Who knows. It was stupid to let myself fall for Ben again after the heartache before. Anyway, I need to move on now and accept that Very

Pretty Girl has a Very Handsome Boyfriend who sends roses to her.

As Ben is firmly out of my Valentine's picture, Tam and I started discussing our card-receiving strategy. Aside from the obligatory card from Mum, which she still signs 'from your Secret Admirer' yet doesn't bother to disguise her handwriting, my Valentine's mail situation is looking very slim. For this reason, I'm going to employ the 'desperate pleading' approach. I'll spend the next four days wandering round sighing and telling everyone, 'I've never got a card before.' The idea is that someone sweet might feel sorry for me and send me lots and lots of cards. The downside to the technique is that I make myself look like a complete loser – but it's the lesser of two evils.

Tam is focusing her Valentine's efforts on Rupert, a guy she fancies in her Spanish class. I'm coming to her lecture on Thursday to check his suitability and see whether he has dangerously pointy ears or any other unfortunate bodily defects that'll lead me to make up cruel and shallow nicknames. If it's the big thumbs-up, then she's going to strike up conversation – and depending on how that goes, maybe even see if he wants to go out for a drink on Valentine's night!

Tam and I have put together a flatmate report documenting our love lives. At least this way, we'll know what to expect on Valentine's Day:

Me: non-existent with Ben, working on 'desperate pleading' card-receiving approach.

Tam: non-existent, but working on date-getting with Rupert.

Suniti: I'm guessing she's also in 'Team Non-Existent', but I'd like to be surprised by a stretch hummer pulling up outside South Hall and Suniti running down the corridors in little black dress and kitten heels, screeching, 'Fuck it, I forgot to do my bikini line!'

Justin: also non-existent but falling badly for Sheree and considering sending a card.

Matt: sleeping with Lu-Lu-the-vocalist, but he assures us, 'She's not my girlfriend'.

Ben: probably sleeping with Very Pretty Girl but assures us of nothing.

Wednesday 12 February

1.30 pm My timetable for the Spring Semester has once again given me Wednesday afternoons off for sport. I wish they wouldn't. Every Wednesday I'm struck with the guilts over my lack of sporting prowess and then compensate by eating chocolate, reading magazines or shopping. Good thing is that Tam is equally unsporty, but she annoyed me today by going for a run in the park. Why even pretend? I'm not caving into sports' afternoon peer pressure and am getting a mag.

3.25 pm. In room. Depressed. I didn't want to do it – the magazine made me. Have taken sex survey, **'How Hot Are You?'** and discovered on a scale of ice to fire, I am lukewarm.

Breast milk and urine are lukewarm.

Surely I'm sizzling, piping, scolding, scorching or roasting? Even simmering or parboiled would do. But, lukewarm?

Think magazine writers are very irresponsible as they make young, impressionable girls like me feel bad for not being engaged in a constant shagfest. The article, after questioning your sex life (or lack thereof), flings statistics at you to confirm how abnormal you are. Have discovered that '86% of women use sex toys'. If I think of a hundred people, then take out thirteen friends and me – everyone else I know has used a sex toy.

Oh, God – Mum and Granny were in my hundred people!

The next stat says, 'The average Brit has sex 135 times a year.' That's two-and-a-half times a week, for every week of every year. That means since starting uni I should have had sex . . . um . . . let me see . . . bloody hell – seventy-eight times!

Is clear that am not going to be able to catch up on the sex stat, but maybe I should buy a vibrator to be part of that gang? Thing is, though, not sure that I really want to use one. Maybe, though, it's like eyelash curlers: all girls like to have one but no one ever uses them.

6 pm Matt has been hiding in my room for last half-hour to escape the sexual grip of Lu-Lu. Of course, he's not admitting it, as how could Matt possibly disclose that he can't keep up with her? Instead, he told me, 'Jos, you and me never get any quality time together. Let's talk.'

Am pleased that someone is having an adverse reaction to too much sex. You see, it's people like Lu-Lu (aka Sahara-desert-in-a-heatwave) who make sex survey results so difficult to compete with. You get a couple of deviant entries like her and suddenly you're lukewarm.

Thursday 13 February
11.15 am. In Spanish lecture trying to spot Rupert. Feels very unusual to bunk my Shakespeare lecture so I can attend another module I'm not even taking. Am quite enjoying

sitting back and listening to lecturer's lovely Spanish accent. Have been closing my eyes and imagining I'm back on a Spanish beach soaking up the rays (this is the edited version where Pablo and his cocktail bar don't feature. OK, maybe the bar can play a small role).

Rupert is sat a couple of rows in front. He is definitely yummy. Looks very public school in crumpled pink shirt with navy v-neck over the top. Bet he's wearing loafers – or deck shoes. Do like his bright green eyes and the messy hair. Yes, I agree with his Top 3 inclusion.

Think Tam must really like him (to look at, obviously, as they haven't spoken yet). Have never seen her make such an effort before leaving the flat. Usually it's all, 'Shitting hell! I've still got my PJ bottoms on!' just as we're going out the door. Today her wavy blonde locks have been washed, Bed-Headed, scrunched and diffused. Her make-up – although looking natural in both tones and texture, has taken one hour and fifteen minutes to apply, and her clothes have been meticulously chosen to get exactly the right 'casual but sexy' look for a Spanish lecture.

Now I've checked out Rupert, there's not much else to entertain mind with and my thoughts keep wandering off into misery about being lukewarm. According to mag, most people in lecture hall must have had sex at some point in the last three days. That means on my row alone there have been seventeen bouts of shagging since Monday! It's making me feel quite nauseous. Despite my attempts to halt time while I desperately scrabble around to find a date for the big One-Four, the loveless day is still hurtling relentlessly towards me (twelve hours to go). I'm going to spend a lukewarm Valentine's Day counting all the people I should have had sex with. Misery!

12.45 pm Oh, bugger, don't think Tam's going to get chance to chat with Rupert. He just read a text message and then got up and left class. Nice arse, though.

Friday 14 February

9 am Valentine's Day has been fantastic! I was woken up by the postman who delivered twenty-seven cards – all from male models. Jared Leto brought me breakfast in bed and I enjoyed being fed peeled grapes and liked the fact he arrived wearing only a bow tie. Then I got a call from Brad wanting to meet for morning coffee. I boarded his private jet and flew to Paris where we ate croissants and drank cappuccino in a fantastic little patisserie. It was wonderful, but I couldn't stay long as Orlando Bloom had booked me in for a lunch date months ago. I spent a lovely couple of hours with him and then ended my day with afternoon tea at Jude Law's house. Yes, he said I dress better than Sienna, but there was no time for pillow talk as I had to hurry back to South Hall where Mr Tubs and an empty pigeonhole were waiting to snap me out of the fantasy world I prefer to live in.

So to summarise:

No – I didn't get any Valentine's cards

Yes – I speak to my teddy bear and make up stuff

No – I'm not surprised I didn't get any cards for the above reason

Yes – Valentine's is a load of commercial bollocks designed to make the happy happier and the lonely lonelier.

But yes – It would still be nice to get lots of cards.

Actually, was horrible at our pigeonholes this morning. No one wanted to look too early as over-eagerness is weakness. I casually mooched down about 9.15 am and found Jasmine and Chloe twittering in skimpy silk dressing-gowns, both with an armful of red envelopes. I smiled pleasantly at them and moved to the end of the pigeonholes. There were red envelopes under Watson, Wentworth, White . . . and then a great empty gaping hole of nothingness under Williams. I did a subtle lowering-my-eyes-to-the-ground, just in case the postman had been slapdash, but there was nothing.

Bloody Mum!! Where's my Secret Admirer when I need her?

'Did you get any post?' trilled Jasmine, struggling to bear the weight of her 377 cards. If she had held them behind her it would have evened out the pull of her boobs.

'No, I didn't,' I said coolly. 'I was actually hoping Amazon may have delivered my *Guide to Vodoo Magic*.'

The bunny-girls looked at me nervously and then recoiled up the stairs.

Just as I made to leave, I found self pausing inexplicably by Ben's pigeonhole. Before I could stop self, I had looked. And there, looking back at me was one red envelope.

Misery.

9.30 am I'm brightened minutely by the sight of Justin and Tam who are also moping around because of empty pigeonholes. Justin's got it the worst – he actually sent a card to Sheree, which puts him in the negatives.

9.35 am Have spoken to Mum and demanded explanation for not sending a Valentine's card. Can tell she's been doing her Samaritan training as she started using active listening and repeating the end of what I said but in a slightly different way. 'So you were annoyed because I didn't send a card?'

After she'd stopped parroting me, Mum said, 'I thought you might find it embarrassing now that you're a student.'

It's interesting that she thinks I'd be more embarrassed by getting a card signed 'secret admirer', over her smoking dope with my friends.

Hmmm.

9.40 am Although things look very gloomy right now, am not going to spiral into self-doubt. Instead, I've decided to bunk lectures and do what all good feminists will be doing on Valentine's Day. I'm going vibrator shopping!

5 pm Tam came with me. We decided to sacrifice lectures and make a day of it, as what else have single gals got to do on Valentine's Day? We started with lunch in a restaurant that was far too expensive for us, so we ordered one dish between us and looked spitefully at the happy, rich couples. We had a little drink to get us in the sex-toy-purchasing mood and then casually strolled into Ann Summers.

They lull you in with the false sense of security that it's all classy underwear and lacy vests. Then you walk three feet further and you're hit by the crotchless knickers and boobless bras (less is more on the sex shop catwalk). Before I knew it, we'd reached the windowless back section where I was surrounded by hundreds of 'toys'.

The shop was crammed with panicky-looking men doing last-minute present buying. What sort of boyfriend leaves it till the actual day to shop? In the company of such inferior species, I was starting to feel relieved, and, well, blessed to be buying a vibrator rather than dealing with the real thing.

Tam smiled encouragingly at me and we began scanning the vibrator section. She picked up a green glittery thing and said fondly, 'This was my first vibrator.'

First? Tam is probably on to round three of her vibrator purchases and I'm still trying to work out if I've finished puberty.

I was amazed at the choice. Vibrators come in all different colours, shapes, widths, lengths and textures. Did start to feel a little nervous when I looked up higher and clocked the two-pronged versions. The Platinum Rampant Rabbit had so many different pulsing and pressure options that it would be like programming a microwave.

After much debating I eventually decided on a baby-pink, one-speed, one-pronged vibrator of a petite size. I got to the counter and felt as though I'd grown as a person. It was a defining moment in my life: I am a feminist student who can go lunching with her girl friend and vibrator shopping on Valentine's Day!

I smiled proudly at the shop assistant as I got out my credit card and then I heard the one thing you never want to hear in a sex shop.

Your name.

'Josie!' cried Matt and Ben.

Good God!

They squeezed up to the counter alongside me and peered across the desk to see my purchase. Thankfully, the shop assistant had already bagged it up.

'What are you doing here?' I cried, full of wild panic and lust for Ben who was stood by the chocolate body-paint section.

'I'm shopping for Lu-Lu,' Matt said casually, 'and Ben's helping me. More to the point, what are you doing here?' he grinned. 'A little Valentine's shopping for oneself, is it?'

'No!' I said edgily. 'I . . . er . . . I'm buying a present,' I said, going crimson.

'Your mum's birthday?' Matt probed.

'Yes.' Fck. Fck. Why did I say 'yes' to that?

'Would you like a receipt, madam?' the sales assistant asked.

'Yes, please,' I replied, trying to sound calm and in control.

'What did you buy your mum from here?' Ben asked, looking round at the product lines.

'Just to let you know, madam,' said the shop assistant, 'all vibrators are non-returnable.'

'You're buying your mum a *vibrator*?' Matt laughed. Then he continued laughing. And then laughed some more. He laughed so hard that he had to put his hand on Ben's shoulder to demonstrate he needed support for his raucous laughter.

'No, Matthew, I am buying the vibrator for myself,' I said defiantly with a little, 'hmmph!' at the end to show I was not embarrassed by this admission. Ben went to say something but I'd slipped into rant mode: 'I have purchased a vibrator because I am a feminist and have come to realise that if I want to be sexually fulfilled, I am better off doing it myself!'

'Hear, hear,' agreed Tam with a dignified nod of her head.

'Well, that's just dandy,' smiled Matt. 'We'll see you two girls and Harry the Hard-On back at the flat. We'll be sure to knock.'

If Ann Summers had been on the top floor of a multi-storey building, it's quite possible I'd have jumped.

6 pm Got home – still stinging from humiliation – and decided to seal up vibrator package and hide away to avoid any further embarrassments. Have now labelled a shoe box with a big sticker saying 'Private' and in it I am storing all things embarrassing, like Jolen supplies and chicken fillets, as cannot cope with any more discoveries. 'Private' box is now stowed safely beneath bed and I'm getting on with rising above the humiliation and focusing on being strong.

6.30 pm Justin has named Tam, him and me the Three Miseryteers. He was quite hysterical with laughter when he devised the name and we humoured him as he's in a bad way due to a lack of Valentine's mail from Sheree.

'Justin, if you sign a card with a big question mark, then how will she even know it's from you?' I asked quite rationally.

'She must know – we had a connection. This means Sheree hated the card and she hates me and I'm going to live alone and then die alongside my Spider-Man collection.'

I now realise why I get on so well with Justin.

To cheer ourselves up, we Three Miseryteers are going to the SU tonight for the Valentine's special (it's the same deal as Halloween except with love songs and red plastic hearts). Justin is hopeful of bumping into Sheree, and Tam and I will just be grateful to immerse ourselves in the alternative reality that alcohol brings.

8 pm I've reached a new level of misery. Secretly, I'd always grasped on to a tiny bit of hope that Very Pretty Girl wasn't actually Ben's girlfriend. There may have been a way to explain the photos or the roses or his visit to London, until ten minutes ago, when all hope and therefore happiness has been smashed to pieces.

We were all bustling about in the kitchen making supper, when Matt interrupted with a question: 'What is the definition of proactive?'

'You don't know?' he tutted when we ignored him. 'OK, I'll tell you: the definition of proactive is . . .' (dramatic pause) '. . . going vibrator shopping on Valentine's Day!'

I flashed him an 'I will kill' stare, Tam sighed and Ben stared vacantly out of the window.

'Are you all in bad moods because of a card shortage? Don't worry, kids, I didn't get a card either. Although I did receive a Valentine's "gift", if you know what I mean?'

'Yes, we do "know what you mean", Matthew, because we can hear every fucking sound,' snapped Tam.

'Jealous bags!' he taunted, in a baby voice.

'Am I supposed to be jealous of you having sex with a cheap and filthy slut, or jealous of her shagging a chauvinistic twat with an IQ in single figures and the maturity and social skills of a two-year-old?'

For a moment, Matt looked hurt. He turned his back on us and busied himself in his food cupboard. A few moments later though, he was slapping Ben on the back, asking, 'Who was your card from, Benny-boy? Don't be coy, now,' he teased.

I was wanting to know the answer, but dreading my fears being confirmed.

'No one you know,' Ben said.

'Is she a ho?'

'Just leave it.'

Ben looked different. His face wasn't warm or open like normal and his shoulders were tense and hunched forward.

'So, she's a bit of a goer, then? Nice one, mate.' Matt gave him a wink and a nudge. 'OK, next. Are we talking bust size B, bust size C, or my favourite – a double D?'

From where I was sitting, I could see Ben's face reflected in the window. He looked cold and serious; his eyes narrowed and, very quietly, he repeated: 'Leave it.'

'Shit, mate, it's not from your mum?' laughed Matt.

Oh no.

'It is, isn't it?!! Benny-boy still gets cards from his mum. How sweet!'

Ben's jaw clenched.

I was willing Matt to stop.

But he didn't. 'Are you a mummy's boy? AreyouBenji? Areyou?'

Ben turned to face Matt and stared at him coldly. A voice, dark with sadness boomed: *'My mum's dead!'*

There was stunned silence. Matt was frozen in the centre of the kitchen, his eyes blinking at Ben's and his mouth trying to catch air like a fish. Ben stared back with heavy eyes.

No one knew what to say.

His words hung in the air.

Ben looked uncomfortable. By way of explanation, he added, 'She died a few years ago,' and then there was again silence.

I wanted to go to him – to hug him – to do anything to try and take that pain away.

A mobile started ringing insistently.

Ben thrust his hand into his pocket and snapped the phone open. 'What?' he said, his voice tired and heavy. His face immediately softened when he heard the voice on the other end. 'Are you OK?' he asked, gently.

Whoever the voice belonged to and whatever they were saying, warmed Ben; his whole body relaxed and his brow softened.

'I know, I know,' he whispered into the phone. 'We'll definitely go snowboarding again next year . . . I'm glad you liked the roses.'

Very Pretty Girl!

Tam looked over to me, gauging my reaction. Hearing Ben speak so tenderly to someone else made my chest ache so deeply that I instinctively pushed my hand hard against it to distract the feeling.

'. . . I'll leave shortly,' he told her. 'I'm looking forward to seeing you.'

Aware that his was the only voice in the room, Ben made his way out of the kitchen. But as the door swung to behind him, we all heard clearly enough as he said, 'I love you, Grace.'

FIFTEEN

Saturday 15 February
11 am. In bed feeling mentally and physically fragile. Misery!
He loves Grace.

Ugh. My head is really pounding. Think I should try and
remain still. Duvet is safe house. Will spend day hiding in
warmth of bed so won't need to look at hideous, single self in
mirror. Yes, duvet, sleep, warmth and Mr Tubs. Mmmm . . .

11.01 am Eek! There is a kebab in my bed!

11.02 am Um, am not too sure how that got there. Oh, crap!
Mr Tubs has got barbecue sauce on his head.

11.03 am Am not entirely clear on what happened last night.
I know I went to the SU and had a little too much to drink. I
believe – oh, God, I believe I was performing a routine on
the dance floor! Think it might have been the one I made up
to '_Locomotion_' when I was eight but I re-purposed it
somehow. Am having flashbacks of incorporating a Buffy
impression midway through. But why? I can remember
Justin trying to usher me off the dance floor and an
unfamiliar, good-looking person smiling politely at me.
Strange.

11.05 am It's whirring back into focus now . . . After hearing
Ben's phone conversation, I went back to my room and
spent twenty minutes telling myself, 'I am a feminist, I do
not need boys.' When the remaining two Miseryteers heard
the chants, Justin pointed out that would make me celibate,

a lesbian or a nun. We then changed the chant to: 'I am beautiful and have a vibrator.' Then Tam shoved a mug of vodka in my hand while Justin rearranged my hair and tried to apply blusher with the wrong end of the brush. They gave me a pep talk about letting go, moving on and not needing Ben to complete me.

'Sweetie,' Justin sing-songed in his Welsh accent, 'we are no longer the Three Miseryteers – that phase is already behind us. So what if we didn't get any Valentine's cards? And so what if you and I are experiencing the pain of unrequited love?' (Hardly think fancying Sheree for about three days compares.) 'We must go out and have fun. It is our duty as students. Plus, there is a whole SU filled with single, gorgeous people waiting for us!'

And they frogmarched me there.

All the happy people in relationships were in swanky restaurants or having intimate evenings in, and the desperate, single people left over piled into the SU. Was scary to look around and actually see the type of people available on my pulling list. They ranged between Chemistry students, people with frizzy, electrified hair and boys wearing nylon shirts. Am saddened by state of the student dating world, and even more saddened to be part of it.

Think I might have been a bit rude to someone from the S.H.A.G. society. They kept doling out handfuls of free condoms to everyone and I pointed out that Valentine's is not the best day for contraceptive deliveries seeing as anybody who is going to need a condom 'would bloody well be at home with their Valentine's date bloody well using them!' Looks like the free stash of condoms I was given can be added to my 'private' box, to gather dust alongside the vibrator.

There weren't many people from South Hall at the SU, which was probably for the best since I spent most of the evening slow dancing with Tam to '*I Will Always Love You*'. There was no sign of the bunnies either, who probably had more glamorous places to be, where attention and presents are lavished on them just for having blonde hair and mid-alphabet-sized breasts. Did see Gil, though. He was wearing a black bandana and his dreads poked out of the bottom. He shoulder-barged his way through the busy bar to reach me and gabbled excitably: 'I've got something for you!'

Was getting nervous when he started digging around in his combat trousers. He eventually pulled out a scruffy red envelope with my name scrawled across the front.

A Valentine's card!

Inside he'd written, 'To sexy Josie, Will you be my Valentine?' and a huge question mark filled the bottom half of the card.

'How lovely to get a card,' I said, with a mixture of delight that I'd received a Valentine's, and disappointment that it was from Gil.

'You haven't had any others?' he asked, looking shocked at the prospect. (He's growing on me.) 'Does that mean I can be your Valentine?'

'Er. Well. Not really, erm, shall we say no? Yeah?' I stuttered, wondering if I could have phrased it more clearly.

'Is that a "yes" then?' Gil asked eagerly.

'Um, no. It's a "no", I'm afraid.'

'Oh, well,' he sighed, 'you can't blame me for trying.' Then he brightened again with another idea. 'How about a consolation dance?'

I agreed to the dance but regretted it when a bump 'n' grind number came on and Gil was thumping hips with me.

231

Still, in the scheme of things, it was worth a little bruising because a card's a card! Hah!

11.30 am Have found a crumpled piece of paper tucked in my handbag. It reads:

Confirmation of £30 deposit for kickboxing membership. Tuesdays, 8–9 pm in the Sports Hall.

Oh, crap! That's what the Buffy thing was about – I joined the kickboxing society!

Sunday 16 February
4 pm Cannot believe I've paid £30 to do a sport! In my drunken logic, being a kickboxer must have seemed like a good idea – perhaps to bring me nearer to Buffy or the good-looking instructor? Wish Tam would join too, as I get nervous about doing things on my own. Was considering backing out, but Tam says it'll be good for me as rather than boo-hooing about Ben being in love with Grace (note: he still isn't back from Valentine's w/e with her, tsk, tsk), I should start focusing more on self.

Yes, definitely. Kickboxing will be great for becoming a more rounded person and there will probably be lots of lovely boys there with good thigh muscles, too.

Monday 17 February
11.30 am. Feminism and Literature. Am having very interesting lecture about the sub-groups within feminism. Dylan, who keeps perching oh-so-causally on the edge of lecture desk to demonstrate he is cool and youthful, has been telling us about Amazon feminism. The idea is to reject gender stereotypes like assuming women to be physically weak and men powerful and instead to celebrate images of

women who show physical prowess. The example Dylan chose to illustrate this was kickboxing, so I am now convinced that me signing up to be a kickboxer was not so much a drunken Friday night 'I'll-give-my-money-away-to-the-nearest-fit-man', more a subconscious decision to do a sport that reflects my lifestyle choice i.e. being an Amazon feminist and not thinking about Ben. Hah!

Tuesday 18 February

7.15 pm Am very much focusing on the Amazon feminist in me by doing serious warm-up for my first kickboxing lesson tonight.

Matt has been trying to thwart training with his special brand of sarcastic abuse. 'Shorty, I think you've made a mistake. You're not signed up for standard kickboxing. You've paid for midget boxing, which is on Wednesday nights.'

Matt is such a sizeist. Hate the word 'short' as it sounds so deficient. Petite gives the impression of being small yet perfectly formed, which is a nice way to be, much like Kylie actually.

'I'm not short,' I corrected him stroppily.

'You're not?' said Matt in mock shock. 'How would you describe yourself then, Shorty?'

'I'm not short,' I raged on hearing that word again. 'I . . . I'm . . . I am Kylie!'

'You've definitely got the cute ass.' Matt grinned.

'Wha . . . well . . . hmmph!'

I tried to ignore Matt and carry on with my important warm-up session, but each time I practised an air punch or a kicking action, he fell to the floor, holding his sides with exaggerated laughter. Was not very helpful for already shaky confidence levels. Don't even like having Matt in my room. Last weekend he was being rude about Mr Tubs and then when he left I found him in a very degrading position under my duvet. (Mr Tubs, that is. Thank goodness.)

Matt insisted I try one of my slayer-kicks on him and kept covering his shins mockingly. Felt very pleased with self when I managed to flick my foot as high as his groin. Hah!

'Ow,' Matt yelped, clutching himself dramatically. 'If you've done this baby any damage, there are going to be a lot of disappointed girls in the world. Do you want that on your conscience? Do you?'

'At least Lu-Lu won't have to come round any more,' I said, continuing stretching my legs.

He put his hand placatingly on my shoulder. 'I think I might need a nurse to take a look. Would you mind?'

'Hai ya!' I said, karate-chopping his arm.

'Ouch! Someone's got a lot of pent-up aggression. I thought Big Boy Roy would have helped sort that out.'

'What are you talk—'

'Zzzzrr, zzzzrr, zzzzrr,' sounded Matt as he strolled out of my room.

10 pm Feel as if I've been ten rounds with Chris Eubank or maybe another similarly punchy man who doesn't sound quite so camp. Our class was held in the campus gym and there were over forty people (including some very lithe girls in Juicy Couture tracksuits who must also have been tipped off about the muscular thighs). The instructor, whom I can now place from Friday night, is very fit but not really my type (OK, it was because his eyes were too close together, I know it's shallow but I found it very off-putting).

We were positioned in two long rows and I stood behind a well-built guy so the instructor couldn't see if I was doing it wrong. Was all fine copying the people in front, doing sequences in the air: (1) right jab, (2) left jab, (3) right elbow (4) left kick. Actually thought I was getting quite good until we had to partner up with the person opposite us: Well-Built Guy!! Was very scary being face-to-face with someone three times your body mass index and then told to 'spar'. Kept focusing on Amazon feminism and being physically equal, but then as I was putting my hair up, sparring partner caught me in the back of my legs and I was down on the floor cowering in a ball.

I staggered home from kickboxing – not in a fit state to defend myself from a sleepy toddler – but resolute that I will be going back again next week to strengthen my inner Amazon warrior. I virtually crawled up the stairs to our flat and hauled myself into the kitchen, where I leant heavily on the sink to gulp a pint of water. Then a voice behind me said, 'All right?' I spun round to find Ben sat gloomily at the kitchen table. 'Where've you been?' he asked.

'Kickboxing,' I replied, trying to wipe away the beads of sweat that had been resting on my top lip.

'When did you start that?'

'I met a guy on Friday who runs the club and I decided to join up.'

'Right.'

'Have a nice weekend?' I asked, pushing back a clump of sweaty hair that'd stuck to my forehead.

'Yeah,' Ben shrugged. 'You?'

'Yeah, it was good,' I lied, thinking of the 'Locomotion' and the kebab.

'Good.'
'Good.'

Wednesday 19 February

10.30 am Think I handled things well with Ben. I have to start pushing him from mind and, like Tam says, focus on myself.

Feel quite good this morning as I've got a sporting hangover. Is very novel to wake on Sports Wednesday with a new feeling of exercise smugness in place of slovenly guilt. It's clear that the pain of yesterday's exertion carries over to today and cancels out the need for further sport. Will have nice coffee and leisurely day reading *Jane Eyre*.

10.40 am Bloody Matt has finished my milk! Am really getting sick of his food-thieving. In the last week these are the things that have gone missing: two Müller Corner yoghurts, a chicken escallop, my last portion of Sugar Puffs, one jar of Dolmio and accompanying pasta serving, a Goodfella's pizza and half a loaf of bread. Then, being the complete fuckwit that he is, he puts back the empty milk carton/cereal packet or final dregs of Dolmio etc. Well, I'm fed up with it – and with our kitchen looking like a pit of filth. The boys are supposedly on a rota system with their washing-up, but it clearly isn't working as sink, draining board and work surfaces are stacked with dirty pans, plates and oven trays. I'm an Amazon feminist and I'm about to kick some serious skank-ass.

10.50 am Hmmm. Didn't go too well as Matt was gripped in a computer game involving scantily clad girls and guns.
'Matt, can I–'
'Busy,' he said without taking his eyes off the screen.

236

I think the point of the game was to drive round in a sports car trying to kill as many 'hoes' with twenty-four-inch waists and FF boobs as you can. I liked it.

I tried again: 'It's about your—'

'Quiet!'

Was very unimpressed by his rudeness and thought shouting might be the best way to get his attention. *'Stop stealing my food and do your washing-up!'*

Matt's eyes flickered from the screen. He checked that I had in fact shouted at him, and then he continued playing. 'I've broken up with Lu-Lu,' he said eventually, as if that somehow excused him.

Yey! No more yo-yo knickers keeping me awake or having to listen to detailed descriptions of their activities over breakfast! 'What happened?' I asked, trying to show a degree of concern.

'Slut!' he bawled at the screen. 'It was getting too serious.'

'Matt, you met her three weeks ago!'

'Exactly. It was meant to be a "sex thing". But you know women . . . Bitch! Put the knife away! . . . Once they snag someone good in bed they don't wanna let them go.' Then he laughed erratically as he gunned down three girls in hot pants.

'That's funny,' I pondered. 'I thought it was because you couldn't keep up with her.'

Matt hit the pause button, spun round and glared at me threateningly. 'Josie Williams, if you ever repeat what you've just said, I will be forced to remove the limbs from your stupid teddy bear.'

Yikes!

Thursday 20 February

12.30 pm. Charlotte Brontë. Just got a text from Tam. She's been at her Spanish lecture and spoke to Rupert on the way out of class!! According to text, actual words exchanged were: 'Sorry, I think I picked up your handout by mistake.' She did add that he gave her a lingering stare, though, and he was holding a leaflet about animal rights. For sake of friendship have texted back pretending all this is very exciting and suggesting that next week she mentions something in passing about being a vegetarian – you know, to build on common ground, etc.

Friday 21 February

9 am Kitchen is more hideous than ever. There's not one clean bowl left. For this morning's instalment of cereal I had the choice between using a side-plate or a mug. Am now sat amidst the squalor, slurping Cornflakes out of a chipped Duff Beer mug. And as usual, it's the boys' handiwork. I know this because Suniti is incredibly neat, always clears up in the kitchen and hardly eats more than a spoonful of sugar a day. Tam does cook, but only uses one pan and then washes it up and hides it at the back of her cupboard, and the only thing I can make is pasta and Dolmio and since Matt stole my last jar, I've substituted it for cereal.

7 pm Oh dear, flat war has been declared! Tam and I decided to speak to the boys about their washing-up. It began politely enough with us suggesting that they clear up the mess, followed by Justin and Ben explaining that they'd been doing the washing-up on a rota basis and Matt missed his turn last week. Things went wrong when Matt threw a hissy fit, insisting he'd only skipped one day of washing-up and 'now there's at least a week's worth of stuff!'

Justin read him his rights: 'The laws of washing-up rotas state that until original washing-up is done, everything thereafter becomes the duty of the named washer-upper.'

Ben agreed. 'Mate, if you'd done yours to begin with, you'd have only had one meal's worth.'

'I'm not doing it!' Matt retorted childishly. 'The girls have put their stuff in the pile too.'

'No we haven't,' I protested.

'Why is there a *Friends* mug with Reef in it?'

'That's one thing!' snapped Tam.

'There's probably loads more of your stuff in there. Josie, I can see three of your plates from here.'

'Only because you used them!'

'Whatever,' shrugged Matt. 'I know you two can't stand mess so you'll wash-up anyway.'

'Oh, you think?' said Tam folding her arms. 'We're not touching any of it!'

'I smell a competition,' Matt grinned mischievously. 'Girls versus boys. First one to crack has a forfeit.'

'That's stupid,' I told him crossly. 'Do the washing-up and the rest of us can have our kitchen back.'

'No can do, babycakes. If you win the competition,' Matt continued, 'we'll do anything you want: cook in the nude, be your sex slaves, lend you my *Slutty Shower Scenes* DVD. But if you two crack first and I find you in your marigolds at the midnight hour, then we can plan a forfeit for you.'

'No way,' I said firmly.

Matt was stood slightly behind Ben and started mouthing, 'I love you, Ben' and pretending to hug and smooch him.

I did menacing eyes at Matt, which only encouraged him. He moved behind Ben's shoulder and pretended to lick his neck seductively while watching my face drain of colour.

Ben looked round and Matt quickly side-stepped away. 'Did you want to rethink, Jos? Do we have a deal?'

'Fine,' I said.

'Good,' replied Matt.

Saturday 22 February

6.30 pm What have I done? Can't believe I've dragged us into a stupid forfeit war when only one mug is ours. Problem is, I think the boys will win. Can feel skin getting all crawly and agitated. I've got to be strong though. It's about the principle. Our kitchen is just a microcosm of the world. It's girls versus boys. Feminism versus sexism. Yes!

Sunday 23 February

4 pm Matt's called me anally retentive. Just because I'm not comfortable eating in a kitchen that smells like rotting pork, it hardly makes me uptight. And so what if I've begun marking my milk to show how much I've used?

Monday 24 February

6 pm Each day, flat becomes more of a health hazard. Suniti's been spending less time than ever in communal areas. Don't blame her as cannot possibly cook food in kitchen without losing appetite. I worry about Suniti as I can literally go a week without seeing her. She's on a different time schedule from the rest of us as she seems to be at the library for most of the day and then grabs something to eat late at night. It's probably a good thing that she's not using the kitchen much as it's so filthy – Tam and I have had to resort to going out for food tonight. We're meeting Sheree at a coffee house for a Danish pastry dinner. Justin asked if he could join us, but we told him, 'we can't mix with them from the other side.'

Tuesday 25 February

11.30 am Have done a cruel, sneaky, yet ingenious thing. Justin leapt on to my bed this morning to get the details on coffee with Sheree. 'Did she say anything about me? What was she wearing? Does she drink latte? Oh, my God, me too! We are so perfect for each other!'

Think I may have slightly manipulated him by, first, confirming that Sheree talked about him a lot (slight fib), and, second, by telling him that Sheree is coming over tonight (total lie). And that wasn't even the sneaky, sneaky part. I later dropped into the conversation that Sheree has very high cleanliness standards. I even quoted her as saying, 'I find men who keep a clean and tidy home very sexy – it shows a mutual respect for both sexes.'

Justin looked concerned and asked what time she was coming over. 'Not till about six,' I told him, and then he scurried out of my room.

5.30 pm Yesyesyesyesyesyesyesyesyes! Justin has done the washing-up! Hah! Is brilliant – now we have a clean kitchen and can choose a forfeit to torture the boys with. Yey! Wonder if we could do a You-cannot-go-out-with-anyone-beginning-with-the-letter-'G' type forfeit? Yes, definitely like the sound of that.

Tam and I kissed Justin's freckly cheeks in gratitude and then burst into Matt's room, turned off PlayStation2, and led him and Ben into our sparkling, pristine kitchen.

'Who did this?' Ben said, running a hand through his hair and looking aghast.

''Twas me!' said Justin, proudly admiring his work.

Matt looked distraught. He kept turning on the spot – surveying the cleanliness with disbelief. 'Nooooooo!' he howled. 'How could you, Geri?'

'You should be thanking me!' Justin snorted. 'I've spent two hours clearing up your mess.'

'Thanking you?' Matt was appalled. 'Don't you see? We've lost to the girls . . . To girls, Justin!! Look at them all smug and smiling now. You can never let girls win. They think they're superior now.'

'Think?' said Tam.

'I shall never live down the shame of this moment.' Matt fell to his knees and wept on the clean kitchen floor.

Ben stretched out a hand to me. 'Fair play, girls. It seems you are filthier than we gave you credit for,' and as he said *filthier*, he shook my hand and I almost exploded with lust (must put more effort into pushing aside Ben feelings).

'When's Sheree coming over?' Justin asked as I walked back to my room.

Oops. 'Er, she had to cancel,' I mumbled feebly. 'She's not feeling too well. Bad latte, I think.'

Wednesday 26 February

11 am Felt guilty about Justin doing all that cleaning for nothing, so during kickboxing last night, I came up with brilliant forfeit idea to make it up to him while tormenting Matt and Ben: Sheree is taking us to a feminist poetry reading two weeks today!!

Cannot wait to break the news . . .

6 pm Ben groaned and Matt said: 'No fucking way are you getting me anywhere near a fucking feminist poetry night. Are you out of you fucking minds? Everyone will think I'm a fucking homosexual.'

It went better than expected.

Thursday 27 February
6 pm Matt and Ben have been sulkily slamming doors this morning, but Tam is skipping round like she's got helium up her arse. She saw Rupert in her Spanish lecture and he's invited her on a date in a couple of weeks! Well, technically it's not a date – it's more of an animal rights' protest. And there'll be about a thousand other people there. And Tam's making me go too. And he didn't exactly invite her. He handed her a flyer about it and then she simpered something like, 'That would be brilliant. For the animals.' So, yes, it's less of a date and more of a long day traipsing around the streets of London in a big group of protesters just so Tam can get slightly nearer to the man she fancies. But hey, she's worn a rubber suit and paddled in ice-cream-headache temperatures to help me out.

Wednesday 12 March
7.40 pm Justin has been hiding in his room for the last ten days as Matt's been threatening to shave his head. This evening, though, he's been running back and forth between my room and his, trying to decide on the right outfit to impress Sheree at the poetry reading. Half an hour ago he had a major crisis of confidence worrying that his staple wardrobe of cords was not cool enough. Eventually he settled on sky blue X-Men T-shirt with beige cords and he's

trying something new with his hair (think it involves wax and twists and is supposed to reflect alternativeness).

Matt and Ben have not made anywhere near as much effort – actually, wasn't even sure if Ben was going to make it as he's been in London since the weekend (he can't quite manage to say the words 'I've been to see my girlfriend'. Why? Why?) and he arrived back this morning looking shattered. I am very much hoping it's not a case of the Matt/Lu-Lu kind of knackered.

Matt's dread of this evening increased when Tam told him the poetry reading doesn't start till 9 pm, which means missing the beginning of Wednesday night Sports Social! 'What am I gonna tell the football boys?' he moaned. '"Sorry, lads, I can't come out drinking as I'm going to listen to some feminists' poems." You do realise how much I'm going to be fined for pulling this sort of stunt?'

Midnight Poetry reading was held in a shady coffee house in a back street out of town. Sheree was already there, leaning back on a red leather sofa with cigarette burns on it, reading the literature about the evening's poets. She looked interesting in long shorts with white tights, brown hiking boots and a big afghan coat. Her newly dyed pink hair was clipped into mini sections with glittery butterflies.

'Hi,' Sheree smiled when she saw us. 'I'm glad you all made it.'

Justin grinned back at her as if he was the only person in the room.

Matt glanced around, taking in the red booths, the low lighting, the smell of Java coffee – and then I saw his eyes finally land on the stage where a blood red banner read, 'The Clitoris's Revolt'.

'Fucking hell,' he groaned. 'Are we the only blokes here?'

'Yes,' smiled Sheree. 'The others couldn't find it.'

Matt fake-laughed at her joke. 'Gosh, I've missed your scintillating feminist wit.' Then he pulled his jumper over his head to reveal a tight T-shirt that read: 'I USED TO BE A SEXIST (BUT THE BITCHES HATED IT)'. 'Pray, do tell me, when do the lesbians begin?'

Watching Sheree's lips tighten into a scowl, Matt added, 'That is why we're here, isn't it – to watch the lesbians read poems to each other?'

'Feminists are not necessarily lesbians,' Sheree snarled.

'Wake up and smell the coffee house, sweetheart; this is a lezzer hot spot. Have you looked at the audience?' Then he leant towards her and whispered conspiratorially, 'That's why they keep the lighting dim.'

Tam, wearing skinny jeans and an old-skool Coca Cola T-shirt, swiftly steered Matt to one side before Sheree could pounce. 'Matthew,' she chided, 'stop being so ignorant. Now, go to the bar, get us some drinks and then sit down and behave.'

'Fine. Come on Benji,' Matt said compliantly, and then the two boys skulked off to the bar with their hands in their pockets.

Am always surprised that Matt obeys Tam. If I'd said that he'd either have ignored me or distracted me by saying something random like, 'Would you agree that Chucklevision ended before its time?'

The poetry reading opened with a thirty-year-old woman taking to the stage and reciting a selection of witty poems and anecdotes. Matt had resolved not to enjoy himself so spent his time fiddling with the drinks mats, which displayed graphic images of women's genitalia as part of a 'feminism in art' experience. Ben was slightly better and refused to look when Matt began shuddering dramatically at a rather rotund woman who walked past dressed in leathers.

The second half was an open-mic session where new-comers are welcomed on to the stage to share their poems. A girl wearing a pink choker and a tight Minnie Mouse T-shirt shot on first with a purple notebook. She held it at chest level and flicked her eyes over the first words and then fixed on the audience: 'My poem is called *Cunt*,' she said sweetly.

Don't really remember much of poem as every time she said the C-word, I was flinching in a Pavlovian type response; it reminded me of listening to Snoop Dog when I was in my rebellious teenage stage (I just played music that I didn't like quite loudly) and Mum would tut at every mother-fucking swear word.

Sheree, sipping on a fair trade mochaccino, explained that the excessive use of the C-word is the purpose of the poem. 'In the English language, "cunt" is deemed as the strongest and most vile word – and it's no coincidence that it's a female body part professing sexuality. By using the word in soft language, the poet is trying to embrace it as a positive rather than negative image.'

Justin was hanging on her every word and he nodded so much I wondered if his freckles might fall off.

Matt nudged me, 'Jos, can you shift over slightly. Your cunt's sat on my jumper.'

Grrrr.

After Minnie Mouse, several more audience members shared their poems as Matt continued to deface the drinks mats. At eleven, the hostess announced there was only time for one last poem. A male voice piped up, 'I've got one.'

My stomach released a flutter of panic as I recognised the voice.

Matt sprang to his feet and bounded on to the stage.

'This is great,' said the hostess. 'It's not often we get the chance to hear a male perspective. Thank you very much.'

I heard a girl in front whisper, 'What a subversive T-shirt.'

Matt smiled brightly at his audience and then positioned himself centre stage in front of the 'The Clitoris's Revolt' banner. He adjusted the mic and cleared his throat noisily.

'Good evening, feminists and lesbians . . .'

Tam and I looked at each other in horror and Justin began to turn pink.

'This evening, I'd like to share a short poem I've recently composed,' he pulled out a drinks mat from his pocket. 'I call this one, "The Penis's Revolt".

Oh! My! God!

> We don't like poetry,
> We prefer porno flicks.
> In fact, we like most things,
> Which stimulate our pricks.
> Feminist moan at us,
> But secretly get their kicks –
> That's 'cos they all want a suck on
> Our big, fat, juicy dicks!

The coffee house fell silent. Sheree's jaw hung open. Justin held his head in his hands and Ben was glancing nervously at Tam and me.

'Thank you, girls, and good night!' Matt strutted off stage giving the hostess the wink and the gun. The audience were silent. Everyone watched as Matt, in his offensive T-shirt, weaved through the crowd back to our table. 'All right, girls?' he said cheerfully. 'That was a great forfeit you chose. Inspired! Do you think we can come again next week?'

SIXTEEN

Sunday 16 March

6 pm. Tam's room. Am sat on Tam's bed watching as she tips up shopping bags, yanks clothes from her wardrobe and flies around her room flinging shoes at the floor. There's a pile of tops on her desk, two pairs of jeans hanging over her chair and I've just found a pink bra under my bum. We've been shopping all day for an 'animal rights' outfit as the protest (with Rupert) is tomorrow. It's taken an entire trip because leather, suede and snakeskin are out, as are all forms of heels with 'march' being in the event title.

We both recognise the importance of this occasion: there is only one more week of lectures before the Easter hols, so if Tam doesn't build the foundations for lurve on the march, Rupert could meet someone else during the holidays. It's point critical.

Even though every surface of Tam's room is covered in clothes, she's convinced that she has nothing suitable to wear.

'Do you think yellow is too garish for winter?'

'Bold colours are in.'

'Mm, but maybe with blonde hair it looks a bit brash? Rupert's posh. I've got to look casual yet classy; dedicated to the cause but stylish; pretty but also capable.'

Tam is one of those annoying people who can shove on a saggy jumper and a pair of ill-fitting jeans and still manage to look sexy. And she doesn't even realise it.

Despite the current clothing panic, Tam and I have been ejoying a very relaxing weekend. We've had the flat to ourselves as Ben's visiting Grace (whose existence he still hasn't admitted, tsk), Matt's playing away in a football match, Justin fled home to Abergavenny after the poetry débâcle and Suniti disappeared with Aja on Thursday and hasn't been seen since.

Actually, Tam saw Suniti and Aja arguing furiously as they were leaving. Suniti was carrying a suitcase and when Tam asked where they were going, Aja just muttered, 'We're seeing friends.'

I don't trust Aja. Tam agrees that there's something shady about him. It's a shame that he's her only relative over here because it seems like he's trying to prevent her from getting involved in university life. Maybe he thinks she's becoming too Westernised? I wish he'd give Suniti some space as she's a lot more relaxed when his smoky Kappa clothes aren't infiltrating our flat.

6.30 pm The peace of spending a weekend with just Tam has been shattered. We heard someone on the stairway bellowing, 'I'm the fucking king!' and then Matt barged in announcing they'd won their match. Did not like the way he then plonked himself next to me – still in stinking football outfit.

'So what's going on?' Matt said, surveying Tam's room and then picking up a pair of see-through black knickers. 'Sweet. Is this what happens when you two are alone?'

'We're going on an animal rights' march tomorrow with Rupert,' I told him firmly.

'Not the posh knob?'

'Shut up,' said Tam, ripping a label off a new Mango skirt with her teeth.

'Don't you think it's a bit sad to go on a protest just 'cos you fancy some guy?'

'Look,' I said irritably, with surfing springing to mind, 'if you really like someone, it's good to make an extra effort to get to know them and their interests.'

'Oh, I see,' mused Matt, picking the mud off his shorts. 'I've got an 'I EAT VEGETARIANS' T-shirt you can borrow.'

'Matthew,' huffed Tam, 'do you think you could leave? I want to try on my new clothes.'

'I'm not stopping you.'

'Well, at least turn away, will you?'

Tam pulled on a pale blue ribbed vest top and then slipped into a lush pair of Miss Sixty jeans from today's shop (totally above budget yet allowed because of slinky fit). She looked casual and very sexy, which I think is the right look for any sort of protest.

Matt, who had been watching in the mirror the whole time, turned round and ran his eyes over Tam. Then he gave a dismissive shrug and said, 'I bet he won't even notice.'

'Haven't you got somewhere else to go?' There was a hint of hurt in Tam's voice but she busied herself by hanging up the new skirt.

'No. I'd rather stay here and laugh at you.'

'You're pathetic.'

'No, you are pathetic,' Matt retorted, with a sudden bitter tone to his voice. 'You're the most desperate girl in halls.'

For a moment, Tam's chin quivered ever so slightly and her eyes dropped to the bottom of her wardrobe. Then she gathered herself, turned to Matt, and with some emphasis said, 'Could you get the fuck out of my room?'

Matt blinked. 'My pleasure,' he finally jeered, walking out and slamming the door behind him.

Monday 17 March

9 am. On coach. We're on our way. Had to boycott feminism lecture to be Tam's protest partner. Is very difficult being both animal rights protester and feminist but I'm enjoying the challenge. Actually, am quite relieved to be missing Feminism and Literature as still feel a bit awkward around Sheree. We apologised for Matt's poetry rudeness, and Sheree did say the hostess covered it up by interpreting his poem as 'a phallic ego being threatened by feminism' – but even so, I saw the look of shame on her face. Think Justin's got his work cut out living with Matt while trying to woo Sheree.

9.30 am Am bit disappointed with the protest turn-out. Hoped Rupert might have other rich, public school friends for me to march (flirt) with, but coach is actually full of scary-looking activist types who are writing 'Die, experimenters!' across their chests. For some reason, I had images of rugged guys marching through the streets of London carrying puppies. Instead, all the boys look under-fed and have weird crispy hair.

10.30 am God, I'm really starving. Without thinking I packed ham sandwiches, but now realise that everyone on coach is vegetarian or vegan. Am fearful of getting attacked if I eat them, but am also very desperate to munch on honey-roasted ham. Mmmm, meat . . .

10.45 am Am eating stealthily. Sandwiches are hiding under *Big Issue* (accessory to go with Tam's outfit). Discreetly rip off small piece, hide it in hand, then cough furtively bringing hand to mouth, and sneak piece of sandwich on to tongue.

11 am 'Hiya, chaps.' Rupert is stood at the front of the coach wearing a brown v-neck and well-cut jeans. 'I'm so pleased you've all made the effort to be here. Today is going to make a big difference and you're all part of that. So, the POA: we'll be dropped off by Leicester Square where we'll meet with the other protesters. Then we'll march peacefully on a ten-mile circuit led by the marshals, and the coach will pick us up at the other end with an ETA of 4 pm. Does that sound OK?'

Sorry, did he just say ten miles? I don't even want to get off the coach – it's freezing and looks like it's about to rain. Tam is smiling enthusiastically; she's been lulled by the plummy tones of Rupert's voice instead of listening to the actual words. I dug her in the ribs and said, 'Walking. Miles. Ten.' But she is smiling and saying, 'Mmmm . . . POA: Rupert.'

3 pm Erm, am writing from cosy King's Arms. Thing is, the march is a fantastic idea and a great cause – you know, people coming together to show support for something they believe in – but Rupert yomped off so far ahead that we could hardly keep up. Then I needed a rest break as my padded bra was restricting my breathing, and Tam's jeans kept slipping down and showing her thong. By the time we'd readjusted, Rupert was out of sight and I had cravings for steak and kidney pie. All of a sudden, we rounded a bend and there before us was the inviting and cosy King's Arms pub.

Decided to nip in for a quick snack to refuel declining energy levels, but that was, er, well, two hours and three pints of ale ago. Oops!

3.30 pm Nice man in a black cab dropped us five minutes before end of march and we strutted over finishing line with big smiles looking fresh and healthy (and a little bit tipsy). We were in the first few to finish and Rupert was waiting there with a big hug for both of us.

'Super effort, girls. Really super! How about we celebrate with a drink while we wait for the others?'

'Sounds super,' hiccupped Tam.

5.45 pm. Back on coach. Feel very good about self, like am finally part of worthwhile cause. Tam and Rupert had good chats in the pub and even swapped numbers (Rupert said it was so he could update her on any further animal rights' activities, but I reckon that's just a polite cover). While they were chatting about Spanish lectures and the advantages of being vegetarian (Tam told a few white ones), I was left talking to Tree Boy. I'm not convinced that he knows much more about animal rights than I do, but he certainly loves to fight the good fight. 'It's my ninth protest this year,' he told me enthusiastically. 'I've been to everything from demonstrations against tuition fees and weapons of mass destruction to protests on gay rights, pro-life and ethnic discrimination.'

Was wondering how a white, heterosexual, middle-class male from Oxford could know quite so much about all these topics, but he assured me it's all about impact in numbers. I like Tree Boy. If I ever start a campaign to bring back *Dungeons and Dragons*, he'll be a good person's number to have.

Tuesday 18 March

11.45 pm Bloody hell! Had been back from kickboxing for about an hour (still enjoying the sense of smugness sporting aches give me), when Tam's mobile rang. It was Rupert!! She quickly shushed me, waving a hand up and down even though I was silent, and then she paced around her room nervously fiddling with her hair.

'Yes, I'm at the flat . . . Half an hour? . . . Sure, I'll be here . . . See you then.'

Tam put her mobile down and cupped her face in her hands. 'Rupert's coming over and he said he's got something "very important" to ask me! I think this might be it, Jos. He's going to ask me out!'

We were both very excited so whizzed round hiding the Ginsters wrappers, shoving leather shoes, belts and bags under the bed, all while trying to change Tam's outfit and applying her lip-gloss in a casual late-night manner.

Half an hour later when perfume was freshly sprayed and make-up reapplied, Rupert arrived. With Tree Boy.

The two of them, masked in balaclavas, had spent the evening breaking into a laboratory. They rescued twenty-three animals, including five dogs, fifteen white rats and three rabbits. Stood behind Rupert's legs was a very skinny brown-and-white beagle wagging his tail in our direction. Oh dear.

Is quite terrible the things that are going on in the lab. This beagle was due to be gassed tomorrow to test the effects of a new drug on the nervous system. Tam and I felt a bit guilty about the whole sneaking-off-to-pub-on-protest thing, as, really, animals are a very important cause.

Rupert begged us to take the beagle. 'It'll only be for a couple of nights while I make other arrangements. We've already got three female dogs at my place so I can't have a male in there.' Rupert looked at Tam with his posh green eyes. 'Tamara, I know you're passionate about this too. Would you take him for us?'

'OK,' she simpered.

OK? Apart from storing a dog in a flat with no dog bowl, dog food, dog bed and definitely no garden for him to . . . er, relieve himself in, if the warden finds him here we'll be evicted from halls – so it's not really *OK,* at all. And just to make things slightly worse, this dog has been STOLEN from a laboratory. It's like hiding a fugitive.

Actually, think Tam is already regretting her decision when Rupert left, the dog got a far bigger hug than she did. We're starting to get the impression that there's only room for animals in his life.

Midnight Thought Mum might take in the beagle as a playmate for Gruff. Forgetting it was late, I called home and she picked up, asking, 'What is it? Where are you? What's happened?'

I asked Mum if she would have a beagle, but she's already having to leave Gruff with Granny during her Samaritans shifts, and we both agree Granny couldn't cope with three dogs. Mum is going to ring round tomorrow to see if she can find anyone to take him in.

So now there is a dog lying under the kitchen table. He has a Kellogg's Cornflakes water bowl and three slices of my honey-roasted ham next to him. I'm really hoping he's not going to need the loo in the near future.

Wednesday 19 March

8.45 am Have just heard this shouted from our kitchen: 'What the fuck?'

Matt has met the dog.

Think we better call a flat meeting.

9.30 am

JUSTIN/MATT/BEN: Why is there a dog in our kitchen?

TAM/JOSIE: Activism. Animal. Fit Rupert. Laboratory. Beagle. Can he stay?

JUSTIN: Does Sheree like dogs?

MATT: Only if we call him Jeremy Beagle.

BEN: Yesyoucan,boy, cantcha?

So the beagle is staying until Rupert's found him a home. Only thing is, Suniti is still away so couldn't include her in flat meeting. When she gets here, I'll introduce Jeremy Beagle very nicely and make him do the soppy eye thing and am sure she won't be able to resist.

Jeremy really is a very cool dog. He smells slightly like disinfectant because of the lab, but that's quite welcome in our kitchen. I like his soft, floppy ears and the way he collapses on his side if you scratch his belly in the right place. Ben is so cute with him: 'You like being scratched, dontchyou? Yessyoudo, yessyoudo.' It's as if he's read the book I wrote on, *Everything Josie Williams Wants From A Boyfriend* (except he missed the chapter where it says, 'You must never kiss, talk to, or look at another girl. Again. Ever. Particularly not Grace. Or Jasmine).

Midday We had to sneak Jeremy out of halls for a walk. It was like organising a military operation. I waited in the courtyard, Tam was at the entrance of South Hall, Justin was positioned on the stairs, Matt was by our flat door and Ben was in the kitchen holding on to Jeremy.

'Clear,' I yelled.

'Clear,' Tam echoed.

'Clear,' Justin sung.

'Gay lord,' Matt shouted at Justin, followed by, 'Clear!'

'Go, boy!' Ben told Jeremy.

And he shot out of the flat, bounded down the stairs, sprang across the courtyard and headed for the park.

Was lovely going for a walk together as though we're a big family (of slightly dysfunctional young people). Tam thought ahead and brought a poo bag as we're trying to be responsible dog-minders. Thing was, she could only find a dustbin liner, so Matt gave an embarrassing commentary as she struggled to open it and then tried to do that clever dog-poo-removal thing where owner wears bag like glove, then grabs poo and does a flick of the wrist and bag magically turns inside-out containing hot poo. Problem with bin-bags is they're more sleeping-bag-sized than glove-sized. Bag got twisted and confused so Tam ended up holding black liner delicately between her thumb and forefinger because poo's whereabouts within bag was very unclear.

8 pm Mum's just called and has heard about a lady who might be interested in a rescue dog. The only problem is, she's away until the weekend but Mum's going to ring me back with any news.

Thursday 20 March

11.15 am. Charlotte Brontë. Am meant to be learning about colonial imperialism in *Jane Eyre*, but can't concentrate as have just seen a copy of student paper. The laboratory break-in is on the front page – with a picture of Jeremy Beagle! The police don't have any details yet but they believe the Animal Rights' Society is to blame. It also says: 'A spokesperson has confirmed that when the animals are found, they will be returned to the lab.'

Feel sick. Matt is on rota to stay in the flat with Jeremy this morning. Really hope he doesn't do anything stupid otherwise Jeremy – and all of us – could be in a lot of trouble.

1.30 pm. Flat. Jeremy is still here, happy and unfound. Matt did quite a good job except he fed him chicken balti for lunch, which could have nasty repercussions. Apparently the flat intercom buzzed five times this morning and Matt had to keep running to his bedroom with Jeremy and locking himself in, just in case it was a warden.

Things aren't so great on the Rupert front. He called Tam to say he still hasn't found a home for Jeremy. 'I've got to be honest with you, Tamara; I'm struggling to find anyone to take him. With the lab break-in all over the press, people would be suspicious. If there's anyone you can think of that could help, please, please let me know.'

Really hope this friend of Mum's is going to say yes. We're all meant to be going home tomorrow for the Easter hols. I suppose if worse comes to worse, I could always try and take him with me until he's found a home. We just need to keep him safe for another twenty-four hours.

Oh, God. Someone's coming up the flat stairway . . .

2 pm It was Suniti. It's all becoming a terrible mess. She'd just got back from 'seeing friends' and I heard her walk into her room. I quickly fetched Jeremy and went to introduce him immediately, so she didn't get a shock when she went into the kitchen. I didn't realise that it was Aja in her room.

'Got any more?' he asked. His hands were shoved in his black tracksuit bottoms and he was anxiously looking out of the window.

'It's Josie,' I said carefully.

Aja swung round. 'What are you doing in here?' he asked accusingly. Jeremy ran straight up and started sniffing him and panting. 'Oi! Get off!' he yelled at the dog who was investigating his bag for leftover food. Aja clutched the bag to him. 'Why the hell have you brought that thing in?'

Really didn't appreciate his tone of voice as had only wanted to speak to Suniti. 'It's not your flat,' I told him crossly, patting an excitable Jeremy on the head.

'Suniti is allergic,' he spat through brown teeth. 'Now keep it away from us!'

Oh.

Aja pushed past me and banged loudly on the bathroom door, yelling at Suniti in Punjabi.

Moments later, Suniti rushed from the bathroom with wide, frightened eyes.

Aja grabbed her bag, locked Suniti's room and then marched her down the corridor.

'Suniti, are you OK?' I called after her as they made their way from the flat. She looked awful. Her skin was pale and languid and her eyes were red and sore.

She didn't answer and let Aja lead her out of the flat.

'I'm sorry about your allergy,' I added, feeling desperately bad about driving her out.

God, I hope Aja doesn't tell anyone about Jeremy! His reaction to the dog was completely over the top; how was I supposed to know about her allergy? I find Aja rather strange. Funny enough, when I was in Suniti's room just now, I noticed something. Aja had told Tam that he and Suniti were going to visit friends but I saw her passport on top of her bag.

Hmmm. Wonder where they've been?

10.45 pm We decided to all stay in this evening so we could keep watch on Jeremy. Tam cooked lasagne as her flat meal contribution, but it wasn't too enjoyable as the kitchen has started to smell very unpleasant since Jeremy's lunchtime curry.

'As much as I love Jezzer,' Matt said, shovelling a generous forkful of lasagne into his mouth, 'I'm not sure I like it when he masturbates on our kitchen floor.' He pointed his fork to where Jeremy lay, contently giving his private area a clean.

'It's only natural,' I said, sticking up for the dog.

'You'd never let me do that in public.'

'That's debatable. I mean, you are a wanker in public.'

'Ah, the Josie Williams humour. By the way, Jos, how is Peter Probe?'

'What?'

'Zzzzrr zzzzrr zzzzrr.'

'Actually, Matt,' I said defiantly, refusing to be embarrassed by his constant vibrator references, 'I've been meaning to have a word with you. I put my underwear on the drying rack this morning and I've noticed a turquoise thong has gone missing. Would you like to own up?'

'The dog probably ate it,' he said with a shrug.

Just then, the kitchen door swung open and Jasmine minced in wearing a tight white pencil skirt and a pink halter-neck top.

'Hi, guys,' she trilled prettily. 'Thought I'd stop by as I, like, haven't seen you all in so long.' She sat herself opposite Ben and, crossing her long smooth legs, asked: 'So, what's new?'

Ben's got a girlfriend! I felt like shouting.

In a breath, Jasmine had leapt to her feet and was screeching, 'Oh, fuck me! What the fuck is that?' She was staring at Jeremy Beagle who had thoughtfully started licking her ankle. (Couldn't help chuckling, knowing where else he'd been licking!) 'Can you get this thing to stop!' She brushed at Jeremy's head and he flinched away.

'S'OK, easy,' I said, stroking a nervy Jeremy.

'Oh, good fuck,' she gasped in realisation. 'That's one of the animals from that break-in, isn't it?'

Tam looked at me uncomfortably.

'It's probably carrying loads of weird diseases or something. I bet this was your idea, Josie.'

Why me? Jasmine always singles me out . . .

'And you know if you're caught, you'll be kicked out of halls,' she told me, adjusting her tight white skirt that had conveniently ridden up her thighs.

'Listen, Jasmine,' Ben addressed her. 'We're just helping out a friend and Jeremy's not going to be here for long.'

'I understand,' Jasmine sang sweetly. 'Anyway,' she continued, 'I actually stopped by to ask if you fancied watching a DVD with me? In my room?' She fluttered her eyelashes and parted her lips slightly for his benefit.

SayNo.SayNo.SayNo.

'Thanks for the offer, but I was planning on getting an early night,' Ben said politely.

Yes!Yes!Yes!

'You big knob-head,' Matt scolded once Jasmine had left. 'You just got invited into Jasmine's bedroom to watch a DVD? Do you realise the importance of this?'

'I didn't fancy it,' shrugged Ben and then leant over to rub Jeremy on the tummy.

Whilst am ecstatic with this rejection of a bunny, I'm rational enough to know it stems from Ben's love of someone even more beautiful.

Friday 21 March

3.30 pm. The Mid-Victorian Novel. Things are getting even trickier with Jeremy. Everyone on campus is talking about the laboratory raid and Rupert called again this morning to say there's no update on a home. Think I'm going to have to try and sneak him out of halls tonight when I leave for Easter – but how will I get him home? Can dogs even go on trains? As soon as I finish the lecture, I better go back to the flat and ring Rail Enquiries.

4.30 pm I walked into our kitchen and froze. Warden-Brian was in the middle of the room. Tam was standing with her back against the window and Jeremy was lying nervously at her feet with his head between his paws.

My heart leapt into my mouth. Jeremy had been discovered! Oh, shit – and we were going to be suspended!

'How interesting,' Warden-Brian sneered through paper-thin lips. 'I was given a tip-off that you were hiding an animal in here.'

I looked at Tam and her eyes narrowed with anger: Aja!

Warden-Brian moved slowly around the kitchen, pausing to look at things. He tapped Jeremy's water bowl with his foot and then pulled up his trousers slightly so he could bend to check under our table for any other hidden animals.

'You probably heard that there was a laboratory break-in on Tuesday night,' he said slowly. 'I'd be interested to know how long you've had this dog for.'

What do we do? What do we do? Panic was flooding through me. Tam was twiddling her hair nervously and staring at me.

'Hello, darling!' Mum trilled, bursting into the kitchen in a grey tweed coat and fitted black trousers. 'Now, where's this dog, then?' Mum stopped short, having noticed Brian standing by our kitchen table and the dog at Tam's feet. Suddenly taking in the situation, she exclaimed, 'Ah, there you are my little darling!' She gracefully leant down to stroke Jeremy, whilst saying 'I'm sorry to leave the dog with you girls, but he was so desperately thirsty from the car journey.'

I looked at Mum in amazement. What is *she* doing here?

Tam took the bait first. 'No problem, Mrs Williams. Jeremy really needed that water.'

Warden-Brian looked at us all suspiciously and ran his freaky fingernail under his chin.

Noticing the warden's name badge, Mum chirped, 'Oh, you must be Brian! Josie's told me all about you.' She beamed at the bemused warden. 'It sounds like you're doing a wonderful job keeping the children safe.'

'Oh. Er, thank you,' he said, touching the top of his head and smoothing over the five strands. 'This is your dog?' he asked.

'Who, Jeremy? Yes. Isn't he wonderful?' Mum was moving towards Brian now. 'I bet you're an animal lover,' she purred.

'Well, I suppose I am,' he said bashfully. 'I don't have a dog . . . but . . . well, I do have two gerbils. Bathsheba and Gabriel.'

'How wonderful,' said Mum, clapping her hands together. 'They're so underestimated as pets; such lovely companions.' Then Mum turned to me and, putting a hand on my arm (I think to nudge me out of gawping), said, 'Now Josie, have you got your things ready? I really should be getting you and Jeremy home before rush hour.'

'Oh, right,' said Brian, looking vaguely disappointed. 'I suppose I should leave you to it.' As he walked out of the kitchen, he quietly said, 'Sorry about the misunderstanding,' and then flashed a last look at Mum before leaving.

'Mum . . . How did you . . . ?'

'Darling, I left you a message to say I was on my way up. How were you planning to get the dog back on your own?'

'But I didn't get any messages . . .'

'Oh, well, it was one of those texts. You know what I'm like. Anyway, the good news is my friend Mary is going to have Jeremy. She won't be home till Monday, so I said I'd collect him and could bring you back at the same time.'

'That's brilliant!' said Tam, looking very relieved. 'Thank you so much!'

'How did you even get into South Hall?' I asked.

'Oh, Hobbit was at the main entrance as I arrived,' Mum paused thoughfully, and then added: 'He's such a lovely boy.'

Oh dear!

'Right then, Josie, I think we best get going before Brian suspects anything. I'll take Jeremy down to the car.'

'Mm,' I nodded, still stunned by the whole situation.

And that was it. I packed my stuff for Easter, gave Tam a hug, and then was driven home with Mum nattering away about Hobbit, and Jeremy lying on our back seat, letting out chicken balti smells.

SEVENTEEN

Sunday 20 April

8 pm. Flat. I've been at home for the last four weeks for the Easter hols. Would have kept up-to-date with diary, except all interesting things ceased to happen as soon as I opened our front door. OK – that's a bit mean, but living on campus with thousands of students is a slight contrast to living with Mum. Actually, must not be horrible as she was the Jeremy Beagle rescuer and, thanks to her, he is now living a very contented life with Mary and her six-year-old Labrador.

It's been the usual routine back at uni: I unpacked, ate pasta and Dolmio while gassing with Tam, then we listened to Matt and Justin having a bitch fight that started about Sheree and ended with them slagging off each other's mothers. Ben's been typically elusive about his Easter hols, just saying he spent most of his time in London. I think we can imagine what he was doing up there. Hmm, and there was me hoping for a tragic break-up during Easter.

I think Suniti had flown home to Pakistan over Easter, because when I arrived back at halls, she was unpacking her suitcase. Don't think the trip can have been a success as she looked terrible: she is painfully thin and her face looks gaunt and tired. She was wearing the same long black skirt I usually see her in, but it was hanging off her hips and I noticed that her fingernails have been chewed raw.

Mum had packed me off to uni with a bundle of food, so I made Suniti a small sandwich as she doesn't have anything in yet, but she ate it in her bedroom and has been locked in the toilet for the past hour.

9.10 pm Oh, no! Think Suniti may have a problem. I've just been for a shower and as I was drying myself off, I noticed a white bottle that had rolled beneath the sink. Turning it round in my hand, I saw from the label that it was high-dose laxatives. Suniti's the only one who's been in the bathroom all evening. I put the bottle back where I found it and as I came out of the bathroom, Aja was standing in Suniti's doorway staring at me. I hurried along the corridor in my towel and went straight into Tam's room, but I could feel his eyes on me the whole way. I can't stand Aja – there's something about him that makes my skin crawl. And I definitely don't trust him since dobbing us in about Jeremy.

Tam and I've been discussing the laxatives and we think they're tied up with Suniti's weight loss. I know she could be taking them for, er, well, digestive reasons – but I don't think it's that. I've read articles that laxative abuse is a form of eating disorder, which would really make sense. Over the past couple of months Suniti's lost a lot of weight and seems more withdrawn than ever. Tam said eating disorders are about people trying to take control of their lives, so we wonder if it's Suniti's way of dealing with the stress of moving here from Karachi. I'm going to try and have a talk with her when Aja isn't around.

Tuesday 22 April

1.15 pm. Sex and Sensibility in *Clarissa*. Lecturer has told us we only have three more weeks of lectures and then a short revision period before exams start in June. Yikes – uni is whizzing by so quickly, and I'm not sure that I've learnt enough to answer exam questions. I must really concentrate in these final few lectures so that exams will be smooth and untaxing.

Oh, but now lecturer is discussing the theme of imprisonment in the second half of *Clarissa* and as I haven't read beyond page 50 (which is actually still the Preface), I think this is a good opportunity to write diary. (Obviously, will catch up with important *Clarissa* work at a later date.)

Managed to speak to Suniti this morning. I waited till Aja had left and then I nipped along to her room. For once, the door was open. Suniti was sat on her bed staring out of the window, so I knocked lightly on the wall to let her know I was there. Suniti jumped at the sound and spun round, her eyes full of panic. 'I . . . er, I'm a bit busy at the moment,' she told me.

I knew it was going to be awkward but this was important. 'Suniti, I'm worried about you,' I said, sitting myself next to her on the pale green duvet. Suniti's room is completely bare. The only signs of inhabitation are her medical textbooks neatly stacked on the shelves and one photo on her desk of her sisters. 'I've noticed that you've lost a bit of weight recently and I'm worred about you,' I said as gently as I could. Looking at Suniti, I realised what a gross understatement I was making. She was wearing a white top that clung to her to ribs and her bare arms looked frail.

'I'm fine,' she replied, looking at the floor. 'I've just been busy.'

'Did something happen over Easter when you went home? Are your family OK?'

'Yes, fine,' Suniti said defensively.

There was a long, awkward silence while I wondered how to approach the laxative issue. Then I blurted: 'I know what's been going on in the bathroom.'

Suniti's eyes remained on the ground but she instinctively brought her hands into her lap and started picking at her nails.

'It's OK,' I reassured her. 'A lot of people go through this sort of thing. But you need to be careful as it could be dangerous for your health.'

I noticed Suniti's chest rising and falling heavily and then her shoulders started to shake as she began sobbing. It was so horrible seeing her upset – the last thing I wanted to do was make her unhappier. 'How do you know?' she stammered through her tears.

'I found the laxatives.'

Suniti turned her damp face to mine and suddenly looked very young and frightened. 'You're not going to tell anyone, are you?' she pleaded. Her hands were grabbing at my arms urgently. 'Please don't,' she begged. 'Aja would kill me!'

That bloody bastard! I knew she was scared of him. 'Listen Suniti, Tam already knows about this, but I promise you it will go no further. We won't tell anyone what's going on, including Aja, but you have to promise me that you'll try and stop doing this.'

'I know, I know,' she repeated. 'I really want to.'

'How bad is it? Are you being sick as well?'

Suniti looked confused. 'No,' she replied, wiping away her tears with the back of her hand.

'Well, that's good. I really admire you, Suniti: you've left your family and moved to a foreign country to study for one of the toughest degrees – it's not surprising that you're having a hard time. But it's important that you take control of this.'

'I haven't got control,' she said desperately, pacing up and down her bedroom and nervously rubbing her mouth.

'You've got to be positive. Having an eating disorder is more common than you'd realise.'

Suniti stopped to look at me.

'OK, maybe it isn't quite at that stage yet,' I soothed, realising that hearing the words 'eating disorder' made it sound too real. 'But the thing is, if you carry on taking the laxatives, then it soon could be.'

Suniti moved away from me and stood by the window. 'I know,' she said quietly.

'You can talk to me whenever you need—'

'Thank you,' she interrupted, 'but I would like to get back to work now.'

Wednesday 23 April

6 pm Ow, ow, ow. Body aches all over from kickboxing last night. Am not sure a one-hour class a week is going to turn me into the Amazon martial artist I was hoping for. Best thing about kickboxing on a Tuesday is that it leaves the whole of Sports Wednesday free for shopping! I asked Suniti if she wanted to come shopping with me to try and bridge the awkwardness after our eating chat. She said she was going to be busy with work, and then added, 'Thank you for your concern yesterday, but I am fine and I'd appreciate it if you wouldn't worry about me in future.' Not sure my chat did as much good as I'd hoped, as I think by 'worry' she actually meant 'interfere'.

I'm not going to give up though. I looked up eating disorders on the web, and am positive that that's what the problem is. I've printed off some stuff that I think might help and I'm going to find out the number for our uni counsellor. It's just picking the right time to give the info to her.

Tam, not being busy with work or sport, came with me for a Wednesday-arvo shopping trip. Suppose it was a bit naughty seeing as it's my birthday in three days (yey!!) and perhaps I should have waited and spread the material joy. Had very pleasant surprise when got to cash machine in town. I asked to withdraw £100 and not only did the machine let me have it, it flicked up my current balance and I did not see the letters DR anywhere, which meant the final instalment of my student loan had just been paid in. Yey!

In celebration, I bought self some very, very cool boots. Think I might be getting carried away with whole martial arts image as they are pointy-toed, below the knee, cream with a three-inch heel: very kick-ass. Am really quite annoyed with Tam, though. We have an unwritten rule for luxury, non-essential item buying: other person is meant to reason with shopper and halt purchase; instead, she coaxed and encouraged: 'Jos, don't even worry about it: the LEA paid for them!'

6.10 pm Am suffering a small amount of post-shopping guilt. Because of this I've put boots back in box and will not look at them until the anniversary of my birth and then can receive them as a gift to self, ceasing all negative guilt.

Thursday 24 April
10.40 am I've given Suniti the stuff I printed on eating disorders. I tried to do it as casually as possible, so just knocked on her door and said, 'Suniti, I've got some info here that you might find useful. Just let me know if you want to chat about anything.'

Suniti smiled lightly and said thanks, but never looked up at me.

Friday 25 April
9 am It's the eve of birthday but am a bit disappointed that there are no cards or presents in my pigeonhole.

Ah, though, it's very possible that all friends and relatives are so organised that they are sending b'day cards today, first class. Yes, that must be it.

3.30 pm. The Mid-Victorian Novel. Am listening to lecturer blathering on about images of lips in *North and South*. Have actually read this book and do not think that when Gaskell described the odd pair of lips, she actually meant them to be 'a semiotic sign where society's anxieties are expressed or, more importantly, concealed'. I mean, really, it makes you wonder what the lecturers are smoking.

Actually, no it doesn't. It makes me wonder how much the lectures are costing me. I'm going to work this out:

6 lectures a week x 11 weeks in a semester = 66

66 lectures x 2 semesters = 132

Tuition fees are £3,000 a year, so £3,000 / 132 = £22.72 per lecture.

Ouch. It's lucky you pay up-front as would not feel very happy about giving the lecturer a twenty-pound note every time I leave class. Ooo, though – I'd only have to miss one week of lectures and would have saved up enough money for boots. The joy!

Saturday 26 April
8 am It's my birthday!!!!!!!!!!!!

8.05 am Post hasn't arrived. Why is no one up yet?

8.30 am I'll check my pigeonhole again.

8.33 am Have one card, two parcels and one letter from Mr Lloyds TSB who seems to have missed the concept of birthday post: you're meant to send cheques, not bills.

8.35 am Er, not too sure what to do. If I was at home, I'd make Mum sit round and watch as I opened each present very slowly. Slovenly flatmates won't be up for another couple of hours and not sure I can make them sit in circle and watch gift unveiling. Mr Tubs might enjoy it, though.

8.45 am The card is from Dad. He sent me another cheque and wrote, 'Josie, once again my present is rather impersonal I hope you know I think of you constantly and am very proud of the woman you are becoming. I will be back in the UK in July, so I hope we can spend some time together then. All my love, Dad.'

I held the card to me as I sat quietly in my room. I was pleased when I realised that for the first time since Mum and Dad's break up, I'm really looking forward to him coming home.

The first parcel was from Mum. Her present-buying skills have greatly improved since Christmas. I got a bottle of DKNY perfume, a lush Miss Sixty top, two CDs and a polka-dot thong. Rang home to say 'thanks' and then got a whole rendition of *'Happy Birthday to You'*, which I found a little embarrassing and expensive since was calling from mobile.

The second parcel was from Granny and am very thankful only Mr Tubs was here to see it: she sent me an electrolysis set. Do-it-yourself hair removal!

What is she trying to say? I'm a hairy gorilla child with moustache, beard and stray hairs sprouting from cheeks! Oh, God, had always thought Jolen was enough and told self that all girls with olive skin were a bit hairy. It is clear now that I'm more like these old women who have full-blown beards without realising! No one's told me before as they didn't want to crush fragile confidence, but on my nineteenth birthday, the Bearer of Doom thought it was time for the truth . . .

This is why I don't have a boyfriend. Possibly, then, Ben did quite like me and was enjoying that kiss – until my beard was exposed in firelight and he pulled away with stubble burn! Birthday is disaster. Entire birth was wrong.

8.50 am There is an electric needle poking out of my arm (tester area). It feels like a scolding current is pulsating through body. There is no way that any product containing electrocuting needles should ever, ever be given as a present. This is going straight into my 'Private' box. Anyway, have checked in mirror and am really not that hairy. Except for legs, but it has been a long winter.

8.55 am Am wearing pink top, my polka-dot thong and smelling of DKNY. Have ruined excitement of birthday newness by indulging in all presents at once. Have now hit a low. Am present addict. Need more.

9 am Ah! My boots! Yummy . . .

9.01 am Who knew they'd look so good with a polka-dot thong?

9.02 am Now there really is no more. Will wait in kitchen till flatmates are awake.

10 am Students are so lazy.

10.50 am Tam has finally gotten up (sloth). She dashed into kitchen, grabbed a piece of toast and said: 'Happy Birthday, sweetie. I've got to run now but I'll see you later to give you your present. Back soon.'

As she made her way to the door, I caught her arm: 'Wait!' I hissed hysterically, clutching her wrist. 'Do I have a beard?'

Tam laughed, gave me a birthday kiss on the cheek and declared, 'Nope. No beard.'

Phew.

10.58 am Can hear movement from boys' rooms . . .

6.40 pm Mmmm, having a lovely birthday! Was bit unsure when Matt and Ben insisted on taking me to the pub before I'd even had breakfast.

'Have you learnt nothing by the age of nineteen?' Matt said, tucking my arm beneath his and marching me down the stairway. 'Tell her, Ben.'

'The best time to go to the pub is opening time,' he smiled.

It turned out to be a decoy to get me out of our flat, as Tam and Justin were decorating the kitchen ready for a surprise lunchtime party! I almost fell over in shock when I returned from the pub and found our kitchen filled with people shouting 'Happy birthday!'

Was so sweet of flatmates to organise it. Justin had even got one of those photo cakes with a picture of me dressed in my slag outfit as the icing! Is so nice having a birthday and feeling special – particularly as you get lots of presents! On top of all of Tam's thoughtfulness she gave me a gorgeous cream skirt from Kookai that falls just below the knee and is a perfect slinky fit. Ben gave me a Frisbee, which was a very cute gift but think I preferred the birthday peck on the cheek I got with it. Matt's present was the pint he bought me at the pub and he added, 'You can come by my room if you want an "extra special" gift', which I don't.

I was most touched by Suniti. Although she didn't come to the party, she left a small bunch of tulips outside my room with a note that simply read, 'Happy Birthday, I hope you have a special day. Suniti.' It means a lot to know that she is thinking of me, even with everything else going on.

7.10 pm So excited! Have discovered cream skirt goes perfectly with boots!!! Knew they were a good investment. We're all going out to Icon tonight, which is a smart club in town where new boots and skirt will fit in very well. Am wearing them now with brown negligee top and hair all loose and wavy. Am looking very boho and tussled in a just-stepped-out-of-bed (yet-questioning-why-I'm-fully-dressed-in-bed) type way. Have slight niggle at back of mind that new boots may be the incyest wincyest bit uncomfy. Am sure it is all in head – a case of shopping guilt trickling out in other ways.

8.10 pm Ugh. Ben's not coming out. We were having some drinks in kitchen when his phone rang.

Grace.

As usual, Ben looked pleased to hear from her. He spoke quietly and looked up to check if anyone was listening so I pretended to get something from the fridge.

'I'll pick you up from the train station . . . It's fine . . . No, no I haven't got any plans . . . I'll see you soon.'

Ben walked over to me and said, 'I'm sorry, Josie, I don't think I'll be able to make it tonight – um, something's come up.'

The bugger! Ditching his flatmate on her birthday for a last-minute romp with his girlfriend. Hmmph.

He moved towards the door and then turned back, 'By the way, you look really beautiful.'

Whywhywhy does he make my stomach flutter??! Is so frustrating when I'm trying to be aloof and over him. Misery.

8.12 pm Right. Must snap out of negative frame of mind. I am an Amazon feminist who is not going to snivel because puffy, red eyes do not go with kick-ass diva boots . . .

Sunday 27 April
11.58 am Eugh!!!!!!! Have been standing in vomit!

Woke up and thought I was dying of alcohol poisoning. Stomach was no longer fluttering and felt more like it'd been dowsed liberally with acid. Staggered to bathroom, locked door, managed to take clothes off without moving head, and then stepped into shower. After a few moments realised feet were wet but had not turned shower on yet. I tilted head gently towards the ground – and then it recoiled in horror. My size four feet were stood in someone else's vomit!

Intense revoltingness has scarred me psychologically. Worse part was, I had to stay there while I turned on shower – my toes squelching in the sick. Was all very awful and experience hasn't helped feelings of dyingness or the three large blisters from new and hellishly painful boots.

Will climb into bed with Tam.

12.05 pm 'Three-in-a-bed rules in your house, eh?'

Oh my God! Pete – captain of the football team Pete – is in Tam's bed.

She looked as shocked to see him as I was. Quickly jumped out of accidental threesome and dashed back to my room. Am now sat on bed trying to rack brains as to what went on last night.

12.07 pm Think. Think. Think.

Oh!

My!

God!

I kissed Matt!

EIGHTEEN

Sunday 27 April (still)

12.10 pm Am horror-struck. I kissed Matt?

What was I thinking? Need water. And possibly also life transplant.

12.17 pm So many sleeping bodies in kitchen that reaching water source is impossible. Half the university football team are scattered across our floor.

What happened last night?

Think . . .

OK . . . well . . . we got a taxi to Icon. I may have gone straight to bar and bought self a very large birthday cocktail to help erase Ben-letting-me-down-on-my-birthday-in-prefer-ence-of-Grace negativity.

Remember being impressed when Gil and Hobbit arrived in proper shoes rather than trainers. They handed me a breakdancing DVD that I've seen in their kitchen (literally, it has a tea stain on the bottom right-hand corner). Ooo . . . and Gil kept telling me how pretty I looked, which I quite enjoyed until he mentioned having another go at that mistletoe kiss (eek!). Now, who else was there?

Ah, Sheree came! Was very pleased as know clubs aren't really her thing. Justin's face sparkled with happiness when she arrived so I insisted on buying their drinks and sitting them in corner together so they could have some 'alone time'. Have a feeling Justin was darting 'Be subtle' warning stares at me.

OK, is good so far. Definitely enjoyed doing plenty of dancing with Tam and also spent lot of time at bar with Matt and the football boys. Remember being bought several drinks, which was nice as was birthday girl after all.

Hmmph! That was it: the bunnies arrived! Was enjoying looking pretty in tussled outfit and having lots of birthday attention, but then both bunnies teetered in wearing designer shoes and low-cut tops. Before I could slur 'cleavage', football boys had gathered round them and were arguing about who'd buy their drinks.

Tam and I huffed off – in a dignified way, of course – and hung out at the downstairs bar. And guess who was bloody serving???

Pablo!!

Think I was a bit tipsy by then as seemed to think Pablo was my new best friend and I kept telling him how lovely it was to see him. Apparently he never went back to Spain and has moved in with someone over here. I'm pleased he looked happy and that things are back to normal between us (like Pablo working behind the bar and me getting free drinks from the bar!!).

Back upstairs I saw Justin and Sheree getting funky together on the dance floor. Loved watching them as Justin, who only comes up to Sheree's shoulder, was doing mad robot dancing and Sheree was happily twirling in her DMs. One minute they were both laughing together – and then the next, they were kissing! (proper, passionate, 'I-want-to-eat-you' kissing!) Think I might have done something childish like grabbed both their bums, as remember Justin trying to shoo me away without taking his lips off Sheree's.

Then what?

Oh . . . ahem, well, as occasionally happens when alcohol's involved, my internal switch flicked from happy to emotional. Must have been triggered by the ginger coupling, as all of a sudden I was telling Tam how much I loved her. Then I told her how much I loved Ben, but that, 'he loves Grace and is with her now but it's my birthday and I love him and he should be with me because I look tussled.'

Next thing I recall is being dragged to the bar by Matt, who'd lined up a row of shots for Tam and me.

Hmmm . . . after that everything is kind of blurry. Think I had a drunken mirage that Ben was there, and then scary flashback memories of leaning against the bar snogging Matt while lots of people cheered.

I've come over all nauseous again.

Don't even know how I got home except for a hazy memory of telling off my new boots for not walking in straight lines. And where did Tam go? Is dangerous really as could have fallen in ditch (although not too many ditches on way back to halls), but I could definitely have exposed myself in front of the night bus.

Feel awful about self.

Have acute bout of alcohol blues and feel weird about kissing Matt. Everyone else has a pleasant, fun evening and I end up pulling my flatmate – and not even the one I fancy! At least Tam can have a good laugh at me. Then I'll have to face Matt who'll be a smug knob-end about whole thing. Don't even know how we ended up kissing. Is all so wrong. Particularly as I've seen the way he eats . . .

12.30 pm Tam is behaving strangely. Maybe alcohol blues have got to her too? I heard Pete leave, so crept into her bedroom full of excitement that they'd got together. Think Tam must feel bad about letting him stay on the first night as she didn't want to talk about it. 'Don't tell anyone,' she warned me. 'It was a big mistake.'

Thought it would perk her up to hear about me-and-Matt kissing! Was expecting a belly laugh and then a mime of a vomiting action, but she just said, 'Are you trying to work your way through all our flatmates? I better warn Justin.' And then she rolled over and went back to sleep.

12.45 pm Oh, crap! Just thought that Grace must be here. Best make self look respectable as cannot lollop around flat looking like I'm decaying as it's not the ideal state for standing next to the most intimidatingly beautiful girl ever. Right, make-up and non-baggy clothes are required. And possibly also a sick bag?

2.30 pm I've met her. Grace was sat at the kitchen table reading the paper and wearing a floaty bohemian skirt, stylish worn cowboy boots and a white bandana. Damn, she's cool. And far more beautiful than her photo. She looked like a slender porcelain doll – that shops in Camden.

'Hi.' She smiled widely at me.

'Hi,' I replied, trying not to scrutinise her face for flaws as conditioned by *OK!*

'I'm Grace.'

'Ben said you were visiting.' I opened the fridge and poked around inside.

'Did he?' She sounded surprised. 'So he's told you about me?'

'Not exactly, but it was pretty obvious,' I said with a sullen voice. I'd hadn't planned to be rude, but for some reason every time I spoke, my voice sounded surly and I kept on doing these kind of shrugging gestures – a bit like when you're thirteen and your mum asks if you had a good day at school.

'I suppose it would be,' Grace said gently, 'what with Ben coming up to London so much.'

'Mm,' I shrugged again. Realising there was nothing in the fridge I wanted, I moved to my cupboard and pulled out a new loaf of bread.

'You're studying English Literature, aren't you?' Grace asked from the kitchen table. 'Yeah,' I replied brusquely. 'You?'

'I'm not a student,' laughed Grace. 'I'm a teacher!'

'A teacher? You're older than Ben?'

'Yes, by seven years.'

A cradle-snatcher!

'How long are you here for?' I probed coolly.

'I've got to get back to London tonight.'

Good. I dropped a piece of bread into the toaster and watched as it slowly crisped.

'Ben has been fantastic,' Grace confided.

I didn't want to hear what a fantastic boyfriend he was. I could imagine. I have imagined. I stared at the toaster, ignoring her.

A thick silence hung between us. I buttered my toast roughly and Grace nervously adjusted her bandana.

Then the kitchen door opened and Ben walked in. The flow of air reached my nose and I smelt the faint hint of Ben – warm soap and mint filling my senses. I was concentrating hard on not letting my stomach flutter or allowing my chest to twinge, still bitterly disappointed that he missed my birthday in preference of Grace.

He looked at Grace and then turned to me. 'Have you two met?' he asked, with a dark voice.

When I said nothing, Grace replied, 'Yes, we have.'

Standing behind me Ben asked leadingly, 'Good night, was it?'

I turned to face him and smiled tightly. 'Yes, it was a brilliant night. Shame you missed it,' I said pointedly, biting into my toast.

'Such a shame,' he replied coldly, filling up a water bottle.

I needed to get out of the kitchen. I was feeling like shit and seeing Grace with Ben only made it worse. I took my toast and left the room, not bothering to say bye to either of them.

Am now sat on my bed with Mr Tubs, feeling ashamed. I behaved like a brat. I suppose seeing Grace in the flesh heaved together all my feelings of hurt and I focused it on her. It's hardly Grace's fault I'm obsessed with her boyfriend.

Oh no, can hear Justin coming down corridor. Not sure I've got the energy to cope with someone else's happiness.

4 pm 'I need to talk to you urgently,' said Justin, shutting my door behind him and climbing on my bed. He was still in his pyjamas and tufts of ginger hair were protruding madly from the centre of his head. He took Mr Tubs from my knee and held him against his chest.

'Josie, I've got two bits of big news,' he told me seriously. 'The first: Sheree and I got together last night . . .'

'I know, you muppet, I saw you.'

'I haven't finished. We got together and it was amazing – the most perfect night and she's such a cool girl. But, I texted her an hour ago to say what a tidy time I had and I haven't heard back!'

I was waiting for him to expand on the big news – but that was it. Justin made me check the message for accidental subtext.

'It's fine. Sheree probably hasn't checked her phone yet.'

'Do you think she regrets it? She never replied to my Valentine's card, but then she did say she didn't realise it was from me. Should I send a recovery text? Maybe I should go round there? Do you think she hates me? Could you ring her?'

I sorted Justin out by confiscating his phone, pushing him off the bed and telling him to go and read three comics before coming to see me again.

'Wait though,' he said, stopping in my doorway. 'I haven't told you the second bit of news.'

Sighing, I slipped down into my bed and pulled the covers over my head. Muffled by the duvet, I asked, 'Did you spill tomato sauce on your Spider-Man T-shirt?'

'It's about Ben.'

In a nanosecond the covers were off and I was sat upright with ears pricked.

Justin perched on the bed again and put his freckly hands on mine. 'Josie, you know how you've been upset with Ben because he's been so secretive about going out with Grace?'

'Yes – because he ditched me, on my birthday to spend the night with Miss 'I'm-Beautiful-But-Natural-With-It',' I huffed sulkily. 'And worse still – I've just met her and I was really horrible,' I confessed. 'Am I bad person?'

'Oh, no!' exclaimed Justin, gripping my hands. 'What exactly did you say?'

'Nothing, really,' I said, nervously. 'I was just unfriendly and then shitty with Ben for not coming out to Icon.'

'But he did come. I know it was only for half an hour but at least he made the effort.'

'Oh, God, I really must have been in a bad way. Is that what the problem is? I was being a drunken knob in front of Ben? I didn't tell him to dump Grace, did I?'

'No, it's a bit worse than that. You see the second bit of news . . . Did my phone just beep?'

'What?'

'It did, didn't it? It must be Sheree.' Justin let go of my hands and was up looking for his phone.

'Tellme.Tellme.Tellme!' I ordered as Justin started rummaging around my room.

'Ah, ha!' Justin spotted his phone on the windowsill. 'Please be from Sheree, please be from Sheree.'

'Justin!' I bellowed. 'The news about Ben?'

'Oh, yeah,' he said distractedly, clicking through to his messages. 'It's that . . . here we are . . .'

'What's the news?' I yelled.

'One new message!' squealed Justin, ignoring me.

'Just tell me!'

'Oh yeah. The big news is: Grace is Ben's sister.'

'Nooooooo!' I cried. 'His sister?'

'Nooooooo!' Justin cried. 'It's from O2!!'

Grace is Ben's sister? Ben is Grace's brother? But it doesn't make sense. 'Give me that,' I snatched the mobile and pulled Justin on to the bed. 'Now listen to me,' I said, slightly hysterical, grabbing his face between my hands. 'I need you to tell me everything. Is it true? How did you find out? I need details, Justin. Details! And why the bloody hell did you tell me this huge news second?? I repeat, this is huge. Sheree not texting you back after one hour is not huge.'

'Because I knew you'd get like this,' Justin said righteously as he removed himself from my grasp. 'Once I mentioned Ben, I knew I wouldn't be able to get a word in, so I planned the order of the news so I could get your advice on Sheree. Now,' he said calmly adjusting himself to sit cross-legged, 'what do you want to know?'

'Everything!'

The details were not good. Ben had introduced Grace while Justin was having his breakfast. 'Josie, I was pretty gob-smacked as well. I almost choked on my Cheerios it was such a shock.'

I had to coax Justin along with the story as he was sidetracked by describing the free toy that came in the Cheerios packet.

'So then what?'

'Then I asked Grace what was wrong with her.'

'What? What do you mean??'

'I thought you'd met her? You know, the losing her hair thing.'

Oh, God! I just thought the bandana was a style statement. 'She's been ill?'

'Yeah, it's pretty bad, actually. She's got some type of cancer and has been having treatment since January.'

I held my head in my hands and sat there trying to make sense of it all. Ben had an older sister. Grace. Grace has cancer. Oh no, his mum! She died of cancer. Grace must be so scared. And Ben and his dad, too. 'I can't believe it,' I said weakly to Justin. 'I thought Ben only had a younger sister.'

'No, it's just him and Grace.'

'But what about when his little sister fainted at school?' I asked, desperate for Justin to have made a mistake.

'I think you got your wires crossed; that was Grace. She's a teacher, isn't she?'

I've messed up so badly. That's why Ben has been going up to London – to visit Grace. I've been horrible to Ben and to Grace and, shit, she's going through such a hard time.

Then Justin's mobile beeped again. He made a dash for it.

'One new message,' he read anxiously. 'It's from Sheree! Sugar, sugar, sugar! Shall I read it? I'm going to read it. OK, here we go. No, you read it.' He shoved the phone at me.

At that point, I couldn't have cared less what the text message said, but Justin was shouting, 'Read it! Read it!' so loudly that I had to make him stop.

'"I had a lovely time too. Do you fancy going for coffee tonite? Sheree."'

Justin squealed with joy and bounced around my room like a mad, Welsh, ginger jack-in-the-box. I got out of bed, opened my door and headed him in the direction of his room and he bounced away kissing his phone.

6.10 pm I went to find Grace to apologise for being so rude, but unfortunately she'd already left for the station. Instead, I found Ben in the kitchen picking over a plate of pasta with his fork.

'Ben,' I said eventually. 'I'm sorry for being rude to you and Grace earlier. I don't know what got into me.'

Ben nodded, and continued toying with his supper.

'Justin told me she's got cancer.'

Ben stared at his plate. 'Yeah. She's having treatment at the moment.'

'I'm so sorry. I had no idea. You should have said something, Ben. I'd have wanted to be there for you.'

Ben looked at me for a moment. 'Grace asked me to keep it quiet. She doesn't want anyone to know, because we're not sure how dad will handle things.'

'He doesn't know?' I asked incredulously.

'Not yet. I think he should be told, but it's Grace's decision. I'm sorry I couldn't tell you, but I don't think it'd be fair to Dad if other people knew when he didn't. I wasn't planning on mentioning it to anyone, except Grace wanted to get out of London for the weekend, and well, with her hair, Justin started asking questions.'

I pulled up a chair and sat next to Ben. 'Is Grace going to be OK?'

'It's a bit early to tell. They caught it in the earlier stages and she's responding well with her chemo, so the doctors think she should be OK. It's just a worry because . . .'

Ben trailed off. His eyes started glistening with tears and he turned his face away from me.

'. . . because of your mum,' I finished for him.

'Yeah,' he said blinking quickly. 'I . . . I just thought we were through all of this. And now Grace.'

'Is it the same type of cancer that your mum had?'

Ben shook his head. 'No, Grace has been diagnosed with non-Hodgkin lymphoma. It's only in the early stages, which is something. The last three months have been a bit surreal – it's like reliving it all again: the visits to hospital, the treatment options, all the tests and drugs.' Ben brought his hand to the back of his neck and massaged it. 'We know what we're dealing with this time round, but it doesn't make it any easier. In some ways it's worse because you know what's coming.'

'How's Grace handling it?'

'She's been amazing. Deciding to keep this from Dad was a huge decision – and I really respect her for making it.'

'So, who else knows?' I asked.

'A few of her London friends and her work obviously. Her boyfriend, James, has been brilliant. Luckily, he works from home so he's always around to look after her during her treatments.'

'What happens next?'

'She's got two more courses of chemo and hopefully that'll be all she needs.'

'If you need me to help with anything, I don't know, like, getting in shopping for you or picking up course notes when you're in London – just let me know.'

'Thanks, that's kind.'

As I was looking at him sat on an orange plastic chair, I got that urge again to just throw my arms around him – to be there for him. I've been messing around getting in petty moods thinking Ben had a girlfriend, when all the time he's been going through this. I needed to explain about the way I'd been acting. 'Ben,' I blurted, 'I want to tell you—'

Matt burst into the kitchen in his faded 'I LOVE LESBIANS' T-shirt, 'I need to talk to you, Josie.'

Ben slid his chair back and picked up his pasta dish. 'I'm just going anyway,' he told us quietly.

I watched Ben walk out, his shoulders slumped and his face heavy.

'Josie,' Matt addressed me, pulling up Ben's empty chair and resting his hands on the kitchen table. 'I don't know if you'll remember this, but we kissed last night.'

This was all I needed. Matt gloating about our drunken kiss. 'I do—'

'Before you say anything, let me apologise.'

Huh?

Matt was different. His face was tense and serious. 'I was being a complete cock and boasting to the football lads that I could pull anyone. Then a bet was laid. And then they picked you. I'm really sorry. I know you were wasted and I shouldn't have taken advantage of you.'

I couldn't believe it. Matt was being mature about this.

'I'd rather we didn't tell anyone about what happened – even our flatmates.' Matt looked deadly serious. 'Do you agree?'

'Mm,' I nodded, realising I'd already told Tam, but I'm sure she doesn't count.

As he sighed in relief, his face started to relax and return to the normal Matt. 'Listen Shorty, I'm about to cook a pizza. How about we go twos on it?'

'Sounds good,' I smiled.

As we were eating supper, Tam surfaced from her room and came to fetch a drink. There was an awkwardness in the air and I'm sure Tam was looking at us both strangely. Matt didn't seem to notice and started cracking up when he got a text message. 'It's from Pete,' he said and started reading it to us with a string of mozzarella hanging from his mouth.

'"What a night! Got beered up, had a shag and then got a blow-job off my ex on the way home. Can't complain! See you Wednesday for training. Pete."'

Tam slowly put down her glass. Her chin ever so slightly began to quiver and then she turned and left the kitchen.

'You idiot!' I shouted. 'Why did you read that?'

'What?'

'Tam was Pete's "shag"!'

As the realisation sunk in, Matt's face grew wild. 'Pete and Tam?'

'Yes.'

'Pete stayed here?'

'Yes. Listen—'

'That fucking cu—'

'Matt, don't tell anyone. Please, promise. Tam doesn't want anyone to know.'

Matt didn't answer. He was up on his feet, his face contorted with anger. He shoved his chair aside and stormed out of the kitchen. A few seconds later the door to the flat slammed behind him.

11.20 pm Poor Tam. She's mortified. 'I feel such an idiot. It was the end of the night and Pete hadn't got anywhere with the bunnies so he thought – *She'll be an easy lay*. And I was.' Tam stopped for a moment to wipe a tear that had trickled as far as her chin. 'Then he went round to his ex's house the morning after. I feel, used. And then you . . .' her voice faded away and she looked out the window.

'And then me?'

'And . . . nothing. That's it. Really.'

Tam said she wanted an early night, so I left and am now sat in my room wondering when everything got so complicated? I thought university was the one time in your life when you have no responsibilities and everything's meant to be easy and fun. Ben's having to deal with more than anyone should, and Suniti's struggling to keep on top of things with her eating. Even Matt and Tam are miserable. Nothing is simple anymore.

Oh, just heard the door slam. Matt's back – I should probably check he's OK.

11.30 pm Matt was sat at his desk, staring blankly at the wall.

'Where have you been?' I asked.

Matt rested his hands on the table in front of him and he hung his head as though he was tired of it all.

I noticed the knuckles on his right hand were pink and swollen.

'You've been in a fight.'

'Josie, don't start.'

'You went to see Pete, didn't you?'

'And?' Matt barked confrontationally.

'And – you punched him.'

Matt slammed his good fist against the table. 'If he's going to mess with Tamara then he's fucking lucky to only get a fist in his face.' His voice was shaking with anger. I've never seen Matt like that before. His jaw was clenched and he was breathing heavily.

'I take it you're off the football team?' I said eventually.

'Yeah,' Matt laughed darkly.

'You did that because of Tam?'

Matt just shrugged and looked away.

And I saw it. Right there in the way he shrugged and then lowered his eyes away from me. 'My God!' I exclaimed.

Matt's eyes flashed at me. 'What?' he said defensively.

'You're in love with Tam.'

He huffed dismissively as though I was way off the mark.

But I stared at his face – and it was all there. His eyes were glazed and kept blinking rapidly. 'You are,' I repeated. 'That's why you felt bad for kissing me, isn't it? And that's why you would punch Pete.'

Matt held my stare. Then very slowly he said, 'Don't make a big deal out of this. I don't want Tamara to know.'

NINETEEN

Monday 28 April

11.30 am. Feminism and Literature. Am finding it difficult to concentrate on the loveliness of Lecturer-Dylan because of massive secret burden I am now carrying: Matt is in love with Tamara. Can't believe I didn't work it out before. Everything makes so much sense now: the way Matt always listens to Tam, how he hated Spock and why he was weird about Rupert.

Oh, God! Maybe Tam feels the same? I'm sat next to her now. She's chewing the lid of a blue biro and gazing dippily into space. She did behave very strangely after I kissed Matt, and she hated Lu-Lu – but then, who wouldn't hate someone that makes animal noises at 3 am? (Actually, think Lu-Lu has dropped out, as haven't seen her in *Clarissa* lectures since the start of semester. You see, too much sex *is* bad for you.)

Talking of jiggery-pokery, Sheree is sat on row in front with a huge love bite on the side of her neck. (I'm guessing her coffee-date with Justin went well.) She keeps twiddling her hair and exposing the purple monstrosity, which is making me feel quite nauseous. Do not like to think of little, innocent Justin in *that* kind of way. Shudder. Am pleased they're happy together, though wish Sheree would stop turning round to whisper things like, 'Justin does the most incredible thing to my ear lobes.' Eek.

Back to The Secret: I'm worried by it. What if Matt and Tam are secretly lusting for each other without either of them realising it? I've a responsibility to make sure that doesn't happen! But on the other hand, I did say I wouldn't mention this to anyone . . . And then what if I tell Tam and she doesn't fancy Matt? And would she even fancy him? I mean – it's Matt!

Wednesday 30 April

11 am Tam and I have spent Sports Wednesday eating brownies and watching *Dirty Dancing*. I would have felt guilty about the laziness, except I did go kickboxing last night and now all my muscles are taut in a frightened 'please-don't-use-me' type way. Plus, I wanted to spend some 'alone time' with Tam so I could subtly figure out her feelings about Matt.

'Hypothetically speaking, would you ever go out with Matt?' I asked, and then stuffed a huge piece of chocolate brownie into my mouth to try and look casual.

Tam peeled her eyes away from Patrick Swayze and looked at me strangely. 'Why? Don't tell me *you* fancy him?'

'God, no!' I almost choked on a choc chip. 'We just haven't done hypotheticals in a while.'

'Right.'

'So?'

'So?'

'Would you ever go out with Matt, hypothetically speaking?'

'Josie, hypothetically speaking, I'd rather watch porn with my dad. Pass me another brownie, will you?'

Yep, I think that's cleared it up for me.

So now The Secret must definitely be kept a secret. It's so hard as would normally tell Tam everything. And I mean everything. Yesterday, I even told her about this hair I found growing on my shoulder: it was on its own, blonde and at least two inches long – I jest not. It was freaky.

'Is there any more news about Grace?' asked Tam, changing the subject.

'Yes, Ben was in London yesterday because Grace started her next course of chemo. Apparently the doctor said she's doing really well and this may be the last course of treatment she needs.'

'That'd be brilliant.'

'Yeah, Ben was really pleased and looked more relaxed than normal.'

Tam and I are going into town later as we want to buy a card for Grace. I'm also going to get her this book on positive-thinking as I read an article about how you can overcome illness through positively channelling your thoughts.

'So Josie,' said Tam, turning off *Dirty Dancing*. 'How do you feel now that Ben is single?'

It's weird because if I'd found out that Ben didn't have a girlfriend under different circumstances, I'd be jumping for joy. But the situation changes everything. 'I've been giving it a bit of thought and I figured that it is not the right time to be confessing my feelings to Ben.'

'You sure?' said Tam.

'Yes. He's got so much more important stuff on his mind – I think he just needs a friend right now. If in the future something's meant to happen, then it will.'

'Does that mean no more mistletoe plans or Spanish lovers to stay?'

'Definitely.' I took the last bite of my chocolate brownie. 'But that doesn't mean I can't dream about his body!'

'Of course!'

It's seems a bit funny talking to Tam about me secretly longing for Ben, when I know Matt is secretly longing for her. I felt sorry for him earlier as we saw him go off for a run rather than to his usual Wednesday football. Tam asked, 'How come you aren't playing in a match today?' and so Matt had to make something up about it being the end of the season and then left the flat looking really down. Ugh, the misery of unrequited love!

Thursday 1 May

6 pm Am feeling very panicked. Gil and Hobbit have been up to my room to borrow the breakdancing DVD they gave me for my birthday (I didn't really mind seeing as I don't have a DVD player and don't like breakdancing), and just as they were leaving, Hobbit asked, 'Where are you living in your second year?'

Haven't thought about this at all. When I said as much, Hobbit did a facial expression that I think was shock but it was difficult to tell behind all that hair.

'You haven't sorted anything?' chipped in Gil, who's now taken to wearing an orange headband over his dreads (it's from the girls' accessories section in H&M). 'You seriously better hurry. Most people I know got their places sorted weeks ago.'

What?? Between Beavis and Butthead they've managed to organise a pleasant house on Sunford Street – right by The Frog – and they've persuaded two other guys from their Marine Biology course to live with them.

Why has no one mentioned house-hunting to me? Oh, God, hope flatmates haven't arranged houses without me because I'm needy and neurotic and seem to be working my way through the boys in our flat?

6.30 pm Am calmer. Have spoken to Tam and everything is going to be OK. Good. Breathe. Felt a bit awkward bursting into Tam's room and asking whether she wanted to live with me again next year. It's sort of like asking someone out on a year-long date. I started rambling . . . breakdancing DVD . . . boys downstairs . . . organised already . . . bit panicky . . . hope not sorted . . . can be neurotic . . . snogged my flatmates . . .

'Josie,' interrupted Tam, who was sat on her bed painting her toenails, 'maybe you should lay off the coffee?'

'What? Oh, no! I was just wondering, well, hoping that you might want to live with me next year?' The end of that was mumbled into my jumper.

'Of course I'm going to be living with you! Who else were you planning on watching *Dirty Dancing* with?'

Yey!! Was sighing huge breaths of relief as had been imagining a dingy bedsit with flickering light bulb and Raymond Noodle suppers for one.

Ah, so all is good! Were both pleased we had each other to live with (although wonder whether I should get it in writing?). Anyway, then we had to work out who else we wanted to share with. I made myself comfy on Tam's bed whilst she did the finishing touches to her deep red toenails.

First of all we talked about Suniti. 'Look Jos,' said Tam, screwing the lid back onto the varnish. 'I don't want to sound mean, but I'm not sure that I want to live with Suniti again next year. I find her quite hard work; she never wants to get involved in flat life and she's not someone I could talk to if I had a problem.'

I understood what Tam was saying. Suniti does prefer to keep herself to herself and she isn't the liveliest of flatmates, but I worry about her. 'The thing is, I've never seen Suniti with any friends, and I'm worried she hasn't got anyone other than Aja.'

'That's true,' Tam agreed. 'She doesn't seem very happy within herself. Do you think she's put on any weight since your chat?'

'It's difficult to tell. I gave her that information I printed off, but I don't know if she's looked at it. Maybe you should try talking to her again?'

'It's really awkward. Last time she completely closed herself off. I think it's best letting her know we're here if she wants to talk about it. I'm not sure there's much else we can do yet.'

We talked about it some more and in the end, Tam agreed we should ask Suniti to live with us. We went to speak to her straightaway.

Knocking on her door, we found Suniti hunched over her desk studying a thick medical textbook. She looked like she hadn't slept in days and she was nervously drumming her left hand against the chair.

'Suniti, we just popped in to ask you about housing plans for next year.'

'Oh,' Suniti said, still focusing on her textbook.

'We wondered if you'd like to live with us again and rent a house together?' Tam ventured.

Suniti stopped drumming and turned to look at us. Her lips spread into a huge smile; 'I would really like that. Thank you so much for thinking of me!' Then, embarrassed by her enthusiasm, she quickly turned back to her book and continued studying.

I'm really pleased we asked Suniti. I'm not sure that she would have had anyone else to move in with, so at least it's one less thing for her to worry about. Back in Tam's room, I commandeered her nail varnish, made myself comfy on her bed and then started painting my toes to match.

'OK,' said Tam, putting both hands on her thighs. 'The boys. Do we want them to live with us too?'

'No. Yes. Yes. I don't know. What do you think?' I said with just a hint of indecision.

'Well, I'm not sure. It's been fun living with the boys. But then they can really piss me off.'

'Yeah,' I agreed, thinking of the jokes at our expense, the sexism, the mess, the noise and the general day-to-day torment of living with someone you fancy.

'But then,' Tam continued, 'would we have as much fun without them?'

'Probably not,' I mused, thinking of the nights out, the nights in and Ben.

We decided to draw up a list of pros and cons of having each of them as housemates:

Justin

Pros: tidy, good cook, enjoys hypotheticals, endearing comic-book fetish, also likes repeats of *The OC*

Cons: recent heavy petting with Sheree scares us, ability to pass out within three pints can be a burden, prone to self-absorbency and tantrums

Matt

Pros: very funny, good entertainment value, protective of flatmates in slightly Neanderthal way

Cons: can fart the *Eastenders* theme tune, untidy, unhygienic, offensive, probably STD carrier, will insist on getting the Adult Channel

(Mental note: also in love with flatmate)

Ben

Pros: his tilty smile, the smell of his neck, the way he . . . Oops, that was just my list! OK, official pros: considerate, feel safe having him round the house, good taste in music, very hygienic, mature, can control Matt

Cons: there is a strong likelihood that if he ever brings a girl back to his room, I will spontaneously combust with misery.

We studied the list in some detail and it didn't make things much clearer. Tam said, 'If we don't live with the boys, they could move in with other girls.'

Immediately we both started bristling.

'So that's that,' I confirmed.

8.30 pm The boys were eating supper in the kitchen when Tam broached the subject of living together.

'So have you got any house plans for next year?' she asked casually.

'Yeah,' said Matt, licking pizza sauce from the sleeve of his 'MANWHORE' jumper. 'We've sorted out an all-boys' house.'

My jaw dropped.

Tam's nostrils flared and she started twisting a finger round a blonde curl.

'Just joking, you pair of goons!' laughed Matt. 'I wanted to see how much you'd miss us.'

For someone who is in love with Tam, Matt really doesn't do a good job of self-promotion. 'What d'ya reckon, Benji?' he smirked. 'Shall we make the wenches' day and agree to live with them for yet another fun-filled year?'

'It'd be cruel not to.' Ben smiled at us both.

'Suniti's going to live with us again,' Tam informed everyone. 'So we need to start looking for a house for six.'

'You might want to make that five,' corrected Justin. He was grating fresh Parmesan over a pasta dish in a very pompous way. 'I've been thinking about moving in with Sheree and a couple of other people I've got a lot in common with.'

'Are they gay as well?' asked Matt.

'Yes, Matthew. I'm gay. My friends are gay. People who are polite are gay. Girls who don't fancy you are gay. And, of course, all people with ginger hair are gay.'

'I knew it!' cried Matt, throwing a triumphant fist into the air.

'I'm sure you can all appreciate my reasons for finding an alternative housing solution,' said Justin, as he put the Parmesan back in the fridge. Then he picked up his meal and retired to his bedroom.

9 pm Traitor!! Can't believe he's ditching us for Sheree. When I went to interrogate him, Justin said that he's grown as a person since he's been going out with Sheree and that he needs to be around people who 'understand' him more than we do! He's only been seeing her for five days! Hmmph! Right, well then, I am going to do some kickboxing practice in my room and I'll be imagining that it's Justin I'm pulverising!

Friday 2 May
5.30 pm Met Sheree for lunch in between lectures and she's just signed for a house with some girl friends from English. No Justin, then! Hah! Apparently they had a 'disagreement'

last night about comics. She told him, 'Some comics can perpetuate harmful stereotypes. The majority of super-heroes are men, and the few female leads often deploy male qualities to make them heroines – else they play the part of the damsel in distress.'

I don't think Justin took it too well.

9.45 pm 'Nnnmmmmggh!' wailed Justin, lying face down on my bed. Once he realised I was ignoring him, he sat up again and wrapped my duvet around him. 'I tried rationalising with Sheree. I told her, "Comic books are revolutionary. What about *Powergirl*?" But Sheree said, "*Powergirl* is a stereotype of radical feminism." If that's what she thinks, then I'll let her wallow in her own ignorance!'

'Mm.'

'It's ridiculous, though. I mean, has she not read *Wonder Woman* or *Tank Girl*? They are cultural icons. You just can't argue against them! They are . . . they are . . . glorious!'

'Uh huh.'

'It was really horrible, Josie. Our argument got so heated that we agreed, for the sake of our relationship, never to discuss comics again. Can you imagine? I can never talk about comics with Sheree. I think I'm traumatised.'

'Mm.'

'Well, anyway,' said Justin, breathing in heavily and folding his arms over the duvet. 'I've considered it and I think I will live with you again next year.'

Hmmm.

10.30 pm Housing plans have changed again. Suniti has just been into my room to tell me she won't be living with us. I heard a feeble knock and opened my bedroom door to find Suniti stood in the corridor with glassy, damp eyes. She quickly explained, 'I am very sorry but I have changed my mind about living with you all. I have already made other arrangements.' When I tried to ask her about it, she immediately stiffened and said she had work to do. And then she sped back to her room where I saw Aja waiting in the doorway.

I sat for a moment thinking about what had happened. It's clear that Aja affected Suniti's change of heart. But why? I wondered again if he might not like her hanging out with Westerners, but it's not as if she sees any Muslim friends either. He's bullying her for some reason and I need to find out why.

I walked along the corridor and banged loudly on Suniti's door.

Aja opened it with an arrogant smirk pasted across his face, but remained stood in my way.

Looking past him, I spoke to Suniti: 'Can I have a word?'

Her eyes were filled with panic and she whispered, 'Not now.'

'Don't be rude,' Aja said sarcastically. 'You can talk in front of me.' He took a step back allowing me into the room, and then closed the door sharply behind me.

Suniti's room smelt of stale smoke. There was a scruffy pack of Rizzlas thrown on her desk and Suniti stood awkwardly with her back to the window.

'Is everything OK?' I asked her directly. 'Why have you changed your mind about living with us?'

'I am sorry,' she said quietly, not answering the question.

Aja moved over to Suniti's bed and lazily stretched himself across it, resting his hands behind his head.

'Who are you going to live with?' I asked, not prepared to let it drop.

Suniti said nothing.

'She's going to be living with me,' Aja delighted in telling me.

'Why, Suniti?'

'It's got nothing to do with you,' Aja spat.

'Yes, it has. It's important to me that Suniti is happy.'

Aja laughed codly. 'Suniti, will you be happy living with me?'

She nodded quickly without looking at either of us.

Aja smiled satisfied. Then he pointed to the door and waved, 'Bye bye.'

Saturday 3 May

2 pm I was actually shaking with anger after my confrontation with Aja! I can see why Suniti hasn't been getting involved in flat life with Aja watching over her. He is a real bully; I don't know where he gets off loitering around our flat and being so rude. I went to see Suniti this morning to check she was OK, but she didn't invite me into her room and stood in the corridor to tell me, 'I will be living with Aja, so please leave us alone.'

It hasn't been a great morning all round. Tam and I had to sacrifice our Saturday morning routine (watching cartoons with tea and toast) to visit the University Accommodation Office. A nice third-year girl who wore her hair in bunches gave us some advice on renting in our second year. She started by telling us to look at the university housing list as all the properties are approved and meet certain safety standards. It all sounded very good until she rooted out the list and found that every last one of the 564 houses had already been rented for next year. Bugger.

After a massive bout of panic, Tam and I were eventually soothed when the third-year explained about letting agents. Apparently they have hundreds of student properties on their books and she's organised an appointment for us on Monday morning. Then we were sent home with an armful of leaflets about renting student houses.

Tam and I have been very proactive and after reading through the housing bumph, we've made a list of all the things we think are important when choosing a house.

'OK,' Tam said, addressing Matt, Ben and Justin, whom we'd called into the kitchen for a House Meeting. 'These are the things we need to be asking ourselves when we look for a house. Is it in a good neighbourhood with bright street lighting? Are there any signs of damp? Is it near public transport? Is the heating system efficient? Does it have internet access? Does the landlord have a current Corgi gas certificate?'

Not sure we were on quite the same wavelength as the boys; Ben was interested to know whether there would be a shed to store his surfboards in; Justin wants a double bed; and Matt said, 'I couldn't give a shit as long as we're near a pub'. Hmmm.

Monday 5 May

5 pm Peroxide-Pam is our new letting agent. She is about forty-five, has bottle-blonde hair, two gold hoops in each ear and wears hot pink lipstick that bleeds into her lip creases.

She asked us questions about what we wanted from a house – location, size, amenities, décor – and then, noting all this down, she grabbed a few sets of keys and took us to see houses that were the complete opposite. Admittedly, we did agree that we wanted to live in a student area, but we didn't realise this would involve being taken into the backstreets of town where every fifth pebbledashed terrace house has a disused fridge in its front garden.

Each house we viewed achieved 'not-in-my-lifetime' status. They bred rats, ran on gas only, or were opposite a kebab shop so you can watch from your bedroom window as a skewered pig spins sadly on a metal roasting pole. Ben was trying to keep up morale by suggesting things like 'a lick of paint' or 'a bright throw', (I thought it was sweet that he tried to buoy up our spirits when he's got bigger things on his mind) but even he knew we'd missed the housing boat: we were left with the accommodation dregs.

At least we're now wise to the letting agent's jargon and have managed to create a dictionary of accommodation terms:

Recently renovated – the landlord put a partition in the lounge and called it a fifth bedroom

Two bathrooms – one of them is outside

Perfect for students – replace 'students' with 'filthy, blind people with no sense of smell'

Front garden – concrete slab piled with bin-bags

Fully furnished – four walls, a ceiling and a table

Quiet neighbourhood – all the shops are boarded up

Lively neighbourhood – you live in between Billy Bahji takeaway and a salubrious massage parlour with blacked-out windows

Pets welcome – house comes supplied with free-range rats.

The final house we saw was the best of the day, except for two things: (1) it was a thirty-minute walk from the SU, which translates to a ninety-minute stumble after a night out, and (2), the fifth bedroom was in the basement with no windows. It was very Stephen King and we all grimaced when we saw it, bar Matt. 'That's perfect. A little gimp room for our gimp. Geri, you'll love it.'

'Fuck you,' scowled Justin, who is still in a sulk about the comic argument.

'Baby, I wouldn't let you kiss my ass, let alone have your wicked way with me.'

And so the day ended.

Tuesday 6 May

1.10 pm. Sex and Sensibility in *Clarissa*. Judging by the new love-bite on Sheree's neck, I think her and Justin have sucked-and-made-up. I'm glad they're both happy, but I am struggling to find joy in their relationship as am consumed by fear that we might actually be homeless next year. There's only a week-and-a-half left of lectures before the revision period – and none of us want to be house-hunting during exams. Ben and Justin had clear timetables this morning, so they've gone looking at other places. Am not holding out much hope since everyone I speak to has already signed for a place next year. Why are we the last? Why?

4 pm Oh, dear. The best place they saw was a five-bedroom terrace house, where the sixty-five-year-old landlord insists on living with you.

Wednesday 7 May

5 pm We all dropped Sports Wednesday for house-hunting. (OK, Tam and I dropped watching *Dirty Dancing*, but the boys would have been doing exercise.) Peroxide-Pam took us to her usual array of filth-holes but just when we were giving up the will to live, we found an almost bearable place on Sunford Street. It's not exactly a home-away-from-home, but there's a pub at the end of the road, it has a shed in the garden and three of the rooms have double beds. The boys were happy.

Tam and I weren't quite so keen on the murky décor; the paint is peeling off the walls, there are brown tiles in the bathroom and all the carpets are a sludgy grey colour. Still, location-wise, it's in a good spot too – we're only a few doors down from Hobbit and Gil and fairly near the SU, so we've decided, we're going to rent it!

Thursday 8 May

6 pm Had to miss Charlotte Brontë lecture to traipse down to the letting agents so we could sign for our house. We stood in front of Peroxide-Pam's MFI desk, ready to hand over our money: we had to pay £210 for the first month's rent in advance, another £210 for the deposit (in case we damage anything) and then £30 for the 'drawing up' fee (apparently it costs that much to print five copies of the 'Assured shorthold contract' and then add our names, hmmm). Anyway, Matt, being the complete wank-head that he is, forgot he'd paid for some Playstation2 games with the rest of his loan. His debit card wouldn't go through. Then his credit card wouldn't go through. And then his other credit card wouldn't go through. We now have to go back again tomorrow once his parents have deposited more money into his account. Hmmph.

Friday 9 May
4 pm Have virtually missed a whole week of lectures just to sort out our house, but we have finally done it! We are now legally contracted to rent 'no.64 Sunford Street'! Is very grown up renting property. And if three people dropped out, it would almost be like Ben and I had our own place. Not that I've been thinking about that at all.

Saturday 10 May
8 pm Oh dear. House relations are already dodgy. We've been trying to work out who's going to have which room in the new place. It's a contentious subject because the two downstairs rooms only have single beds, whereas all the upstairs are doubles. The real point of debate is bedroom 5 upstairs. It's en-suite, looks over the garden and has a king-sized bed. Tam and I thought we were quite clever by suggesting that girls should automatically have an upstairs room because of safety issues. When Justin asked us to specify these 'issues', it was a struggle to convince him that baddies would be less likely to attack the house if there are boys downstairs.

There was a good hour of bickering, right the way through *X-Factor*, which was annoying. Ben, of course, was being a gentleman and said if we feel more comfortable upstairs then he's cool with it. Matt wasn't exactly making allowances for Tam, although he did offer to take a downstairs room – but only if we agreed to naked Fridays. Hmmm.

We were going to pick names out of a hat to help us decide until Gil trundled into the kitchen with a different idea. 'For a huge decision like room-choice, it can't be left to chance. You need to do something competitive that involves skill, endurance and concentration – and a very bendy back.' (Uh-oh.) 'You can play Twister!'

8.30 pm Am limbering up in my room. After my rubbishness at limbo, I'm unconvinced that playing Twister is the right way to go about this . . .

10 pm We pushed the kitchen table back against the wall and stacked the orange chairs on top of it to make room for Gil's Twister mat. The five of us waited nervously by the window, while Gil and Hobbit – our independent adjudicators – smoothed out the mat and positioned the Twister board on the work surface. I was wearing jeans, no shoes and a tight white T-shirt top that would allow for stretchy positions without exposing stomach/boobs etc. Justin, being a complete fool, kept his socks on.

I felt bad when Suniti came into the kitchen to get a glass of water; we were all bouncing around, excited about Twister and the new house, and I wondered if she felt left out. I wanted to check she was OK, but Gil wouldn't let me leave as he was announcing the rules. 'This is gonna be pretty full-on. It's sudden death. The first person to fall will have the last choice of rooms. Then the second person to fall will have the second to last choice of rooms. You can see where this is going. But I'm gonna be strict – only hands and feet are allowed to touch the mat, otherwise I'll disqualify you. Let the twisting commence!'

Hobbit muttered something to Gil.

'Oh, yeah,' Gil added. 'The judges' decision – that's me and Hobbit – is final.'

Hobbit took over. 'Ben, dude, you're on first.' Hobbit reached for the Twister board and started spinning. 'OK, we have Right Foot Green . . . ' and we were off.

Once all five of us were on the mat, personal space barriers had to disappear. I was in a compromising position with Tam (her low-cut vest top would have made a lesser friend blush). Matt was struggling to concentrate, as out of the corner of his left eye he was assessing the girl-on-girl, but from his right he could see Justin's arse, which was centimetres from his face. He was desperate to move nearer to Tam, but the next spin meant his face would be pressed up against Justin's behind. Matt couldn't handle the proximity: he fell.

In a strop about being the first contender out, Matt made a desperate plea, 'Guys, I'm sure we can sort out rooms without playing such an immature game. How about we organise it via size; Justin, of course, you get the small room by the lounge. I'm going to have the big room as I need a king-sized bed for obvious reasons—'

'To fit your giant ego in,' suggested Tam from the Twister mat.

'Tamara, when I'm looking down your top, I really don't think you're in the best position to be making jokes.'

Justin was the next to fall because his socked-feet skidded on the way to reach Right Foot Blue.

'That's so unfair,' sulked Justin. 'I'm the only one in a relationship so I should get a double bed.'

'Geri, don't worry about it,' said Matt. 'Sheree will soon discover that you've got no genitals and then you'll be single, too.'

From what I could hear, there was tussle to the side of the mat, but all I could focus on was Ben. He was stretched virtually the full length of the Twister mat in a press-up type stance. And yes, I could see his biceps tensed and, yes, it was very distracting. I was trying to clear mind of these self-indulgent thoughts as I'm not meant to be fancying Ben. The next move put Tam in a crab position over Ben's left leg, and I was twisted into a complicated knot of limbs with her. It was very Kama Sutra. The judges insisted coming in closer to 'inspect'; they had to be sure that our hands and feet were in the correct positions, of course. Tam got the giggles and it probably wasn't helping that I was doing come-to-bed eyes. Her arms eventually gave way and she collapsed on to the mat. Leaving Ben and me.

On Ben's next move he had to turn his body to face upwards while balancing on one hand. He managed it with a feat of sheer muscle power and he came to rest directly below me. I was given Left Hand Green, which meant my arms had to be splayed wider, lowering my body down towards Ben's . . . mmmm. My arms started to tremble and heart was drilling at my chest. I was poised an inch above Ben with our faces virtually touching.

There was silence from the spectators and Ben's eyes were fixed on mine. I could smell the soapy warmth of his neck and my stomach began to flutter madly. I kept repeating instructions to my body: heart – do not beat so loudly; pupils – no dilating; saliva gland – please don't dribble.

'Ben: Right Foot Yellow,' instructed Gil, with a sullen-ness to his voice.

Ben had to move his leg further into the centre of the mat, lifting his waist closer to mine. Um. It was rather pleasant and am sure I'd have enjoyed the moment intensely had five other people not been watching. There was something so delicious about Ben being beneath me, looking up into my face, with our waists touching.

Matt wolf whistled loudly, which distracted my attention, allowing the force of lust to get the better of me. I simply went weak at the knees. Only problem was, as my legs and arms weakened, my body collapsed on to Ben's and the two of us tumbled to the floor with me lying rather intimately on top of him.

I quickly jumped up and brushed self off as it looked a bit like I'd manoeuvred him to the ground and was about to consummate my girl-on-top position. 'Sorry,' I mumbled awkwardly.

Hobbit grabbed Ben's arm and thrust it into the air. 'We declare you King of the Twister mat! Please, go ahead and announce your choice of rooms.'

Ben stood up and looked round for a moment. 'Er, didn't Josie win? I touched the mat first.'

'Oh . . . um, I dunno, man,' fumbled Hobbit.

'Re-match!' bellowed Matt.

'No way,' said Gil firmly. 'Josie fell first, and she brought Ben to the ground. You're not allowed bodily contact with other players, so Ben's the winner and Josie gets second place.'

'If you're sure?' said Ben, checking no one minded.

'Go on then. Pick your room,' said Matt.

'OK, well then, I think I'll go for the middle bedroom upstairs.'

'Mate, that's not the en-suite,' said Matt.

'I know.'

'You don't want the en-suite?' Matt asked in disbelief.

And Ben said (swoon): 'I'm not too worried about having it. I'm happy with one of the others.'

He knew I had next pick and that I'd love the en-suite . . . he did that for me! Omigod!Omigod!Omigod!

'You complete dick!' snorted Matt. 'Now Josie'll get it. You could have deferred it to me.'

'I think it's safest this way,' said Ben casually. 'Imagine what it'd be like having your own bathroom with Jos around. She could burst in at any time or mistake you for a dead body when you're showering. I'm doing this for the good of the flat.'

And that just made it sweeter. Mmmm . . .

Am light-headed with happiness! Will luxuriate in Twister daydreams forever. Ben is wonderful and I have an en-suite!! Yey!

TWENTY

Sunday 11 May

11.30 am. Launderette. Am watching my whites circle in the campus launderette. It smells like cabbage in here and there's a lone leaflet pinned to the door about joining the Tolkien Society. I saw Suniti heading down here with her washing, so decided to do mine at the same time to try and get things back on track between us after the Aja run-in. Think this forty-minute wash-cycle is the longest we've spent in the same room. We haven't done much bonding though; I tried to chat about various things – families, our courses, what we're up to over summer – but I got a few muted replies and now she's reading her textbook.

Think the whirr of the washing machines has mesmerised my mind as keep replaying Twister scenes, pausing on visuals of me hovering over Ben. We had a nice chat late last night and Ben is looking a lot more positive recently. He said Grace's chemo is going well and she hasn't had such bad side effects this time round. I'm pleased he feels he can come and talk to me about things. Have to admit, I am finding it tricky to think of him purely on friends level, and after he left I fell asleep and had a very yummy dream which was set in my new en-suite room and featured Ben, me and some very intimate twisting.

2 pm. Flat. Hmmm. All my washing has been hanging on the drying rack in our corridor. When I went to fold it away, I noticed an empty space where my polka dot thong should have been – and Matt had just been kicking a ball around in the corridor! I haven't forgotten the turquoise thong that

316

went missing when Jeremy was here! Now I've bloody gone and signed a contract to live with him for another year! I bet he's selling student thongs on e-Bay or something sick . . .

2.15 pm Matt was sat on his bed with Ben, the two of them gripped in a computer game.

'Have you stolen my polka dot thong?' I interrupted.

'What?' he grunted, eyebrows dipping together.

'That's the second one that's gone missing recently and you're the obvious suspect.'

Matt paused the game and the two of them turned to face me. 'Why me, Poirot?'

'"*Sex Machine*" . . . shimmy shimmy . . . you wearing Tam's black thong?'

'Oh, that was a joke. It might come as a surprise,' he continued, 'because I know you're into some kinky shit, but I really don't have a thing for women's underwear. Unless it's on my bedroom floor, of course,' he added with a smirk.

'I think we need to get to the bottom of this – if you'll excuse the pun,' said Ben. 'Are you sure they are both missing, presumed stolen?'

'Yes. Well. No. Today's definitely went missing and then when Jeremy Beagle was here, I'm pretty sure someone stole a turquoise one.'

'I see,' mused Ben, stroking his chin in a detective gesture.

He was being cute with me! First, giving me the en-suite and now flirting? Ooo! 'And,' I said, keeping up the conversational momentum as I was enjoying seeing him being so chirpy, 'today when I was on my way back from doing the laundry, I had the feeling that someone was watching me.' (I kind of did, actually, but I was hoping it was a passing boy thinking, 'Oh, she's pretty.')

'Right, Miss Williams, I think I've found the problem,' announced Ben. 'You have a stalker!'

I got the impression that Ben wasn't taking my missing thongs very seriously. But he was flirting with me, so I can forgive the rest. 'And what expertise leads you to deduce such a thing, Detective Adams?'

'I've recently finished a psychology paper on the personality profile of stalkers. This has all the trademarks.'

'I see,' I replied wistfully, imagining Ben ploughing intelligently through his psychology textbooks. 'And what sort of personality profile should I watch out for?'

'It's a good question. They are usually loners, people who can't form strong emotional relationships, and most of the time, it's someone you know.'

'So like I said – it's Matt.'

Matt raised his eyebrows at me in an 'I-know-you're-flirting-with-Ben' kind of way, so I gave him a pursed-lipped smirk that read 'You-better-not-say-anything-as-I-know-you're-in-love-with-Tam'. And then we both smiled at each other half pleasantly.

Ooo . . . would be fun if Ben was the thong-thieving stalker!

3 pm Bloody hell! I think Aja might be the thong-thief! (I have no evidence, apart from Tam agreeing with me.) I didn't realise that he's been in the flat since lunchtime, giving him full access to my drying rack! Tam said she saw him lingering around in the corridor looking shifty, and then when I passed him on the way to the bathroom, he was stood in Suniti's doorway and stared at me with a long and insidious

318

look. Now that I think about it, Aja was in the flat when my turquoise thong went missing!

Oh, God, so what if I have creepy Aja thinking perverted thoughts about me? Is hideous idea – and why *my* thongs? Maybe it was that overfriendly hug I gave him on my first day? No, I think it's part of his weird power games. Yikes, this is starting to freak me out . . .

Monday 12 May
11.30 am. Feminism and Literature. Am trying to push aside thong-thieving suspicions and focus on work as it's my final week of lectures. After this, we've got a three-week revision period – and then exams start! I'll be sad to finish Dylan's class. Has been good learning about feminism, and although I haven't exactly changed the world with my new knowledge (or even Matt's approach to washing-up), it's more about how you behave as a person. Yes, definitely.

4 pm I know this might seem psychosomatic because I was talking about stalkers yesterday, but I swear that Aja actually is stalking me! After Feminism lecture I nipped into town to buy a new tub of Jolen. (Am not too sure if a true feminist would worry about trivial issues like bleaching, but since Granny's electrolysis present, I've become a bit paranoid and started bleaching my arm hair, too.) As I was walking alongside the park, I had a strong feeling that someone was watching me. I quickened my pace, but all the time could feel someone's gaze on me, following every step I made. I stopped and looked round sharply. And there he was: Aja was stood about fifty feet away. He was wearing a dark hoodie that was pulled over his black hair, shading his face. He had his hands in his pockets and his eyes were fixed square on me. He looked surprised when he realised he'd been spotted and, pulling the hoodie further over his face, he fled across the park and disappeared behind a clump of trees.

So he's was following me! And he probably has my thongs. And . . . Oh, God, I really do have a stalker now!

6 pm Told Tam about seeing Aja in the park. She thinks he's probably trying to scare me so I don't get involved in Suniti's business again. Problem is, I can't do anything about Aja as I don't have any proof other than a couple of missing thongs and him hiding from me in the park. It does make me feel nervous though, as Aja is such a weirdo and I don't know what he's capable of. Tam suggested I buy a personal alarm – 'just in case'. Think the SU sell them really cheaply so am going to pick one up tomorrow after Brontë lecture. Am also going to make a real effort to focus in kickboxing class tomorrow, as then can protect self if necessary. Watch out, Aja! I am a nineteen-year-old stalked kickboxer who will be alarmed and dangerous. Yes! Good.

Tuesday 13 May
7 pm No further stalking incidents to report – yet. Did a thong count and currently no more have gone missing.

Thursday 15 May
4 am. In Tam's bed. Oh, God! Aja was in my room! Staring at me whilst sleeping. All stalking fears are horrifically coming true . . . Could have been murdered in middle of night . . . Nowhere is safe!

All the boys went off to Wednesday night Sports Social; I didn't feel in the mood since the most sporting thing I'd done all day was run from the kitchen into Tam's room to tell her that the *Neighbours* theme tune has changed. I knew Aja was in the flat with Suniti, but I tried to put stalking fears out of head and get an early night. It must have been around 3 am when the sound of my bedroom door creaking woke me.

Had this anxious sixth sense that there was somebody else in my room. Was trying to get a handle on over-active imagination, so tried to think rationally about who would possibly be in my room in the middle of the night. Then entire repertoire of horror movies sprang to mind: it could be the Scream mask, or Freddy Krueger, or Chucky . . .

Hot, panicky tingles began darting around body and heart was beating rapidly. I tightened my grip on Mr Tubs and kept eyes firmly closed (as obviously that makes me invisible).

I thought I could smell a faint tinge of cigarette smoke. And then I heard somebody breathing. It was the deep, heavy breathing of a man.

Adrenalin took over and forced eyes open.

Stood beside my bed was a large, dark figure – watching me sleep.

'Aaaaggghhh!' I screamed. The intruder stumbled backwards into my desk, and then ran from my room and out of the flat, thundering down the stairs.

Within moments, Tam was in my room waving a pair of GHDs threateningly ('It was the only heavy thing I could find'). My lungs were on fire and I could hardly speak with shock and kept pointing at bedroom door saying, 'Stalker'!

'Was it Aja?' asked Tam, turning circles in my room.

'Yes! Well, I don't know,' I told her breathlessly. 'I couldn't see very clearly, but I'm sure it was!'

Am sleeping in Tam's room now and we've locked her door from the inside. Why was he in my room? Was so scary waking up to see someone watching me. Am also upset that kickboxing lessons have not been best investment. In retrospect, don't think shutting eyes and screaming is quite as successful as leaping out of bed and kicking groins, jabbing throats and punching eyes. Hmmm . . .

11 am This morning I told the boys what happened. Matt just said, 'You probably dreamt it, freak-girl'; Justin thought it was petrifying and is sleeping with his door locked from now on, and Ben was the only one who seemed genuinely concerned. He made us call Warden-Brian to report the intruder and said he's going to sleep with his door ajar so he can hear if anything is going on. (Is it possible for him to be any lovelier??)

Warden-Brian was here fifteen minutes ago and I explained about the intruder and said I had suspicions that it is Aja. As expected, the warden proved completely useless and spent more time asking about Mum than working out how to help me. He asked questions like, 'Had you been drinking?' and then, rather than tracking down Aja (who, unsurprisingly, was nowhere to be seen this morning), he ended up telling *me* off for keeping the entrance door propped open with the fire extinguisher! OK, so it means other people can come in and out, but at least it saves us having to get out of bed when people forget their keys. Anyway, I'd rather the door be open than be locked in the flat with stalker-boy Aja.

All that's happening is Warden-Brian's going to have a word with Suniti because Aja hasn't been signed-in as a visitor. Great, so now Suniti will get in trouble and rather than banning Aja for coming here again, Brian's going to make it OK by signing him in!

Saturday 17 May

6 pm Things are getting stranger. Suniti and I went to the supermarket together this afternoon. I wanted to talk to her about Aja, as I haven't properly seen her since Wednesday night.

'Suniti, did the Warden speak to you about signing-in Aja when he stays?'

'Yes,' she replied, looking confused about how I knew.

'I was the one who mentioned it to him. I didn't want to get you in trouble, but Aja has been here quite a lot and to be honest with you, he makes me feel uncomfortable.'

Suniti didn't look at me and was fiddling with the sleeve of her jumper.

'A couple of my things have gone missing – and I'm not suggesting it's him, but we need to keep track of who's coming in and out of the flat. I hope that's OK with you?'

Suniti just nodded and then we left the supermarket in silence. As we were walking back to South Hall, I got the feeling again that I was being followed. I guessed it would be Aja, so I picked up the pace back to the flat. Once I was safely in the kitchen, I watched out of the window – and sure enough, five minutes later, Aja strolled through the court-yard.

As soon as Suniti buzzed him into the flat, she scurried off to her room behind him and they started arguing. I slipped into the bathroom so I could hear more clearly through the wall. I couldn't make out everything as they were fluctuating between English and Punjabi, but the last thing I heard as he walked out of her room was, 'I'll be back on Tuesday,' and then heavy sobbing followed the sound of Suniti's door clicking to.

When I got back to my room, my underwear drawer was open slightly and my favourite pair of white French knickers had been stolen!

8 pm. Tam's room. I've been sat with Tam all evening working out what I should do. She agrees that Aja is a threat and that we need to get him barred from halls. As Warden-Brian prefers counting his strands of hair to protecting his students, we're going to take matters into our own hands. We need to get evidence to show that he's been stealing my underwear, and Tam – being very wise – has devised a plan. We're going to sneak a mousetrap into my underwear drawer! If Aja's coming round on Tuesday like he said, then I'll leave my bedroom door open and pretend to be out. If he takes the opportunity to root amongst undies – snap! The trap will get him and I'll have evidence that he's my stalker!

10 pm Erm, where do you buy a mousetrap from?

Monday 19 May
4 pm A pet shop. I found it slightly weird that they were selling mice for £3 each, and then a couple of aisles down they were selling mousetraps for £5. I bought one of those traps that has a metal bar that snaps down when activated, squashing the poor mouse. Think the shop assistant thought it strange when I asked, 'If someone accidentally put their finger inside, it wouldn't break the finger, would it? I was hoping for mild bruising.'

Tuesday 20 May

Midday. Tam's room. Trap is now in place! Tam and I have done quite a nice job of camouflaging it with my prettiest undies. I've put it right in the centre of the drawer being the first place Aja's dirty little hands would reach for. Aja arrived at the flat about ten minutes ago and when he was in clear earshot, I said to Tam, 'My door's open so help yourself to that nail varnish. I'm going out now and won't be back till about four.' Then I snuck into Tam's room and we are staked out in here.

12.15 pm Nothing's happened.

12.30 pm Still nothing's happened. I'm bored.

12.31 pm And hungry. We had a pack of Minstrels in here but it got a bit back-and-forth-ish and now they've all gone.

1 pm Tam's view is also of the Telecom pole, only I can see it from a slightly different angle, which is surprisingly interesting.

2 pm Tra la la. Boooooooring. Tam said we could use time to start exam revision but I looked at her with a face full of evil.

2.30 pm Am starving. Why has Aja not snuck into room yet? Is very annoying. Or possibly he has, but is so quiet – literally like a mouse – that we haven't heard? But no, if trap had snapped, am sure there would have been yelping.

3 pm We've been comparing Top 3's to pass the time. There hasn't been much change from the usual. I still like Ben – who gave me the en-suite (still yey!) – but he has got a lot to deal with at the moment, so need to keep reminding self not to think about him.

I was gabbling on about this to Tam, getting very deep and meaningful and talking about fate and saying, 'If it's meant to be, then the universe will conspire to make it happen.' I paused, waiting for Tam's equally poignant response, and then she looked up and said, 'Have you ever had an in-growing hair?' Hmmm . . .

Tam's Top 3 is also bleak. Sadly, Matt didn't feature at all. She still thinks Rupert is cute, but he hasn't been in touch again this term, which suggests he really does prefer animals to girls. Am obviously not insinuating he prefers animals in that kind of way, as bestiality is wrong and definitely very against principles of animal rights' activist.

3.05 pm Can't stop thinking about bestiality. Is it real? Do people really do that sort of thing? Surely is modern urban myth to make people feel sickened about state of society?

3.06 pm Tam says to stop going on about it. Wonder if there is an equivalent form with inanimate objects like teddy bears? No. Must stop thinking immediately. Will never be able to sleep with Mr Tubs again. I mean 'sleep' as in 'fall asleep in bed', obviously. Other type of sleeping together is wrong and disturbing. Just stop, brain. Stooooop! Eugh!

3.30 pm Plan has failed.

Heard Suniti's door open and Aja saying, 'Come on, we're leaving.'

Was no point hiding any longer, so Tam and I casually stepped out of room as if we hadn't been hiding from him all day. We saw Suniti walking along the corridor with her suitcase. 'What's going on?' I asked.

Suniti mumbled, 'I am going home for a few days.'

I noticed that her eyes were wet and bloodshot. 'Is something wrong?' I asked.

'No,' Aja spoke for her.

'Why are you going so suddenly, then?' I questioned Suniti. 'You've got exams coming up.'

'Her brother's ill,' Aja told me impatiently and continued walking.

I looked Suniti straight in the eyes. 'I didn't know you had a brother?'

'Y . . . ye . . . yes, I do,' Suniti stammered, but her face told me something else.

Aja grabbed her by the arm and yanked her away firmly. 'Come on – you'll miss your flight!'

Why would Aja lie? It doesn't make sense. What power does he hold over Suniti? I was scared to interfere any further in case I make things worse for Suniti.

6 pm Shitting hell! Am in Casualty with Justin. I killed his index finger with my mousetrap!

Feel awful. Had forgotten about trap and was in kitchen making tea and toast while mulling over possible stalking conspiracies. All of a sudden, there was a high-pitched scream followed by hysterical cursing coming from my bedroom. I raced in to find Justin flailing about with the mousetrap attached to his finger! He was virtually fainting with pain (although, am sure he was being a little over-dramatic).

Anyway, was still terrible as could see Justin's finger getting redder and redder and he was really screeching by now and there was blood coming out of his fingernail. No one else was in as Tam had gone to buy more Minstrels and Matt and Ben were playing football in the park. Realised I'd have to handle situation myself so I ordered Justin to keep still, then with a steady hand I tried to prise open the metal bar that had snapped on to his finger. Was all very tricky as Justin kept convulsing at the sight of his blood.

I managed to lever it open just enough to free the finger. And with that, Justin verbally abused me! He suggested things like I am sadistic and a danger to society.

What happened next, I admit, may have been the influence of watching too many high emotion American dramas. I slapped Justin round the face with the aim of knocking some sense into his hysterical ramblings. To both our surprise, it worked. Justin was so shocked he fell quiet and I was able to bundle him out of the flat and into a taxi heading for casualty.

We were sitting in the waiting area when I broke the silence.

'How's the finger?' I asked, looking straight ahead and wishing the doctor would hurry up.

'Painful,' Justin replied.

'Sorry about that.' There was another long silence. Eventually I said, 'If you don't mind me asking, what exactly were you doing in my underwear drawer?'

Justin inspected the damage to his finger and breathed out shakily to indicate his intense pain. 'I was trying to find out what size you were as I wanted to buy Sheree a present.'

'Right,' I said, mulling this over. 'Only, Sheree's at least a foot taller than me and we have completely different body shapes.'

'Oh,' said Justin, his eyes shifting slightly to the side.

'Um, so do you want to tell me what you were really doing?' I asked, sounding as polite and breezy as I could.

Justin thought for a moment. 'I'd gone into your room to borrow something . . . and then I thought I saw a mouse in your underwear so I went to investigate.'

'Right,' I said. 'Just one more thing, though, how did you see the mouse if the drawer was closed?'

'I said I heard a mouse.'

'You heard a mouse in my underwear drawer?' It wasn't plausible and Justin knew it.

'Yes. Well, you put a trap in there. There must be mice!' He huffed and then folded his arms, except it hurt his finger.

'I put a trap in there because I've had three pairs of pants stolen and I thought it was Aja who'd been taking them. Justin,' I said calmly, 'have you or have you not been taking my underwear?'

Justin hung his head. 'Have.'

I smiled and put my arm round him. 'Look, I totally understand,' I said, attempting to be cool and liberal. 'It's perfectly normal. You have an underwear fetish. Big deal. It doesn't make you a sexual deviant.'

Justin shrugged my arm off him and threw me a look that suggested he might put me in casualty. Luckily the doctor arrived . . .

So Justin's finger is now being X-rayed and I'm sat in the waiting area thinking about what this means.

1) Justin is the underwear thief
2) I was wrong about Aja

3) There is finger blood in my underwear drawer

Hmmm. Things aren't looking good.

7 pm. Casualty still. The doctor's finished. Justin is coming my way. There is a white bandage. He's not looking very happy. Oh no . . .

8.30 pm. Flat. He has a small fracture and it'll take at least six weeks to heal. I admit that it's not ideal timing with exams coming up, but at least it wasn't his writing hand. I thought it might help if I encouraged Justin to look at the positives. 'Sweetie,' I said gently as we made our way back to halls in another taxi, 'this could be a good thing as at least everything is out in the open. I've always suspected that you were gay. Now you don't need to worry about this Sheree front any more.'

Justin started snarling at me: 'You think I'm gay?'

'Well, you know, maybe just a little,' I backtracked.

'A little "gay"?' he questioned, his Welsh accent getting stronger.

'OK, we don't have to say 'gay'. You're just more "sensitive" than most boys. I think it's nice.'

'Josie, I'd have thought that you out of everyone might understand.' This wasn't going well and Justin's cheeks were pink with anger. 'Firstly, taking your underwear is not a fetish. It does not thrill me sexually.'

'Oh.' Well, that's quite a relief, I suppose.

'Secondly, just because I occasionally like wearing women's undergarments or clothes, it does not mean I'm gay. The majority of crossdressers are heterosexual.'

'Right.'

'And thirdly, I am going out with Sheree because I really like her. And Sheree knows I like to crossdress occasionally, and she encourages it.'

'I see,' I said, thinking, *My un-gay flatmate is a crossdresser who goes out with my feminist course mate who encourages him to crossdress, but it isn't a fetish.* I didn't really see at all. And anyway, what's wrong with Sheree's thongs?

'They're too big.'

Oops, I think I said that last bit out loud.

Thinking about it, I was sure I'd seen a glimpse of red satin when Matt wedgied Justin at my flat meal. That's probably why he flipped out and punched Matt!

Justin went on to educate me; 'Women can wear men's clothes and no one raises an eyebrow, but if a man wears a skirt, he's laughed at. Dressing in female clothes is liberating for me as I feel as though I can pass into the feminine world.' Then with a toss of his head he said, 'I thought you were a feminist!'

'I am!'

'Well, you should be supporting this.'

'I should?'

'Yes. Society's attitude to transvestism tells us about its attitude to women. Society can't understand men who voluntarily surrender their masculinity for the less valued femininity. Crossdressing breaks down essentialist notions of gender.'

Was bit staggered listening to Sheree coming out of Justin's mouth. I felt terrible. I'd injured Justin and been an ignorant feminist and only bred harmful stereotypes. I felt ashamed to call myself a student. 'I'm very sorry, Justin,' I said earnestly. 'I'm sorry about your finger. I'm sorry I thought you were gay. And I'm sorry for being a rubbish feminist.'

'And I'm sorry about wearing your underwear. Do you want them back?'

'Nah, you're all right.'

'How about your cream skirt?'

Hmmm . . .

TWENTY-ONE

Monday 26 May

4 pm Justin devised a cover story for his bandaged finger: 'Josie was dancing in front of her mirror to Kylie, doing some type of hip swirls and arm waves. I stuck my head round the door to see if she wanted anything from the shop, and as I made to leave she tried an ambitious rotation, only she wobbled off balance and fell heavily against the door, which slammed against my finger!'

I'm not sure why the story had to involve me mirror-dancing or the elaborate details about hip swirls and rotations, but Justin seemed to like that version. Still, I promised not to tell anyone the crossdressing truth, on the proviso that he doesn't mention to Ben I've sewn extra padding into my bras. Sheree wasn't impressed with the 'accident', but I think I've made it up to them both by taking them on a shopping expedition to La Senza – so now Justin has his own drawer of pretty underwear.

It's been almost a week since the 'accident' and I've had time to reconsider the stalker thing. Even though Justin accounts for the missing thongs, am still convinced that Aja was following me. For a start, he did hide from me in the park and follow us back from the supermarket. And what about the guy in my bedroom? What I don't understand is why he'd lie about Suniti having a brother? And where was she really going? Suniti looked terrified when they left. Her medic exams start in a couple of weeks and I know she wouldn't leave uni in the middle of revision period. When she gets back we definitely need to have a talk as it can't go on like this.

Tuesday 27 May

11.30 am Must settle down and do some work. I've had a very unproductive week of revision and realise now that it's my working environment that's been holding me back. I've had a bit of a tidy round as is difficult to concentrate in messy surroundings. I did get a bit carried away and started reorganising drawers, shelves and entire summer wardrobe. Mmmm . . . do love summer clothes. Lovely floaty skirts and skimpy tops; pretty flip-flops and anklets; loose hair with chunky jewellery. Tried on a few outfits and ended up mincing round room in bikini, but think that is all part of getting it out of system ready to revise. Is good really as now that my room's tidy, revising will be a much smoother process.

11.45 am Think it'd also help if I nip to shops quickly and get a couple of dividers etc. to help organise revision notes. Yes, definitely.

3 pm Am now owner of five different shades of highlighter, two glitter pens, ten pink files, a hundred plastic wallets, a set of pastel-coloured dividers and a frog hole-puncher.

6.30 pm Ooo . . . just discovered that reading set texts aloud in different accents is good way to make revision entertaining while developing accent portfolio. Do think *Jane Eyre* has a whole new subtext when read in Jamaican.

7.15 pm Oh crap! Have only managed twenty-three minutes of actual work today and have to leave for kickboxing soon. Must escape from distracting room and exhibitionist self by being surrounded with other people: tomorrow I'm going to the library!

Wednesday 28 May

1 pm. Library. It's so big! Feel knowledgeable just being in its presence. Is very busy here. Think it's a bit like church; no one goes all year and then the guilt pangs creep in. Before you know it, it's Christmas/exam time and you're lining up to take Holy Communion/ask the librarian how the referencing works.

Am sat in Law section as didn't fancy English area because the students tend to be a bit hairy and arty-looking. Am quite enjoying watching all the smart, affluent Law boys; although, if I'm honest with self, they are still no comparison to Ben. Since he gave up the en-suite for me, lots of potential literary thoughts have been knocked out of brain by bathroom-related fantasies . . . mmmm.

Thursday 29 May

3 pm. Library. Tam's joined me today as she wanted to check out the Law boys too. We also thought working together might help revision process as we could inspire each other to do productive work. After the essay-writing-while-drunk incident, should have realised this wasn't a good idea. We arrived at 11 am and have managed one hour of revision to three hours of hypothetical conversation.

'Jos, how much would you have to be paid to wear a snorkel and mask around the library?'

'Are you allowed to address the fact that you're wearing it?'

'No. If anyone asks, you say, "What snorkel? This tube helps me breath".'

'Thirty pounds,' I said.

'Cheap.'

'Yep.' Then it was my turn. 'Who would you rather have sex with: McGibbon or Warden-Brian?'

'Ooo . . . tough. Ok, well Warden-Brian might be into perverted things with that freakishly long fingernail or make me comb his dwindling hair so by default it'd have to be McGibbon, but I'd insist on an anti-spittle clause.'

Friday 30 May

2.45 pm. Library. Once again, it's been another unproductive day. Before I'd even left the flat, Matt was baiting me by calling me geek-related names because I've been spending so much time in the library. (I guess in Matt's world, two days is a lot.) I was very assertive and informed him intelligently: 'I really don't have time for a sarcastic tirade of verbal sparring. Some students have actually come to university to work. I realise this concept is lost on you; therefore, I'll try and articulate it in a way that you can comprehend. I am going to the library to sit at a desk and learn so that I'll pass my exams and won't have to repeat the fresher programme with delinquents like yourself!'

'For someone so short, you know a lot of big words.'

To torment me further, Matt turned up at the library an hour later and joined Tam and me. He's been giving a running commentary on all the girls in Law section. 'Hello, curvaceous blonde at six o' clock with her back to us. That's it, sweetheart, turn round for Matty . . . Oh, good God! Come in, Scotty, we've got a body-off-Bay-Watch-face-off-Crime-Watch on aisle five. Over.'

When he'd finished his little performance, I caught his eye and raised my right eyebrow very slightly while tilting my head towards Tam. The look said, 'Nice cover-up, Matt, but I know you love Tam, so why don't you shut your big, gaping mouth before I open mine and tell her. Thank you.'

Matt scowled at me and then got on with his work.

Saturday 31 May

11 pm Aja and Suniti are back. Suniti looked awful: her clothes were hanging off her and her skin was blotchy and red. She hurried past me, not wanting to talk and then locked herself in the bathroom. Aja walked along the corridor and stopped right in front of me and stared into my face. He was so close that I could smell the stale cigarettes on his breath. He looked like he'd been sleeping rough; the same Kappa hoodie was filthy and stained, and his nails were black. Then he ran his eyes down my body, leered and walked back to Suniti's room, slamming the door.

I'm so pleased everyone's staying in the flat tonight (except Matt who was calling us all 'Larrys' as he left for the SU), as I wouldn't want to stay on my own with Aja here. I'm keeping my door locked and sleeping with my alarm under the pillow, just in case.

Sunday 1 June

10.30 am Am in complete shock! Last night . . . well, it's just unbelievable . . . it was so frightening . . . don't know what to think any more . . . it's like entire flat life has been a lie . . .

Was very nervous about Aja stuff, so I positioned my personal alarm under pillow for easy access and put Mr Tubs on guard ('on guard' meaning Mr Tubs was on the outside of the bed because the person nearest the door is always killed first). I drifted into a restless dream about Aja: I was alone, walking through the empty park. I heard a creaking sound above me and slowly looked up. Aja was casually sat on a branch of a thick oak that overhung the pathway. A flush of panic danced through me: I was completely alone.

Aja waved at me and then jumped down from the tree.

I started running. I fled from the park, heading back towards campus with the soft sound of trainers falling quickly behind me. I was starting to sweat as the footsteps were gaining. In the dream the running seemed to go on and on; past empty shops, through alleyways, along deserted streets and finally, eventually, I was running across campus, through the courtyard, into South Hall, up the stairs towards our flat. I desperately fumbled with my room key trying to unlock my door, but my fingers were moist with the heat and the key slipped to the ground. I heard Aja's voice shouting behind me as he flew up the stairway. My bedroom door opened and I ducked inside, slamming it behind me and locking it. There was pounding on the other side of the door and furious shouting.

Gradually slipping away from the dream, I pulled myself up in bed, hot and tingling with fear. But I could still hear knocking and voices shouting. It took me a few moments to realise there was someone banging loudly on our flat door. Bugger! I remembered I'd double-locked it from the inside, which meant Matt wouldn't be able to get in. I clambered out of bed in a sleepy haze and felt my way to the door in the dark.

As I undid the latch, a group of figures barged past me, shouting, knocking me hard against the wall.

Out of instinct, I slammed my hand against the light switch and the bright strip lighting flashed on, illuminating five men and one woman storming their way into our student flat.

My head pounded with questions. *Who are they? Has Aja set this up?*

My personal alarm was still under my pillow and I was stood in tiny bed shorts and a skimpy white vest top. The man nearest to me was unshaven and wearing a black jumper and dark jeans. His eyes were searching the corridor and then he moved towards me and gripped my bare arm in his thick fingers.

Adrenalin shot through me like gunfire and I launched my right foot hard at his groin. The intruder blocked my kick with his leg and then gabbed my arm and twisted it behind my back, pinning me up against the corridor wall.

'Aaaaggghhh!' I screeched.

Out of nowhere I saw a heavy fist flash past my head. It was Ben – wearing only his boxer shorts – his eyes dark and his hand surging forward. There was a painful-sounding crack as the fist reached my captor's face. The man staggered back, clutching his hands to his face. Then a dark trickle of blood edged from his nose.

Ben's hand was on my shoulder, 'Are you . . .'

A second intruder with a goatee grabbed Ben roughly and shoved him to the ground, pushing a knee into the small of his back.

A woman's hands were on me now, shoving me against the corridor wall. Other loud voices were shouting, 'Police!'

I blinked hard, trying to make sense of the word. They weren't police. They weren't in uniforms and they looked dangerous – it was something to do with Aja! 'They're not,' I screamed at Justin and Tam, who emerged from their rooms looking petrified. 'Help us! They're not police!'

Clad in Spider-Man pyjamas, Justin shuffled forwards and yelled in a broad Welsh accent, 'Stay back – I've got pepper spray!' (Was actually Nivea deodorant.)

The intruder with blood dripping from his nose ran down the corridor towards Justin.

Tam, wearing only her thin Rainbow Bright T-shirt, began screaming as well. She tried to girlie-slap him as he passed.

'Out the way!' Bloodied Nose demanded and Tam stopped immediately.

Justin and Tam edged back into Tam's doorway, clutching each other's hands.

Bloodied Nose and two other men had surrounded Suniti's room.

Woman Intruder was holding me.

Goateed Man was kneeling on Ben.

Man with No Name was blocking the entrance to the flat.

There was no escape.

Bloodied Nose started thumping heavily on Suniti's door. 'Police! Open up!' he shouted in a commanding voice.

There was no reply and the door was locked.

Police? Why would they be colluding with Aja?

I saw Ben being roughly handcuffed, then pulled to his feet by Goateed Man and dragged out of the flat.

What is going on? Is this really the police? Woman Intruder let go of me and I slunk over to Tam's doorway and stood huddled with her and Justin in various states of undress.

'Suniti Gallahad and Aja Malik,' hollered Bloodied Nose, 'we know you're in there. Open the door!'

So Aja hadn't set this up?

'Josie,' hissed Justin, 'did you report Aja about the stalking thing?'

'God! You don't think it's about that?'

'Open up!' shouted Bloodied Nose.

Again, there was no reply.

Bloodied Nose and another man slammed a metal battering ram into Suniti's door. It thwacked, but didn't budge.

'Again!' The door powered off its hinges, hit Suniti's wardrobe and crashed deafeningly to the ground.

Through the doorframe we saw Suniti and Aja stood together by the window with wide eyes darting round the room.

It was like *The Bill*. Except this was happening in our flat.

In a blur of movement Bloodied Nose ran at Aja, who darted quickly to his left and attempted to head-butt Woman Intruder who was blocking the doorway. There was a rumble as she managed to grab on to his shoulders, put a leg behind his knee and force him backwards over it, bringing him heavily to the ground.

Aja was shouting aggressively in Punjabi as Bloodied Nose took over and slapped a set of handcuffs over his wrists. Holding him by the scruff of his Kappa top, he was hauled to his feet and held against the bedroom wall. 'Aja Malik,' said Bloodied Nose, 'we are arresting you for importing controlled drugs. You don't have to say anything but it may harm your defence if you do not mention when questioned something which you later rely on in court. Anything you do say may be given in evidence.'

Justin, Tam and I stood shocked in Tam's doorway.

The Woman Intruder (whom I was starting to realise was not actually an intruder, but a police officer) had hold of

Suniti and was putting handcuffs on her whilst she was read her rights, too.

Suniti looked petrified, but she made no attempt to protest.

'I think you've got this wrong,' I said desperately. 'Suniti's a medical student. Suniti – tell them they've made a mistake.'

Suniti remained silent while a thickset man with cropped black hair started searching the room, pulling out Suniti's drawers, knocking textbooks off her shelf, checking behind the curtains, looking through her cupboards and pulling up a corner of the carpet. I couldn't believe he was ransacking her room and Suniti wasn't trying to stop him.

'Please, Suniti,' I begged, 'tell them it's not true.'

Tam placed a hand on my arm to stop me going to her. The man continued searching. He lifted up Suniti's mattress, but there was nothing there. Then he searched Aja's rucksack, pulling out a T-shirt, Rizzla's, a pack of tobacco. He unzipped an inside pocket and tucked snugly inside was a small polythene bag filled with white powder.

'Oh, God!' gasped Tam.

'Is that yours?' Bloodied Nose addressed Aja.

Aja said something to Suniti in Punjabi.

Suniti was searched by the woman officer. She patted her hands down Suniti's arms, her waist, her legs, then Suniti's shoes were removed. In the toe area of her left shoe, the woman pulled out a tiny bag of white powder – it looked like a condom with a knot in the end of it. And then two more were found in the right shoe.

Suniti's eyes filled with tears.

This wasn't a mistake? My head was spinning. I was trying to think. *Suniti. Drugs. Aja. Police.* It didn't make sense. *Why would she have drugs?*

'Let's get them to the station,' ordered Bloodied Nose.

Suniti didn't even look up as she was led from her room. Aja followed behind her, dragging his feet and throwing himself around, needing two men to hold him.

The man with the cropped black hair began cordoning off Suniti's room with tape. The rest of us were told we were going to the station for questioning. I wasn't sure what they wanted with us – they'd already handcuffed Ben and pinned me against the wall; what else was going to happen?

'Wait,' I said as we followed them onto the stairway. It was the middle of the night and I was only in bed shorts and a vest; 'Can I get a jacket?'

One of the officers took me back to my room and waited while I quickly grabbed my long duffle coat and a jumper for Tam, too. It was strange to have someone accompany me, just in case I decided to run off.

There was a small crowd of students loitering outside in the courtyard, waiting to see who the police cars had come for. It was embarrassing being taken away as though we were criminals. Justin and I were put in the back of the first police car, and Tam was directed to a second one, where I could make out the silhouette of Ben in the back seat.

Both cars were driven to the local station. It felt so surreal and in the silence I realised my heart was hammering. How disorientating to wake up in middle of the night to a police raid!

I've never been in a police station before. It reminded me slightly of a dirty hospital – it was the same plastic flooring and garish overhead lighting. We were sat on cold,

343

plastic chairs in the waiting room, alongside a drunk 40-year-old who looked like he'd been in a fight. I found the whole situation weirdly funny; Justin was in his Spider-Man pyjamas, I had on nothing more than a long coat and Tam was in a jumper of mine that was too small. Ben, who'd been given a blanket since he'd left the flat in his boxers, had already been taken away for questioning.

When it was my turn, I was led into a small, square room with no windows. I immediately felt claustrophobic and my heart began thumping again at my chest. I was interviewed by Bloodied Nose, who he introduced himself as Officer Waite. I looked at him closely in the bright lighting and decided he was probably about thirty-five. His face looked older – very lived-in with thick lines indented in his forehead and large, open pores on his cheeks. He explained , 'I work in the drugs wing of HM Customs and Excise and tonight's raid was a joint agency effort led by Customs with the support of the police and immigration.'

I think I was in the questioning room for less than twenty minutes, although it felt like hours and hours. I sat still, trying not to think about the lack of windows or the door with the heavy lock on it. Officer Waite went through numerous questions with me: Had I seen anyone coming in and out of Suniti's room? Did she seem to have a lot of money? How often was Aja here? What was their relationship? Had we seen Aja with anyone else? Had he offered us drugs? Do you think Suniti used drugs? How often did she go back to Pakistan? How long were her visits?

I answered his questions as best as I could. I explained about Aja being at the flat a lot as they're cousins; how Suniti seemed nervous around him; how she disappeared quite often and left abruptly to visit a 'sick brother' under Aja's duress. I talked about how I thought Aja was watching me and hid from me in the park, and finally I told him that Suniti was very gentle and conscientious and I couldn't imagine she'd be involved unless she was pressured into it.

Once Officer Waite was satisfied with my answers, he explained what he knew. 'Firstly, Aja is not Suniti's cousin. He is from Pakistan but moved over to Britain eight years ago on a fake passport. We don't know how he got in touch with Suniti yet, but he's been using her as a drugs mule.'

A drugs mule? The officer said it so matter-of-factly that it was hard to believe it was Suniti he was talking about.

'The ring that run the mules,' Officer Waite continued, 'look for people with valid reasons for coming in and out of the UK. Suniti's got a perfect excuse: she is studying here so it'd be normal for her to go home a few times each year – and she has a valid passport. We've looked into her bank accounts and she hasn't been paying for her uni fees or rent. We know she isn't on a scholarship and suspect Aja's been paying them in return for her flying back with the heroin.'

It was so much to take in. Suniti smuggling heroin? Although a few hours ago the idea would have seemed insane, for some reason it was starting to make a bit of sense – to explain some of the things that had been happening.

Officer Waite then asked, 'And what about your flatmate, Ben?'

I wasn't sure what he meant at first. Ben's not involved.

'Assaulting a police officer is a serious offence.'

Oh, yes. That's right – Ben came to my defence! Wow, that was some sight, seeing him launch his fist through the air at my attacker – and all in underpants! But, God, what if he's charged? 'Ben didn't mean to punch you,' I blurted. 'Well, he did mean to, but I don't think he realised what was happening. None of us did. I know you were shouting 'Police!', but it didn't really register as we'd been asleep. And there'd been all this other stuff going on the night before . . . I thought Aja had crept into my room in the middle of the night, so Ben said he'd sleep with his door ajar to listen out for me. And then when you burst in, I thought you were something to do with Aja, so I panicked and screamed . . . and tried to get away from you . . . and I think, well, I think Ben saw me and thought I was being attacked. He's not like that normally. He would never punch anyone. He's the most caring and gentle—'

'OK, OK,' said Officer Waite. ' I get the picture. Luckily for him I'm in a generous mood – and that's rare.' I believed him. 'I might decide against pressing charges.'

What a relief. The last thing Ben needs is to have a criminal record.

As I was leaving the interview room, I asked, 'What will happen to Suniti?'

'She's in another area of the station at the moment. A specialist doctor will be with her as she could have more heroin to pass.' I didn't know what he meant about a doctor, but before I could ask, Officer Waite continued; 'She'll be questioned and charged, then after that there'll be an initial hearing at the Magistrates Court, which should happen in the next couple of days.'

'Will she go to prison?' I asked.

The officer nodded. 'She could be sentenced for anything between seven and twelve years.' I think my eyes must have bulged forwards as he quickly added, 'But I'd hope they'd be lenient. This is a familiar story; someone is desperate for the money so they agree to do it as a one-off.

Then once they're involved, it seems impossible to get out again.'

I was still stunned by the idea that Suniti would be going to prison.

Officer Waite handed me a card. 'Give me a call if you think of anything else. One of my colleagues has spoken to the student authorities, so they'll be informed of what's gone on.' Then he steered me back out to the entrance area, where I sat in my duffle coat waiting for the others to finish.

It was three in the morning when Ben, Justin, Tam and I were sat in our kitchen holding on to warm mugs of tea. Matt still wasn't back from his night out and Suniti's room had now been cordoned off as a crime scene.

The four of us sat in the quiet of the kitchen listening to the hum of the fridge and trying to make sense of things.

'I just don't get it,' said Justin, his Welsh accent soft with tiredness. 'If Suniti was importing heroin, how come they didn't detect it at the airport?'

'She was body packing,' said Ben. 'You know, ingesting it. The officer said she'd have been swallowing it in knotted condoms.'

'Isn't that dangerous?' I asked.

'Totally,' said Ben. 'I was talking to Officer Waite about it and he said Suniti could have swallowed around forty condoms. If one of them had leaked, the heroin would be absorbed straight into her stomach – and could have killed her.'

Tam breathed out in disbelief.

Justin put his hand up as if he were at school, 'But what happens once she's swallowed it? You know, how does she get it out again?'

'What do you think?' said Ben. 'She's probably been spending a lot of time on the toilet.'

'The laxatives!' said Tam.

'Of course!' I gulped. 'That's why she was taking them, to help pass the drugs quicker.'

Justin and Ben didn't know what we were talking about so I explained about finding Suniti's laxatives and worrying that she had an eating disorder. 'I guess that's why she behaved strangely when I tried talking to her about it. And it explains why Aja was always hanging about the flat after she got back from Pakistan.'

'Jos, I think this whole thing is why you thought Aja was stalking you,' said Tam. 'Maybe he thought you were onto him – or were getting too involved with Suniti?'

'That makes sense,' agreed Ben. 'Except why would Aja have snuck into your room last night?'

'God, I don't even want to think about it. It was so scary seeing someone stood over my bed. At least he's locked up now.'

We fell silent remembering that Suniti would also be locked up. Somehow it didn't seem right.

I finally climbed into bed at 4.30 am, but couldn't sleep. I lay in the dark, staring at the ceiling, with Mr Tubs curled into my neck. All of a sudden there was another thundering of feet up the stairway, followed by loud knocking on the flat door.

What now? I thought. Is Tam going to be arrested for being a member of the Mafia? Not wishing to have a second door broken down, I quickly jumped up to open it – taking my alarm with me this time.

I turned on the hall light and blinked at the man in uniform stood in the doorway. It was a drunk and keyless

Matt rolling in at 5.15 am, wearing his 'FBI (FEMALE BODY INSPECTOR)' T-shirt. He gave me a beery kiss on the cheek and said, 'Thanks, Shorty, you're an angel. Are you going to tuck me in?'

At a time when all my expectations had been turned on their head, Matt's drunken lechery was comfortingly reassuring. I said, 'Bed. That way,' and pointed to his room.

I had to smile as he slurred, 'Do you think Tam might want to tuck me in?' and then he tried to give me a knowing wink and staggered right past Suniti's missing door and into his room.

TWENTY-TWO

Sunday 1 June (still)

4 pm We're being treated like celebrities; the student authorities have been buzzing around all day and most of South Hall have visited to get the inside story.

Despite not even being there, Matt is acting like he orchestrated the whole operation and is giving blow-by-blow accounts of how the police burst in. I think Sheree might have heard a slightly embroidered version too as she keeps squeezing Justin's arm and calling him, 'My brave little soldier'. I'm surprised I haven't seen Chloe or Jasmine. I thought they'd make a particular effort to prance around looking like the picture of concern because the student press have been here.

Warden-Brian bustled in this morning as we were trying to eat breakfast and adjust to the new day. Immaculately dressed in his pressed bib, he started pointing his fingernail at things and trying to look important. When he realised there was nothing to be done other than buy a new door for Suniti's room, he made a big show of looking busy and saying things like, 'Everyone stay back, this is a crime scene!'

After sufficient mincing, Warden-Brian interrupted my cereal to ask, 'Josie, is your mother aware of what's gone on?'

'I haven't spoken to her yet,' I said, hoping he might go away as he was putting me off my Cornflakes.

'If she wants to chat to me about anything – anything at all – then here's my number.' Warden-Brian pulled a neatly folded piece of lined paper out of his trouser pocket. It was still warm when he handed it to me.

He then looked at me intensely as if waiting for a reaction.

'Er, sure, I'll pass it on,' I said eventually.

Brian was satisfied and, as he left the kitchen, he ever so slightly skipped on his right foot. Heinous images of Mum with the Warden clawed their way into my mind and I sadly lay down my spoon, realising the Cornflakes would have to be binned.

Soon after, Gil and Hobbit came up to the flat and spent six minutes standing in Suniti's doorway repeating, 'No way, man. No way.'

Gil was acting strangely. He kept following me round the flat, constantly checking that I was OK and asking weird questions like, 'Have you been alright the last few nights?' and 'Don't waste any time being scared.' I really needed my own head space, so I told Beavis and Butthead that I was going to lie down and I padded back to my room. I lay on my bed, eyes closed, enjoying the quiet. What a surreal 24 hours! I couldn't quite believe that Suniti had been arrested – and is facing a prison sentence. I felt a dull ache in my stomach; sadness maybe, or even guilt perhaps for not being able to help her. The vibtration of my mobile interrupted my thoughts. It was mum. Her unhappiness radar had honed in on me again!

Hearing her voice reminded me how much I needed her right now. I began explaining what had happened and she listened carefully, asking me questions to get the full picture. 'It doesn't seem fair, Mum. Suniti's been pressured into this one thing and then a nightmare chain of events unravelled around her.'

'In life,' Mum told me, 'you always have choices and although there would have been a lot of financial pressures to encourage Suniti to get involved in this, she did have the opportunity to say no.'

'But she's in prison, Mum. She's a good person.'

'I'm sure there are a lot of good people in prison – a lot of good people who have made some bad choices.'

'So what do I do?'

'She may want visitors, or you could write to her. Other than staying in contact, there isn't much you can do, darling. You've got to try and get on with your life and be there for Suniti if she wants you to be.'

Think Mum is a good Samaritan.

5pm. There's just been a tentative knock on my bedroom door, followed by a head of dreadlocks peering in. 'Hi Jos. Er, I just need to speak to you about something, if that's cool?'

Gil shut the door behind him and sat himself on my bed.

I felt nervous. Why was he still in our flat? What was coming next? And why had he shut the door? I didn't want any more surprises.

'Matt told me you've been a bit freaked out as you thought you were being stalked by that Aja dude.'

'Yes.'

'Um, well, I've got something to confess.' Gil pulled distractedly at a thick blonde dread. 'Right, so you know how you thought Aja was in your room one night?'

'Yes.'

'Well, he wasn't.'

'He wasn't?' I repeated. 'How do you know?'

'This is gonna sound a bit random OK, but, er well, I'm just gonna say it: It was me.'

'What?' I gasped.

352

'I'd been drinking Absinth,' Gil said, as if that explained it.

'And?'

'And, I guess I was pretty out of it. I must have climbed up an extra flight of stairs into your flat – I didn't realise, you know, as your room is directly above mine.'

'Why didn't you tell me straight away?'

'I dunno, man. You started screaming. I was pretty scared myself. Once I realised what had happened, I was worried that you'd think it was a bit weird, you know, me standing in your room in the middle of the night.'

'Yes, there's always that.'

'Sorry about scaring you.' Then Gil wrapped his arms round me and gave me a big hug – which went on a little longer than I thought was polite.

6 pm It's been a strange day. I admit, at first, I was enjoying the drama the night had brought. Now, though, I just feel really low about everything. I mean, this is Suniti – our flatmate – who's going to be sent to prison. Her whole world has changed and we're all in the flat enjoying the brief stardom of living with a criminal.

I stayed in my room for most of the afternoon, gazing out of the window and thinking that the Telecom pole and the one tree wasn't such a bad view afterall.

'Hey, Jos.' Ben was stood in my doorway wearing a pale blue Bench T-shirt and jeans. His hair was messily scuffed over his face and he smiled his tilty smile at me. 'I just wanted to check you were OK.'

'Oh, thanks,' I said, warmed by his concern.

'I didn't really get to know Suniti that well,' Ben said, remaining in the doorway,' I guess none of us knew her properly – but you seemed to make the most effort with her. You're probably going to feel this the hardest out of us all. If you need to get out of the flat and go for a walk or anything, just let me know.'

'Thanks,' I said softly, touched that Ben has the capacity to worry about how I'm feeling when he's got his own worries.

Ben gave a small nod and then turned to go back to his room.

'Ben,' I called after him. 'Thank you for what you did last night. You know, punching Officer Waite for me.'

Ben laughed. 'That's cool. I feel a bit bad about his nose, though! All I saw was a bloke hurting you. I didn't really have time to work out was happening.'

My chest started to flutter. All Ben thought about was protecting me. Mmmm.

'At least if I hear you screaming in the corridor again, I'll be sure to check for wetsuits and police officers before launching my attack!'

I smiled.

'I best go,' Ben said. 'I'm waiting on a call from Grace.'

'How is she? Are you OK?'

'She's doing really well, thanks. And I am, too. Grace's finished her treatment for now. She said the doctors are going to assess her in another month or so, and after that, fingers crossed she'll go into remission. Then Ben looked past me, out of my window and said almost to himself', It's been a weird ride, hasn't it?' And then he walked back to his room.

Monday 2 June

4 pm. Library. I'm working back in the library again. Matt, Tam and I are sat together on a communal study table and it's sweltering in here. Why is it always boiling during exam time? It's been weird trying to carry on with stuff as though nothing's happened; we're still wandering around the campus while Suniti's locked in a cell. One of Officer Waite's colleagues called earlier to check that everything was OK. He told us that Suniti hadn't applied for bail and is going to be in custody until her trial next month.

4.30 pm Ben has just joined our library study group, which isn't exactly helping my concentration. I've been reliving the moment when he leapt across the corridor in his pants and punched my 'attacker'. Mmmm . . .

He's sitting opposite me right now as I'm surreptitiously diary-writing/perving/diary-writing. I don't often get chance to look at him up close. Tam said that when I concentrate, I poke my tongue out of the left-hand corner of my mouth. Doesn't sound like the sexiest of looks, so am concentrating on not concentrating on Ben.

He really is handsome, though. I love watching him study as his brow furrows when he's focused on something – and if he's really concentrating you can see two small knots of muscles work above his jaw-line. I love everything about him; the way his thick sandy hair falls messily over his face, how his smile tilts slightly to the left and his hands – God, his fingers are long and sexy – with wide strong palms and . . .

Ow! Matt has thrown a ball of screwed-up paper at my head. It says: 'Stop staring. Pervert!'

Matt is sat opposite Tam, drooling at her in a summery yellow dress that falls prettily off her shoulders. I'm sending the note back: 'Pot. Kettle. Black.'

Thursday 5 June

1.05 pm. Library. Only four days till exams start. I feel totally unprepared. Wonder if we'll get special consideration because of recent events? Suppose the drug raid is not entirely to blame for lack of revision. For example, right now I'm squashed around study table with: Tam (picking her split ends), Matt (having pen-spinning competition with himself), Ben (looking like Adonis), Justin-and-Sheree (holding hands, stroking legs and smiling sappily), Gil (doodling on file), Hobbit (making a roll-up on lap).

Think I'd get more work done at flat because every ten minutes someone interrupts the silence with a piece of wisdom. Tam might start with something like: 'This is a record-breaking hair: seven split ends.' Then someone else – hungry for non-work related thoughts – manages to take that statement and turn it into an opportunity for a chat: 'Talking of record-breaking, did anyone read about that flexible dude who managed to hide inside a big traffic cone for twenty minutes?' And then we're off . . . Fifteen minutes later – once all traffic cone and body contortionist topics have been exhausted – we go back to doodling/pen-spinning/texting and thinking how it'll feel when we fail our exams.

Friday 6 June

4.15 pm Oh, dear . . . our study days in the library were short-lived. We had all squeezed around a communal study table like yesterday. There's a big area of these stretching 200 feet across the library, and directly to their left are private study booths. Study booth workers are the real hardcore; they're the people you see carrying 'Reference Only' textbooks, or rooting through the dusty journals and periodicals at the back end of the library. The communal study tables where we sit is for the softcore; it's filled with people like us who only discover the library in exam time and tend to enjoy reading the interesting table graffiti, such as, 'Martin blows goats'.

Tam and I were sat next to each other today and, unfortunately, that put us opposite Justin and Sheree. As usual, they started petting at the table. I was looking around the library to keep my eyes anywhere but the ginger coupling – and then I saw Rupert. He walked straight past our table without noticing us and into the study booth on our left. I nudged Tam and whispered, 'Rupert's in the booth there, shall we say hi?'

Tam took one look at Justin who was nibbling Sheree's ear lobe and nodded.

There's only a tiny window in the door of the study booth just so you can check whether it's occupied, but it's small enough to remain private. I saw the back of Rupert's head hunched over the desk and so I quietly opened the door.

'Oh, my God!' I cried.

It was Pablo . . .

'Shitting hell!' Tam shrieked.

Snogging Rupert . . .

Justin and Sheree stopped petting and our whole table strained to see what was going on in the booth.

Rupert swiftly removed himself from Pablo and straightened out his chinos.

'But what . . . you – when?' I stammered, utterly confused.

Pablo was still sat on the chair and Rupert was pressed against the desk looking baffled: 'Gosh, erm, this is rather awkward. How does everybody know each other?'

'Hosie is the lady I stay with.'

'Oh,' Rupert said, pulling down his lips in a 'yikes' type action.

'I'm very sorry for the kiss of Rupert,' Pablo told me. 'But he is my boyfriend and I love him!'

I heard sniggering from Matt and glanced over my shoulder to see that we had attracted a small crowd.

'We are homosexuals,' Pablo announced rather too loudly, seeing as we were in the 'Absolute Silence' section of the library.

I looked at Tam. Tam was staring at me. 'Lovely,' I whispered eventually. 'Wonderful. Um, only – well, what about in Spain? And coming to visit me?'

'I explain,' said Pablo, pressing two fingers against his brow. 'Hosie, I have known I am the homosexual since age twelve years. I am sorry to explain that the romance in Spain was my parents.'

Rupert leant his head towards Pablo and said something in Spanish. I dug Tam in the ribs for a translation but I don't think she had concentrated quite as hard as Rupert in their lectures.

'What Pablo means,' Rupert explained, 'is that his parents suspected he was gay and so he tried to pretend he was straight by having the romance with you. They found out the truth eventually and, sadly, they threw Pablo out.'

'Yes,' agreed Pablo, lowering his eyes miserably. 'This is truth. I come to England and I know only you, Hosie. I thought I pretend to not be the homosexual, then you might let me stay. It is very bad of me, I know. And then at the party—'

'Halloween,' interjected Rupert.

'I meet Rupert – the skeleton—'

'You're Funny Bones!' Tam exclaimed at Rupert.

Bugger, my mobile started ringing! I'd forgotten to put it on silent; I dashed to my bag on the library table and rummaged inside.

'Well done!' said Matt, slapping me on the shoulder. 'You've managed to turn Pablo gay. What an achievement!'

BEEEEEEEEEEEEEEEEP BEEEEEEEEEEEEEEEEEEP BEEEEEEEEEEEEEEEEP!

There was a piercing ringing. I'd pressed my personal alarm by mistake! My phone was still ringing and the alarm was sirening at full volume.

'My ears!' cried Matt, standing up and then falling dramatically on the table clutching at his head. Then encouraged by the noise and drama, he shouted above the ringing, 'Geri, why don't you join the boys in the study booth – I'm sure they'd make room for a little one.'

I could see a matronly librarian marching over from the other end of the library floor.

'Don't speak to him like that,' Sheree interjected defensively.

'Pipe down, wench.'

'Don't speak to her like that!' parroted Justin, grabbing Matt's folder and throwing it childishly to the floor. He looked triumphant as the papers spilled everywhere.

Pablo had poked his head out of the booth, watching the ruckus between Matt and Justin – probably with a sense of déjà vu.

'Pick that up, you twat!' Matt ordered.

Sheree butted in: 'Pick up your own folder, you sexist, ginger-bullying bastard!'

Oh, God! Was all getting hideously out of control. Tam was helping me struggle with my alarm; Ben was on his feet trying to calm things; Justin and Sheree were snarling at Matt; Rupert and Pablo were squeezed into the study booth doorway and Gil and Hobbit were still in their seats mesmerised by the whole thing.

'Tell your dyke-friend to butt out!'

Justin made a leap for Matt's throat while yelling, 'Take that back!'

The librarian was only feet away . . .

Matt flicked Justin off, but accidentally caught his fractured index finger at the same time. Justin yelped spectacularly and Sheree jumped up to tend to him.

The librarian had reached us.

I threaded the cord back into the alarm.

'Enough!' she bellowed.

Finally there was silence. A hundred faces stared at us across the library. We were then accompanied out of the building and had our swipe cards removed.

Sunday 8 June

5.15 pm The exams start tomorrow and being barred from the library has not really helped. This is what I've learnt during the revision period: Tam's record number of split-ends on a single hair is eleven; Gil can fit eight fruit pastilles in his mouth in one go but encountered difficulties when chewing; Hobbit can make a roll-up with one hand behind his back; when Ben smiles he shows six teeth, but when he laughs I've counted ten; Justin and Sheree can publicly kiss for three minutes before realising we are all cringing; Matt looks at Tam an average of eighteen times in a ten-minute period; and finally, our ex-flatmate is a drug smuggler and my ex-lover is gay.

It's all very useful knowledge, but not exactly what I was hoping my tuition fees would go towards.

Only worthwhile thing we've done in revision period is plan an end-of-year flat party. We've decided to boycott the official Summer Ball as the tickets are £90 – ouch! Some people had already bought their dresses, so we're going to hold our own version, the Alternative Summer Ball. It's free entry, bring your own and dress to impress. Can't wait! Is possible that our final weekend pre-exams should have been spent revising, but sometimes a break can help. And anyway, it'll be our last night as freshers so it's our duty to make sure it's a good one.

Really must try and focus on revision now. First exam is at 9 am tomorrow. Will prepare exam materials as organisation always provide sense of calm. Yes. Good. Wonder if other students will be taking mascots? Mr Tubs is the obvious choice since examiners don't know we can communicate. Hah!

7.15 pm Justin read a report that said eating fish makes you brainy. After failing to do any substantial amount of revision, we're all cooking fish fingers for supper . . .

Monday 9 June
4.30 pm Hmmph! Shakespeare exam did not go well. Had forgotten about strict exam hall protocol where pasty moderators sit you in long rows of nervous students, then instruct you to remain silent while they wander around

peering over shoulders. Started to get that thing again where I panic in case brain malfunctions and I start shouting. Also, was very off-putting when I'd eventually got into my flow and Mr Examiner walked round the entire 828 people in the hall and decided to stand by my desk to bellow, 'Fifteen minutes to go!' Was so loud that wondered if *I'd* shouted, and then pen flew from hand and landed three rows in front.

Wednesday 18 June

6 pm Have been unable to write diary over past ten days since middle finger has developed hideous growth from over-writing. Have been trying to counter disfigurement issues by covering it in cotton wool during exams to ease pen-on-lump pressure. No matter how securely cotton wool is attached, within five minutes of starting the exam, whole thing has slipped and spend rest of time making readjustments.

Can't say exams have gone that smoothly. In Brontë, I was sat behind Speed Writer of the Year who'd reel off a page every three minutes. Was very difficult trying to concentrate with her frantically shooting her hand up and down asking for more paper in a loud, showy-off way. Mr Tubs and I were totally unimpressed.

There have been all the usual dramas this past week. Matt missed an exam. He says he got the dates muddled but I don't think it was a coincidence that an England World Cup match had the same kick-off time. Then Tam was upset as she missed a question on the back page of her Spanish paper. Was quite sweet, actually, as she was crying in the kitchen and Matt rushed over to ask, 'Are you all right, Tamara? What's happened?'

'I'm fine. I had a bad exam – I'm being a baby about it,' she smiled.

'God, I thought something awful had happened. Come here, you,' and he enveloped her in a big hug.

I've also been struggling to keep unrequited lust under control since all feelings for Ben are flying back at full pelt. As the weather is warmer, he keeps walking round with no top on. Brain is melting with desire. Cannot even escape to library to work because of ban. Keep drifting off into daydreams where Ben is my boyfriend and every few hours we have sex breaks. Mmmm . . .

Last exam tomorrow. 'Sex and Sensibility in *Clarissa*'; this is when I find out whether reading a two-page synopsis of the book is as good as reading the whole thing.

Thursday 19 June
4 pm Answer: 'It isn't.' Still, I've finished my exams now and that means no more essays, lectures or McGibbon for three months! Summer's here! Waaahooooooo!!!!!!!!!!!

Friday 20 June
11 am Mmmm . . . is so lovely waking up with no exams to consume mind, leaving head free to luxuriate in final party preparations for tomorrow night. Tam and I are in charge of decor; think will nip into town to buy party bits and pieces – and possibly have the tiniest browse for party dress! (Bank balance has told me that I should definitely not do this since already have plenty of clothes in wardrobe, but don't think bank realises that existing dresses have been on numerous outings and are getting rather bored.)

6.30 pm Tiniest browse turned into five hours traipsing round town having mini-breakdowns in every changing room when realised that body shape has been bypassed by clothes-makers and that no even-numbered sizes fit me.

Finally came across a boutiquey-shop I hadn't noticed before and moped inside full of self-pity. And there it was: the most perfect, beautiful, ridiculously expensive dress. It's chocolate brown in a shimmery, slinky material and comes just below the knee. It's completely backless and just has two tiny straps that weave over the shoulder and down into the side of the dress. It screams 'I-exude-hot-sultry-sexiness-but-am-sweet-with-it', which is exactly the look am going for. Do not know how wardrobe coped before this purchase.

OK, it was a little over-budget, but I can justify it because am actually saving money by not going to the official ball; therefore, dress is a reward for disciplined thriftiness. Plus, what else is your Egg card for?

Saturday 21 June
10.30 am In my pigeonhole this morning, there was a letter from Suniti.

Dear Josie,

I hope you don't mind me writing to you, but I felt you all deserved an explanation.

Please do not think that everything has been a lie. I truly did wish to study medicine in the UK and I'd been accepted to receive a scholarship. Unfortunately, two months before I was due to arrive the scholarship programme I had applied through was shut down. My parents couldn't afford the full amount to assist me, so a friend told me about someone he

364

knew who'd moved to the UK who might be able to help. This was Aja.

As you may have found out, Aja is not really my cousin. He offered to pay my fees if I ran an errand for him. At first it sounded like a good solution – but he didn't tell me all the details. He made it sound easy and convinced me that I wouldn't get into any trouble.

As soon as I'd made the first journey, I realised how dangerous it was. I looked on the internet and discovered how long you could be imprisoned for importing heroin. I was so scared. I immediately told Aja that I didn't want to do it again, but he said I had no choice as he'd tip off the police about my involvement and tell my family, which would bring great shame to them all. That is why I had to continue making the trips.

I am very sorry for what I have done and I accept the prison sentence I'm given. If you are able to forgive me, I would be very grateful if you would write to let me know how you all are. Although I haven't involved myself in university life, it doesn't mean I haven't watched and observed. I feel like I know you all, even when you feel you don't know me.

Suniti.

The last part of the letter really choked me. It's true, I don't know who Suniti is. Maybe we should have tried harder to include her. Would she have opened up to us if we had? At times I felt like she was wanting to let me in, but perhaps she was scared to. I wish I'd pushed harder and insisted, rather than letting her get in deeper and deeper with Aja.

It's funny how many things make sense now that I know the truth. All the time that we thought Suniti was just shy and private, she was actually keeping us at arms length so we wouldn't find out her secret. I've shown the letter to the others. Even Matt was quietened by it and said he feels like an idiot for making all those 'she fancies me' jokes. We've agreed we're all going to write and keep in touch; in different circumstances, maybe we'd have been closer.

4 pm Felt bit subdued after Suniti's letter but have been busying self with decorations for the Alternative Summer Ball. Kitchen is looking as chic as I can make it with leftover Christmas tinsel and mini night-light candles. Have redeemed self, though, by making delicious vodka jelly. It's so easy; I just got a packet of strawberry jelly and added vodka and hot water. Perfect. Now, Mr Oliver, if you'd mentioned a simple, easy and delicious pudding like that, we might have got on a little better this year.

Think we're almost organised. The boys have been out buying crates of alcohol and Gil and Hobbit are bringing up their decks soon. I just need to get ready . . .

7.30 pm Am very pleased with The Dress. Only problem is, I can't wear proper bra because of backlessness. Have been mincing round, trying to stick on chicken fillet things to enhance cleavage and all got rather tricky with sticking double-sided tape over boobs. Am not looking forward to pain implications when removing them! Still, think it's worth it as The Dress looks very good and have complemented it with dishevelled ringlety hair.

Tam looks so beautiful. She's wearing a stunning green corset dress that flows out to the floor. She looks like a mermaid with her hair tumbling down her back. I want to cry with joy and hug her tightly (but worried make-up will run and boobs will fall off). Told Tam I love her and she says she loves me – and this is before the alcohol.

So, the final checks: we have lippy on, we're smelling tasty, our toenails are painted, our legs are smooth and we have vodka jelly chilling in the fridge. This is it: our last night as freshers!

TWENTY-THREE

Sunday 22 June

4 am It's four in the morning and I'm still wearing The Dress. It's been a long night; there's been breakdancing, men in uniform and romping – exactly what we were hoping for from our Alternative Summer Ball.

I'll start from the beginning. The night began in a civilised way with pre-party drinks with flatmates. I felt a strange surge of pride seeing the three boys in their smart tuxedos. I don't know whether it was the tailoring of the jackets or because they were stood chatting amicably together, but our dappy flatmates suddenly seemed very grown up and sophisticated.

Ben looked incredibly handsome. I think he'd attempted to style his hair, but a few blonde locks had managed to escape and tumbled over his face in a cute, messy way. Ben watched me as I took the vodka jelly from the fridge and began dividing it into shots. 'Jos,' he said softly, leaning towards me, 'you look really beautiful.' My stomach fluttered madly and I sort of laughed, smiled and blushed all at once, while managing to mumble, 'Thank you.'

All flatmates congratulated me on the delicious vodka jelly and agreed it was the best thing I'd made all year (which I think was a slightly loaded compliment). It was strange that, on our final night as freshers, our sixth flatmate was missing. I know Suniti probably wouldn't have come out of her bedroom, or she'd have disappeared to the late-night library, but just knowing her room was empty didn't feel right.

The remaining five of us grabbed a spoon and raised a wobble of vodka jelly. 'To Suniti,' I toasted.

'To Suniti,' everyone replied and we swallowed the jelly.

Justin had made a 'First Year Album' with all our favourite tunes on. He turned it up and, fuelled by edible alcohol, we all had a dance. Justin entertained us with some classic Michael moves, complete with crotch-grabbing, 'ow'-ing and a bumpy attempt at the moonwalk; Ben body-popped to *Digable Planets* and Matt flashed his tux open to *Le Freak* and exposed a white T-shirt that read, 'I'M GOING COMMANDO'. I decided that the boys hadn't changed that much over the year – it was the suits after all.

Gil and Hobbit arrived in second-hand tuxedo jackets, coupled with boardshorts and Reefs. They set up their decks in the kitchen and South Hall started to beat. It was like a mating call; within half an hour the flat was bustling and humming with people. Could hardly tell we were students as everyone looked so stylish arriving in sexy dresses and suave suits (although carrier bags full of chinking £2.99 wine bottles may have given it away).

Sheree had glammed-up and looked amazing. Her hair was smoothed down into a feathery bob and she wore a pretty white dress with strappy pink heels and even a dainty silver bracelet on her wrist. Think Justin might have liked the change as the moment she arrived, he grabbed her hand and whisked her off to his room. Hmmm.

Rupert and Pablo came to the party. I'd called Pablo to apologise for the library fiasco and said I'd really like it if they both could come. Have to say, they do make a dashing couple (I just hope Rupert is a fan of body hair, eek!) Think Tam is quite relieved that Rupert is gay as it means her powers of seduction are still intact! The four of us had a nice chat and we've planned to go out for dinner when we get back in September. God, Mum would be surprised if she knew how my holiday romance had unfolded!

It was so much fun chatting and mingling with everyone and was pleased that The Dress was a hit. Was becoming bit of a compliment junkie, no longer blushing and stammering but taking sweet, if not drunken comments, in my smooth-legged strides; when you've fleetingly got it, you've gotta flaunt it.

After a long stint on the decks, Gil and Hobbit took their chance to shine on the dance floor. We formed a circle around them as they put their DVD-viewing to use and breakdanced for the crowd. Hobbit started by running at our kitchen wall and managing to flip his legs over his head and land on his hands, which, quite amazingly, turned into a headspin. Then Gil high-fived with Hobbit and took over centre-circle. He seemed to bounce down on to the kitchen floor and then do something like spinning on his bum, but obviously it was much more technical than that as there was lots of clapping from the crowd.

Probably imagining the applause was for them, Jasmine and Chloe strutted in wearing expensive black ball gowns, with their blonde hair spilling over their shoulders. 'We're not stopping,' trilled Jasmine over the music, 'we're off to the Summer Ball, but we just wanted to see how your little party turned out.'

Ugh! They were the last people I wanted to see. Was having a rather lovely end to our first year and bunnies were definitely not on the guest list.

'Josie, that dress is so divine!' Jasmine gushed insincerely. 'Have I seen it in New Look?'

Bloody bunny-bitch! Wanted to think of cutting/witty reply but I was interrupted by Gil who flipped up too quickly from a head spin and stumbled dizzily against the kitchen side. His suited elbow knocked a full plate of vodka jelly from the surface, which toppled towards the floor – landing jelly-down on Jasmine's black Marc Jacobs shoes.

'Eeeeeeeeek!' she cried, blinking at her feet in horror. 'You idiot!'

Gil flushed bright red and stooped to the floor, desperately trying to knock off the red jelly with his hands. 'I'm so sorry . . . sorry,' he kept repeating as it started squelching between her toes.

'How awful!' Chloe screeched.

Jasmine jabbed Gil in the shins, yapping, 'Stay back!'

Gil limped over to the sink and nervously ran a hand over his dreads, leaving behind a blob of red jelly.

'My shoes are fucking ruined,' raged Jasmine above the music.

'I'll pay for them . . .' Gil tried to offer.

'As if you could afford to,' she spat, bending over to dab dramatically at her shoes. It was not an accident that everybody in the kitchen could see down her cleavage.

'You shouldn't speak to people like that,' I said, watching Gil standing awkwardly by the sink with flushed cheeks.

Jasmine stood up straight, smoothed her dress and peered down at me. In her heels she was almost a foot above me – her breasts right in my eyeline. 'Yes, you're right of course, sweetie, but then you can't count a pathetic fuck like that as a person, can you?'

Gil, in tux and shorts, with red jelly on his head, looked as though he might cry.

'Jasmine,' a male voice said from the kitchen doorway. It was Ben. His broad shoulders almost filled the doorframe and his face looked serious. Jasmine turned round to look at him. 'I think you should apologise to Gil. It was an accident.' His voice was loud and strong and cut above the music, grabbing the whole room's attention.

Gil gave a shy nod in agreement with Ben.

'Do me a favour,' laughed Jasmine arrogantly and then with a flick of her hair, she made to leave.

'Fine. Then I'll share with everyone the true meaning of 'pathetic'.'

Jasmine's painted lips screwed into an unattractive ball and she stared darkly at Ben.

Ben spoke above the music to the room; 'You've probably all read about the lab break-in a couple of months ago? Well, our flat looked after one of the dogs for a few nights, but when Jasmine found out she decided to share it with the Warden.'

The room seemed to gasp.

'Your selfishness could have meant our whole flat was expelled from halls and a dog was sent back to the laboratory to be gassed.'

'You awful girl!' Rupert exclaimed, dismayed to hear what had gone on.

Jasmine's powdered cheeks turned deep red. She let out a tiny choked sound of insolence, her glossed top lip flickered and she spun on her jellied-heels and darted out – with Chloe a step behind.

I can't believe what that bloody bunny-bitch tried to do! I'm so proud of Ben for standing up to her. Mmmm . . . was wonderful the way he handled it. Seeing Jasmine put in her place by Ben almost makes up for their kiss. Almost.

The party got back on track and Gil was telling everyone he did the jelly-shoe thing on purpose. I smiled later when I saw Matt in our corridor swigging wine with Yanni and Hesperos and still finding it funny to shout 'malacas' with them both. It was a fantastic night and everyone was enjoying a great end to the year.

Around 3.30 am, people gradually started to filter out. Gil was calming down the beat with some chill-out tracks and the few people left in the kitchen were getting coupley. I scanned the room looking for Ben, hoping maybe for an end-of-year dance. I felt that familiar stab of disappointment when I couldn't spot him and was going to make do with a boogie with Tam – until I saw Matt spinning her round happily. Everyone had coupled up: Sheree was nuzzling Justin, Tam was laughing with Matt, and Rupert and Pablo were slow-dancing.

Then, Justin, whom I can only assume had been drinking obscene amounts of Red Bull, broke away from Sheree and jumped on to the kitchen table, excitedly announcing a game of hide and seek. He began counting as an elated Sheree leapt about, giggling, 'Yey! I love hide and seek!' (Must note: I'd always thought Sheree was above the conventions of gender, but put her in a dress and heels and you've got instant girlie! Oh, although, maybe it was a subversive experiment to 'demonstrate the performativity of gender'? Hmmm.)

People started disappearing from the kitchen, flicking the lights out on the way. I was going to hide in my room but that would be too obvious. Then I dithered around in Tam's with her and Matt, but they shooed me out saying we'll all get caught as I'm a clumsy hider. Hmmph!

Could hear Justin getting nearer to a hundred, '62 . . . 63 . . . 64 . . .' so nipped further along the corridor into Ben's darkened room and leapt under the duvet in starfish stance.

'Ow!' came a muffled sound from beneath me.

'Oh, crap!' I froze still.

'68 . . . 69 . . . 70 . . .'

'Still ow!' said the voice beneath me.

'Who's that?'

'Ben.' Long pause. 'Who's that?'

'76 . . . 77 . . . 78 . . .'

'Josie.'

'You do know you're on top of me?'

'Erm . . . yes.'

'Do you mind me asking, why?'

'83 . . . 84 . . . 85 . . .'

'I'm hiding.'

'Right.'

'88 . . . 89 . . . 90 . . .'

And then I added, 'I'm playing hide and seek.'

'Well, you're pretty terrible at it.'

'92 . . . 93 . . . 94 . . .'

'So are you!'

'I wasn't hiding.'

'What were you doing?'

'Sleeping.'

'Oh.'

'98 . . . 99 . . . 100 . . .'

'Jos, do you think you could just move your knee slightly to the left?'

'I'm coming . . . ready or not!'

Hiding-adrenalin had made me overlook the fact I'd jumped on top of Ben, who was asleep in his bed, in his

374

boxers, and now I was lying on top of him with one of my limbs in a very awkward place. The reality of the situation suddenly thundered into focus. 'God! I'm really sor—.'

'Ssh, Jos – he'll find us.'

I stayed completely still. My body pressed against Ben's unclothed skin; my face inches above his; both of us lying in the dark beneath his duvet.

We heard Justin jump down from the kitchen table and then elephant-foot it down the corridor. 'Watch out, boyos! I'm after you—.' he screeched.

I suddenly felt a surge of bravery in the darkness. 'Ben,' I whispered in the still of his room, 'as this couldn't really get any more awkward, and my knee is in your groin, do you mind if I ask you something?'

'Sure,' he whispered back.

'I know it's probably stupid to bring this up now as it happened months ago, but . . .'

We heard Justin push open the bathroom door and start clattering about, searching for people in the dark.

'It's about that night on the surf trip,' I said hesitantly. 'You know, when we, er, we kissed?'

Ben's body was completely still beneath mine. I could feel the warmth of his skin radiating against my body. In the dark I couldn't make out his features properly, but I could almost taste his minty soap smell, mixed with a hint of aftershave.

'I remember kissing you, yes.'

'Well, erm, I just wanted to know –' I was speaking in a hushed whisper, '– just so it's straight in my mind: why did you go off with Jasmine afterwards?'

There was no answer.

I couldn't see his reaction in the dark. What was he thinking? The quiet dissolved my bravery and I started whispering nervously. 'I know we only had one kiss, but Jasmine is so horrible . . . oh, well done for your speech in the kitchen – I really liked it. I can't believe she reported Jeremy. What an idiot! She's also been really mean to me at Halloween and, oh, so yes, what I was saying was, erm, why did you leave me to kiss Jasmine?'

The bathroom must have been empty as we heard Justin move into Suniti's room. He started burrowing around, slamming cupboards and giving a running commentary on his search.

'Is that what she told you?' Ben said quietly. I could feel his breath against my face as he spoke. It smelt of fresh toothpaste.

'I saw you both kissing outside the caravan.'

'I've never kissed Jasmine,' Ben said earnestly. 'She tried to kiss me and I turned away from it. I virtually had to carry her inside the caravan, she was so drunk.'

'Oh.' Yey! Yey! Yipee! Am idiot. Wahoo!

My face was still hovered just above Ben's. God, I just wanted to lower it an inch and kiss him.

'Not behind the curtains . . . not in the wardrobe . . . but I'm getting warmer!'

'As I remember it,' continued Ben, his mouth whispering quietly below mine, 'you were the one who left me to swim naked in the sea with Gil.'

'Oh.' No! Boo! Hiss! Am idiot. Crap! 'I'd hoped you hadn't seen that.'

'It was difficult not to when you ran down the beach taking your clothes off.'

'But I misheard – I'd got water in my ears because of the shark . . . well, there wasn't . . . but . . . I didn't want to skinny-dip, but I thought everyone else was going to and if I was the first one in then . . . well . . . it all went wrong.'

There was silence between us.

'Have you ever fancied Jasmine? In truth and dare she asked who you'd most like to kiss – and you chose her.'

'She actually asked, "Who would you like to kiss in this room?"'

And I'd left to go to the bathroom. Oh my God! Was Ben implying he would have picked me? Was that it? Ben's warm skin was pressed against mine and I could feel his chest rising and falling beneath mine.

'Would you have chosen me?' I asked shyly.

Justin burst into Ben's room.

Ben and I froze. My legs were between his; our bodies hot beneath the duvet.

Justin floundered around in the darkness as he opened Ben's wardrobe and punched in a hand to check for hiders.

I felt Ben shift slightly beneath me and my body seemed to sink further into his.

Justin got on all fours and started prodding around beneath the bed.

My was heart racing with longing. Would he have picked me?

'No way!' slurred Justin, plonking himself on the end of the bed, narrowly missing our legs. 'There's got to be people somewhere.'

I held my breath. I didn't want Justin to find us. I needed to hear Ben's answer. Would he have picked me? Does he like me?

Justin bounced up and chirruped, 'Not in here. I'm coming . . . wherever you are . . .' and he swept out of the room.

Ben and I stayed motionless, our bodies still entwined.

I needed to know. Eventually I whispered, 'So, would you?'

Ben moved his left arm from underneath me. I felt his hand feel its way round my waist and on to the small of my back. He pulled my body into his, our middles pressed together, our faces so slightly apart.

'Gotcha!' yelled Justin from his room. Sheree had been discovered and she screamed coquettishly, followed by slurping noises and the sound of bedsprings creaking.

'Josie,' Ben said quietly, the heat from his hand shooting tingles up my spine. I felt my breathing flutter as he slid it further along my back. 'Ever since that moment at the freshers' ball when you told me I "inspired the notion of sterilisation", I haven't . . .

And then there was an ear-splitting noise!

B R R R R R R R R R R R R R R. B R R R R R R R R R R R. BRRRRRRRRRRRRRRR.

B R R R R R R R R R R R R R R. B R R R R R R R R R R R. BRRRRRRRRRRRRRRR.

It was the fire alarm wailing aggressively! My first thought was, fucking fuck fuck! What was Ben going to say? Was it, 'I haven't been able to have sex because you maimed me?' Or, 'I haven't been able to stop thinking about you?' What? What? My one big moment with Ben ruined!

Then an icy panic flitted through me. I knew there wouldn't be a practice drill on the last day of semester.

This time it was for real.

I scrambled off Ben and we both rushed into the corridor where Justin was trying to wipe Sheree's lipstick off his face. The sound of the alarm was deafening and the emergency lighting was filling the corridor with a garish brightness. Tam's door was locked – she must have snuck off to bed. I banged loudly on it. 'We've got to get out, Tam – there's a fire!'

'I'm coming,' she called back and seconds later she stumbled out in a skimpy dressing-gown.

I could already smell the smoke. 'Hurry up!' I shouted, grabbing her arm. 'Ben, where's Matt?'

'I don't know, he's not in his room!'

'I'm sure he'll be fine,' said Tam. 'Let's just go.'

'He could have passed out somewhere,' I said. 'This isn't a practice . . . there's a real fire!'

'There is?' said Matt, bursting out of Tam's room.

Briefly registered Matt in just a pair of boxers and his bow tie, but then Ben hastily ushered everyone outside. 'Come on! Get out of here!'

'I don't think we need to panic,' said Tam calmly. 'It's . . . '

'Go! Go! Go!' I yelled.

Outside, the first fire engine screeched into the courtyard. The blue flashing lights kept illuminating the scene as students milled around uneasily. I began doing headcounts to make sure we hadn't missed anyone.

Grabbing my arm firmly, Tam said, 'You don't need to panic. I don't think it's a real fire.'

'Of course it is. I could smell the smoke.'

'Erm, yes. That's because we had just blown out a couple of candles.'

'We?'

'Well, Matt and I—'.

'Matt and you?!'

'Yes, we thought it'd be ni—'

'You and Matt? Candles? Oh my God!' I squealed, delightedly.

'I think I've got some explaining to do,' said Tam.

'Yes,' I said, eagerly moving closer for the intel.

'I meant to the fire officers!'

'Oh, of course.'

'Come with me?' Tam implored.

We approached a well-built fireman, who must have been in his mid-thirties and looked straight out of a Chippendale show. 'Hi,' Tam said nervously. 'I thought you might want to know that this isn't a real fire.'

'It isn't?' he replied, adjusting his helmet to see Tam more clearly in her skimpy dressing-gown.

'I think I may have accidentally set the alarm off.'

'Is that right, Miss? And what flat are you from?'

'Flat 2. I had a couple of candles burning,' she admitted guiltily.

'I see,' he said, sucking in the night air.

'I'm very sorry,' Tam apologised genuinely. 'Am I in a lot of trouble?'

Gil bounded up to the three of us, panting. 'Sorry, excuse me, dude, yeah – um, this is not a real fire! – I think, well, it's from our flat.'

'Oh, really,' said the fireman. 'And which flat are *you* from?'

'Flat 1.'

'And why did the alarms go off?'

'Erm, well, yeah, there was some smoke.'

'Yes, that's usually what sets fire alarms off.'

'Right, totally. Yeah, we were kinda having a smoke, if you know what I mean?'

'I think I do,' said the fire officer, with a hint of a smile. 'So, you were lighting candles upstairs.' He nodded at Tam. 'And you were smoking downstairs?' He nodded at Gil. 'Well, I'm pleased you've both cleared your consciences, but it wasn't either of your flats that triggered the alarm.'

'It wasn't?' Tam said incredulously.

'Somebody from the top floor was cooking a pizza but they passed out with it still in the oven.'

'So we're not going to be fined?' Gil asked.

'I think we can let you off.'

As the fireman made his way back to the others, he passed two figures who were cowering shamefully against the side of South Hall. I realised, to my everlasting delight, it was Jasmine and Chloe – with no make-up, kinky hair and saggy pyjamas. At last!

A quarter of an hour later, the firemen pulled away tooting their horns to lots of female cheers. A girl in a crumpled blue ball gown, bellowed, 'Don't go! There's a fire in my heart, baby!'

We were allowed back in the flat and Justin and Sheree quickly slunk off to his room, and Matt and Tam made a similarly fast retreat before I could extract the full candle-related details. Ben and I were left alone in the corridor, him still in his boxer shorts and me in my creased chocolate dress. The emergency lighting was beaming overhead and there was a raw awkwardness to the situation.

'I guess we should get to bed, really,' Ben said, staring at his feet.

There was a long silence as he waited for me to say something.

I needed to hear the rest of 'I haven't . . .' but the mood had been broken. Ben looked faintly embarrassed and I wondered if he was regretting the intimacy.

'I guess we should,' I said quietly. I gave him a nervous half-smile and said, 'Night, then,' before pulling my bedroom door shut behind me.

TWENTY-FOUR

Sunday 22 June (still)

5.15 am What the bloody hell was I thinking????

I didn't want to say, 'Night, then' – I wanted to say, 'Would you mind if we got back in your bed, in exactly the same position as before (me on top of you, your hand on my back, my legs between yours) and then you can tell me what exactly *you haven't* . . .' But I didn't. At the last minute the hideous fear of being rejected took over and, quite simply, I wimped out. And now I'll never know what Ben was going to say.

There's no point even trying to go to sleep. Don't think I'll ever be able to sleep again after lying on top of Ben; God, it was ridiculously erotic. I'm just going to sit here savouring the few sweet moments of being in the same bed as him, and after that, I'll move forward and face the fact that I'm going to become a sad and lonely old lady with seven pet guinea pigs, who still looks back on this night, thinking, 'I wonder what Ben was going to say?'

5.20 am Can't believe that Tam and Matt are together – I mean, bloody hell, if Matt can persuade Tam to share his bed after she told me, 'I'd rather watch porn with my dad', then surely I could have kissed Ben? It's too late now, though – it's been over an hour since the fire alarm. He'll be sleeping – in those delicious Calvin's, stretched out in his bed under the duvet . . . mmmm.

5.22 am This isn't what an Amazon feminist would do! I need to take control, seize the opportunity – look fear in the face and say, 'Er, Ben – do you fancy me as much as I fancy you?'

Must find out what Ben was going to say to me! I'm going to wake him up and demand to hear the end of his answer and then if it's a good answer I'll kiss him and if it's a bad answer then I'll, well, I'll try and leave in a dignified way and then I'll come back to my room and cry a lot. But that's it. That's what I'm going to do. I'm going to do it right now. I'm just going to go. The pen is going to be put down, my door will be opened, Ben's door will be opened and . . . oh, God, it's too scary!!

5.23 am Mr Tubs has called me a pathetic wimpish loser. So I can't stay here with him. I'm going . . .

10 am I tiptoed down the silent corridor and knocked gently on Ben's door. It made me jump when he said, 'It's open.'

Ben was sat at his desk in the semi-darkness.

I closed the door behind me but remained standing by it.

Be calm. Breathe. You are confident and brave, I kept telling myself. 'Ben . . . I . . . I just wondered, well, I wanted to ask – you know that thing you were talking about . . .'

And as I started mumbling, Ben got up from his chair, walked across his room towards me, put both his big hands gently around my face and kissed me. He kissed me so deliciously that if I hadn't been leaning against the door, I think I might have toppled over with pleasure.

Ben and I smiled into our kiss and our teeth clinked. It felt so wonderful to be kissing that perfect tilted smile at last!

'Jos,' Ben said, as he picked up my hand and led me to sit down on his bed. 'Are we now clear on what I was going to say?'

To be honest, I always like clarity and still would have rather known, but then a kiss is a whole lot better than that.

I moved on.

Feeling more confident now, I gently pushed Ben down on to the bed and kissed his neck, his cheek, his forehead, his nose, his lips. Mmmm . . . was so lovely in his bed. Was enjoying more delicious kisses and the feeling of Ben's strong hands moving gently down my neck and tracing the straps of my dress, his fingers stroking against the bare skin of my back. And then I panicked!

The fake boobs!

I had to get rid of them before Ben realised I'm a fraud! Think it would be rather off-putting if my breasts fell off in his hands. Actually, was very awkward trying to slip my own hands down front of dress while carrying on kissing Ben. When I had them in my grasp, it was so painful tearing them off that I accidentally bit a little hard on Ben's lip. Tried to pretend it was part of a feisty kissing action I was experimenting with, which he seemed to like.

Then what to do with the chicken fillets? Ben's hands moved from my back, over my shoulders, along my arms and . . . aaagh! . . . towards my hands which were harbouring two boobs. Yikes! Just lobbed boobs erratically at side of bed and hoped they'd stay pinned by wall. Then had to pretend again that lobbing action was part of my feisty technique, which all got rather tricky.

Was OK in the end. Ben did not notice missing boobs and we carried on kissing for a long, long, delicious amount of time. Eventually when we snuggled down into his bed and talked about the night.

Or maybe it was me that was talking, as after about half an hour or so, I think Ben started to get bit tired of me.

'Ben?

'Mm . . .'

'You know Grace?'

'Mm . . .'

'Did you know I thought she was your girlfriend?'

'I did,' said Ben quietly.

'Is that why you were cross with me when I was speaking to her in the kitchen?'

'No. I'd seen you kiss Matt the night before.'

Oops. So Ben *had* been at Icon. 'It was just a bet,' I explained.

'I know – he told me later.'

'Guess it could have looked bad.'

'Jos – '

'Yup?'

'Is there anything else, or do you think I can go to sleep?'

'I think that's it,' I said, snuggling down into his flat-packed pecs. 'Oh – just one more thing.'

'Mm . . .'

'I really like your chest.'

This morning has been lovely too. I woke up with an amazing happy floaty feeling. Love just breathing in, as every breath feels so calm and light. Ben rolled over and kissed my nose and said, 'Morning, my little skinny-dipper.' So nice that things are natural and non-awkward. However, am realising that nothing is ever perfect.

Ben asked, 'What's that on your arm?'

Looked down to find one chicken fillet boob stuck to top of arm. Quickly whipped it off in hair-removing action and winced, 'It's a . . . dressing. Yes. To cover a cigarette burn,' and then I mumbled on about smoking bans, government fat cats and nicotine tax profits etc.

Was eager to see signs of life from Tam's room as desperately wanted to hear about her night (and possibly mention mine!!). When I saw Matt duck out carrying his tux under his arm, I climbed into bed with her. Lots of screaming, giggling and 'O.M.G-ing' ensued (love being a girl).

Am so happy for them both! Apparently, she's liked Matt since Christmas. The 'porn' answer was a cover as she thought I might march her to the psychiatrist for fancying him!

I then relayed Ben-me-starfish-hide-and-seek-get-together to lots of excited squeals and hugs. Would love to have exhausted every detail of evening, but we both had to get on with packing . . .

2.45 pm Mum will be here in just over an hour and haven't got much further. Keep getting distracted by student memorabilia: clitoris revolt beer mat, kickboxing receipt, lei of flowers from Hawaiian party, and of course the sex wax, which leads me to Ben . . . and mmmm! Whole night was perfect. OK, well, not perfect, but it ended very nicely. Cannot stop thinking about him! Everything I pack is so full of memories that I keep stopping and stroking objects longingly as though am leaving uni for ever.

3.30 pm We've all had a last cup of tea together in our kitchen. Except we had no milk and we'd packed the sugar.

Was touched when Matt brought out a blue carrier bag and said, 'I know how envious you all are of my T-shirt collection – so I got some specially printed for you.'

It was such a sweet thing to do. He pulled out the first T-shirt which was bright red. Splashed across the chest in bold orange letters, it read, 'GINGER DOESN'T MEAN GAY'. 'There you go, Geri.' Matt smiled.

'Do you want another punch?' joked Justin, who actually seemed quite pleased with his offensive T-shirt.

A pale blue T-shirt came out next and Matt slid it across the kitchen table to Ben. He unfolded it and held up the T-shirt so we could all read the front. In white italic writing it said, 'WANNA WAX MY STICK?' Ben smiled and put his hand on Matt's shoulder and gave it a firm squeeze. 'Cheers, mate, that's really nice of you.'

Matt looked awkward with the praise and quickly pulled out the next T-shirt. 'This one's for you, Tam,' he said, handing her a bright yellow T-shirt. In neat green letters it read, 'GIRLS LIKE PORN TOO'.

Matt waited nervously for her response.

She tutted disapprovingly, but then her lips parted into a smile. She held the T-shirt across her chest and gave Matt a naughty look. 'Maybe they do . . .'

Matt's eyes sparkled and he put a hand on Tam's thigh and whispered something into her ear.

'Ahem. There's still one more person to go,' I reminded them.

'Oh, yeah,' Matt said, pulling the final T-shirt from the bag. 'You were a tricky one. I went through a few options, like, 'I TALK TO MYSELF', or 'HIGH MAINTENANCE'. I thought 'ASK ME ABOUT MY VIBRATOR' was quite nice too – except I wasn't sure you'd wear it enough.'

Hmmm, was starting to wonder what atrocity I was going to be branded with.

'I wanted to get something that really sums you up, so I decided on this.' Matt unfolded a dusky pink T-shirt, and in small white letters it read. 'I'M NOT SHORT! I'M KYLIE!'

I loved it!

We all put our T-shirts on and I suddenly wondered if I might cry. It was sad to look round our bare kitchen: there were no posters, no toaster, no washing-up left on the side – just six orange chairs and five faces. I didn't want it to end.

We've all promised to keep in touch over the summer. Tam is coming to stay in August and Matt's even threatening to give surfing a go with Ben. With my boyfriend, Ben. Well, sort of *boyfriend*. We didn't discuss titles but hope it's official as Ben would be perfect boyfriend and . . .

Aaagh! Mum is here!

5.15 pm It took nineteen trips to load the car!! How is it possible that I have double what I arrived with? Was hoping that Hobbit wouldn't be lingering around with a spare joint to corrupt Mum again, but unfortunately he heard her voice and came to say 'Hi'. I watched nervously as they had a meaningful spiritual hug and chatted about mantras – thankfully no sneaky drug transactions were made.

Another of Mum's fan base made an appearance on the stairway: Warden-Brian.

'Hello, Josie's Mum,' he bumbled awkwardly.

I could tell Mum had no recollection of Brian.

'I thought I'd pop by to pick up Josie's room key,' he said, running his fingernail up and down the stitching of his bib. 'I knew it would save her the trouble of coming to the Accommodation Office.'

Seeing as Warden-Brian hates me, his ulterior motive was quite clear.

Mum's eyebrows raised as she remembered the Jeremy Beagle encounter. 'That's awfully kind of you, Brian,' she cooed.

'Haven't got the dog with you today?' he enquired, desperate for conversation with Mum.

'No, I left him at my mother's – I didn't think there'd be room as Josie has that much stuff!'

'I can help you to your car with these bags,' Brian offered.

And so, Mum, clearly being a non-feminist, let Warden-Brian struggle up and down the stairs with my various loads of bags. I felt very awkward seeing him carrying my 'private' shoebox, knowing all the embarrassing things that it housed. He rested it on the car roof and then leant against the boot on his elbow. I think he was trying to look smooth. 'Well, I think that's everything.' He smiled at Mum.

I left Brian to schmooze (it was making me queasy) and went to do a final check of my room. It looked small and unfamiliar. There were no posters or photos, and no Mr Tubs on my bed. Someone else is going to be living here next year. Someone else will discover you can get an entirely different view of the Telecom pole from next door. Someone else might drink red wine while writing about *Winnie-the-Pooh*. Someone else might wonder about the stain on the carpet or cry about the boy three doors down. Somebody else has all this ahead of them.

I wandered down the stairs, past Gil and Hobbit's empty flat, and out into the courtyard, where Mum and Warden-Brian were waiting. I handed over my room keys and in return Warden-Brian gave me my deposit back. How much friendlier things are now.

'Have a safe drive,' he said, stealing a final look at Mum and then trundling off through the courtyard.

I think I might even miss him.

5.30 pm Am in the car. Can't see out of the back window and a chair leg keeps poking me in the neck. My flatmates waved me off in front of South Hall. Justin, wearing his new T-shirt with pride, planted a big kiss on my cheek. I quietly threatened him with further finger damage if he doesn't keep in touch over summer.

'Out of my way, Geri,' said Matt, stepping forward and placing both hands on my shoulder. 'Now, are you going to be good over summer?' he said, in an unusually motherly tone.

'Erm . . . yes,' I replied, looking at him strangely.

'Because I don't want you two girls gossiping together about the size of our willies, you hear me?'

'Shut up,' I hissed crossly out of the corner of my mouth, hoping Mum hadn't heard. How is Tam going to manage with him?

Matt grinned cheekily and then bear-hugged me so tightly I thought my air bra might pop.

'How about letting me in for a turn?' smiled Tam.

When I noticed her eyes had a glassy film over them, I had to try really hard to swallow the lump in my throat. 'I'm going to miss you,' I told her.

She stroked back my hair and replied, 'Me too. So make sure you call me – ' then she hushed her voice and whispered ' – because I need to get the rest of the Ben details, you little minx!'

We giggled naughtily and after giving me a big squeeze and a kiss, she moved to the side and stood with Matt.

Just leaving Ben.

I admit, I did want a starry-eyed, romantic goodbye – the one where it begins to snow, but we're so madly in love he simply picks me up, swirls me round, kisses me passionately and tells me he loves me – but, then, it's June, and this is Ben. And my mum was there. So I got a brief but delicious kiss and Ben said, 'Have a safe drive, Jos. I'll call you soon.'

So, just out of interest, how soon is 'soon'?

EPILOGUE

5.45 pm 'Erm, Mum . . .' I said, loosening my seatbelt and twisting round to face the back seat. 'Do you remember the shoe box that was on the car roof?' I was scanning my eyes over the clutter of suitcases, bags, cardboard boxes and loose clothes that filled the back of the car.

'Yes.'

'You did put it in the boot, didn't you?' I asked, panicky tingles starting to spread throughout my body.

'No,' mum replied, 'I thought you had.'

Nooooooooooooooooo!

'That is a shame, was there anything important in it?' She asked lightly.

I visualised the contents of my 'Private' box and couldn't manage an answer. I thought I'd come so far from the nervous fresher who stumbled in on day one, hugging a non-flatmate, whimpering about prison cells and wanting to go home. As everyone waved me off this morning, I felt a real sense of pride – like I'd finished my first year in a blaze of glory!

But now I realise my flatmates were actually waving the car down – and rather than leaving behind a blaze of glory, I've actually left a trail of contraceptives, two chicken fillets, one electrolysis set and a pink vibrator . . .

THE END